THE OPEN ROAD

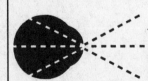

This Large Print Book carries the
Seal of Approval of N.A.V.H.

THE OPEN ROAD

M. M. HOLADAY

WHEELER PUBLISHING
A part of Gale, a Cengage Company

Farmington Hills, Mich • San Francisco • New York • Waterville, Maine
Meriden, Conn • Mason, Ohio • Chicago

LIBRARY OF CONGRESS CIP DATA ON FILE.
CATALOGUING IN PUBLICATION FOR THIS BOOK
IS AVAILABLE FROM THE LIBRARY OF CONGRESS

ISBN-13: 978-1-4328-4749-4 (softcover)

Published in 2018 by arrangement with M. M. Holaday

Printed in Mexico
1 2 3 4 5 6 7 22 21 20 19 18

For
Jeff
Eric
Reid
Kathryn

ACKNOWLEDGMENTS

I want to thank friends and family who offered encouragement to me repeatedly throughout this project. I am grateful to all of you. I would like to acknowledge a few people by name: my sister, Bek, who read my earliest draft while on our own open-road adventure; Pamela Winnick, for guidance early on; Kathie Johnston, for continuous wise counsel; Susan Uttendorfsky for first-rate copyediting; Andrew Lockhart and Marsha Hayles for insightful advice; Beth Plunkett and Mary Kay Wolfe for astute feedback; and the excellent editors at Five Star.

Finally, thank you to my husband, Jeff, and our children, Eric, Reid, and Kathryn, for bringing such joy to my life by just being you.

CHAPTER ONE:
WINSTON AVERY

*Missouri River Landing, Council Bluffs, Iowa,
Spring 1865*

Winston Avery stepped off the steamboat
onto a crowded pier. Passengers waiting to
board moved aside to let him pass and then
jostled back for a place in line, nudging
against him like nervous ponies in a corral.
Win elbowed his way through the acrid
smell of too much humanity and headed for
shore, carrying his saddle in front of him.
Surely he'd knock someone into the water if
he tried to hoist it onto his shoulder.

General Lee had just surrendered at Ap-
pomattox, yet it seemed the nation had
already turned its attention to the West. The
war had delayed the audacious idea of a
transcontinental railroad, but now steam-
boats chugged upriver to the Omaha Landing, loaded with ex-soldiers newly employed
by the Union Pacific Railroad. The soldiers
who remained in military service gathered

in units awaiting orders to fight an old, persistent enemy on the Great Plains. Prairie schooners congregated on either side of the Missouri River, filled with families, or fortune hunters who had heard about gold in Montana. A fellow passenger aboard the sidewheeler that brought Win east from Dakota Territory predicted that the frontier would be settled in his lifetime. The assessment troubled Win. He imagined masses of people trampling across the unspoiled prairie the way schoolboys head for freshly fallen snow, each racing to be the first to make his mark on it.

He could hardly blame those drawn to the West. Even now, the wind whispered in his ear, blocking out the noise and beckoning him back from where he'd just come. He gazed at the western horizon, the line where sky and land meet seducing him for a moment. He suppressed the impulse and instead headed up the street, wondering how he'd manage the final leg of his journey. His return home to visit the Dawsons was long overdue.

A row of storefronts stood where a grove of gnarled, old oaks once shaded a sleepy river landing with a decent fishing spot. Win caught a glimpse of his sand-colored reflection in a dry-goods shop window. Wind-blown grit from the Sandhills coated him, but Mrs. Dawson wouldn't mind. His best friend's mother would stand in the doorway and smile broadly, ignoring the dirt as she welcomed him with open arms. Still, he tried to brush the dust from the parts of him he could reach.

Most of the businesses catered to settlers trekking west, but, at the doctor's office, an empty buckboard stood out from the schooners equipped for overland travel. Hank Brady, Win's long-time neighbor, emerged from the office with a package and climbed wearily into his seat.

"Mr. Brady! It's Win Avery. How are you?"

The farmer squinted. "Win? By golly, didn't recognize you. It's been years."

"Four. You headed home? I could use a lift to the crossroads."

"Throw your saddle in the back."

Once Win settled in, Mr. Brady whistled to his mules. "You been fightin' Johnny Reb?" he asked.

"No, sir. It's good to hear it's over, though."

"Lee surrendered. The Union's preserved." Brady sighed with satisfaction, as though he'd won the war himself. "Where've you been all these years?"

"West."

11

"By golly, the frontier stirs the soul, don't it? We're living in a young time, Win, if time can be seen as such. Oh, I know the world is old and full of people of all different ages, but there are times when the circumstances suit a particular type of man, and this is a time for young men. There's plenty of opportunity for a healthy young feller to build a new life. If I weren't so old and Mrs. Brady wasn't ailin' . . . Well, our time for that kind of adventure has come and gone. Our biggest dream now is to see our Tom come walking down the road." Mr. Brady's voice cracked with emotion. He cleared his throat.

"Have you heard from him?" Win had seen a dozen Union soldiers lined up at the river's edge, staring vacantly ahead as they awaited transport. Several had a white bandage at the tip of a missing appendage flagging their incompleteness.

"Yep, he's ok. On his way home, thank God. We got word the same day the Dawsons were killed. Mary and I were as high and as low as a person can be, all at the same time." Mr. Brady glanced at Win. "Aw . . . you didn't know? I thought that's why you came home. I'm sorry, son."

"No . . ." Win felt stabbed in the heart.

"Jeb was away at school. Got back yesterday for the funeral," Mr. Brady said.

Win shut his eyes, a futile attempt to keep the truth from arriving faster than he could accept it. Images of Sarah Dawson smiling as she worked around the house tumbled through his mind.

"I didn't know they were —" Win stopped. "What happened?"

"There's no way to know for sure, but from the way the bodies were found, the sheriff thinks Frank Taylor showed up at the doc's office, wounded from a knife fight. Doc and the missus were tending to him when that hothead, Henry Davis, burst in looking for him. Taylor pulled his gun and tried to use Miz Dawson as a shield. Davis fired at Taylor, hitting Miz Dawson instead. The doc got caught in the crossfire, too." Brady shook his head.

Win sat in silence, recalling a day Dr. Dawson had dissected a fish Win and Jeb brought home from the river, giving the boys a brief lesson in anatomy. He remembered how expertly Jeb's father handled the knife and his steady hand.

"Here you go, son." Brady slowed his team to a stop. "I'm sorry you had to find out this way. I'd take you all the way to the doc's, but Mary needs this." He patted the package next to him.

13

Win jumped down and lifted his saddle from the wagon. He heard himself say, "It's real good news about Tom. Please give my best to Mrs. Brady."

Mr. Brady nodded and turned his team south. Win stared at the wagon as it rolled away, his purpose for coming home gone like the breeze carrying away the dust stirred up by the wheels. It had taken four years for Win to fully appreciate all they had done for him. He'd come back to tell them that.

Win looked west — once again tempted. But Mr. Brady said Jeb was back for the funeral. He wanted to see him. Maybe he could convince Jeb to come with him. Win heaved his saddle onto his shoulder and headed down the road to the Dawson home.

Jeb wasn't there, but the door was unlocked, so Win let himself in. The house still had the familiar smell of baked bread and coffee, but it lacked the cheerfulness Jeb's mother brought to it. Win couldn't remember a time when Mrs. Dawson wasn't there, in good spirits and busy. He almost called out, hoping she'd answer. He wandered through the rooms in silence.

Win entered the front parlor, his favorite room of the house. Oddly grateful that its contents had been undisturbed, he picked up Mrs. Dawson's sewing and admired the fine needlework. Bookshelves lined the parlor walls; his heart ached with memories. Mrs. Dawson often read to them at night. Win could read well, but it was more fun to close his eyes and listen to her. She was good at it. She read Walter Scott and Charles Kingsley — adventure stories for boys like you, she'd say. Win wondered if Jeb's mother had enjoyed the adventure stories as much as they had. Light would dance in her eyes when she read. He and Jeb would drift off to sleep planning high-sea voyages and dreaming of daring sword fights.

There was one book that sparked particular memories. Win scanned the shelves and spotted it — *The Last of the Mohicans*. The hero of the story, Natty Bumppo, had a magnificent nickname: Hawkeye. Win often daydreamed in school about Hawkeye living in the frontier. The stories stayed with him when he crossed the plains. When his boss on the wagon train, Clint Sanders, told him that he'd befriended an Arapaho, Win imagined the Indian to be like Hawkeye's friend, Chingachgook. Win expressed eagerness to meet his own Indian friend and his boss laughed so hard, he broke wind. "As a group, they ain't to be messed with, kid,"

Clint had said, and started calling Win "Mohican."

Through the parlor window, Win spotted Jeb slip through the row of budding poplars. He must have been at the Blankenships' neighboring farm. Jeb's shoulders sagged, sadness strapped to him like sacks of grain on his back.

Jeb had the blue eyes and fair coloring of his mother and his father's quiet, confident manner. In school, Jeb earned high marks, while Win often fell into mischief. Smarter than his teacher recognized, he bored easily and made trouble. Jeb not only kept Win from falling too far into a mess, he managed to smooth the feathers Win invariably ruffled. He wondered if his friend would hold it against him for being away so long. Jeb did not hold grudges, but anyone could change in four years. When Jeb noticed Win standing at the front door, his face brightened and his shoulders relaxed a bit.

"Win, you are a sight to behold." Jeb strode toward him, his hand extended, as Win descended from the porch steps. "How'd you hear? I didn't know where to reach you."

"I didn't know 'til just now. Hank Brady told me. I'm sorry, Jeb. I'm real sorry." They abandoned the handshake and exchanged

16

bear hugs.

Jeb nodded his thanks. "I was in Keokuk myself. Sheriff Baumgartner sent word to the dean at the medical college. He tracked me down." He sank onto the wide, wooden porch steps and leaned forward on his elbows. "Got here just in time for the funeral."

Reticent by nature, Jeb never strung too many words together at a time. But by his fourth sentence describing the funeral, as he talked to Win like he'd been gone a week rather than four years, Win felt assured that Jeb harbored no ill will for his long absence. Win pulled a flask out of his saddlebag and handed it to Jeb. He took off his faded trail hat and ran his hand through his long hair to keep it from falling into his eyes as he sat down next to his friend.

"The two men who killed my folks both died, too, so there's nothing more to be done about it." Jeb took a swallow of whiskey and passed it back to Win. "No trial, no sentencing. Leaves me unsettled."

"It isn't fair at all," Win said. "Your folks were the best people I've ever known. They were always there with open arms . . . helped me through tough times. They were your parents, Jeb, but you know what they meant to me."

Jeb nodded. "I remember when Ma stood up to that new teacher who called you 'wild.' She said a boy who loses a mother to influenza and a father to the bottle ought to be given some leeway. She was in your corner."

"I tested her patience."

"Maybe, but she liked you. Ma said your natural charm would get you out of most of the trouble that found you."

"The lessons I learned from your folks kept me alive and out of jail. I owe them a lot."

Jeb turned to Win. "Where'd you go? What happened to you?"

Win watched a hawk hang in an air current overhead, a reminder of his own earth-bound limitations. Four years earlier, he left Rockfield to join the Pony Express. The company had advertised for good riders, orphans preferred. He considered himself both and signed up. But the Central Overland Express was already on its last legs and folded as soon as telegraph service reached California. That short time racing cross-country ignited a smoldering ember in his belly, however. He told Jeb nothing in his life had been more thrilling, prior to or since. "When my job as a Post rider ended, I sorta wanted to come back, but, at the

18

same time, didn't want to," Win said. "I knew I'd be welcome, but drifted instead . . . looking for what, I'm not sure. Maybe I wanted to find something as exciting and as single-minded in purpose . . . Maybe I just didn't want to come back a failure." It wasn't a great explanation, but Jeb had always valued honesty over excuses.

Jeb nodded. It didn't really matter whether he agreed or was simply acknowledging that he had heard. Win had forgotten how easy it was to be in Jeb's company.

"I rode for the COE only six months," Win said. "They went out of business and most of us didn't get paid, so I was broke. I drifted a bit until I met Clint Sanders, a wagon train captain who escorted settlers across the prairie. He's coarser than your pa, but I liked him, maybe 'cause he gave me a job. I was a cook's helper the first trip, but got to scout for him the second time."

Jeb turned to Win. "You've been to California *twice* since I last saw you?" He leaned back, turned his face to the sky, and closed his eyes. "I got jealousy boilin' inside me, Win. I just might have to hit you."

"You did the right thing, staying in school."

Jeb rose abruptly. "How long are you staying?"

19

Bound by no schedule, Win hadn't planned past the day. Craning his neck to look up at his friend's tall frame, he said, "As long as you need me, Jeb."

"I've gotta feed the stock." Jeb started toward the barn. Win followed.

Old Daniel, a faithful workhorse of the Dawsons for as long as Win could remember, plodded over to the corral fence. Win greeted Old Daniel while Jeb disappeared into the barn. Then the velvet nose of the sorrel he used to ride, Hippocrates, brushed against Win's shoulder. He nuzzled with him before reaching over to stroke the neck of Galen, a bay that had been Jeb's. A dying patient bequeathed a pair of young foals to Jeb's father, who named them after two prominent figures in medical history and then assigned Jeb and Win the task of raising them. Win figured they must be almost ten years old by now — still young and healthy. It wasn't the welcoming party he'd imagined, but a welcome sight nonetheless. Jeb came out with three buckets of oats.

"Adam Blankenship's been looking after the stock. He said Pa rode these two regularly on house calls," Jeb said. He held up a feed bucket for Galen. "He said he'd be happy to buy them . . . Old Daniel, too."

Win winced inwardly as he held a bucket

for Old Daniel. The thought of selling Galen and Hippocrates felt like a stomach punch. He'd become a capable horse handler caring for Hippocrates. The training had served him well. The Express ponies seemed to favor Win and ran hard for him. On trail, he sweet-talked the cook's cantankerous mules into cooperating, which elevated Win's status from nobody to muleskinner overnight. Jeb couldn't sell Hippocrates and Galen.

When the horses had finished eating, Jeb reluctantly turned to the house. "I guess it's time. I haven't been in his office yet."

"Let's go together." Win walked with him to the house. With the key stored on top of the doorframe, Jeb unlocked the door separating the living quarters from Dr. Dawson's office.

Neighbors had tried to clean up the mess. Someone had stacked Dr. Dawson's medical journals neatly on his desk. Broken glass had been swept up, but there were bloodstains on the wooden floor that could not be scrubbed away, and they were sobering to look at. Win wondered what possible words he could say that would offer any comfort. "Your pa must have been looking forward to you practicing with him."

Jeb said nothing.

"I'm sure he was real proud of —"

"I quit."

The words hung in the air, suspended on thin silk threads.

"Quit what?" Win asked. "Medical school?"

Jeb nodded. "Being a doctor was Pa's dream, not mine. A man follows his own dreams, not someone else's."

"Aw, hell, Jeb. You're gonna make a damn fine doctor. Give yourself a little rein."

Jeb held up his hand. "I dropped out four months ago. I should have told Pa. I wish I had. It's a lie I can't fix now."

Win stared at Jeb. "What made you change your mind?"

"A lot of little things, I guess. It took a while for my gut and my head to agree, but in the end, I knew it was right. I've been working at a sawmill. It's the hardest work I've ever done, but it feels good. I'm grateful the dean of the school tracked me down when the telegram came about Ma and Pa."

Win handled the news the way he'd learned to handle most things, which was to stay on the light side of heavy matters. Tragic events early in life taught Win to be adaptable and thick-skinned, qualities that sometimes made him seem cavalier. But, in reality, he simply found it less painful not to get too invested in anything. So now that Jeb, the responsible, obedient son, had dropped out of medical school, naturally his confession amused Win. He reached over and squeezed Jeb's muscular arm. "Damn, you're a beast." He grinned. "I thought you looked bigger than I remembered. You've got at least twenty pounds more muscle on you. I guess you don't get that way sitting in a library."

Jeb shook his head. "I guess you haven't lost your peculiar sense of humor."

Win woke the next morning to the aroma of coffee. For a peaceful moment, he was a boy again at the Dawson home, with Mrs. Dawson cooking breakfast in the kitchen. Win's thoughts drifted to a day a decade earlier. He was eating supper with the Dawsons, something he did almost every evening that year.

"Miz Dawson, what's a Corja Bull?" Win had asked Jeb's mother as he'd scooped a second helping of potatoes onto his plate. Mrs. Dawson said she had never heard of that kind of bull. Dr. Dawson speculated that it might be a new breed, and asked where Win heard about it. Jeb explained that their teacher, Miss Palmer, called Win a "Corja Bull" after he fell out of the schoolhouse window.

Mrs. Dawson had placed a reassuring hand tenderly on his shoulder. She asked if Miss Palmer called him "incorrigible." Win said yes and asked what it meant. "Win, you dear boy," Mrs. Dawson had said, "incorrigible simply means that sometimes you are just too lively and curious for some grown-ups."

Win's mind cleared; he remembered Sarah Dawson was dead, and the ache returned. He pulled on his clothes, combed through his unruly hair with his fingers, and shuffled downstairs into the kitchen to find Jeb attempting to cook breakfast. He was trying to pick pieces of eggshell out of a hot pan.

Yawning, Win waved his friend away from the stove and took over. "I did this every morning for five months straight." Win cleared the gravel from his throat. "Don't even need to be fully awake." He scraped the pan clean, tossed in a dollop of lard that sizzled, and broke fresh eggs into it. Then he sliced some bacon and threw it in the pan with the eggs.

Jeb poured coffee into two cups and sat down at the table.

Win glanced at him. "I've been thinking. You should come west with me."

"And do what?"

24

"We could go on that adventure we always talked about as kids — sleep under the stars, ride the open prairie . . ."

"I mean for work. I've already got a job. Besides, we were going to join a ship's crew and sail the seas, not that it matters."

Win paused from stirring the eggs. "It's so big out there, it's like the ocean. The sky is huge and the land goes on forever. You've got to see it, while it's still there . . ."

"Where's it going?"

"I mean while it's still wild." Win was wide awake now as his idea took root. "You've got to see the wide, open space before it gets cluttered with people. At the rate folks are headed out there, the whole country will look like Council Bluffs Landing in a few years."

"Boss gave me four days. I've got to be back by my shift on Friday," Jeb said.

"Why?"

"Ice is breaking upriver. We've got to get the logs out before they jam up."

"No, I mean why go back? You've got to come with me and see the frontier. It's gonna disappear, Jeb. You can't go back to that mill."

"I can't just walk away from a good job."

"Sure you can. Besides, I've been thinking about going to Denver to look up my old

25

boss. He'll give us jobs. He doesn't pilot wagon trains to California anymore; he has a freight company. He said he found a gal who can tolerate him and wants to spend his nights lying next to a warm, soft woman instead of on the cold, hard ground." Win smiled at the thought. "We could go cross-country, take Galen and Hippocrates — save them from a boring existence in Rockfield, too. Hell, a stage could get us to Denver in a week, which just shows you how fast the country is shrinking, but what's the fun of that?" Win envisioned riding through the prairie again. This time he wouldn't be alone. "Why not take a couple of months instead?"

"Sounds irresponsible."

Win stirred the eggs. "Exactly! If there was ever a time to take to the open road and be irresponsible, it's now. Come on, what do you say?"

"Let me think on it."

"That sawmill job is nothing, and you know it."

"You're like a dog with a sock." Jeb sounded annoyed. He gripped his coffee mug tightly. "Drop it. I don't change directions as fast as you."

Win dished up two plates and set them down on the table. Jeb said it was the ugliest mess of eggs and bacon he'd ever seen. Win figured he was just feeling ornery. Jeb arrived at decisions at his own pace, and pushing him only brought out the mule in him. Win dropped the subject of going west and asked about the neighbors he could remember. "Remember that Harvest Festival the year before I left . . . when Hippocrates won the horse race? I've forgotten why Ben Richards was so sore at me."

Despite his criticism of Win's cooking, Jeb had no trouble eating it. Between bites he said, "Your memory is lousy. Galen won that race. You were too busy kissing Ben Richards's daughter to remember anything."

Win threw his head back and laughed. "Whatever happened to Sally?"

"She married Virgil; they've got a kid already."

"No shit . . ."

Four years earlier, classmate Sally Richards had stared dreamily at Win for the better part of a week before he took her behind the schoolhouse at recess and kissed her. The incident became known during the Harvest Festival, irritating classmate Virgil Peters, who challenged Win to a fistfight. Win had spread his arms out in a gesture of astonished innocence and told Virgil he had no reason to fight him, adding that Sally

27

would probably be more than happy to kiss him, too. At that point, Sally's father appeared and took off after him.

"Maybe I should go visit ol' Sally Richards while I'm here . . . see how she's doin'," Win said with his mouth full, the memory of Sally's soft lips lingering with him.

"It's Sally *Peters* now, and if you value your health, you'll steer clear. Virgil grew some after you left." Jeb stabbed at a piece of bacon. "How can the sky be bigger than here? Seems to me the sky is the sky."

"Ha! That's why you gotta see it, so you know what I mean," Win said, pleased that Jeb was already returning to more relevant matters. With his fork, Win pointed at the west-facing window. "No trees to block the view. You can see for miles." He pointed at the ceiling. "At night, the stars hang so low, you swear you can touch them."

Jeb ate in silence. Finally, he said, "Aren't you going to say it?"

"Say what?"

"That stupid ass motto of yours, the one that always got us in trouble. You know . . . 'Sometimes you gotta do something crazy, just to feel alive.' "

Win hadn't used his favorite argument for quite some time, primarily because Jeb was

28

right; it was a stupid ass saying that usually got him into trouble. But the fact that Jeb brought it up was as good as announcing that he'd decided to come with him. Win tried to contain his excitement, but a broad grin escaped anyway. "This is different. This isn't crazy; it's the best idea I've ever had."

Win helped close up the house. He was boxing up books in the library when Jeb appeared in the doorway holding a brand new lever-action, breech-loading, repeating Henry rifle. Win whistled in astonishment.

"That's a beauty."

Jeb handed the rifle to him. "It's for you. I just found it buried in Ma's trunk. I got one just like it two years ago at Christmas. From the bill of sale, it looks like she bought them together and planned to give this one to you."

A pang of guilt hit Win in the chest. She'd been waiting two years to give him that fine, handsome rifle. Staying away for so long seemed ungrateful. The Dawsons had shown him far more kindness than he deserved, and he had no way to repay them.

Jeb, not without emotion, but with no-nonsense purpose — now that he'd agreed to travel with Win — brought out a box of odds and ends, saying they looked like they might have some value.

"We should sell some of this and get ourselves a couple of .44 Colt revolvers. With a revolver and a repeating rifle apiece, we'll be as well-armed as guards protecting gold on its way to the San Francisco mint."

Win thought about the Colt Dragoon revolver he'd taken off a dead man, which was stolen from him two months earlier. It had been a good gun. Too complicated a story to tell at the moment, Win decided against mentioning it. "Good idea," he said.

They sold the chickens and packed away Dr. Dawson's medicines. The neighbor ladies came for Mrs. Dawson's dresses, although Jeb saved the handkerchiefs she had embroidered, combs she wore in her hair for special occasions, and her wedding ring. He also saved his father's kit of medicinal powders and a few surgical instruments.

Jeb left the key to the house on the kitchen table. He'd arranged for Mr. Blankenship to come by the next day to lock up and take Old Daniel back with him. When the house sold, he'd forward the money to the Denver National Bank. They had known Adam Blankenship all of their lives — his word was all that was needed.

Win and Jeb left Rockfield the next day.

They packed provisions and took one last look around their childhood home. Sadness and excitement braided together so tightly, Win couldn't feel one without the other. Running off four years ago seemed unappreciative, but he could make amends. Jeb needed rescuing now . . . and Win was just the man to do it.

CHAPTER TWO:
JEB DAWSON

Nebraska Territory, Spring 1865

Jeb groaned as he eased his sore body out of the saddle. He didn't know of a muscle in his legs or backside that didn't burn. "I guess there's a difference between riding and riding *all day.*" He arched his back, stretching out the stiffness.

"That'll go away; another day and you won't feel it." Win dismounted with an agility that Jeb envied. The way he went to work setting up their evening camp reminded Jeb of how his mother had hung laundry or kneaded bread dough — habitual tasks repeated so often that no conscious thought was required.

Win had aged more years than he'd been gone, Jeb thought. He was capable and confident, and even though he'd joked about Jeb adding twenty pounds of muscle, he, too, had filled out and grown taller. While Jeb hobbled the horses and unsaddled them, Win made quick work of building a fire and cleaning the chicken he had bought from a farmer. Soon he had it roasting on a spit.

Despite his sore backside, Jeb loved every minute of their days on trail. The splendor they traveled through awakened his senses dulled by grief. They crossed the Missouri and Platte Rivers on crowded ferries, but, as they were not encumbered by oxen and prairie schooners, they quickly separated themselves from the commotion once on the west side of the Platte. Win let out a whoop and Hippocrates galloped straight for the setting sun as though trying to catch it. Jeb and Galen chased after him into wide-open country. The clay shell encasing his heart cracked and broke away in chunks like the clumps of dirt kicked up by the horses' hooves. Win's idea to head west wasn't youthful stupidity at all. It was brilliant.

Jeb lowered his stiff body down next to the fire. The smoke masked the rich, earthy aroma of a prairie springing to life. The sun dropped, painting the clouds red and gold.

"See that sky?" Win leaned back and gazed at the colorful display. "I once saw a girl with hair that color. When I was riding for Russell, I got a special assignment. It was some kind of secret dispatch, 'cause it couldn't be telegraphed, and I got permission to go off route and ride to Omaha. The fellow gave me twenty bucks and said if I got it there in time, the gentleman on the other end would give me twenty more. As you can imagine, I took the job. Anyway, I was on my way back with forty dollars in my pocket and nervous as hell I would get robbed — now that I had something worth stealing. Out of the blue comes this other rider, tearing out like Indians are after him. At first I thought he was coming after my forty bucks, so I spurred my horse to get away. I'm pushing my pony as fast as I dare. I look over and see that the rider isn't chasing me at all; he's riding alongside of me, like he's racing! But then his hat flies off his head and I see that he isn't a *he* at all, he's a *she*! She's a wild little thing, her hair in two braided pigtails, but most of it loose and blowing around her head. Her hair was that color," he said, pointing to a cloud. "I've never seen anything like it. I've never seen a girl ride like that, either. She kept racing me 'til finally I tipped my hat to her, which was hard, 'cause I could barely hang on. A big ol' grin spread across her face and then she let up, like that's what she'd been waiting for. She waved to me and turned around to lope back to wherever she came from."

"Did you ever see her again?"

"Nope." Win intertwined his fingers behind his head and stared at the sky.

The girl must have made quite an impression, as Win sounded disappointed. Juices from the chicken dripped into the fire and sizzled. Jeb carefully lifted their meal from the flames.

"Here, grab a leg." Jeb held the chicken for his friend.

Win came out of his musing and pulled off one of the legs. "At some point, we'll join a train. Even well-armed, crack shots like us would be fools to cross the territory alone these days. We don't want Inkpaduta to get us," he said, laughing.

As a boy, the most terrifying stories Jeb heard were about the murderous Inkpaduta and his band of followers, who massacred settlers in northern Iowa and took three women and a girl captive. Different from the adventure stories that took place at sea, these horrific accounts were real, and close to home. The renegade Dakota eluded capture and became the subject of many a tall tale in the schoolyard.

"Don't worry, Jeb," Win said, grinning. "Flash floods and twisters, now that's scary shit." When Jeb didn't laugh, Win abandoned his teasing and assured Jeb that they'd look for a large wagon train — one with at least forty wagons. Large trains with extra men greatly reduced the threat of an Indian attack.

"By tomorrow, we'll be at Salt Creek." Win chewed the chicken leg to bare bone and tossed it in the fire. "I bet we'll see a train crossing there and be welcomed like family. A couple of fellows like us, with our own horses and guns — hell, they might even pay us."

Jeb pulled the meat from the bone and wondered what it would be like to be Win, a seemingly unconcerned dandelion seed blowing in whatever direction the wind took it. He guessed he was finding out.

As Win predicted, several wagon trains congregated at the Salt Creek Crossing. A community of blacksmiths and wheelwrights had formed at the river's edge, where trains naturally stopped. Dry goods salesmen made a decent living there, too. Prices were higher than even just thirty miles east, but unless a family wanted to lose two days of travel to get a better price, there was little they could do but pay. Merchants sold just about anything: essentials like flour, sugar, and tools; non-essentials like erroneous guidebooks and elixirs with questionable ingredients; and downright unsavory items like Indian scalps, necklaces of human bones, and other souvenirs confiscated from encounters with hostile Indians.

Win eyed several groups and, for whatever reason, passed them without a word. When they came upon a large train crossing at a wide, shallow spot in the river, Jeb saw what Win had been searching for.

Men on the near side cajoled the oxen into the water, while others on the far side saw to it that the oxen didn't balk once they crossed and were required to scale the riverbank to solid ground again. The whole operation was calm and well organized; several wagons carried children.

One man sat on his horse, supervising. His clothes were practical and well suited to him, his hat was perfectly shaped to keep rain off his neck and sun out of his eyes, his handsome palomino quarter horse was alert and ready for his command, and his age — seasoned, but not ancient — identified him as the boss.

Win said he had a good feeling about this train and approached the man. "Pardon me, sir, are you the trail captain?"

"I am." He didn't volunteer any more

information. Jeb felt himself being sized up immediately.

"Were you hired or elected?" Win asked. "If you don't mind the question."

Settlers who hired a trail boss rather than elect one from their group generally fared better — at least that's what Jeb had gathered from Win. Professionals knew what they were doing and where they were going. Travel was safer, and the petty conflicts fewer.

"It was a mutual agreement," the pilot said as he looked Win over carefully. "It is correct that I have been hired to escort these folks to California, but I'm particular about who I wet-nurse across the prairie. Don't take no simpering city folks, and no Mormons. You ain't Mormon, are you?"

"No, sir," Win said.

"You ain't going to the gold fields in Montana, are you?"

"No, we're —"

"Don't matter where you're going, as long as you ain't Mormon or going to Montana. Only fools go to Montana, and Mormons are peculiar." He spoke with a tone that didn't invite further discussion. He pointed to his train. "These here folks are tough, honest farmers who can handle their own teams and know which end of a rifle to point. Could get there without me, truth be told, but are smart enough not to try. You been through Sioux country before?"

"I have — twice," Win said. "My partner hasn't, but he can handle it."

The trail captain eyed Jeb again and then turned back to Win. "Who was your pilot?"

"Clint Sanders. He's as good as they come."

The lines on the captain's weathered face softened. He pushed his hat back and leaned on his saddle horn. "Shew, that ol' sonofabitch. Clint and me go way back. Scouted together in '50, when we was just pups." He extended his calloused hand to Win.

Win leaned over and shook the man's hand. "Win Avery, sir. This is my partner, Jeb Daw—"

A scream and a splash interrupted their job interview.

While their potential new boss opined about Mormons, Jeb had been watching a wagon enter the river. The husband, Jeb assumed, rode on horseback next to the family's oxen. His wife drove the wagon. Her hair was light colored and she wore it like Jeb's mother had, in a low twist at the nape of her neck. From the back, she looked exactly like Sarah Dawson and, for a confused moment, Jeb thought it might be her. His head cleared, however, when he saw a young girl at the back of their wagon wrestling with a squirmy, little, black dog. The girl screamed when the dog wiggled out of her arms and dropped into the river. Jeb signaled to Galen, who lunged forward and held himself steady as Jeb stretched down from his saddle to fish the soggy little animal out. The girl, who had leaned out too far calling to her dog, lost her balance and tumbled out of the wagon. Jeb jumped off Galen to pluck the sputtering girl from the river before she washed away. He stood in water up to his thighs with the dog tucked under one arm and the girl under the other, both soaking his shirt. The man on horseback arrived to take the girl from him and, reluctantly, the dog as well. Win was grinning ear to ear as Jeb sloshed back up the riverbank, Galen following calmly behind him.

"Shew, I guess I gotta bring you along now." The captain did not offer so much as a thank you or an inquiry into Jeb's condition. "I'm Dutch Ferguson. The boys on this train are stand-up fellas. The rules are that this ain't a democracy — everybody does what I say. No swearing, spitting, or scratching in front of the women. Can't pay you, but we'll feed you in exchange for a good day's work. If that sounds fair, you're welcome to join us."

Jeb pulled off his boots to drain the water as he considered the arbitrary nature of the journey he and Win had begun. Loose dandelion seeds, they'd blown across the path of Dutch Ferguson's train and latched on to it. He stuffed his feet back into squishy leather.

"That sounds fine. Much obliged," Win said. "We'll go as far as we can with you. We're headed for Denver."

Dutch nodded. "You're smart to come this way. It'll take you longer, but you've got a better chance of arriving with your scalp. You heard about them Cheyenne and Arapaho at Sand Creek, I take it. That crazy bastard Chivington stirred up trouble for all of us when he attacked. Plains were safer twenty years ago than they are now. Indians are out for revenge. We'll stay sharp and try to be polite if we run into any." Their new boss then entered the river and crossed with the last wagon.

"And, by the way, thanks for saving that little girl," Jeb muttered to himself as he squeezed water from his shirttail. Win burst out laughing, not *at* Jeb, but with elation, as though having Jeb along broke up some

41

low-hanging clouds of his own. Jeb had to admit that, despite getting soaked, hearing Win let loose helped massage some feeling back into his anesthetized spirit.

Jeb dried out completely that evening at the cook's campfire, where he and Win met the other hired scouts. Win turned quiet; Jeb figured he was feeling out the group. They met Bill Foster, who was working his way back to his home in California, where a wife and teenaged daughter waited for him. A fellow named Toby seemed capable enough, but fidgeted. When he sat on the ground to eat, he'd bounce his leg up and down. Rolf Peterson was a big man, tall and thick — the kind of fellow men want on their side in a fight. A big kidder, Rolf teased Jeb more than once about saving a dog, although his tone was friendly.

The only scout Jeb didn't like was Robert Dale, who stated unequivocally that complete removal of the Indian was the only way to ensure peace and prosperity in the West. Jeb noticed that Win stayed away from him.

The mother of the little girl who had fallen into the river peeked around the corner of Cookie's wagon, her face illuminated by the fire. The men rose; they all looked ill at ease in the company of a woman except for Bill, who welcomed her by name. Jeb removed his hat when the woman approached him, carrying a dish covered by a cloth.

"Mr. Dawson, my husband said it was you that pulled Patches and Lizzie from the river. I don't know how else to thank you, except to offer you this." She folded back the towel, revealing a warm berry cobbler. "Lizzie should've known better than to lean out of the wagon like that. We'll try to be smarter at the next river crossing," she said with an apologetic smile and tilted her head the way his mother used to. Jeb asked her name again, forgetting how Bill addressed her. "Grace Moberg," she said. If their conversation had been private, he might have shared with her that he'd just lost his mother, and he responded so quickly because he'd been noticing how much alike they looked, and even though he'd been living on his own, he missed her. He might have even told the woman a little about Sarah Dawson, how she was graceful and kind and full of life. But, surrounded by trail hands, he just thanked her. She smiled again and left.

Each man produced a fork, indicating that Jeb would be sharing his reward. Jeb took as big a bite as his fork could hold and passed it to the next in line. By the time it came back to him, he scraped the remaining last crumbs from the pan. More banter ensued from Rolf, this time encouraging Jeb to save Patches again at the next crossing, as that Miz Moberg made a fine cobbler.

Nebraska Territory in May looked like a rolling, green sea. Jeb had heard that some people became terrified by the vast emptiness of the prairie, but he saw sacredness in its beauty.

Hippocrates loped up to him, falling in alongside Galen. "There's our ocean," Win said.

"This is far better than swabbing a deck. You're right, Win, the sky is bigger." Jeb breathed in the earthy scents of the prairie. "You were right about a lot of things. I'm never going back. I belong out here. When did you first feel it?"

"Hmmm . . . That's a hard question. I envy you, Jeb. Maybe not at this particular time, but, in general, you are a man with a content disposition — a man at peace. Me, on the other hand, I'm always trying to find something, and I don't even know what I'm lookin' for. And it gets in the way of . . . well, appreciating things. It is beautiful out here, no doubt about that. It can turn on you, though. This country is the harshest I've ever seen. Sometimes the evil and beauty, the ugliness and splendor, get kind of jumbled together."

"That's what draws you to it."

"Maybe so."

Word came from one of the scouts that Fort Kearney had reported cases of measles. Dutch said he was more afraid of measles than Indians, because at least he could see Indians coming and knew what he was up against. Measles spread silently and could wipe out a train before anyone knew what hit them. He ordered the train to change course and head for Midway Station instead. Win took the news in stride, so Jeb did, too — not that he had any say in the matter.

The men began taking turns on a night watch. At midnight, Toby kicked Jeb and Win awake, saying it was time for their shift. Win grabbed his rifle and motioned to Jeb to follow him. They walked about a hundred yards away from the wagons to a little rise where they could see in every direction.

"What do we look for?" Jeb whispered as they settled in.

"Anything sneaking up on us," his friend said, keeping his voice low, "but with this full moon, there's nothing to worry about."

Win produced a handkerchief filled with biscuits that he'd stuffed inside his shirt, obviously stolen from the cook's wagon. He pulled them apart and gave half to Jeb.

"Cookie'll have your hide if he finds out you stole these."

"Better eat up, then," Win said.

Jeb destroyed the evidence by stuffing it in his mouth and looked around. He could see for miles on the moonlit prairie. Win seemed to know what he was talking about. Nothing could sneak up on them.

"There was a fellow at the mill who hated Indians," Jeb said after a while. He spoke quietly — voices carried at night. "Like that Robert Dale. He told story after story about terrible things they've done to settlers. It'd make your blood run cold."

"Hmmm . . . I've heard those stories, too. Pretty damn scary."

"Have you ever seen any?"

"Only from a distance." Win laughed quietly. "I heard someone say that sympathy for the Indian is directly relative to the distance one lives from them. He was talking about folks out east who think of the Indian as a noble savage living in consort with nature. He said Indian-lovers are people who just haven't met one yet."

"Seems to be Dale's opinion."

46

Win shook his head sadly, his eyes scanning the landscape. "White folks can be ruthless, too. I was ashamed when I read in the papers about the execution in Mankato. Thirty-eight Dakota hanged."

"President Lincoln reviewed the trial records himself to determine which ones committed rape and murder of civilians. Hundreds were released."

"The Indians left the reservation in the first place because the government didn't send the food they promised. They were starving. Wouldn't you leave and fend for yourself?"

"Yeah, but raiding for food and carving up people are two different things."

"I agree. It's just that there's a lack of understanding on both sides. A lot of hate comes from ignorance, but neither side seems to want to listen to what the other has to say."

"The Swedes and the Irish at the sawmill hated each other, but I knew men in both camps who were decent fellows."

"My old boss, Clint, told me about an Indian who saved his life. He said he was a decent, honorable man. They're still good friends."

"Don't know why we all can't just get

along." Jeb felt naïve saying the words out loud.

"Yup. It's a complicated mess." They were quiet for a while, listening to the crickets. "Lose much tonight?" Win asked finally.

"Two bits; haven't played poker in months. I'm a little rusty."

Win removed his hat to scratch his head. "Well, when Rolf's bluffing, he glances at everyone first. If you've got anything better than a pair, call him. And just fold if Toby ever stops bouncing that damn leg of his."

"You've got a keen eye. What else have you learned out here besides thievery and poker?"

"Well, let's see. Clint taught me enough of the Arapaho language to get me into trouble. And I've spent some interesting nights with whores. I learned a fair piece of knowledge from them, and they're more fun to talk about." He grinned at Jeb with one eye closed in a wink.

"You always were good at learning when you put your mind to it."

Win laughed quietly. "Yeah, the subject captured my interest, for sure. How 'bout you? You been with a woman?"

Jeb snorted, giving away that the experience had not been all he had expected, something he'd admit only to Win. "The

48

boys at the mill went drinking every Saturday night, once they collected their wages. I never saw the point of working so hard all week just to lose it in one night. I went along a couple of times, though, so they wouldn't think I was unfriendly. They visited a bordello and talked me into going. Got kind of a young, pretty one the first time, but the next time I got one that was . . . coarser. Just didn't seem right."

"Huh," Win said. Jeb wondered if Win was recalling his own experiences. Coyotes yelped from a fair distance away.

"How'd you feel? You know . . . afterward." Jeb scanned the grasses as they rustled in the breeze.

"After being with those women?" Win asked. "Hmm . . . educated. I got a really good one once. Believe me, she was different from most. I paid her extra to show me what to do — you know, what women like . . . It isn't something a proper wife talks about, I guess."

"Didn't you feel . . . I don't know . . . guilty?" Jeb shifted in his seat. "I felt kinda bad, like I used her."

"You paid her, didn't you?"

"Yeah, two dollars."

Win waved his hand as though to absolve Jeb's lingering guilt. "Consider it paying for a type of education you can't get anywhere else. Believe me, that knowledge is gonna come in handy someday. Look at Glenn Moberg . . . his wife is so sweet and nice. Why? 'Cause he knows what he's doing, that's why. I'll bet if you asked him, he'd say he got helpful experience from a sportin' gal before he ever met that nice woman. How else are you supposed to know what to do?"

Win had an unconventional, yet oddly pragmatic, view of the world. Jeb figured it came from being shuffled around from home to home when he was young. Maybe he had seen and heard more than boys should and drew conclusions that may not have been accurate, but had been etched in his young mind nonetheless.

Jeb considered Win's view of the Mobergs. Mr. Moberg was a pleasant, contented man, who had an equally pleasant wife. His own parents had been happy that way, too.

"That Grace Moberg sure looks like Ma, doesn't she? Goddamn outlaws. Why couldn't they have just shot each other? Why'd they have to take Ma and Pa with them?"

Win nodded. "Hmm . . . I don't blame you for asking that. But, you know, Pa kept questioning why my ma got sick. He couldn't get an answer, and it ate away at him. Influenza took Ma's life, but then Pa let the bottle take his. Hard to say what my fate would have been if your folks hadn't stepped in. I'm not saying you can't feel the way you do, but you'll never get an answer to your question. Eventually, it'll come down to this: are you going to let those men take your life, too, by letting grief swallow you up? Or are you going to beat them by living your life in spite of what they took from you?"

Often full of bullshit, this time Win made sense.

By mid-afternoon the next day, their luck with good weather had run out. Jeb smelled the change in the air. He and Win rode the back left flank of the train, watching the clouds build on the horizon. The breeze switched directions and picked up speed. Storm clouds billowed and the sky lost its brilliant blue color, fading into a hazy white. The air became heavy.

Win stood tall in his saddle and craned his neck in the direction of the approaching storm. "That's gonna hit right about sunset."

Lightning was the biggest danger out in open country. Dutch turned the lead wagon

51

and headed for a low area. No guarantee, but it was safer than the top of a ridge. Orders came to hustle along. Galen snorted and whinnied nervously when the bank of clouds stuck on the horizon broke loose and rolled closer. Distant, rumbling thunder warned of the power trapped inside the large, dark anvil blocking the late-afternoon sun. Dutch motioned to the men to circle up.

The animals were herded inside the corral of wagons, men tied down every flap, and women piled trunks on top of each other to make room for their families inside the only shelter on the open prairie. A bolt of lightning and clap of thunder sent everyone scrambling. Jeb unsaddled Galen inside the corral and tried to stash his gear inside the supply wagon, but other men had already claimed the spot. Win grabbed some wooden crates, shoved them under the cook's wagon, and showed Jeb how to squeeze himself and his gear on top of them. As soon as the rain began, water ran under the wagon, but the men and their gear stayed dry.

"How many miserable rainy nights did you spend before you figured this out?" Jeb propped his head up against his saddle.

"Only took one."

Jeb lay quietly and listened for the roar of a twister hidden inside the storm, since he couldn't watch the sky while tucked under the wagon. He'd seen only one tornado in his life, but witnessed the destruction it caused many times and knew the wagon was no shelter against its power. Lightning illuminated the wagons encircling the livestock. Many of the horses congregated together. Galen and Hippocrates stood next to each other. Jeb wondered if it was intentional — if they felt safer together — or if it was just a coincidence.

Win then produced a deck of cards and, to Jeb's surprise, some jerky and a bottle of whiskey. "We can't drink too much, or Cookie'll notice."

"I swear, Win, you're gonna get caught someday and then what —"

Win sat up in surprise, cracking his head on the underside of the wagon. "Look at that!" He pointed past Jeb to the horses inside the circle of wagons. Blue light tipped the horses' ears, like ethereal, blue flames. "Remember that book your ma read to us about the ship that glowed with blue light during the storm?"

In the story, electric discharge at the ends of the mast and crosstrees caused the tips to emit a pale-blue light. "I remember," Jeb said. "Ma called it St. Elmo's fire."

"Out here, they call it 'foxfire.' "

"I guess that's some of that splendor mixed up with the harshness you were talking about."

A flash of lightning illuminated Win's face. Jeb could tell by the way his eyes shone that Win believed every word as he said, "It's a sign. Something good's gonna happen. Foxfire always brings good luck. You'll see."

The storm raged on, the wagons a ring of isolated ships on the prairie sea. After a swallow of whiskey apiece and a half-hearted attempt at a card game, the two friends stretched out on the wooden crates, listening to the rain. Jeb wondered what other evil and splendor was out there, all jumbled together.

CHAPTER THREE:
MEG JAMESON

Nebraska Territory, Spring 1865

Meg Jameson gripped her legs around her horse's belly as the mare thundered across the prairie at full gallop. Terrified by the men chasing her, she had to keep reminding herself to relax her hold on the reins, allowing her rescuer unrestrained movement. Biscuit, her beloved companion for nine years, was faster than the wind when allowed to stretch out. Meg let her, because at the moment, Biscuit was the one in greater danger.

Her guardian uncle had threatened to kill Biscuit. His breath on Meg's neck, his doughy hand moving too close to her breast, the smell of powerful cologne making her eyes water — all of it was repulsive. But the words he'd whispered, "Let me touch you, or you'll find your precious horse gutted in her stall," induced her to act. Meg escaped on her horse that night.

John Sutter, a heartless soul who did all of her uncle's dirty work, had picked up her trail in Omaha City. She had no choice but to abandon the road and flee into open country. For days, following tributaries and using the shrubbery along the riverbank for concealment, horse and rider traveled upstream. When they climbed out into the open again, Meg was lost, and a long way from home.

The sun slipped below the horizon. The blanket of twilight would allow her to travel a while longer before the heavier quilt of darkness enveloped them, but Meg saw a good hiding spot in a thicket along a stream and decided to stop. She unsaddled Biscuit and ate some jerky. She pulled down her breeches and relieved herself. The buttery soft, deerskin breeches protected her legs from chafing, and she was glad she had had the sense to grab them before she fled. She wore them under her skirts whenever she rode. Sore from so many hours in the saddle, skin abrasions would have made matters worse. Gus had given her a new pair of riding breeches every year since she was eight years old. Dear Gus. She'd give anything to be with him right now.

She shivered as the humid night air condensed into dew. Afraid that a fire would give away her location, Meg grabbed a blanket and wrapped it around her head and shoulders. The nocturnal animals began to stir. Crickets chirped loudly to each other, as if seeking companionship in the dark. Meg leaned against the saddle and held the loaded rifle close. Exhausted, but unable to sleep, she watched the stars come out, pulling the blanket closer and wondering what Gus would say about all this. *You're in a pickle,* he'd say; *a goddamn pickle — that's a fact.* The old stableman didn't sugarcoat words. He always spoke the truth and set her straight. She relied on him for everything, and he'd never let her down. Meg loved Gus. He was the father and mother she lost a decade earlier. He was her whole world. Once she came of age, her inheritance would be released to her. She'd be free from her depraved uncle, and planned to buy a spread of land and take care of Gus in his old age — like he'd taken care of her.

Often she and Gus took the ferry across the river and rode into the wilds past Omaha. Once when they were out riding, Gus pointed out a rider cutting across a long, flat stretch of prairie. He told Meg he was a rider for the Pony Express — he could tell by the special saddle. He said they were the fastest riders ever to cross the plains. Meg took off after the rider before Gus could stop her. The rider spurred his horse into a gallop once he spotted her coming. She rode alongside of him, pushing Biscuit hard, exhilarated by the race. The rider finally tipped his hat to her, at which point she grinned and slowed down, letting the rider continue without her. Why she wanted to challenge the fastest riders on the prairie she couldn't say, but she rode back to Gus triumphant. With pride and delight in his voice, Gus quoted some philosopher. What had he said? He said friendship was a single soul dwelling in two bodies. She and Biscuit were a single soul, he said. You and I are a single soul, too, Gus, she thought. I miss you.

Gus cared about her more than anyone else — of that, she was certain. When she told him how her uncle would leer at her, try to touch her, and say scandalous things to her, Gus smoothed his wiry, white mustache, squinted sharply at her with his piercing, blue eyes, and said, "Meggie, darlin', I won't let that bastard scrape away your sparkle." He showed her how to kick a man to disable him and how to jam the back of a chair under a doorknob. Perhaps most helpful of all was just knowing Gus was on her side.

She wished now that she hadn't panicked and run away before finding him.

The moon was up, so full and bright it cast shadows. Biscuit grazed quietly nearby. Her indifference to the night sounds gave Meg some assurance that all was well. A breeze swirled around her, and the scents of the prairie soothed her. The grasses, the flowers, even the soil itself had an aroma that, despite her circumstances, drew her in and calmed her. She drifted to sleep.

Biscuit's soft nose tickled Meg awake as the sun first lightened the eastern sky. Startled, Meg sat up abruptly and spun her head in all directions, looking for danger. She and Biscuit were alone.

The breeze rustled the stately, big blue stem and airy switch grasses, each catching the wind differently, the movement captivating Meg. Pasque flowers, the first to bloom in the spring, were beginning to fade as new flowers emerged. Meg plucked several prairie violets and stuck them in Biscuit's coarse mane as she tried to decide if it was safe to turn back.

Biscuit directed her ears forward, then back, then forward again, as if searching for a sound. Meg thought she heard something, too, and quickly mounted, preparing to flee if necessary. But the sound was that of a child crying. Meg told herself it must be her imagination playing tricks on her, or the grasses whispering, perhaps, and yet she heard it again. Biscuit snorted nervously, her ears pointed straight ahead.

Meg stood in her saddle and looked around. Only the trees and bushes hugging the riverbank broke up the endless expanse. She pulled her rifle from its sheath. "Hup," she whispered, and the horse advanced toward the sound.

Biscuit snorted again. The crying stopped abruptly. Meg peered into the tall grass in front of her and saw the frightened face of an Indian child not thirty paces away. She and the child both gasped. Then the child disappeared in the grass.

"Wait!" Meg called, startled by her own voice. She could see the child trying to scramble away. She rode over to a young Indian boy, about ten years old — probably Pawnee, considering she was in Nebraska Territory. He turned and produced a knife, ready to fight. She pointed her rifle at him.

He wore only a breechcloth, and both of his ankles were badly swollen. He tried to look fierce, but Meg could see that he was just frightened, and in pain. His cheeks were stained with tears. It was hard to imagine someone was worse off than she, out in the middle of nowhere, but it seemed to be the case. She felt a little braver for it, and bolder. Gus always said that most people were decent if treated with a little respect. He also said that kindness had a way of circling back to itself. She lowered her rifle. The boy looked relieved. She put it back in its sheath and pulled out some jerky. She showed it to the boy and tossed a piece to him as a gesture of goodwill. Keeping a wary eye on her, he felt for the jerky, sniffed it, and wolfed it down.

Gus would try to help the boy, she thought. She certainly couldn't just ride away, seeing he was hurt. "I'll find some sticks for a splint," she said. He jumped, as though her voice startled him. Meg pointed to his ankles and gestured for him to wait there — which seemed a little silly, since he couldn't go anywhere anyway.

She rode over to the stream, cut cattail leaves and hemp stems with her own knife, and gathered moss and as much mud as she could carry on a mat of leaves. When she returned, he'd disappeared in the tall grass. Meg and Biscuit meandered back and forth, scanning the area, until suddenly his hand popped up, waving. She felt oddly flattered that he'd signaled to her and hurried over.

Together they fashioned crude splints for both of his ankles. The supple grass secured the thicker stems used to brace the ankles in place. When she packed mud around his ankles, his expression softened a little, as though the coolness eased his pain. He pointed to her face and said something she couldn't understand. She touched the tender area where her uncle had struck her. Apparently, she had a black eye.

"Do you speak any English at all?" Meg asked. The boy looked at her blankly. She pointed to herself and said, "Meg," and then pointed to the boy with a questioning look. The boy responded with a long string of sounds. She furrowed her brow. The boy leaned forward and spoke slowly, emphasizing each syllable patiently, as if speaking to a stupid child.

"Wa-sha-nee-ko-mo-se-ma."

"Wa . . . sha . . . nee . . . o —"

"KO-mo-se-ma."

"Wa . . . sha . . . nee . . . ko . . . mo . . . se . . . ma?"

The boy nodded and pointed back at Meg. "Mig."

"Meg," she corrected him.

"May-g," he said, imitating her emphasis. She nodded. Close enough.

She stood up and patted the saddle. "Washaneekomosema," she said, indicating that he would sit there. Then she held the reins, as if to lead the horse. The boy nodded and allowed her to help him into the saddle. He blinked rapidly as the blood rushed to his ankles. He grabbed Biscuit's mane tightly. Meg knew he must be in pain, but there was nothing else to do. Meg pointed out into the prairie. "Which way?" she asked. He pointed. Meg led Biscuit north.

Although thankful for the company after being alone for so many days, Meg worried about the direction they were headed. The Pawnee lived on a reservation along the Loup River in the central part of Nebraska Territory, and if they were going there, she had wandered too far north. But Pawnee men served as scouts for the US cavalry, so maybe he was taking her to a fort.

The boy began to chat. He pointed to Meg's hair and then touched his own. Meg couldn't understand him, but figured he had never seen hair the color of hers before. She knew it was unusual, mostly because none of the girls at school had ginger-colored hair and seemed to resent her for it. Meg never understood what all the fuss was about. She shrugged at the Pawnee boy, who laughed, pointed at the sun, and said something else she couldn't understand.

A moment later, he pointed at the horizon, where she saw a mustang pony, presumably his, grazing next to the stream. Meg figured the boy must have hurt his ankles falling from the pony. She whistled a low, soothing melody the way Gus did when he had to calm skittish horses. The mustang lifted its head and perked up its ears. Meg led Biscuit slowly toward the mustang, whistling softly. The boy's pony walked right over to her. She gently grabbed the rope around its neck and stroked its nose affectionately while the boy, agile even with mud and grass boots, transferred himself to the pony's back. Meg then climbed into her own saddle, relieved to be back on Biscuit again.

"Gus would be pleased that you climbed right back on to what bucked you off. Shows grit; he likes that in a person." She knew he couldn't understand her, but enjoyed pretending that he did. "Well, I'd better go before your family finds you. They must be out looking for you. I don't think I want to meet grown-up Indians."

No sooner had she said the words when three Pawnee men appeared. The boy called to them before Meg could stop him. Her instinct was to flee, but as fast as Biscuit was, Meg didn't think she could outrun them.

An older man and two young men approached on horseback. By the way the boy greeted them, she assumed they were his family. Reluctantly, she followed the boy as he rode over to them. When they crested a small hill, their village came into view. At least twenty domed earthen structures dotted the north side of the riverbank, their long passageway entrances facing east. Smoke rose from the opening at the top of each of the lodges, all of which stood well over ten feet high and over forty feet wide. Meg could see people moving about. The village looked peaceful, even serene, in the early morning calm. The three Pawnee men did not, however, and loomed large as they approached. Necklaces rattled against their bare chests. The younger men's heads were shaved, except for a strip of tufted hair down the center. The older man was missing an ear, but several earrings dangled from the other. The men looked fierce; she held her breath, her heart pounded. The boy cheerfully greeted them as their eyes traveled from her to the rough splints on his feet and back to her again. Meg gripped her reins as they studied Biscuit, worried they might take her. The youngest of the men spoke harshly to the boy, but Washaneeko-mosema ignored him and chattered away to the older man, gesturing to her and to his feet. The boy whistled the same melody she used to call his horse. All the ponies pivoted their ears toward the boy. Meg assumed he was giving them an account of what she had done, and was glad she had helped him.

The boy finally pointed to her and said, "May-g." They all stared.

Meg felt the blood drain from her face. She felt woozy, but managed to utter the only Pawnee word she knew. "Wa-sha-nee-ko-mo-se-ma," she said carefully, pointing back at the boy.

The boy laughed with delight. His family remained stoic, so he quieted and looked back and forth from the older man to Meg. The older man had not taken his eyes off her.

The Pawnee spoke among themselves. Meg remembered Gus telling her Pawnee weren't as hostile against white people as their enemies, the Cheyenne and the Lakota. She wondered what they were saying, if she could do anything to help her situation, or if her fate had already been sealed. The boy didn't seem concerned; Meg hoped his account of her actions would weigh in her favor.

66

The older man pointed to a notch on the horizon, where two sets of rolling hills converged. Then he waved her away, as if to shoo flies from food. He said something to her she couldn't understand, but it appeared he wanted her to go in that direction. The boy smiled at her and raised his hand. Meg automatically raised her hand to wave, thinking he was waving good-bye, and felt embarrassed when she realized he, too, was pointing to the notch. The Pawnee family turned to head back to their camp. Meg galloped away as fast as she dared.

For the rest of the day, Meg angled her way south and west across softly rolling terrain. She scanned the landscape for a line of vertical telegraph poles directing her to a relay station or a road leading to a stagecoach station or a farm. With a burst of renewed hope, she loped to the crest of a high hill. Surely from such a vantage point, she'd be able to see something. She gasped when she saw the hills roll out endlessly in front of her and cried out in despair.

"Oh, my precious girl, what are we going to do?" Meg leaned forward to hug Biscuit. She watched the sun dip behind storm clouds gathering in the west. She'd spend another scary night on the prairie — undoubtedly, a wet one. Her heart sank.

But as the clouds blocked out the sun's glare, they allowed for a clearer view of the landscape. A white line in the sea of grass caught her attention. A wagon train! Behind the train, and only about five miles away, a lone prairie schooner appeared to be chasing after the rest of the train. It must have fallen behind, she decided. She looked for the fastest route toward it as the wind shifted and the sky darkened.

By the time she reached the wagon, the wind had picked up and light rain fell. A young couple waved to her, but didn't stop.

"Wagons!" the man shouted so the wind couldn't carry away his voice. He pointed west.

"I saw them!" Meg shouted back, a gust of wind sucking away her breath. "I'll ride ahead and tell them to wait for you!" The man nodded and Meg signaled to Biscuit. A few miles ahead, she came upon a river. The wagons were nowhere in sight, but the ruts left behind in the sand showed where they had crossed.

She rode back to the couple. "There's a river up ahead. They already crossed!"

"We've got to get across before the rain!" The man slapped the reins hard. The scrawny oxen seemed to go at the same speed regardless of how much encouragement they were given. A low rumble of thunder warned of the rain that soon followed. Meg found herself riding along next to them, not knowing what else to do. After days of solitude, an encounter with Pawnees, and now a storm, she was grateful to be with people who spoke English.

"I'm Beth!" the young woman shouted through the rain. "This is my husband, Jim! What's your name?"

"Meg!" The wind took her voice away.

"We just got married!" Beth shouted, trying to make conversation, but after Jim said something to her, she shrugged at Meg, a gesture indicating she was postponing pleasantries for the time being.

When they reached the river, rain poured from the sky; the water level had already risen to the top of the bank. "I don't think we should cross," Meg shouted to Jim. "It looks dangerous."

"If we don't cross now, we'll never catch up," he shouted back.

"I'm sure they will wait —"

"We aren't part of their train. They don't know we're here."

"We just eloped, 'cause my parents didn't approve," Beth shouted, as if that explained everything. So they were runaways, too.

Jim looked haggard. "It's the first train we've seen. We've got to get across."

"But the water . . ."

"It hasn't been raining that long." Jim had made his decision. He jumped down from the wagon and led the oxen into the water. Lightning flashed and thunder boomed overhead. Hail pelted down on them briefly — chunks of ice hurled from the sky, startling the oxen, which lurched forward in a panic. Meg hunched over Biscuit to protect her. Biscuit danced about nervously, but followed her command and waded into the river.

The river spilled over its shallow bank. With every step, the other side of the river moved farther away. Meg saw only gray; the opposite bank disappeared completely as the water and the sky became the same color. The water rose quickly and rushed faster and faster. Meg felt the river wash over her feet, tugging at her stirrups. Biscuit slipped, and regained her footing, but snorted in protest. Meg turned back. Only a fool would cross a river so swollen. She wasn't going to risk it, even if it meant being left behind. The oxen bellowed at Jim, who was now chest deep in water. Water spilled over the sides of the wagon. Beth called to her husband, who tried in vain to get the oxen to move. Biscuit clambered up the muddy bank to safety. Meg turned around just in time to see the wagon tipped sideways by the rushing water, pitching Beth into the river. She screamed; Jim dove into the water after his young wife. Meg watched in horror as the oxen lost their footing and were swept downriver, the weight of the wagon pulling them under. Meg rode along the bank in the pouring rain, trying to keep up with the wreckage and the drowning couple, shouting their names.

CHAPTER FOUR:
WIN

Nebraska Territory, the next morning

At daybreak, the dark-haired girl in Win's dream lingered momentarily, smiled at him, and then scurried away with the rest of the night's images. Win emerged from his makeshift shelter under Cookie's wagon and slipped the whiskey bottle back into its hiding place.

The storm had passed and it looked to be a clear, cool day, the kind of day made for the unencumbered. No worries about the future, no plans to figure out yet — just a day to be savored.

Jeb appeared, combing his hair with his fingers. Cookie made extra pancakes for the men and put bacon in the beans, as there had been no dinner the night before. Dutch came by and assigned Win and Jeb the job of scouting the river for a place to cross. Toby had seen a train cross just before the storm, and Dutch wanted to know if the

72

spot they chose was still passable. They shoveled the last forkfuls of food into their mouths, drained their coffee cups, and saddled up.

Raindrops clung to the patches of tall grass and glistened in the sun. Win watched with amusement as Jeb closed his eyes and breathed in the fresh scent of prairie sage after a storm. Jeb looked up at the blue sky, squinting. "This is a fine day, Win. I'm glad we didn't take a stagecoach. It would've been a shame to miss all this."

They rode to the crest of a hill to get a good view of the river. It had indeed flooded its banks, widening into a shallow lake. Crossing would be difficult and muddy, ruining Jeb's fine day.

Win turned north. "Let's go upriver a bit, see if we can find a place to cross. Otherwise, the boss will want to hold up 'til this dries out. There's nothing worse than digging out a wagon stuck in the mud."

Galen and Hippocrates trotted along the ridge. In the distance, Win noticed a figure. As they got closer, he saw a girl on her knees, digging. Her horse tossed its head and whinnied; the girl dropped the piece of wood that was her makeshift shovel and pulled a rifle from its sheath. The men immediately slowed down. Win raised his hand to show they meant no harm.

Soaked through and caked with mud, the girl's clothes hung heavily on her. She swayed slightly, as though she might topple over from the weight. Her long, thick braid seemed to pull her head toward the ground. She had wild primitiveness about her.

"Do you speak English?" Win asked.

The ferocity faded, replaced by a tired, puzzled expression. "Of course."

"We're from a wagon train a couple of miles back . . . just checking the river. My name is Win Avery. This here is Jeb Dawson," he said. Jeb touched the rim of his hat politely, a gesture Win found amusing given the circumstances. Win leaned forward in his saddle. "What in the world are you doing out here?"

"These folks drowned in the river last night. I couldn't just leave them." She nodded toward two corpses lying next to each other, positioned tenderly to look as though they were sleeping.

Win was taken aback; she was digging a grave. "Are they your kin?"

"No." She stared at the bodies, her brow furrowed.

Jeb dismounted. "You've had quite a time. Let me dig for a while." He picked up the broken piece of wood and began to scrape the ground.

The girl stared at Jeb, and then turned to the bodies. "I couldn't get to them. The river was too fast. If they hadn't gotten snagged in a log jam, I never would have caught up to them." She told Win and Jeb that she'd found the couple at first light, drowned, bobbing face-down in a tangle of branches at the curve in the river. She'd met Jim and Beth the day before, just as the storm hit, but the river pulled them under when they tried to cross. She tried to pull them out of the water, she said, but they were too heavy, so she wrapped the torn canvas bonnet from the wreckage around them and had Biscuit drag them to higher ground. She said she hoped it wasn't disrespectful. Win thought it was resourceful.

"What's your name?" Win asked.

She stared at him for so long he wondered whether she was so traumatized she couldn't remember, or if she was fabricating a lie. In either case, her hesitation gave him an opportunity to get a good look at her. Underneath all the mud, she was pretty. She had rather large blue eyes and freckles spattered across her nose and cheeks — or maybe it was just dirt, Win couldn't tell. She had a black eye that he wondered about. Her cheeks were pink from digging in the chilly morning air. There was something familiar about her, too. And her horse, which bothered him nearly as much. He seldom forgot a horse that had taken his eye.

"Meg Jameson," she said finally.

As though her name reminded her to do something, Meg stumbled over to a tangled mess of river debris and picked up another plank of wood. Without a word, she sat down hard, pulled the knife from her boot, and began carving letters into it. The girl intrigued Win, despite the grim circumstances. He glanced at Jeb with a raised eyebrow, expecting Jeb to shake his head at him, an affable warning to steer clear of guaranteed trouble. But Win caught Jeb stealing a glance at the girl, too.

"You still haven't said what you are doing out here. Where are you from?" Win asked.

Meg sighed heavily, as though tired of his questions, and didn't answer. Win exchanged places with Jeb. Between the two of them, they dug the grave in a fraction of the time it would have taken the girl. Once they buried the couple, Meg took the plank on which she had carved "Jim + Beth 1865" and stuck it in the ground.

"I wish I knew their family name," she said.

"You'd just met them." Jeb had a way of

stating the obvious that never sounded ridiculous, just comforting.

Meg nodded. "All I know is they had just gotten married and her parents didn't approve." She shrugged, perhaps feeling absolved.

Win and Jeb removed their hats. No one said anything. Win glanced at Jeb, wondering if he was recalling standing over his parents' graves not so long ago. He also studied the mystery girl, but she revealed nothing else about who she was or where she'd come from.

After a moment of silence, Win returned his hat to his head and cleared his throat. "Well, come on, we'll take you back with us. Cookie'll give you something to eat." When the girl hesitated, Win spread his arms out, palms up — a gesture indicating she didn't have much of a choice. "Miss Jameson, what else are you going to do? You're a mess, and you can barely stand up."

"You don't have to be afraid of us," Jeb said.

He did it again, Win thought, obvious and comforting . . . damn him.

Meg pulled herself onto her horse and followed them. If hunger and exhaustion competed against wariness of strange men, the former won.

Dutch scowled when he saw the girl. Win rode ahead to explain, but Dutch was ready with his own questions and held up his hands to stop her before she got too close.

"Hold up, there," he called to the girl. "What train are you from? They leave you 'cause you're sick?"

"I'm not from a train. I'm . . . traveling alone," she called back. "I'm not sick."

"Jeb and I found her burying a couple who drowned in the river, sir." Win dismounted next to Dutch. "They didn't seem to be with a train, either, from what we could tell. Her name is Meg Jameson."

"How's the river?" Dutch directed the question to Win, but studied Meg carefully.

"You mean the lake? Crossable upstream about two miles."

Dutch nodded. "I figured. We'll take the wagons upriver . . . camp today, rest and dry out." Then he muttered, "This should be interesting." He walked over to Meg as she dismounted. "That's a fine bay you're riding, miss. Is she yours?"

"Yes, sir, Biscuit's mine."

Despite her exhausted state, she raised her chin proudly, causing Win to smile.

The trail captain smiled slightly, too.

"What are you doing out here alone? How'd you get that shiner?"

Meg's hand flew up to her cheek. She lowered her eyes. "Does it matter?"

Dutch folded his arms across his chest. "It matters if you've got trouble on your tail and it's coming our way."

She paled. Curious as he was to hear her answer, Win felt sympathy for Meg. Her eyes darted to the eastern horizon. Clearly, she was in some kind of trouble. The question was whether it was of her own making.

Meg had no chance to answer. Grace Moberg pushed through the group of men, practically shedding feathers as she put her arms around the startled girl. "Gracious, child! You poor thing!" she clucked. "Surely your questions can wait, Mr. Ferguson." Apparently, news that Win and Jeb found a girl on the prairie had already spread among the settlers. She asked Meg when she last ate and offered her breakfast. She was about to whisk her away, but Dutch stopped them.

"Just answer this. Where're you from?"

"Council Bluffs, sir."

He squinted. "You ain't Mormon, are you?"

"No, sir."

Grace raised her eyebrows and gave him a look that stopped further inquiries. As they left the circle of men, Meg glanced back at Win and Jeb.

"She didn't say what she was doing out here," Dale said after she was gone. He seemed perturbed by her presence, but Dale seemed perturbed about everything.

"Take it easy, Dale. Let's give her a chance to eat and get cleaned up," Dutch said.

Dale wandered off. Before Win left, he heard Dutch mutter to Cookie, "Two young bucks and a single pretty doe; if that ain't a smoldering cinder next to a powder keg, I don't know what is."

CHAPTER FIVE:
JEB

Nebraska Territory, same day

Jeb scraped the mud from the hooves of Meg's horse, killing time while he waited, along with the other men, for his turn at the river. The river's edge was the women's private territory for the time being. They gathered at the bank to wash clothes and bathe. The men occupied themselves by repairing torn canvas and greasing wagon axles, keeping their eyes respectfully averted.

He admired the lines of Biscuit as he checked her for injuries, the only thing he could think of to do for Miss Jameson. She was tougher than she looked — like a durable willow, seemingly delicate, but, in truth, could not be blown down. Beneath the mud and exhaustion lay power that unnerved him. He was the one who felt rescued.

Jeb grabbed a handful of oats and cupped it under Biscuit's nose. "This would be a bribe, pretty girl, if I thought you'd tell me about your owner."

Biscuit wolfed down the oats and then nuzzled Jeb affectionately, perhaps to thank him — or perhaps to weasel more oats from him. Either way, the mare shared no secrets about Meg Jameson.

The Mobergs' girl, Lizzie, had taken a shine to Jeb ever since he plucked her from the river and gravitated toward him when the train made camp. Even though she chattered excessively at times, he didn't mind her company. Win often slipped away when he saw her coming, but Jeb thought she was funny and she had an infectious smile. Now that Grace had Meg under her wing, Jeb was particularly interested in any news Lizzie had to share, and didn't mind at all when she spotted him and ran over.

"She's real pretty, Mr. Dawson," Lizzie said of Meg as she climbed on the wheel of the supply wagon and balanced precariously on one of the spokes. Jeb nearly reached out to grab her, thinking she would fall, but she jumped down safely and turned to climb up the wheel again. "Her hair is red and gold and sparkles like sunlight on water," she said in a wistful way that made Jeb smile. "Ma made sure Meg had something to eat, and then took her down to the water. Ma said she wished she could wash away her troubles along with the mud. Once we got her all cleaned up and in one of Ma's dresses, Ma sent me away, and you know what that means . . . *grown-up* talk." Lizzie jumped down from the wheel again. "Can I give Biscuit some oats?"

Jeb passed the bucket to her as he imagined Meg bathing at the river.

Lizzie cupped oats in her hand for Biscuit. "I bet she got in a fight, just like Johnny Novak and Molly Stapleton did back home. I bet that's how she got that black eye."

"I guess she'll tell us if she wants to." Jeb unsaddled Meg's horse and laid the wet blanket in the sun.

"Molly socked Johnny right in the ol' kisser," Lizzie said with a dramatic flair. "At least, that's what Betty Ann said. I didn't see it, but the next day at school, Johnny's lip looked like this." She curled down her bottom lip and puffed it out to make her lips look twice their normal size.

"Elizabeth Ann Moberg." Lizzie's mother came up behind her, hands on her hips. "You know it's not polite to gossip."

"Aw, I ain't gossiping about Meg, just Johnny and Molly." Lizzie mirrored her mother, putting her hands on her hips.

Grace ignored the excuse. "The Spencer

83

boys are out collecting buffalo chips. Go help and stay close to them. No wandering off." She handed her daughter a basket.

"Yes'm." Lizzie ran off to find the boys.

Grace turned to Jeb. "Did Miss Jameson tell you what she was doing out here?"

"Nah. Hardly said a word, but my hunch is she's running from something."

"I got that feeling, too, so I asked her if she had man trouble. It's usually men who cause most of the trouble women face. No offense."

"None taken, ma'am," Jeb said, although inwardly he winced at the thought of a man causing Meg's trouble. He wondered if a husband gave her that black eye. It would be a damn shame if she were married. "Does she, um . . . have man trouble?"

Before Grace could answer, Win arrived at the makeshift corral and announced that Dutch had assigned the task of providing the crew's dinner meat to Win and Jeb. Jeb sighed heavily. The trail captain kept the two of them so busy, Jeb wondered how anything would've gotten done if they hadn't joined his train.

Win turned to Grace. "How's Miss Muddy?"

"Well, that's what I came to tell you." Grace addressed them both. "Meg will join

84

our family until we get to someplace civilized. Glenn's already told Mr. Ferguson we'll take full responsibility for her."

"What's her story?" Win asked.

"She's had quite a time, let me tell you." Grace leaned toward them as if sharing something confidential. "Poor thing. She's scared to death of a man called Sutter. He rides a piebald with three white legs and a black one, so be on the lookout. He works for her uncle, and, my gracious, the stories Meg told me about both of them! Her uncle threatened to kill her horse if she didn't . . . Well, all you two need to know is she's a good girl and needs our help. She's done nothing wrong, and you should be proper gentlemen around her, not that I have to remind the two of you."

"Yes, ma'am," Jeb said.

Mrs. Moberg tilted her head and smiled at Jeb. "If more men were like you boys and Glenn, I wouldn't have to say the disparaging things about them I did earlier."

"What did she say earlier?" Win asked Jeb.

"That men cause most of the trouble women face in this world," Jeb said.

"Is she married?" Win turned abruptly back to Grace.

"No, no husband." Grace smiled and patted Win's arm with motherly affection.

85

"Now, you'd better go before the boss finds yet another job for you. I've seen how he relies on you two. Cookie gave Meg his tent, bless his heart, so she can have some privacy. I'd better check on her." With a friendly wave, Grace left.

Win and Jeb took their time saddling their horses. Jeb figured Win felt the same as he did — that if they finished one chore too soon, they'd just be given another. "Lizzie saw Meg all cleaned up," Jeb said as he checked his rifle. "Apparently, without that layer of mud, she's kinda pretty. And her hair . . . it's the color of that prairie sunset you talk about."

"Yeah?" Win was cinching his saddle and jerked his head up in surprise. "No kidding? Maybe she's the girl from my pony-riding days. She seems familiar. She said she was from Council Bluffs. That's just across the river from where that girl raced me years ago . . ." Jeb hoped it wasn't true. If it was, then Win would have seen her first, and by the unwritten rules between friends, she'd be his. "What I don't get is her goddamn uncle," Jeb said, hoping to hide the jealousy that crept over him unexpectedly. "What kind of man threatens to kill a girl's horse?"

Meg appeared at the corral. She wore a dress Grace had given her and had pulled her clean hair back into a single, thick braid. Jeb glanced at Win, disappointed to see that she captured his attention, too. Win and Jeb had competed against each other all of their lives, but only in shooting or riding contests — never for the same girl. This new territory had not yet tested their friendship.

Jeb removed his hat. "I took the liberty of seeing to your horse, miss. I unsaddled her and checked her for injuries. Got most of the mud off of her."

"Mrs. Moberg told me. Thank you, Mr. Dawson. I appreciate it."

"It's Jeb, miss," he said. "My pleasure."

"I came to collect Biscuit's tack. I should get it oiled before it stiffens."

Win jumped up and landed on the supply wagon like a frog to a rock. "There should be oil in here somewhere. Let me get you some." He disappeared under the bonnet.

"I understand you gave Biscuit some oats," Meg said to Jeb. "What do I owe you?"

Jeb slid his rifle in its sheath. "Oh, nothing . . . my treat. She's been through a lot."

A shadow drifted across her face, like an airy cloud that changes the sun's intensity for a moment, its brightness returning almost instantly. "Well, thank you, again. That was very kind," she said. Win emerged from the wagon with a bottle of oil. "Thank you for this morning, too," Meg said to both of them. "I'm not sure what I would have done if you two hadn't come along."

Win opened his mouth, perhaps to ask again where she was from, or maybe to ask if she'd ever raced a Post rider, but Dutch arrived at the corral. Jeb wondered if they'd ever be able to finish a conversation, the way folks wandered in and out of everyone's business on this train.

"I figured something was keeping you two from finding dinner." The trail boss looked directly at Meg. "Glenn tells me you'll be traveling with them." He pointed his finger at her. "You bring trouble to our traveling community and you'll be answering to me, you hear?"

She nodded quickly. "Yessir. I won't cause any trouble, I promise." She stuck her hand out to shake hands with him, as if to settle a contract with him. Startled, the trail boss took her hand. Meg shook it firmly, like a man.

Dutch flexed his hand after she released it and turned his attention back to Win and Jeb. "You expectin' dinner to wander into camp by itself?"

"No, sir," they both said together and mounted up. In unison, they tipped their hats to Meg and rode out.

"It's Jeb, miss," Win mimicked sarcastically once they were out of earshot.

"Grace said to be gentlemen."

"Right." Win snorted.

Jeb wondered if the trouble Dutch warned her about hadn't already arrived.

Meg had her tent folded and Biscuit saddled long before the rest of the train was ready the next morning. She lifted Lizzie onto Biscuit's back and showed her how to hold the reins. With their daughter in Meg's care, Jeb saw Glenn and Grace slip into their wagon for some private time together before the bell clanged the signal it was time to move out. Jeb wondered if Meg realized the favor she had done for them and the reason for the satisfied grins on the couple's faces when the train got under way. Win rode leisurely past Jeb with raised eyebrows and a big smile; Win never missed a thing.

Dutch led the train across the river. He assigned Jeb to the near side to help any wagon that got into trouble, apparently since he was so good at water rescue. When the Moberg wagon crossed, Lizzie sat in front of Meg on Biscuit, beaming with excitement. She waved at Jeb as they entered the river, shouting to him that she wouldn't

89

get wet this time. Meg handled her horse well crossing the river, walking through the water like a stroll in a park. When they got to the other side, Lizzie called and waved to Win, who had been teamed with Toby and Dale to keep the wagons moving up the riverbank. Once during the morning, Jeb saw Biscuit loping — Meg holding Lizzie securely with one hand while holding the reins with the other as casually as any other woman would hold a pair of gloves. Lizzie shrieked with delight.

At midday, Dutch signaled for the train to stop for a rest. Grace called to her daughter; Meg eased her down to the ground. Lizzie ran past Win and Jeb on her way to her wagon, stopping briefly to tell them what she learned from Meg that morning.

"Hey, Mr. Avery, Mr. Dawson, guess what? Miz Meg said she learned to ride when she was my age, and she's gonna let me ride Biscuit all by myself sometime!" Lizzie's eyes sparkled. "I asked her how she got her black eye, but she won't tell me. I told her about Molly Ferguson and Johnny Novak, but she said it wasn't like that. Well, gotta go!" Lizzie waved and ran to her mother.

Meg radiated happiness as Jeb and Win rode up to her, a transformation from the day before. "Isn't the prairie beautiful this morning?"

"It is indeed. You captured Lizzie's heart, by the way, letting her ride with you. Of course, you know she's dying to find out how you got that black eye," Win said.

Meg laughed. "She's a walking newspaper, that one. Told me far too much about everyone on the train."

"So, how did you get that shiner?" Win asked.

"Oh, it's nothing," she said, her back stiffening. She stuck out her chin slightly. "It doesn't matter." Jeb wished Win would let it go. Obviously she didn't want to talk about it, and he was going to ruin a perfect morning.

Win cocked his head, a sign he was a little exasperated. "Aw, c'mon, Miss Jameson. You can trust us. Jeb and me, we're good people — ask anyone in Rockfield. That's close to Council Bluffs, you know. We're practically neighbors."

"I'm sorry. I don't mean to be secretive."

It surprised Jeb that she didn't bristle. Win could get pushy at times.

"At least I'm not Mormon," she said smiling, revealing a sense of humor. "I have that going for me, don't I? What does Mr. Ferguson have against Mormons?" She still hadn't explained her black eye.

"Good question, but I don't know. I never asked," Win said.

"Thousands came through Council Bluffs, as I'm sure you know, being from Rockfield. From my bedroom window, I used to watch their wagons being ferried across the river. Gus and I used to ride over on the Omaha side to see their trains stretch out and dream about going, too."

"Gus? Who's Gus?" Jeb wished he hadn't blurted out the question so fast; he sounded like some kind of jealous nitwit.

"He ran the stables where I kept Biscuit. He's my friend."

"And you two rode over on the Omaha side often?" Win asked.

"Oh, yes, we loved the open space across the river. Sometimes I wanted to just keep going and never look back."

Win squinted at Meg, no doubt waiting to judge her reaction. "I was in Omaha once, when I rode for the Pony Express. I was assigned to deliver a special dispatch . . . in '61, I think. This little girl in pigtail braids came chasing after me. Rode like the wind, and wouldn't let up until I finally tipped my hat to her. The age would be about right . . . and the hair color."

Meg's eyes grew wide and her hand flew

up to her mouth. "You were that rider?"

"I've been wondering if that little girl was you. You seemed familiar." Win smiled broadly.

Jeb's spirits sank, but Meg's face lit up as though she had been reunited with a long-lost friend. "This is remarkable! I've thought about that day so many times."

"You were fast. You would've been a good Post rider," Win said.

Meg was full of questions. What was it like to race across the country? What part of the route did he ride? Win had the opportunity to build himself up in front of her, but surprisingly, he didn't take it. He waved off her questions and said that truthfully, he spent a lot of cold, scary nights in the bunkhouses and often wished Jeb had come along with him.

She turned to Jeb. "You two have been friends a long time?"

"Since we were kids."

"You're lucky to have each other." Her mind seemed to travel elsewhere for a moment.

"Yup." Win didn't elaborate, perhaps afraid the conversation would drift off topic. "Now, see? This isn't so bad, is it? Talking friendly like this, eh, Miss Jameson?"

"Please call me Meg. After all, you've

known me since I was twelve!"

Win smiled and nodded. Jeb made a quick calculation in his head. That made her seventeen, just three years younger than he and Win.

"You know, Jeb beat me hands down last time we raced. You'll have to take him on next." Win jerked his thumb in Jeb's direction.

She grinned and said she'd welcome the challenge.

Grace called to them, offering cobbler. Win raised his arm, indicating they heard, but no one made a move to leave. It seemed to Jeb like something important had just happened. A breeze swirled around them, as though mixing their fates together. He was too embarrassed to express such a mystical thought, but he sensed Win and Meg felt it, too, because they also lingered. Meg looked content, almost happy, and Win smiled at the western horizon, lost in thought.

Win and Jeb found themselves at the Mobergs' campfire every night after that. During the day, Meg rode with them whenever Dutch didn't have them working, but those times were rare. He kept the boys constantly busy. The train passed through an area Win called the Sandhills. What looked like easy passage across gently undulating hills turned into tortuous slugging through sandy, shifting soil that immobilized many a team of oxen. The scouts had to dig out heavy wagons sunk deep. Jeb was covered in grime and sweat most of the time — hardly a condition that favored courting a girl. But he looked forward to the evening, when the chores were finished; he cleaned himself up a bit and called on the Mobergs . . . and Meg.

Dutch had been right about this group of settlers. They were smart, worked tirelessly, and their spirits remained high. One evening, someone brought out a fiddle and folks began to gather for a dance. Jeb never learned that particular social skill, having pestered his mother to read pirate stories instead. Dance instruction had been postponed until the opportunity vanished. Jeb regretted it, as now, nothing would please him more than to hold Meg in his arms. Win disappeared; Jeb figured he couldn't dance, either.

Under the fear of humiliation, Jeb offered to take Glenn's guard duty. He lingered for a moment, however, mesmerized by the mysterious new girl who watched the dancers as the music started, her toes tapping time.

Glenn grabbed his wife's hand and twirled her around. Bill Foster, the scout with the wife and daughter in California, showed up, sporting a clean shirt and slicked-back hair. "Learn to dance, boy." He hiked up his trousers. "There's nothin' like a little music to brighten a young lady's spirits . . ." Perhaps Foster sensed Jeb's misery, because he changed his tone. "Now, don't go fretting. I ain't no competition, but just watch. Tonight, you're gonna wish you was me, 'cause I'm gonna get a pretty girl to smile at me." Then he sashayed comically over to Meg, bowed to her, and appeared to ask her to dance. She smiled, took his proffered hand, and they joined the dancers. Bill proved to be quite nimble on his feet. As he turned to face Jeb, he raised his eyebrows and gave him an "I told you so" look. Jeb laughed out loud at himself. The old man was right; he should learn to dance. He also wondered if his infatuation with Meg was as obvious to everyone as it was to Bill.

Later that week, the train moved into Sioux country. Attacks at Mud Springs and Julesburg earlier in the year by the Cheyenne and Sioux made Dutch jumpy. Jeb hardly ever saw him when he wasn't scanning the horizon. He kept the wagons and crew close.

Late one afternoon, Win waved to Jeb from the top of one of the rolling hills. Meg saw him, too, and followed Jeb. "You ready for that race?" she said as they arrived at the crest, eagerness in her eyes.

"Ha! You two can race later, Meggie," Win said. "Right now, you should see this. Take a look." Win pointed to the valley, where thousands of buffalo grazed below. The dark mass looked like a cloud's shadow in the vale until Jeb spotted the individual giants grazing.

"Oh my!" She gazed at the herd. "They're magnificent!"

The wind carried an occasional grunt or bellow with it as it whistled in their ears. Something stirred the massive herd into motion and it ran in silence for several seconds before they heard the low rumble and felt the ground tremble.

Robert Dale, the Indian-hating scout, rode up to them. "The boss wants you closer to the wagons, Miss Jameson." He glared at her. "We need to stay alert, and you did promise the boss you wouldn't cause trouble."

"For crying out loud, Dale," Win said. "Camp Rankin is just over the next hill."

"No, he's right. I'll go." Meg turned to Win and Jeb. "Thank you for sharing that with me." Meg rode slowly down the ridge toward the Moberg wagon. Even Biscuit's head hung low, as though chastised.

Dale didn't even wait until she was out of earshot. "She's bad luck. She'll bring trouble. I can feel it."

"Go to hell, Dale," Win said. "She's fine, and we're on the lookout for your goddamn Indians."

The surly scout leaned over his saddle horn. "You go to hell. If you care what happens to that gal, you'd watch for Indians instead of watching her. Indians got strange ways, and the farther I am from them, the better. It's inhuman, what they do — cut off a man's privates, stuff it in his mouth, make him watch while they rape his wife and cut her up. They're crazy bastards." Dale rode away without waiting for a reply.

Jeb felt sick. Win glanced at him and said, "You look white as a sheet. Clint could tell you plenty of stories with different endings, Jeb. They're just people, and we're frustrating the hell out of them. Dale's the bastard; his stories are meant to scare."

"It worked."

Dense fog rolled in overnight. When Jeb

woke, he thought he might still be asleep, as he saw only gray mist. He sat up, large beads of dew rolling off his blanket. In the middle of the low-lying cloud, Jeb could barely see beyond three wagons.

The day broke quietly. Cookie didn't clang his bell announcing breakfast. Instead, he gently kicked the men awake. The scouts quietly ate breakfast as they waited for the fog to lift, not talking, as though everyone was helping those on guard duty listen for danger, since no one could see beyond the camp. Muffled voices mixed with hinges squeaking and oxen lowing as the settlers prepared for the day. Jeb glanced at Meg's tent. Catching a glimpse of her first thing in the morning would start his day off right.

Win arrived at Cookie's fire, scowling. "Meg's horse is gone," he quietly told Jeb. The warm coffee Jeb had been savoring turned to acid in his stomach.

Chapter Six:
Meg

Camp Rankin, Colorado Territory, a day later
Meg regretted her rash decision to run away
from Dutch's train almost as soon as she
had done so. She'd been relishing the kindness the Mobergs had extended to her. She
liked the way Win called her "Meggie." Gus
called her that. She liked the way Jeb quietly
looked out for her, without making her feel
weak. She missed them already.

The evening before, Dale had approached
her when she checked on Biscuit, and had
frightened her. "I saw riders today," he said.
"I've been watching the horizon for you,
'cause I heard some men are after you." The
skin on the back of her neck prickled. Meg
asked if one of the riders had a piebald
mount, with three white legs and one black
one. "Now that you mention it, yeah, one of
them was definitely riding a horse like that."
Then he leaned in close and said, "Sure
would be a shame if innocent folks got hurt

trying to protect you — like that little Moberg girl, for instance."

In a panic, Meg escaped to her tent, changed into her riding breeches, and waited for the camp to settle down for the night. She knew Grace and Glenn, Win and Jeb, and even that sweet old Bill Foster would try to protect her. She couldn't let anyone get hurt on her account.

Fog had rolled in by the time she peeked out of her tent. Without a sound, she made her way over to Biscuit, who was waiting for her at the closest end of the makeshift corral like a faithful conspirator. Meg saddled her quietly, tiptoed out of hearing range, and then climbed into the saddle and slipped into the mist.

Her pace slow and cautious, and unable to see ahead more than a few yards, Meg couldn't determine how far she'd traveled when the sound of clinking metal rings and bit mouthpieces announced white riders. No Indian made that kind of noise. Filled with dread, she drew her rifle, ready to shoot Sutter as soon as she could see him. The rumble of horse hooves grew louder. Biscuit snorted nervously. Then, Meg saw the faint outline of the distinctive Kossuth hat worn by cavalry officers. She lowered her rifle at the same moment she material-ized in front of the officer's horse, which reared up in surprise, nearly tossing its rider to the ground. Once he recovered and hol-stered his own weapon, the rattled officer asked what, in heaven's name, was a white woman doing out here alone with war par-ties afoot? She blurted out that an evil man named Sutter was after her and he had a dangerous group of men with him, and that she'd left a wagon train to protect the good people she'd met. She told the officer that she'd return to the train with the regiment, though, as Sutter couldn't cause trouble with the cavalry there. But the officer wouldn't hear of it. A Cheyenne war party had moved into the area. If they ran into them before reaching the train, he said, she would be in the way. Without any more delay, the officer ordered one of his privates to escort her to the fort. He and his men continued on as Meg opened her mouth to protest.

Meg arrived at Camp Rankin with the cavalryman, who turned her over to a gruff-looking sergeant. The sergeant barely glanced at her before ordering her to join a group of civilians gathered at the flagpole. "They're leaving any minute for Valley Sta-tion," he said, and started to walk away.

"But I need to send a telegraph message . . ." Meg said. Everything was spinning out of control. She wanted to wait at the fort until she heard from Gus. Dutch's train might be ordered here, too, and she could reunite with Win and Jeb.

"Can't. Line's been cut. Do it at Valley Station," the sergeant said, "twelve miles down the road." He pointed at the group of civilians again. "All non-military's gotta get." He turned to leave.

"Wait, please. I've got to at least mail these . . ." Meg pulled out letters she had written to Gus. Grace had told her the first night she'd spent with the Mobergs that Gus would be worried sick about her and to write to him in case an opportunity came along to post a letter before finding safe passage back. It seemed Grace was right, and Meg was grateful for the good advice. She wished she were back in her company to thank her.

"Give 'em here." The sergeant held out his hand. She clutched the letters; they were too important to hand over to someone who might use them to light his next cigar. Her concern must have been transparent, because he softened his tone. "I'll see that your letters get in the mail bag, miss." She had no choice but to hand them over and join the group.

Meg expected only military men at the fort; she was surprised to see so many civilians. A disorderly mass congregated around three schooners, a stagecoach, and a freight wagon, all hitched with teams and ready for departure.

Again, she regretted running away. She already missed Win and Jeb. Win was charming and fun; she liked the attention he showed her. Jeb was quiet, but she sensed depth in his stillness and felt safe around him. Now she was traveling with people she didn't know in a direction she didn't want to go. Here she was, in another goddamn pickle.

CHAPTER SEVEN:
WIN

Dutch Ferguson's train

Win wiped the blood from his cut lip with tender, bruised knuckles. He surveyed the damage to Jeb's face, whose left eye was already swelling shut. Considering how his own head throbbed, Win figured he looked the same as Jeb. Their day had begun with a fight with Dale.

Grace had peeked inside Meg's tent when repeated calls didn't rouse her. She found only the dress Meg had borrowed, neatly folded.

Word spread quickly. No one had seen Meg, or heard anything suspicious. Dutch concluded that she left on her own accord, since no one taken against her will would fold clothes and leave so quietly. Everyone who had met Meg looked concerned or disappointed, except Dale. He looked neither, and that made Win suspicious.

"Do you know something about this,

Dale?" Win asked.

" 'Course not. Why would I?"

"You don't seem too surprised, is all." Jeb squared himself opposite him.

Foster stood up next to Jeb and glared at Dale. "I saw you talking with Miss Jameson last night. What did you say to her?"

"Nothing . . . except to warn her to keep an eye on the horizon. Something you all should be doin'." Dale pointed an accusing finger at Win and Jeb. "I swear, those two pay more attention to her than watchin' for Indians."

"You scared her away, didn't you?" Jeb spoke through clenched teeth.

"The safety of this train comes first!" Dale shouted as Jeb charged him. The two wrestled in the dirt. Bill and Win tried to separate them, but Win caught a few blows himself, which he returned. Finally, Dutch stepped in.

"Where did she go, Dale?" Dutch growled as he pulled him off Jeb.

"How the hell would I know?" Dale wrenched himself free of Dutch's hold and sneered at them all. "I was right. She brought trouble."

"Goddammit, Dale, you're the one stirring up a hornet's nest." With a weary voice, he said to Win and Jeb, "Shew . . . you'd better find her. Get going . . . She can't be far."

But a US cavalry regiment clamored into camp and changed their plans. Lieutenant Carter, from the 7th Iowa Cavalry, informed Dutch and the gathered settlers that Cheyenne warriors were in the area. They would escort the wagon train to Camp Rankin.

Dutch rubbed his face in exasperation. The safety of the settlers came first, but Win knew he was weighing the time a detour in the opposite direction would take against the risk of continuing on. The lieutenant didn't look happy about it, either. Win figured he'd rather advance than backtrack, too. So, it didn't surprise Win when the officer dismounted and the two men stepped out of earshot to discuss the matter privately. Soon, the two men shook hands and returned to the group. The officer announced that the train could continue to Ash Hollow as planned, accompanied by the cavalrymen. Dutch looked pleased. "We welcome your company."

"We'll add whatever protection we can. By the way, are you missing a young woman . . . Miss Jameson?" the lieutenant asked.

Grace ran up to him. "Oh, dear heavens, is she all right?"

107

"Yes, ma'am." The lieutenant touched the rim of his hat. "She's on her way to Camp Rankin with one of my men." Relief spread through Win's body like a shot of whiskey, followed by the frustrating realization that they wouldn't be headed in the same direction. To add insult to injury, the lieutenant continued, "She told us where you were and said to watch out for some outlaw named Sutter. She said Robert Dale had seen him." The lieutenant scanned the group to see if the man might identify himself and share more information, but Dale had disappeared.

Jeb was quiet as the train broke camp. Once underway, Foster rode up next to Win. "I think your friend is either lovestruck or has a death wish. My bet is the former." He jerked his head toward Jeb, who was riding away in the direction of Camp Rankin. "You'd better stop him. Want company?"

Win nodded. Together, they caught up to Jeb and blocked his path. "Where do you think you're going?" Win asked.

"To find Meg." Jeb turned his head slightly to look out of his one good eye.

"Without saying good-bye?" Win couldn't keep the sarcasm out of his voice.

"I was coming back. You said Rankin was just over the hill."

"It's a bit farther than that. And the lieutenant won't let us go after her; I already checked."

"Since when do you follow orders?"

"Since I heard the Cheyenne are gathering into war parties!" Win spread his arms, exasperated at Jeb's uncharacteristic foolishness. "Don't be an idiot. This isn't the time or place to be traveling alone, partner."

Jeb peered at the southern horizon, as though calculating the odds of slipping past Indians undetected. "I'm goin', Win."

"The hell you are." In one swift move, Win pulled the bridle off Galen and let it drop.

Jeb swore under his breath and dismounted. While Jeb gathered the bridle, Win dropped a lasso around Galen's neck. Jeb glared at his friend, who remained unfazed. "We've got to get through this dangerous corridor, Jeb. It's like the cave on Hank Brady's farm. Remember the ledge we had to squeeze past, with the fifty-foot drop? Safe on either side, but that one spot . . ."

Jeb had been more afraid of that one spot than anything else Win could think of. He couldn't stop shaking, even when they emerged safely into the sunlight. Jeb would never go back in the cave again. Win hoped the memory would place the appropriate level of fear on meeting up with Cheyenne dog soldiers.

"You said Indians are just people, like the rest of us," Jeb said.

"Not dog soldiers; they're unrelenting. No retreat. No mercy. We don't want to run into them. Look, pretty soon we'll turn south and be in Colorado Territory. The gold rush settled that area years ago. Lots of little mining towns in the mountains; some brave souls are even farming the plains . . . Hell, Denver's got nearly five thousand people living there. But here . . . this is Cheyenne country. We don't want to be here, especially alone."

"She's out there alone, Win."

"She's safe at Camp Rankin, son. Listen to your friend," Bill said.

Jeb finally nodded reluctantly. "Give me your word," Win said. "Say it."

"You have my word, goddammit."

Once Jeb gave his word, he stuck to it. Confident that Jeb would stay and relieved he wouldn't have to fight his bigger and stronger friend, Win's spirits lifted. He removed the rope from Galen's neck. "Hell, I'll bet Meg's got everyone turned up on end at the fort by now. Got their heads spinning, poor saps."

"I guarantee you that pretty little thing is safer than any of us right now," Foster said.

The truth in Foster's comment unnerved Win, but he continued to joke nonetheless. "I don't know if I'd call her pretty. She's kind of a mess, really. Even cleaned up she's got all that hair . . ." Win gestured around his head, indicating the way her wavy tresses blew around her face.

"You don't fool me, Avery." Foster shook his head and chuckled.

Win wondered what Foster meant by his comment, and if it would bother Jeb. Win caught Jeb glancing southward. That Jeb showed concern at Meg's absence was not as surprising as the ferocity of his anger at Dale. Win couldn't remember one time from their youth when Jeb lost his temper. Win could tell Jeb liked Meg. Hell, she was pretty and fun. What was not to like about a girl who can ride a horse like she could? But maybe Jeb's feelings for her went deeper than Win realized.

The thought needled at him like a prickle weed caught inside his shirt, aggravating him almost as much as Dale. Maybe he was just out of sorts because he felt trapped by their circumstances. He gave Hippocrates a verbal "Hup!" and galloped up to the front of the train. It felt good to break loose a bit, and he wanted to see open land for a change, not the backs of prairie schooners.

As he rode, the sun slipped to the horizon, setting the clouds on fire.

The cavalry escorted Dutch's settlers as far as Ash Hollow, a favorite resting spot on the trail. Getting there required the help of every available man, as each wagon had to be pulled up a steep hill, then, with windlasses, eased down a long, sharp decline. The men spent the day with ropes wrapped around them, pulling against the weight of the prairie schooners. At first, Win's back and arms were on fire — later, he could barely move his sore muscles. The reward was worth the effort, however. Ash Hollow was a peaceful, green oasis where they sat beneath shade trees and drank the first fresh, clean water they had tasted in weeks. Jeb muttered to Win that he wondered how the train could have managed if they hadn't come along, but Win attributed his sour mood to missing Meg. He had been true to his word and not gone after her.

A cavalry scout reported that the Cheyenne dog soldiers were heading for the Platte Bridge Station. The lieutenant assured the settlers they would have safe travel to Fort Laramie, and then led his troops in pursuit. No longer under military control, Win and Jeb said good-bye to the Mobergs and left the train.

Without discussion or conscious planning, Win and Jeb took their time making their way to Denver. However slim the chances, Win hoped they might run into Meg. He looked for her in every little town they passed through.

CHAPTER EIGHT:
JEB

Colorado Territory, a week later

Rudderless ships at sea. Once they left Ash Hollow for Denver, Jeb and Win drifted with the wind. Not that Jeb minded. Enthralled by the Rocky Mountains, a striking contrast to the flat prairies of the Nebraska Territory, Jeb had never seen such snow-capped magnificence. The mountains sang to him, drawing him in like dangerous and mythical Sirens.

He wondered if the Rockies called to Meg, or if the soothing whispers of the prairie spoke to her. Where was she . . . Which way did she go?

Unlike the unpopulated expanse of Nebraska, little towns had popped up everywhere in Colorado Territory. Gold fever had peaked in '59, but it was far from over, and folks still arrived in a steady stream. The Cheyenne, Arapaho, and Sioux left the area as white people rushed in. Anywhere miners found gold, a shantytown materialized. But Jeb also noticed that on the route between Denver and Cheyenne — the junction site of the Union Pacific line of the transcontinental railroad — farmers and ranchers were investing in the future. Farms and ranches dotted the countryside along the frontal range, as did towns that supported them with dry-goods stores, blacksmiths, and lumber mills. Freight traffic and stagecoach lines crisscrossed, overlapped, and intersected with each other. Camp Rankin grew into Fort Sedgwick, and its protection, along with Forts Lyon, Garland, and Morgan, encouraged settlement. But Meg Jameson was not at any fort, town, way station, or village. Galen and Hippocrates plodded along, perhaps missing the company of Biscuit as much as their riders missed Meg.

Stuck in the ground alongside the road, a hand-painted wooden sign read "Paradise," with an arrow pointing west to the base of the foothills. The word "Paradise" had been scratched through, and underneath it was written "Hell." Scrawled in smaller letters was the word "Salvation," with a fresher arrow pointing east. Why no discussion between them occurred Jeb couldn't say, but he and Win turned west at the same time,

115

pulled by something invisible. Perhaps Sirens were at work, maybe they thought they'd find Meg, or maybe the name and editorial remarks on the sign were just too beguiling to bypass.

Paradise consisted of two buildings facing a third, as if in an attempted start of a main street. The blades of a windmill squeaked rhythmically as they spun in the constant breeze. No real roads led to the little hamlet — just a wide, worn path from the east made by heavy-footed oxen pulling schooners.

A giant blacksmith plunged a glowing horseshoe into a barrel of water as they passed by. He nodded amicably. A small, wiry fellow, half the height and width of the blacksmith, sat outside a saloon. He stood up and leaned against the porch supports. "Howdy, strangers. You come from LaPorte? Yer headed for Denver, ain't ya?"

"More or less," Win said.

"Mick! You owe me two bits!" the small man yelled across the street at the store. The blacksmith laid down his work and lumbered over. The storeowner appeared at the doorway.

"You dang Scot! You can't ask 'em until I hear the answer same time as you!" The storekeeper, identified by the dang Scot as

Mick, marched over with clenched fists like he was ready to fight him.

"Honest question, honest answer." The small fellow remained unperturbed, his chin jutting out defensively. "Just cuz you don't like what they say don't make it a lie." He held out his hand. Mick slapped a coin into it. The man cackled cheerfully and pocketed the money.

Mick pointed a finger. "Next time, I get to ask."

"You old buzzard, you always get to ask . . ." and so the argument continued. The two paid no attention to Win and Jeb.

A woman appeared at the door of the trading post. She swept across the narrow street, carrying herself with more poise and elegance than one would expect from a woman in the middle of nowhere. "Mick Carter and Angus McPherson, if you two aren't the orneriest souls on the face of this Earth!"

Angus McPherson ignored the woman. "I told you, Mick, folks goin' from LaPorte to Denver will take this route. It makes more sense than what that goofball Holladay's doin' east of here."

"Holladay can do whatever the hell he wants. He says his way is safer." Mick stuck his face in Angus's.

"Bah! Sayin' it don't make it so!" Angus held his ground. The faces of the two men were inches apart.

"BOYS!" the woman shouted at them, then turned pleasantly to Jeb and Win. "Please excuse them. I'm Georgia Carter. Welcome to Paradise."

Jeb touched the rim of his hat and introduced himself and Win.

Georgia smoothed her apron as it billowed in the breeze. "Nice to meet you. I try to keep these fools in line so people don't think we're peculiar, our brains turned queer by the abundance of vast, open country and the lack of human contact. Sometimes I wonder if it hasn't already happened." She gave her husband and Angus a stern look. "What can we do for you?"

"Just passing through. Maybe buy a meal, if that's possible."

"We can accommodate you."

Mick brought their horses over to the water trough by the well; Georgia invited Win and Jeb to follow her into the store. The blacksmith and Angus joined them as though invited as well. She put the coffee on and told them to make themselves comfortable at a large round table in the living quarters at the back of their store.

"You get a lot of business out here?" Jeb

asked the blacksmith, who had settled at the table with them.

Mrs. Carter thought the question had been directed at her, however, and launched into the history of their little town. She said their blacksmith had been on his way to California when his wagon train was delayed. Blackie, as she called him, spent the winter repairing wagons and shoeing mules for everyone. When it was time to leave, he had grown to like it here and decided to stay. Blackie looked scary, with arms as big as tree trunks, but Georgia said he was just an old softie, winking at him, causing him to clear his throat, embarrassed.

Angus McPherson had been traveling with the same train and opted to stay put with Blackie. After crossing the dry, dusty plains of the eastern Colorado Territory, he hankered for a good shot of whiskey and figured others would surely feel the same way. So he set up a saloon right next to the blacksmith and found that everyone who stopped for repairs also stopped in for a drink. If a large train passed through, he could fill two poker tables at night.

She and Mick, Georgia said proudly, owned and operated the trading post. With their children grown and married, the couple had headed west, eager to see California. But once Georgia caught sight of the Rocky Mountains, she had second thoughts about crossing them, saying she'd just as soon look at them. They ran into Blackie and Angus, twenty miles west of the Latham Station and thirty miles south of LaPorte, and felt like they had stumbled upon the perfect spot for an outpost. They'd just celebrated their first full year at this spot. It was Georgia's idea to name their little town Paradise.

"Say, did you see our sign? How's it look?" Mick asked. He'd come in the back door in the middle of his wife's report.

" 'Paradise' was scratched out, and 'Hell' was written underneath," Win said.

"Vandals." Georgia sighed and shook her head. "We find a perfect spot and give it a perfect name, and folks just can't stand it. Jealousy . . . pure jealousy."

"Anyone else live here?" Jeb asked.

The four residents glanced at one another. "No, it's just us," Mrs. Carter said. "Only a few unlucky prospectors lived up in the mountains when Blackie arrived, and they left with their pockets empty soon after we got here. We settled here for the business that travels through — wagon trains, mostly. What kind of work are you boys in?"

"Nothing yet, but a friend of mine has a

freight business in Denver. I think he'll have jobs for us."

The mention of freighting started another brief argument between Mick and Angus about routes, and whether a regular stage and mail route could run through Paradise instead of Lyonsville, ten miles east.

"Since most of our business comes from settlers coming through in wagon trains, I don't know what will happen once the railroad lays track this far. We might be able to become a depot, but I doubt it. Lyonsville will get the stop, I'm betting."

"No one'll take your bet, Mick, 'cause it's a sure one," Angus said.

"Ben Holladay's got his stage going through Lyonsville . . ."

"Aw, he don't know everything. He could take a half day off that route if he came through here. Just like that gal and —"

Jeb jerked his head up. "What gal?"

CHAPTER NINE: MEG

Northern Colorado Territory

When Meg arrived at Valley Station with the civilians from Camp Rankin, the telegraph operator announced the lines had been cut. Anyone needing telegraph service had to go to Fort Morgan. Taken farther and farther away from everyone she knew and loved, Meg felt very alone.

Perhaps loneliness was the reason she fell into the dubious partnership with Carl Pitts. The well-dressed gentleman approached her as she brushed down Biscuit in the small town next to Fort Morgan. "I saw you ride in," he said, his voice like caramel. "You look beautifully at home in a saddle."

Meg shrugged. He looked like the kind of man who lived in her uncle's world, men used to getting their way. His clothes were made of fine fabric. She glanced at his hands — no calluses from hard work. She continued to brush Biscuit, hoping he'd go away.

The man leaned casually against a tree. "Have you ever raced?"

Meg shook her head. She had no reason to share her experience racing Win as a Post rider.

"Want to show me how fast your horse runs? Say, for . . . ten dollars?"

Ten dollars, properly managed, could go far, and she was low on cash. She squinted at him, lifting her chin. "All I have to do is ride my horse, and you're going to give me ten dollars."

He nodded, grinning.

"Fine." Meg jumped up onto Biscuit and followed the man to the edge of town. He showed her where to run. Meg took off. He was looking at his watch as she completed the loop and reined Biscuit to a halt.

"Excellent! That was excellent! How would you like to earn some money?"

"I just did. You owe me an eagle."

He produced the gold coin. "You could make a lot more of those."

"What do I have to do?"

"Just ride your horse. Simple as that."

"I'm going to Denver. People are expecting me," she lied. She didn't want him to think she was alone and without a plan.

Denver was the first town to pop into her head.

"I'll escort you. We'll race in each town all the way there. You'll arrive rich."

Both Gus and Grace had cautioned her about men like Pitts, no-goods who took advantage of women in desperate situations — gamblers and flimflam men. Meg told herself that she was no fool; she could handle him. Biscuit was fast, and she could use the money. What harm could come from earning some cash along the way?

It didn't take long for Meg to realize that she'd made a mistake, and regretted her decision. The first town they came to, Carl struck up a conversation with the locals, twisting and turning folks' words until a race was set and bets placed. Carl did the same in the next town, talking people into betting and losing their hard-earned money.

Carl failed to work his charm on Meg, however. She insisted on her own hotel room, an issue he'd argue about every time they arrived in a new town. "Think of the money we could save," he would say. "You can trust me," he always added. But she didn't.

They had only been traveling a few days together when someone knocked on her hotel-room door and told her she had to

124

get her father, or whoever he was, from the saloon, as he was too drunk to move on his own accord. Meg went down and, amid the stares of all the men, draped Carl's arm over her shoulder and lugged him back to his room. When she dropped him on the bed, he pulled her down with him. A swift jab with her knee, like Gus taught her, stopped further advances. Carl sobered up quickly, writhing in pain with his legs drawn up to his chest. She wedged a chair under the doorknob in her own room when she returned to it.

The next morning at breakfast, Carl stumbled downstairs and joined her in the hotel restaurant without ceremony. He grimaced at the plate of eggs, bacon, and biscuits in front of her and motioned to the waitress that he needed coffee.

"Here are the rules, Carl," Meg said, speaking sharply to the man nearly twice her age.

Carl winced at the sound of her voice. "Shhh, Meg. Come on. Can't you see I'm suffering?"

"From your own doing! Now listen carefully." She pointed the butter knife at him. "If you ever have your way with me, don't ever plan on sleeping again, 'cause once you're asleep, first I'll cut off your manhood, and then I'll slit your throat. Are we clear?"

"Jesus, Meg," Carl said as he rubbed his temples. "I just wanted to have a little fun, for crying out loud."

"Well, have your fun elsewhere." She slapped butter on a biscuit like a schoolteacher disciplining a child with a ruler. "Men think they can just have their way, like we don't count for anything. Well, we do, goddamn it, and you'd better show me some respect." Meg had picked up swearing from Gus and found that using bad language helped drive home a point, particularly when speaking to men like Carl.

He waved his hand as though to make her stop talking.

Carl wasn't mean, he just couldn't be trusted. He provided protection for Meg on the road. As long as she could protect herself from Carl, she'd be fine. She knew what she was doing.

But they weren't getting any closer to Denver. Carl's treatment of people made her feel uneasy. Gus used an expression when something wasn't illegal, but wasn't right, just the same — wide of the mark, he'd say, and that's what he'd call this racing business. In the beginning, she didn't mind zigzagging across the territory, as she figured she might run into Win and Jeb. But she hadn't. And when they passed through Paradise, a tiny place pretending to be a town, Meg saw herself through new eyes. A kind woman, Georgia, had rubbed her back tenderly, called her "honeybee," and asked if she was all right. Her gentleness was like catching a fever. Unaware she'd even been infected at first, Meg started feeling odd soon after they left town. Common sense spread steadily through her until she could no longer ignore it. Meg didn't know what she was doing after all. She and Gus had always dreamed of coming west. She was here, and the perfect land for their ranch was just outside of Paradise. The money to buy the land was tied up in a trust, but no matter. They could get by until she turned twenty-one. Four years wasn't forever. What was she doing, wasting precious time traveling around with Carl Pitts? She'd lost her way. For Biscuit's sake as well as her own, Meg decided to end it. It was time to get back on the mark.

"Carl, you keep saying we're headed for Denver, but you and I both know this isn't the way," she said. "I'm tired of this." They'd left a town in a hurry and were riding east.

"There's a town a few miles from here.

We'll rest there, my dear."

"I'm not your dear, and I don't want to rest. I don't want to do this anymore. It feels wrong."

"Well, you can't very well travel alone. You need me."

Meg figured the opposite was more accurate. Carl couldn't play his game without Meg to race for him. She felt used. "I don't need you, Carl." She didn't know if she said it aloud, or just to herself.

They arrived at the edge of LaPorte, a thriving business and supply center for wagon trains. Protected by Fort Collins close by, which also protected the Overland Stage route to Virginia Dale, LaPorte boasted four saloons, two livery stables, a brewery, a butcher shop, two blacksmith shops, a feed and seed warehouse, a lumber-yard, a dry-goods store, and a large hotel and restaurant. All had as much business as they could handle.

The Annual LaPorte Founder's Day Celebration was in two days, and part of the festivities included a horse race. Lots of people would be in town — a chance to make some good money, Carl said, and left to enter Biscuit without even asking her. After securing two rooms at a hotel, Meg rode to the livery to start her plan to sever ties with Carl. She felt her fever break, and whatever had been festering inside faded with her resolution. The day already seemed brighter.

At the end of the main street, a young boy emerged from a livery with a wheelbarrow of manure. She rode over to him. He put down the wheelbarrow and waited.

"Hello, there. Are you the liveryman?" she asked.

"No, ma'am." The boy laughed. "Mr. Townsend is. I work for him."

"Is he good to you?"

"Oh, yes, ma'am," the boy said, standing straighter. "He gives me four dollars a week; that's as much as Tommy Fallon makes over at the newspaper! He sets the type for the *LaPorte Herald*."

"Hmmm . . . Do you keep a clean stable?"

"You betcha. That's one of my jobs. I muck out the stalls twice a day."

"You ever have cockfights?"

"No, ma'am." The boy scratched his head. "Boss don't like cockfightin'. Says it riles the stock."

"What's your name?"

"Henry. Henry Deener. You gonna keep your horse with us? She's real pretty." He stroked Biscuit's neck.

Meg smiled. "Yes, I'll board her here,

Henry. Her name is Biscuit."

"Sure thing! Let me just dump this load and I'll be right back!" Henry grabbed the wheelbarrow handles and disappeared. An older man walked out of the livery.

"You must be Mr. Townsend," Meg said.

The old man nodded. "I's wondering what got Henry so excited. Now I see." He stroked Biscuit's nose. "I got a nice box stall in the corner. How long you stayin'?"

"I'm not sure, but I'll need someone to keep a close eye on Biscuit . . . um, to make sure she leaves with no one but me."

"A dollar a day will buy you a clean stall, food, and all the attention she can handle from Henry." Mr. Townsend jerked his head in the direction Henry had gone. "He'll see to it."

"Sounds perfect." Meg felt her luck had turned.

Leaving Biscuit with Mr. Townsend, Meg headed for the dry-goods store. She found a readymade dress similar to the one Grace had loaned her — a pretty calico print with a feminine neckline. She held it up to her in front of a mirror. For the first time in weeks, she liked the person she saw looking back at her.

Meg left the store with a parcel under her arm and ran back to the hotel, where she bathed, washed her hair, and put on her new dress. She was brushing her hair dry when Carl strode into her room. She was annoyed at herself for not remembering to lock it. He tossed his hat on the bed, leaned against the bedpost, and looked her over, smiling. "Well, now, what have we here? My, my, my . . ."

"I didn't do this for you. I did this for me. I've had enough."

"You're beautiful."

"I'm leaving; did you hear me? I'll find my own way from here."

"Come here, baby . . ." Carl opened his arms and moved closer.

Fear rose inside her and gripped her unexpectedly. "No." Her voice sounded like she was underwater; the pounding of her heart filled her ears. Instinctively, she backed away.

"Don't put me off, Meg. We spend every day together, and every night alone. I'm a man, for Christ's sake! What do you expect? I want you. I'll marry you if you want, I promise."

"I don't want to marry you. I don't love you."

"Just let me touch you. I've touched you in my mind so many times, I —"

"Stop it!" She clenched her fists. "That

was never part of our deal!"

"Then I'm changing the deal!"

Meg ran for the door, but he grabbed her waist and pulled her toward him. She panicked as he pressed her body against his. She raised her knee to kick him, but ready for her this time, he grabbed her thigh before she could inflict any damage. He shoved her knee away and threw her down on the bed. She scrambled backward, but he caught hold of her legs and yanked her back. He climbed on top of her. She squirmed, repulsed.

"C'mon, baby, just this once. I'll make you want to stay." He reached inside the open neckline of her dress. Nausea swept over her as his hand found her bare breast.

Too heavy to push off, Carl's weight pinned Meg to the bed. She cringed and cried out as his hand traveled down her dress to the inside of her thigh. Her skirt, twisted tightly around her legs, prevented further exploration, so he rolled to his side just enough to free the tangle. As his hand disappeared beneath her skirt, Meg saw a small bulge in his vest pocket — his derringer.

With speed and agility born from desperation, she lifted the gun from Carl's pocket and pressed the barrel to his neck. "Get off me, you bastard."

Carl froze. "Easy, now, baby . . ."

"You'll bleed out fast."

He grimaced when she moved to point the gun at his face. The derringer wasn't a very powerful weapon, but Carl was self-absorbed enough to not want his pretty face spoiled. Slowly and carefully, Carl raised himself so Meg could scuttle out from under him. He rolled over, sat on the edge of the bed, and ran his hands through his hair.

"Well, you've certainly learned a few things." Moving cautiously, Carl got up, splashed some water on his face, and dried it with a towel. He straightened his clothing and brushed his hair with her brush. "You're right; we're done. Saturday is our last race. You'd better be there, or you'll regret it; I've paid the entrance fee." He picked up his hat. "By the way, who said anything about love?"

After he slammed the door behind him, Meg wished for the hundredth time that she hadn't run away without Gus, or left Jeb and Win. Carl's threat echoed in her head. She wasn't sure what he meant by it, but didn't want to find out. If she raced one more time she wouldn't owe him anything, not even the entrance fee. She wasn't sure how much it was or what amount of money he'd already wagered, but it could be sizeable. She might be better off racing than risking what might happen if she didn't. Saturday was their last race; Carl had even said it. Her split from Carl near-at-hand, Meg broke into Carl's room and counted their money. She took exactly half.

On race day, Meg was eating breakfast when Carl arrived in the dining room wearing his traveling suit. Her anger had cooled; indifference replaced it. Just a few more hours and she'd never have to look at him again.

"How can you eat so much and be so skinny?" he asked as he joined her — without her permission.

At one time, his rudeness would have been annoying. Now she didn't care. His question wasn't relevant, nor was it the apology she deserved. But Meg sensed his irritability was the closest she'd get to any expression of remorse. An apology from Carl would be meaningless, anyway.

She glanced up at him as she cut her steak. "I burn it off being nervous around you, you dirty bastard."

He smiled wryly. "I see you've already taken care of our accounting, you thief."

"I'm only a thief if I take more than my

share, and I didn't."

He leaned forward suddenly, with an urgency that seemed both desperate and pathetic. "Change your mind and come with me. I'll never do that again, I promise. You can wear pretty dresses; I'll take good care of you. Come with me on the noon stage."

She stared at him, incredulous.

Chapter Ten:
Win

Once Georgia mentioned how a sweet girl passed through just a few days earlier, traveling in the company of a man not suited for her, Win and Jeb excused themselves from the Carters' table and left Paradise as quickly as proper manners would allow. No longer in stagnant doldrums, the prospect of finding Meg took the helm. It unfurled their sails and set their course for LaPorte, leaving a dusty wake behind them.

Banners strung across the main street announced the Founder's Day Celebration. Families gathered to picnic; women passed jars of jellies and preserves back and forth. Older men sat together, enjoying a leisurely smoke. Until the picnic food appeared, boys ran from one contest to another, while the youngest children and girls stayed close to their mothers.

A stable boy led Biscuit through the crowd. Win pointed. "There! Come on," he said and worked his way over to the lad. The boy's full attention was focused on a coin in his hand.

"Excuse me," Win said, pulling the freckled-faced youngster out of his reverie. The boy looked up sharply. "We know this horse. Her name is Biscuit. Where's her owner, Miss Jameson?"

"Didja see the race?" The boy's eyes grew wide. "Biscuit was greased lightning! She won by two lengths! And Miss Jameson gave me this *double eagle* for looking after her." He held up the twenty-dollar gold piece proudly.

Win whistled in admiration and glanced around quickly. "What's your name, kid?"

"Henry. Henry Deener."

"Well, Henry Deener, have you got a good pocket? One with no holes?"

"Yessir."

Win winked at the boy. "I suggest you keep Miss Jameson's generous tip out of sight and in your pocket. Where is she, by the way?"

"Over at the fair, settlin' up with dumb ol' Mr. Pitts, I 'spect," Henry said, wrinkling his nose as he looked behind him. He stuffed the gold piece deep into his pants.

"She asked me to brush down Biscuit, seeing's how I done such a good job takin' care of her already." He stood a little taller.

"You taking her to the livery?" Win asked. Henry nodded as he led Biscuit away.

Jeb was already scanning the crowd. "There . . ." He pointed to where Meg and a man stood opposite one another. She wore boy's clothing and was covered in dust. The man counted out paper bills and handed them to her. Meg stuffed the bills into her pocket without recounting and then stepped back, distancing herself from him.

"I can't wait to hear what she's got to say about him," Win said, forcing a cool demeanor, as he'd have thought a little bird had slipped under his shirt the way his heart began to flutter. They made their way through the crowd, but when they arrived at the spot where they had seen her, she was gone.

Win held out his arms. "She's a goddamn apparition!"

"Well, she won't go anywhere without Biscuit. Let's wait for her at the livery," Jeb said.

They waited for what seemed like hours, Jeb finally wandering outside. Win leaned against the stall and took inventory of the clutter in his brain. For someone who preferred free-range travel, Win didn't know how he felt about their recent single-mindedness. He felt as though he'd boarded a train without checking its destination, and was now barreling down the tracks at high speed. It felt dangerous — different from other danger he'd experienced. He could jump off the train, but he wanted to see where it headed, and he didn't want to be left behind.

He heard Jeb call Meg's name, so Win hustled out of the barn. Meg had bathed, changed into a dress, and had Jeb's arms enclosed around her.

"Meg!" Win stretched his own arms wide.

After she embraced Win warmly, she beamed at them both. "I didn't think this day could get better, but now it's perfect. I was so hoping I'd run into you two again."

The barreling train jumped the rail, sending Win flying through the air. He loved the feeling.

CHAPTER ELEVEN:
JEB

Founder's Day celebration, LaPorte

"You know what this reminds me of?" Win surveyed the festivities from the blanket he lounged on.

"Harvest Festival of 1860," Jeb said without hesitation. He'd been thinking the same thing. Five years ago, although Jeb had won that festival's horse race, Win had somehow wrangled a congratulatory kiss out of Sally Richards.

"This pie tastes sweeter than any kiss of Sally's." Win licked the gooey blackberry filling from his fingers.

Jeb laughed, his contentment caught in a silvery net. Meg had purchased a pie from a church booth and, relaxing in the shade on horse blankets borrowed from Mr. Townsend, they were enjoying the fair together. Banners and tablecloths billowed like sails in the gentle breeze. A loosened strand of Meg's hair waved like their ship's flag.

"You didn't have to run away, Meg," Jeb said. "We would have protected you."

"That's exactly why I had to leave. John Sutter is pure evil. I didn't want you getting hurt on my account."

Win spread his arms out in protest. "We can hold our own —"

Meg held up her hand to stop him. "You don't know what he's capable of. Once I saw a woman so badly beaten, one eye was completely swollen shut and she could barely see out of the other. Her husband owed my uncle money and my uncle sent Sutter to collect it. When the man couldn't pay, Sutter beat the man's wife bloody, right in front of him." She shuddered. "I ran away because my uncle got mad at me and threatened to kill Biscuit. He said I'd find Biscuit gutted in her stall. I believed him."

Win let out a soft whistle. "What'd you do to make your uncle so mad?"

"It's what I wouldn't do." Meg looked away.

Jeb remembered the black eye she had when they first met. He hoped Win wouldn't make her uncomfortable by pressing her.

"I am sorry I let Dale scare me," Meg said. "I should have known not to believe him. I was so frightened at the time, I didn't think it through." Meg sighed heavily and squinted at the sun. "You know, this is a pretty sad topic for such a fine day. Tell me about Grace, Lizzie, and the rest of the train."

Win filled her in and said he and Jeb had been drifting a bit, taking their time getting to Denver. Jeb was glad he didn't mention they'd been looking for her. He didn't want to look like a couple of moony-eyed idiots, even though, at the moment, he felt like he was floating on a cloud.

"So, who was the man we saw you with earlier today?" Win asked unexpectedly.

"It's too long a story . . . and boring." Meg tried to shoo away the pesky subject with her hand.

"We've got time."

Meg bit her lip hesitantly, but finally told them about meeting Carl and how they traveled from town to town, racing the locals. "Was that wrong?" She looked directly at Jeb and waited for him to answer, as though his opinion mattered. "It didn't feel right. That's why I stopped."

"Aw, hell, sometimes you gotta do something bad just to know you're alive." Win let his favorite motto slip out without thinking. But when Meg gasped, Win quickly added, "Look, people can wager or not, it's their choice. You didn't do anything wrong."

"Yes, but Carl had a way of talking them into it. It bothered me."

"Is he gone?" Jeb asked, hoping.

"He left on the noon stage."

Jeb leaned back. "Then I wouldn't give it another thought." He liked the way she was opening up, putting her trust in them. "Did Biscuit ever lose?"

She gave Jeb a sideways glance. "Sometimes. Carl couldn't always control where the horses raced. If the terrain was too rough, I wouldn't push her, and we'd lose. He'd get mad, but I didn't care." She shrugged. "I'd never risk hurting Biscuit."

"But on the flats?" Win asked.

Meg grinned wickedly. "She's *very* fast — as fast as any Post rider."

Win threw his head back and laughed. "You should come with us to Denver."

Jeb jerked his head up in surprise, but immediately turned to Meg to see her reaction, hoping she'd agree. He hadn't thought past seeing Meg again, but clearly Win had.

"This running-away thing you do would have to stop, though," Win said, with one eye closed in a wink. "Too damned hard to keep up with you."

Meg rolled her eyes, but accepted the charge against her with a sigh.

"Whatever comes our way, we'll figure it out together. What do you say?" Jeb asked.

She stared at Jeb with an expression Jeb couldn't quite read. "I would like that very much. I'll wire Gus before we leave. He can meet me in Denver."

"Great! It's settled." Win turned his attention back to the fairgoers. Jeb detected a hint of the smile he was trying to suppress.

At Townsend Livery on the morning after the festival, Henry Deener mucked the stalls as Jeb and Win saddled their horses. Jeb spotted Meg striding down the street toward them. She sported a smart, new, wide-brimmed hat to shield her face from the sun, a handsome Eton jacket cut for a woman's figure, and a full riding skirt. However, her most captivating feature by far was her luminous smile.

She waved a piece of paper in the air. "Gus got my letters! I sent a telegraph last night and received his reply this morning. He knows I'm safe and will write to me in Denver. I'm so happy!"

Win tossed a saddlebag packed with provisions across Hippocrates's rump. "You look mighty pretty this morning, Meg."

"New clothes for a fresh start." Meg looked down at her outfit. "The seamstress stayed up late to have these ready by this morning."

"You gonna be needin' a sidesaddle, Miss Jameson? How you gonna ride in a skirt?" Henry dragged the manure shovel behind him and scratched his head.

"Henry! That ain't polite," Mr. Townsend scolded. "I apologize, Miss Jameson. Henry plum lost his manners."

"Oh, Mr. Townsend, it's all right. I had my share of questions when I was Henry's age." She turned to Henry. "Riding sidesaddle is nearly impossible — and impractical, if you ask me. I've worn buckskin britches ever since I learned to ride." She lifted her skirt just slightly to indicate she had them on underneath, modestly revealing only the ankles of her riding boots. Mr. Townsend cleared his throat. Meg ruffled Henry's hair and kissed him on his forehead. "I'm going to miss you, Henry Deener."

Jeb thought Henry would keel over. Apparently, Meg Jameson captivated men of all ages. Securing his bedroll to the back of his saddle, Jeb tried to get the image of her breeches out of his mind.

Once out of town, Win cried, "Ah! The open road! Is there anything that stirs the soul more than this?"

Jeb could have argued that their company might be appropriate competition, but he agreed that mystery and beauty lived in the beckoning foothills that tumbled from the high mountain peaks.

"I can't take my eyes off those hills," Meg said, apparently in concord. "It would be grand to ride through there." Jeb wondered if the surroundings or their company brought her more happiness. Either way, she looked free of all care or concern. Perhaps, like Win, the open road stirred her soul.

"Let's do it." Win tipped his hat back to see the view better. "Sometimes you gotta do something crazy, just to —"

"You said 'bad' before. 'Sometimes you've got to do something *bad,* just to know you're alive,' " Meg said.

Jeb smiled. "Win changes his motto to suit the situation."

"Are you saying it's crazy to ride in the foothills? Do you think there are Indians up there?" Meg gazed at the mountains.

"Hard to say," Win said. "I've heard the Indians have been pretty well pushed out of Colorado Territory."

"Biscuit would favor the cooler, less dusty route."

"You aren't afraid?" Win asked.

"I'd be foolish not to be wary, but roads aren't necessarily safer." Meg spoke as though she could back up her opinion if required.

Jeb agreed it would be a shame not to ride through such beautiful country. They headed toward higher elevation.

En route, Meg revealed a surprise. "I met some Pawnee Indians when I was lost in Nebraska. A little boy had fallen from his horse and hurt his ankles. He couldn't walk, so I put him on Biscuit. We were on his way to his village when his father and brothers found us."

"They let you just ride away?" Jeb asked.

Meg nodded. "I don't think his father and brothers thought much of me, but the boy didn't seem to care that I was white. Gus says you'll find good and bad people everywhere."

Gus again. Jeb reproached himself for feeling jealous of someone he'd never met.

"It's hard to hate a whole group of people once you get to know one of them," Win said. "My old boss, Clint Sanders, told me about an Arapaho who saved his life in the desert, and they became friends. Just a chance meeting — a fluke, you know? But it changed his entire life, and from what he's told me, he changed the Arapaho's, too.

147

He'd agree with your friend, Gus, that there are good and bad people everywhere, white and Indian alike. The trick is in knowing which they are before they get too close."

LaPorte faded behind them and disappeared completely once they slipped behind the closest foothill. Jeb felt as though they were the only three people on Earth. They came to a wide, flat valley between two ranges, stretching out for several miles. Meg said something about the race they owed her and gave Biscuit a quick "Hup!" Biscuit took off. Jeb let out a whoop and chased after her, with Win close behind. Biscuit ran with abandon for a while, but then slowed. Galen and Hippocrates raced past her.

Neither willing to concede, Jeb and Win raced each other, leaving the reason for their competitiveness far behind. "Surrender?" Win shouted when they were neck and neck.

"Never!" Jeb shouted back. He wondered if Meg really cared who won, or if she'd think they were being stupid. Good sense finally won out over his desire to best Win. Hippocrates inched ahead and Jeb granted Win the victory. He slowed and turned, and caught a glimpse of Meg in the distance.

She wasn't watching their race. She was riding Biscuit at a slow lope, her legs tucked around the horse's belly. She had tilted back her head, let go of the reins, and stretched her arms out wide. The sun on her face, she rode without worry or restraint. That singular act, that embodiment of bliss — it was worth losing the race to witness such perfection in motion.

The three stopped at the edge of a small stream lined with cottonwoods to let the horses drink and cool off. Win found a large, flat rock warmed by the sun, perched himself there, and gazed intently into the hills. Meg, full of energy, took everyone's canteen to the river's edge. Jeb sat down next to Win. "What are you looking at, partner?"

Win scratched his head and returned his hat to his head. "I don't know. My gut tells me we aren't alone. Do you feel it?"

"I'm too distracted by the company we *can* see to be thinking about who we can't."

Win squinted at the rock outcroppings. "Yeah, I know what you mean." But he peered at the shadows, obviously pre-occupied by something in addition to Meg. Jeb looked in the same direction, trying to see what Win was searching for. Finally, Win gave up, turned, and surprised Jeb with an unexpected question: "What are we gonna do about Meg? We both like her; that's easy to see."

"You saw her first, back in Omaha."

"I appreciate that, but it doesn't count. She was just a messy little tomboy then. She's all grown up now — well, sort of. Still a little messy." Win looked in the direction of the stream. "I figure we should make a pact. Let's agree that regardless of who she chooses, we'll stay friends."

Win typically joked about his feelings for a woman. Jeb played along. "Ha, you want a pact with me? It's Saint Gus you should be worried about. I'd like to know where we stand next to him. He's all she talks about!"

"You're the only friend I've got, Jeb," Win said, remaining serious. "Pretty soon, she's gonna have us stomping around like a couple of prairie chickens. It'd be nice not to completely lose our dignity, as well as our friendship."

A male prairie chicken during nesting season did look ridiculous, Jeb thought. On the booming grounds in western Iowa, males charged each other, jumped into the air, and made strange booming calls to attract the females. The silliest part of their mating ritual was to stamp their feet, like impatient boys having tantrums, demanding attention. Jeb did not want to look like a desperate prairie chicken.

They had relied on each other for as long as Jeb could remember, except for the last few years when Win had to test his mettle on his own. And it wasn't hard to imagine how a girl could upset the balance between loyalty and competition, and ruin a perfectly good friendship. Jealousy was corrosive. It'd be a shame if things became strained between them. Besides, who said she especially liked either of them anyway? She sure didn't make eyes at them, or giggle nervously the way other girls did. She didn't flirt. Nothing he could spot, anyway. Win was right — they shouldn't let a girl come between them.

Jeb extended his hand. "Agreed." They shook on it as a thought came to him. "Maybe we could share her — you know, like those Mormons."

Visibly less troubled, Win's sense of humor returned. "You've got it backward, partner. It's the Mormon men who have more than one woman — lucky bastards — not the other way around."

"Lucky? They've got more than one *wife*," Jeb said. "Seems like a lot to take on."

Win threw his head back and laughed loudly. A splash came from the creek. Meg had stumbled, slipping into the water just past her knee. Win shook his head. "I wonder if she ever gets through a day without getting in a mess."

Jeb heard her cuss as he made his way down to the creek. He grabbed her outstretched hand and pulled her up onto solid rock, taking the canteens from her. Behind him, he heard Win drumming his hands on his thigh, presumably imitating an aroused prairie chicken. Jeb tried not to smile for fear Meg would think he was laughing at her.

"That was clumsy of me." She wrung the water from the bottom of her skirt.

"Are you hurt?"

"No, just wet." She sloshed back up to Win and pulled off her boot and stocking. "Damn, that water is cold."

Jeb watched Win grin broadly, and then stretch out, pulling his hat over his face, presumably to mask it. "It's warm and peaceful here. I feel a nap coming on while Meg dries out."

"What about . . ." Jeb didn't want to alarm Meg, but Win had said he didn't think they were alone.

Muffled by his hat, Win said, "If anybody was around, we'd have known it by now."

Jeb took Meg's boot, shook the water from it, and set it in the sun.

"Thank you, Jeb. I confess, I'm quite jealous of you both. You're here with each other and I miss Gus so much. When I heard Win laugh just now, I got such a pang of loneliness."

Jeb wondered if Win would ask what her situation was with this Gus fellow, as he certainly wasn't shy about asking questions, but Win lay still.

Meg wiggled her toes in the warm sun. "This area would be good for a ranch, don't you think? Maybe not so good for most crops, but I bet timothy would grow in the valley. Gus and I talked all the time about coming west and running a ranch. He'd love it here."

"Have you known Gus a long time?" Jeb asked. He hoped he sounded like he was making casual conversation.

She cocked her head at Jeb. "Well, not as long as you and Win. Can't go too far back when there's a forty year age difference, but I've known him since I was real little. Most people just see an ornery old man with a missing hand, broken down by life." She turned and squinted at the sun. "But he's been good to me. He takes me the way I am. He watched over me all those years I didn't have anyone; made me feel like I had a home and family. I'm going to do the

153

same for him and buy him some land for a ranch. I passed through a town called Paradise a few days ago. I'm going to buy land around there."

Jeb wondered how she could afford to buy enough land for a ranch, and also wanted to hear more about the forty-year age difference and what that meant, exactly. Win, however, sat up and pushed his hat back. Here it comes, Jeb thought.

"How did he lose his hand?" Win asked.

"Well, that depends on who asks him," she said, "or on how much he's had to drink. He can tell a pretty tall tale. I've heard him tell folks that he lost it fighting an Indian, stopping a runaway stage, getting run over by a locomotive, and getting stampeded on a cattle drive. If he likes you, though, he'll tell you the truth. He had a dog along with him on the Shawnee Trail — he called him Buddy. He loved that dog. One night, Buddy strayed from the camp and got surrounded by a pack of wild dogs. Gus tried to save poor Buddy and got his hand so torn and chewed up, nothing could be done to save it. He saved Buddy, though. That dog stayed by his side when they took off his hand and all the time while he healed up, and then for five more years on the trail. Broke his heart when old Buddy died. Not many people know the real story. He says most people would think he was a fool for saving some dumb dog."

"But you don't think he was," Jeb said. "Not someone who escapes into the wilderness to save her horse."

Meg fixed her eyes on Jeb. "That's right. I don't think he was a fool at all. Protecting what you love is as natural as breathing."

Win pulled his hat back over his eyes to resume his nap. "Amen to that."

"I saw some fish in that stream," Meg said. "Who wants to camp here tonight and have fish for dinner?"

"Sounds wonderful. Try to stay dry," Win said from under his hat.

Jeb found it uncanny how alike Meg and Win were. Resiliency and loyalty lay beneath their lighthearted exteriors. He wondered if they noticed how similar they were. He decided not to draw their attention to it.

"Let's go fishing." Jeb rose. Meg pulled on her boot and scampered out of earshot. Win mumbled quietly from under his hat that Jeb was a bastard.

Jeb whispered hoarsely, "Hey, our pact didn't say we can't be nice to her. We just can't fight about her."

Stretched out comfortably, hat over his eyes, Win simply raised his hands in a brief surrender. Jeb smiled and followed Meg down to the creek.

Jeb didn't want her to come between Win and him, either. Jeb owed Win everything. Looking back, his initial reluctance to give up his job at the sawmill was a bit unsettling, and most certainly depressing. He would have missed the endless stretches of land and the herds of antelope and buffalo. He never would have seen how bright the stars are on the prairie at night. He never would have met Meg. Win's good idea of the pact ensured that neither relationship would be at the expense of the other. At least, that was his hope.

Chapter Twelve:
Gray Wolf

Foothills of the Colorado Rockies

Gray Wolf, the leader of a small band of Arapaho living in the mountains, climbed to a rocky outcropping to check on the two men and a woman who had camped that night just below him. He watched the taller man with light-colored hair come back from relieving himself. He had gone much farther from camp than necessary. Gray Wolf concluded from the man's modesty that the young woman did not belong to him. From the way they moved about camp, he concluded that she didn't belong to the darker-haired man, either, but neither was she a prisoner. They piqued Gray Wolf's curiosity.

The tall man had jumped up to help the young woman with flame-colored hair when she slipped at the creek. Gray Wolf was astonished by the ease with which she had ridden the day before, her arms outstretched, revealing both bravery and unity

157

with her horse. But her clumsiness then surprised him, making him laugh. The other man had peered curiously into the hills. Gray Wolf sensed his presence had been felt and, strangely enough, he respected the man for his astuteness.

The recent fighting between Indians and whites made Gray Wolf wary, but these intriguing travelers were not military men in blue coats. They reminded him of his own youth, when he raced his friends across the plains, all of them showing off their riding prowess and their skills as worthy fighters. A fierce warrior, he counted coup to prove his bravery, and had many eagle feathers as evidence. When he was their age, the world was different. It had been a grand time to be young then.

Twenty summers ago, Gray Wolf's name was Many Stars. He'd gone into the desert to fast and seek guidance from the spirits, a ritual expected of young men his age. He'd fasted four days when a white man, near death, stumbled into his prayer circle. The young man had no food or water, and no weapon. Weak himself, Many Stars dragged the white man into the shade, brought him some water, and stayed with him. The Arapaho had a vision of himself as a wolf, not attacking the man, but protecting him. He prayed to the spirits and became a wolf. He saw the world through the wolf's eyes, and heard himself growl and bare his teeth. Many Stars brought the white man, Clint Sanders, back to his village where he regained his strength. His kinsmen gave Many Stars the new name of Gray Wolf because the wolf spirit had entered him.

Gray Wolf and Clint became friends. They taught each other their languages and customs. Gray Wolf didn't understand much of the white people's ways. Gold in a place beyond the mountains called California made white people race across buffalo land, disrupting the herds. The Fort Laramie treaty of '51, as Clint called it, separated Indian nations into geographic areas. Gray Wolf thought location was a strange way to think about tribes of people. If a Shoshone stepped into Arapaho territory, did he become an Arapaho? Of course not; nor did a line drawn on paper keep white people from traveling into Arapaho country to hunt for gold. While Gray Wolf believed what Clint told him was true, little of it made sense.

Clint sympathized with his friend's confusion, and warned Gray Wolf not to sign the Fort Wise treaty, which gave away the land designated for the Arapaho a decade earlier.

Hohacache — or Little Raven, as Clint called him — wanted peace, and signed the treaty along with Storm, Big Mouth, and Shave-Head, leaders from the southern tribe. But their signing did not bring peace.

Gray Wolf's heart ached as he recalled the day last winter when runners — fleet-footed braves who delivered messages back and forth to camps — reported that many of his Arapaho brothers, including his friend, Left Hand, had been slaughtered at Sand Creek, murdered without cause or mercy. A white soldier named Chivington had issued the order.

In retaliation for the Sand Creek massacre, many of his Arapaho kin joined the Cheyenne, who rampaged against white settlements. Over the past winter, Cheyenne and Arapaho attacked places the white people called Julesburg, Mud Springs, and Rush Creek. In the spring, the warriors attacked outposts and stagecoach stations in an effort to drive away the invaders and preserve what was left of their hunting land and way of life. Even now, his warriors joined other Arapaho, Lakota, and Cheyenne warriors for an attack on what white people called the Platte Bridge Station. The summer of warfare was far from over.

The Arapaho living on the northern plains

had additional troubles. More gold had been discovered in the north, and it seemed there was no stopping the white man's lust for it. White men used Indian trails to get to the gold that was in Indian country, brazenly trespassing on land the white government said belonged to the Arapaho, Shoshone, and Lakota nations. Gray Wolf asked Clint why white people came onto Indian land when Indians were not allowed on white land. His friend had no answers for him, except to say in the white man's eyes, the land always and only belonged to white people. Montana Territory, as Clint called it, first belonged to the French, who sold it to the United States. Once gold was discovered, President Abraham Lincoln quickly created the Montana Territory, despite the fact that all land west of the Mississippi was Indian land, according to a promise made years ago by the Indian Removal Act of 1830. Gray Wolf argued with Clint, saying that no one can own the Earth, just as no one can own the sky, and it made him very angry that white people were scaring away the game and telling the Arapaho where they could and could not go. Clint agreed; it made no sense to him, either.

His friendship with Clint complicated Gray Wolf's role in the fighting. He didn't hate all white people, like some in his tribe, and he didn't believe that killing innocent white people avenged the deaths of Arapaho. He believed in killing the men responsible. He would cut out the heart of the blue coat leader Chivington, if he could, to see if it was as black as he imagined it to be. Gray Wolf wasn't afraid to fight, but to kill helpless white women made him no better than the white murderer. There was no honor in it, and he would not do it. Gray Wolf chose his own path.

Clint warned him that there would be no stopping the white settlers. Gray Wolf would have to fight them all, and there were too many. If he fought until he was dead, how would that help his family? Clint said Gray Wolf's best chance for survival was to escape into the mountains. Clint offered to help any way he could.

So, when the white government started rounding up Indian nations and escorting them to reservations, Gray Wolf moved his family behind the first range of foothills. The hidden valleys and protected canyons teemed with wildlife. White people had already searched for gold there and, finding none, had gone. Gray Wolf and his people lived here now, and he intended to stay — living in peace, and on his own terms.

Gray Wolf watched the two men pack up and prepare to leave. Too curious to ignore them, Gray Wolf decided to meet these white people. Perhaps he would hear important news. He slipped away to gather his hunting party.

CHAPTER THIRTEEN: MEG

Foothills of Colorado Rockies

A flock of birds burst from the trees in unison and flew away, a warning to Meg that something, or someone, was close. She wished they had the same ability to remove themselves so easily. Win warned her not to run if Indians appeared — something she was prone to do, he reminded her. Just as he was explaining how Indians had an eerie ability to stay invisible, a group of seven Arapaho materialized.

The Arapaho approached with confidence, but not aggression, riding toward them at a pace that suggested peaceful business. All seven wore deerskin breechcloths, fringed leggings, and eagle feathers — or *Bee'etei'l*, as Win called them — in their hair as recognition of bravery in battle. The feathers floated in the breeze at the back of their heads. A few men held spears, also with eagle feathers tied to the ends indicating warrior status, as did the marks on the spear shaft from counting coup, a tally of battle success. Five were bare-chested; the two oldest men wore deerskin shirts. One wore the claw of a hawk around his neck and the other, the obvious leader, wore a wolf pelt on his head, the snout of the wolf coming down over his forehead. His leggings were decorated with beads. They looked as magnificent as the scenery from which they emerged.

The leader rode up to them and raised his hand, a gesture Win returned.

"Heebe," Win said. *"Teeteeseihnoo ceitei-hiiho'."*

The Arapaho reacted with surprise when they heard Win speak their language. A few of the men behind the leader talked to each other. The leader stared.

"What did you say?" Jeb asked Win.

"I hope I said hello, and that we are just passing through," Win said. He didn't sound completely sure of himself, and didn't take his eyes off the leader.

"Maybe you should introduce us," Meg whispered.

"Good idea," Win said quietly, almost to himself. *"Nenee'eesih'inoo* Win Avery." Win touched his chest. He pointed to Jeb and Meg and stated their names.

165

Again, the leader stared. Meg got the feeling his silence was due to thinking hard, rather than anger, fear, or intimidation. His brow wrinkled into a deep furrow.

"Did Clint Sanders teach you something like 'we're good people' or 'we don't mean to trespass'?" Jeb asked. "Did Clint teach you the word for 'friendly'?" The Arapaho leader looked sharply at Jeb.

"Jeez, Jeb, give me a second . . . um . . . *Niico'ouuteenebeen,*" Win said. "I think I just said 'I respect you highly' . . . I think."

Instead of responding to Win, the Arapaho leader squinted at Jeb. "Clint Sanders?"

Jeb nodded. "Win, how do you say Clint Sanders is your friend?"

"Ah . . . um . . . Clint Sanders *neiteh'ei.*"

The hard lines on the Arapaho leader's face softened and the furrow in his brow disappeared.

"This is incredible." Win looked as shocked as the Arapaho leader. "Are you Gray Wolf?"

The Arapaho leader nodded his head slightly.

"Unbelievable," Jeb whispered.

"*Neheicoo',*" Gray Wolf said to Win.

"He wants us to follow him." Win turned to Meg. "You all right with that?"

She really didn't have a choice, did she?

But Jeb's reassuring words from the day before, that they would figure out together whatever came their way, rang in her ears. She didn't feel afraid. She nodded.

Win, Jeb, and Meg followed the Arapaho party down a path to their camp. Gray Wolf and the other older man sat down and indicated that they should join them. The leader introduced his second in command as Sharp Eye. Standing Horse and One Who Waits were introduced after they tended to the ponies and joined the group. Gray Wolf did not introduce the three youngest braves, who left to hunt for dinner.

Gray Wolf spoke slowly and deliberately. Meg assumed he was trying to recall English words. He was pretty good at it. Gray Wolf asked if Clint Sanders sent them to find him in the mountains. Win said no, they were on their way to Denver to find Clint. He told Gray Wolf he knew the story of how Gray Wolf saved Clint's life in the desert, and Clint had taught him the few Arapaho words he knew.

"Why do you ride here, and not on the roads the white people built?" Gray Wolf asked.

Win tried to use as many Arapaho words as he could — out of respect, Meg suspected. First he spoke in Arapaho, then in

English: "Flatland is dusty, the hills are green and beautiful."

"A white woman who rides like Arapaho is new to my eyes." Gray Wolf glanced at Meg.

"Her father, a good man, gave her the horse when she was a little girl." Win put his hand over his heart. "Riding makes her happy." Meg liked Win's explanation and was pleased that no one made fun of her, although Standing Horse and One Who Waits talked spiritedly between themselves. One Who Waits extended his arms out wide and tilted his head back just as Meg had done the day before.

"What are they saying?" Meg asked Win.

Gray Wolf answered. "You are *neséihit*."

Win thought for a moment and then said, "There isn't an equivalent word for it in English, but Gray Wolf gave you a compliment. He says you are wild, but in the best sense of the word. He says you . . . fit, or belong here. He means —"

"How do you say 'thank you'?" Meg asked.

"*Hohou*," Gray Wolf said.

"*Hohou*," Meg repeated. She liked Gray Wolf. His eyes were kind.

Gray Wolf nodded to Meg and then turned to Win. "I meet a stranger and he tells my

168

own story to me. I meet a white woman who rides like an Arapaho. These are signs that spirits are at work. Our meeting is for a purpose."

A shiver traveled down Meg's spine, but not from fear. She trembled with excitement.

CHAPTER FOURTEEN:
WIN

Gray Wolf's camp

Cool air from higher elevations cascaded down the mountain to mix with the sun-warmed pines and send a fragrant breeze wafting through Gray Wolf's camp. It swirled around Win and Gray Wolf as they sat across from each other, both searching their memories for words in the other's language. Jeb and Meg sat with them, joined by Sharp Eye, the other elder Arapaho, and Standing Horse and One Who Waits. Win floated on a cloud of exhilaration.

Communicating with the Arapaho took time, but Sharp Eye spoke some English, and Jeb and Meg helped guess at words, too, so the conversation proved productive. Gray Wolf confirmed what Clint had said about his Arapaho friend; he was a spiritual, mystical man, deeply concerned for his people. He also had difficult questions.

Why did the white government tell them

to stop hunting and promise to provide food, when they could feed themselves if left alone to hunt? Why were white hunters so wasteful to kill large numbers of buffalo and scatter the herds? The Arapaho could no longer hunt buffalo together, Gray Wolf said, and their traditions and ceremonies surrounding the annual buffalo hunt were disappearing. Losing their traditions bothered him; he worried the Arapaho were becoming shadows. He asked why lines were drawn on paper to show where the Indians could not go. Gray Wolf said the white government made promises they did not honor. He would never sign a treaty with the government, nor move his family to a reservation. Sickness, hunger, and death lived at the reservations. Here in the mountains, he could protect and provide for his family. He would live here with his family and any Arapaho who also wanted to live in freedom.

Gray Wolf paused then. His eyes narrowed thoughtfully at Win, Jeb, and Meg. "Do you know the coyote and the badger? They both eat . . ." He turned to Sharp Eye and asked if he knew the English word for *honi'*. Sharp Eye shook his head.

"Oh, I know what you mean." Win turned to Meg and Jeb. "*Honi'* is a small burrowing animal, like a ground squirrel, or a prairie dog."

Gray Wolf nodded and continued. "You would think the coyote and the badger would fight over the *honi'*, but each has a different gift, so, instead of fighting, they give their gift to each other. If the *honi'* is above the ground, the coyote chases it. If he catches it, it is his. But if the *honi'* is too fast and escapes underground, the badger, with his sharp claws, digs it out of its burrow and it is his. If it escapes out of its burrow, the coyote is waiting to pounce. When the coyote and the badger hunt together like this, they are well fed. It is . . ." Gray Wolf paused to find the word, ". . . unexpected . . . for two kinds of animals to eat their fill when both are after the same meal, but I have seen it. It is a good partnership."

Gray Wolf invited them to camp with his hunting party for the night. Win lay awake long after he heard the steady breathing of sleep. Too energized to close his eyes, he reflected on their extraordinary day. And the story of the badger and coyote.

Spirits seemed to whisper the story over and over in his ear. Perhaps spirits had brought them together, as Gray Wolf said. One of the Arapaho snored loudly, but where Gray Wolf lay, it was silent. Win wondered if the Arapaho leader was awake as well, unable to sleep.

Win stared at the stars in the inky sky. No thunderstorms, but Win felt electricity in the air. When he finally drifted into sleep, the dark-haired girl who often visited Win in his dreams asked him the name for the blue light at the tips of the pines, glowing like St. Elmo's fire on a ship's mast at sea. "Foxfire," he told her.

"No," she said, "the Arapaho name."

He didn't know.

CHAPTER FIFTEEN:
JEB

Gray Wolf's camp

Win finished a private conversation with Gray Wolf and signaled to Jeb and Meg that he was ready to leave. Jeb tipped his hat to Gray Wolf and Sharp Eye. Meg waved to the Arapaho men. *"Hohou."*

One warrior waved back.

Once they had left camp, Meg gazed all around, taking in the mountainous terrain and the lush green river valley. When she sighed and said, "I belong here," Jeb's heart fluttered with excitement.

"Even with Indians?" Win asked.

"I feel bad for them. Our government has broken so many of its promises. It isn't right." Meg furrowed her brow.

Jeb turned to Win. "What were you and Gray Wolf talking about just now?"

"Oh, you know, stock prices, investing in commodities . . ."

Meg laughed. "Seriously, Win . . . Tell us."

174

"Well, One Who Waits took a fancy to you and wanted to take you back with him. I had to do a little fast talking on your behalf." Meg gasped. "Oh, don't worry." Win waved his hand. "I told him it was a bad idea because you would make a bad squaw. I said you were a lot of trouble, had a stubborn disposition, wouldn't obey a husband, and would embarrass any brave who dared take you as his wife because you'd never listen —"

"Oh, for heaven's sake!" Meg lifted her chin and straightened her back.

"I was doing you a favor!" Win spread his arms out innocently. "There's more . . ."

Meg took off on Biscuit, apparently unwilling to listen to Win's foolish talk.

"Ah, you sweet talker, you." Jeb watched her lope ahead of them.

"Well, the way you've been attending to her . . . being all sweet-like . . . shit. She's gonna get all self-possessed if we both go moony over her. I've got to give her a hard time once in a while."

"I'm not being moony."

"You go on thinkin' that."

"Fine by me if you keep annoying her. It'll work in my favor."

"I didn't annoy her. Besides, I'm twice as smart as you, and ten times better looking."

"Now who's self-possessed?" Jeb said.

"Just stating facts."

Jeb rolled his eyes and changed the subject. "What were you really talking about?"

Win seemed ready to drop the banter, too, and became serious. "Well . . . Gray Wolf asked a lot of questions. He must have been up all night trying to remember English words. He asked that I tell Clint he has furs to trade. He seems worried that he'll have to move his family again, and while I don't blame him, I don't know what we could do about it."

They watched Biscuit lope up a steep rise. "Meg sure was a good sport," Win said, "the way she laughed at herself when Standing Horse mimicked her falling in the stream . . ."

"She did well, didn't she?"

"Yep, no acting high and mighty like some women get, and didn't panic. She didn't even get squeamish when they took apart that deer. Pretty fascinating the way they washed out the bladder."

Meg crested the hill. Biscuit reared up as she screamed, "Run!"

CHAPTER SIXTEEN: MEG

On the road to Denver

Meg panicked as soon as she saw the piebald with three white legs and one black tied with the other horses. In the time it took her to shout a warning to Win and Jeb, a barrel-chested man jumped from his hiding place and pulled her from Biscuit. Meg fought him like a wildcat, but he grabbed her by the wrists and spun her around, pressing her back to his chest. Then he pinned her arms to her sides with one arm and with the other hand, grabbed her hair and jerked her head back. She tried to kick him, but was unable to gather enough force to inflict pain. She heard scuffling and grunting behind her. She couldn't see what was happening, but she knew Win and Jeb had ridden straight into the fight. Apparently, Sutter had picked up help on his way to find her. She couldn't tell how many.

Sutter, never a patient man, drew his gun

and fired it once in the air. The sound of fighting stopped when he lowered his gun and aimed it directly at Meg. She heard the sickening sound of a rock thump against a head, followed by what sounded like a heavy sack of potatoes thrown from a cart.

"Barney, take their guns," Sutter said.

More scuffling came from behind her. Meg tried to turn around, but the man holding her lifted her by her hair, making her stand contorted and awkward, like a doll hanging from a hook. Sutter swaggered into view and holstered his gun. "You're a hard girl to find."

"I beg you, Mr. Sutter, don't kill Biscuit." Her voice sounded quivery and high-pitched — not her own.

Sutter scoffed. "Why the hell would I kill your horse? You gotta ride somethin' back to Council Bluffs." He paced back and forth in front of her. "Your uncle is dead," he said, sneering as he looked her over head to toe, as though considering a purchase.

Confusion surfaced, despite her panic. "Then what do you want?"

"I ain't been paid for some time now. You're coming back with me so I get what's owed me."

"My aunt will pay you. You don't need me."

He snorted. "She's dead, too. Want to know how? Want to know *why*?" He stood in front of Meg, his right hand resting on the holstered revolver slung on his hip. "The old lady found out your uncle preferred fillies to mares. He sure got distracted by you, didn't he?" Sutter traced a line from her eyebrow down her cheek, a dead tree branch of a hand brushing against her in the dark of night, the kind of touch that causes a cold shiver. He continued drawing a line down her throat and stopped at her breast, where it lingered. She recoiled, only to press her back against the man holding her. She felt sick to her stomach. Sutter smiled and let his finger drop.

"Jealousy must've made her lose her mind. She found him in the library, and you know what she did?" In a swift and sudden move, Sutter pulled his gun, pointed it in Meg's face, and shouted "BANG!" Meg flinched and shut her eyes as she cried out. "Your auntie shot him dead."

Meg felt the blood drain from her face as his words registered.

Sutter continued to pace. "After your aunt killed her husband, she tried to cover it up by setting fire to his library. Only thing is, she used a little too much kerosene, and it made such a smoky mess she didn't quite

179

find her way out before the whole place burst into flames."

"You're lying," Meg said.

He smacked her hard across the face. "No, I ain't."

The sting from his strike made her eyes water, but it knocked resolve into her, as well as defiance. "I'm not going back with you. You won't get a cent of my father's money."

Sutter ignored her, motioning to a man Meg didn't recognize to bring Biscuit over. They were going to take her away. Biscuit, loyal as always, danced about nervously as the unfamiliar man tried to manage her.

Someone behind Meg said, "Darryl cain't never get no female to mind him."

"Shut up, Barney," the man called Darryl replied.

Sutter growled at Meg. "Control your goddamn horse." The barrel-chested man holding her released his grip. She pushed him away and faced Sutter squarely. "Go to hell."

Sutter raised his hand to wallop Meg again, but she turned away, covering her face. Instead of hitting her, he grabbed her arm and shoved her toward Biscuit.

Meg buried her face in Biscuit's mane, wrapping her arms around her neck. Biscuit lowered her heavy head and nudged Meg with it as she rubbed her neck — perhaps to return comfort, perhaps as a signal of encouragement. Inside her saddlebag, tucked just inches away from her, opportunity waited. Opportunity for Win and Jeb to get away, at least.

"Why you wastin' all that sweetness on a horse, girl? She cain't give you the kind of attention you need." Meg turned briefly toward the ugly voice of Barney. The retort ready on her lips escaped her as she saw him thrust his hips at her. "You need a man, girly girl," he said. "I got something you can rub." He started toward her.

"Stay away from her!" Win shouted.

A quick glance showed Jeb in a crumpled heap on the ground, unmoving. Win was face-down in the dirt, with an enormous man she remembered as Big Bull sitting on him like he was a park bench. In a fleeting moment, she wondered how many of Win's ribs Big Bull was crushing.

Distracted, Barney pointed at Win, enjoying the power briefly in his possession. "What are you squawkin' fer? Nothin' you can do but watch."

The few seconds of diversion was all the time she needed. When Barney turned his attention back to Meg, she had Carl's derringer pointed at his groin.

She'd forgotten to give the little gun back to Carl. Win had seen it back in LaPorte and had joked, at the time, that a weapon that size couldn't do much damage. *It all depends on where you aim it,* she had replied. She saw in Win's expression momentary relief that she'd been able to get her hands on the gun. But other than maiming Barney, the little weapon couldn't take them all on.

Barney laughed nervously. "What you got there, honey?"

Meg was about to tell Big Bull to get off Win or Barney would lose his manhood when she heard a swish in the air and a *thup*. Barney stopped laughing and stared at her with wide-eyed surprise. An arrow stuck out of his back. The tip poked out of his chest — not far, but far enough for blood to spread like a blossoming flower on his shirt. His knees buckled and he fell to the ground. The man who'd held Meg reached for his gun — two arrows hit him at the same time, one in his heart, the other in his stomach. A blood-curdling war cry pierced the air just before Sutter fell. The man Barney called Darryl, who couldn't manage Biscuit, sprinted away. Big Bull, a giant of a man, heaved himself off Win and tried to escape,

182

his weight and size working against him. Both Big Bull and Darryl met their fate out of view from Meg. She heard two sharp cries, grunts, muffled thuds, and then silence.

Stunned, she couldn't move, but in a dream-like state watched Win retrieve his gun and kneel over Jeb. He turned him over and put his ear to his chest. Relief on his face, Win motioned her over to him. She saw his lips form her name, but she couldn't hear anything. She felt like she was swimming underwater as she tried to move toward him. He reached out to her and pulled her down next to Jeb. Then Win crouched over both of them, spreading his arms over them like protective wings. He had his revolver in one hand, the other rested on her shoulder. She could feel the warmth of his hand through her jacket.

Gray Wolf, Sharp Eye, and One Who Waits rode into view.

Meg cried out with relief and reached up to squeeze Win's hand. They were safe. Win stood and holstered his gun. Gray Wolf dismounted and walked around to each of the fallen men, while the other Arapaho picked them clean of anything valuable. One Who Waits yanked the arrow out of Barney before he turned him over and took his gun.

Standing Horse appeared, carrying guns and a knife, his forearms spattered with blood.

"These are bad men." Gray Wolf pointed to Sutter.

"Yes, they were going to take Meg away," Win said.

Gray Wolf nodded slowly, as though pondering Win's words. "They take her to a reservation."

"Something like that. We're grateful to you."

Meg looked around her at the dead men with arrows lodged in their bodies. Two more lay a few yards away, hacked to pieces. Gray Wolf and his braves had just killed five white men. She could feel Gray Wolf watching her.

"Our people hang when they kill white men," Gray Wolf said.

"You were protecting us," Meg said. But she knew Indians were treated differently under white laws. The Arapaho may have saved their lives, but ruthless white men still commanded a higher status than a principled Arapaho.

"No one needs to know about this," Win said. "We are indebted to you. There is no need to report this to anyone."

Jeb stirred. Meg sat on the ground and

cradled his head in her lap. "You all right?" Win asked his friend, bending over him.

Jeb squinted. "Yeah, great." He tried to stand up, but winced in pain and fell back.

"Wait, take it slow." Win felt Jeb's head. "You aren't bleeding, but that's a nasty bump."

Win helped Jeb to his feet. Meg remained on the ground and watched two Arapaho braves pile the dead bodies. What they were going to do with them, she couldn't guess. Sharp Eye checked Sutter's horse for a brand, while Standing Horse tested the strength of a lariat. She felt no remorse, no fear — only relief. She hoped the Arapaho would get good use out of the treasures they collected.

Gus spoke to her, then, in a memory. *There'll be moments in your life, Meggie darlin', when who you are and what you believe are forever etched into your soul.*

The moment etched itself into Meg's soul. Her life would never be the same. Nor would Gray Wolf's. They would forever be linked.

CHAPTER SEVENTEEN: WIN

Denver, Colorado Territory, August 1865

When Win arrived in Denver with Meg and Jeb, she insisted that Jeb see a doctor, while Win found his old boss and secured work for Jeb and himself. She'd find rooming houses, she declared, and left before they could protest.

Ever since her rescue from Sutter, Meg had appeared to be on a quest, her determination more transparent than the reasons behind it. When Win had asked her what she was up to, she'd simply put her hands on her hips, cocked her head, and said if he and Jeb could have a secret pact, she saw no call for full disclosure, and raised her eyebrows like Grace Moberg, preventing further inquiry about what she was doing. Jeb must've slipped about the pact; he was never good at pretense. Win found Meg both amusing and befuddling at times, but always had the sensation he was aboard that locomotive again, careening out of control.

Win left to search for his old trail boss. He first met Clint in the spring of '62, after the Pony Express had gone out of business. Win drifted into Independence, looking for work, and saw wagon trains forming. He knew right away he wanted to attach himself to a train so he could head west again. One trail captain impressed him with his quiet authority: Clint Sanders. Win hung around, trying to figure out how to get hired, but got a little too close and felt Clint's iron grip on his shoulder.

"Why are you hanging about? Every time I turn around, there you are."

"I'm trying to learn . . . 'cause I need a job." Win squared himself in front of the man, holding on to the last of his pride. "I figured if I knew something before I asked, you'd have reason to hire me."

Sanders looked him over head to toe. Win knew he looked mighty pathetic. He hadn't eaten in a while, his hair was long and dirty, and he smelled ripe. But Win looked his prospective boss straight in the eye, hoping he showed grit and intelligence. It worked. The trail captain tossed him a dollar and told him to get a bath and haircut, clean clothes, and a meal before reporting back.

"When you get back," Clint had added,

"find Cookie and tell him Sanders sent you. He'll take you on, as long as you ain't too irritatin' — so don't be irritatin'."

"Thank you, sir. You won't be sorry!" Win ran off to do as instructed. He returned in a couple of hours, clean, cut, fed, and ready to work.

The cook hired Win as his helper. Win cleaned the fresh game brought in by the scouts and scrubbed the dirty pots every night, all the while steering clear of the crusty old cook so as not to irritate him. He got along with the other hired hands, once he proved he could stand his ground in a fight. When payday arrived, Win paid back a dollar to Sanders.

When they reached California and the train disbanded, Win roamed awhile. But he eventually worked his way back to Independence, where he hoped to find Sanders organizing another train west. This time, Win showed up in clean trail clothes, carrying his own saddle and grinning broadly.

"Mohican!" Sanders thrust out his hand. "Where the hell have you been?"

"Trying to stay out of trouble, sir, and succeeding . . . mostly." Win shook the extended hand.

The trail captain studied him. "Well, I see you've got your own saddle. I need scouts, and you're a good rider," he said, "You've got a job if you've come lookin' for one."

"Thank you, sir. You won't be sorry."

Sanders slapped Win on the back. "Wasn't the first time. Go find a fella named Pete over at the corral and tell him I said you're riding Sophie. She's smooth as butter. Welcome back, son."

Now Clint was somewhere in Denver. Win asked around and was directed to the warehouse district. He spotted his old boss outside one of the shipping warehouses, making notes on the back of a stage schedule. Clint hadn't aged a day — maybe even looked younger without the burdens of trail life weighing on him. Or maybe the lack of a handlebar mustache he'd once sported gave him a more youthful appearance. He looked up, the way people do when they sense someone is looking at them.

"Well, I'll be damned," Clint said as Win walked up to him. "You just keep turning up like a bad penny. Can't seem to shake you loose."

Win extended his hand. "It's great to see you, too, Clint."

"How the hell are you, Win?" Clint asked, his grip strong as ever. "What brings you to Denver?"

"You, frankly. You're the best boss I've

ever had, though Dutch Ferguson comes in close. He says hello."

Clint threw his head back and laughed. "Dutch, that old sonofabitch. We had some times, he and I."

"That's what I hear. I rode with him to Ash Hollow with a friend of mine. We broke off there and headed this way."

"That wouldn't be your old friend . . . What was his name? Jeb?"

"That's right. He's over at the doc's. We ran into a bit of trouble between here and LaPorte."

"What kind of trouble?" Clint squinted at him curiously.

"Well, I think you need a glass in your hand to hear it. Can I buy my old boss a beer?"

"How 'bout you buy your new boss a beer? I got work, if you want it. First, you gotta meet Mandy."

Clint brought Win by his home to meet Amanda, a woman Clint's age, who looked as though she lived unapologetically, a trait well suited for Clint. She greeted Win with a kiss on the cheek that was maternal and yet not, which seemed to amuse her. When they left, Clint confessed that he'd never been happier and would die a contented man, as that Mandy was a peach.

At the saloon, Win told Clint about heading west with Jeb and finding Meg on the prairie. Clint laughed heartily when he heard how Meg had raced Win when he was a Post rider. Clint was a good laugher. He made the person telling the story feel like he was telling a good one. When Win got to the part where they met Gray Wolf, Clint sighed with relief.

"I was worried when you said you had trouble, 'cause I know Gray Wolf just moved his family there. He stays out of sight, mostly. The fact that he approached you is interesting."

"He said we met for a purpose," Win said. "He thinks spirits are at work."

Clint smiled. "He's funny that way, but he's no fool, and very practical. He sees war being waged on his people and knows he's out-powered. But he isn't gonna let our government push him 'round, neither. I don't blame him for avoiding the reservation. He may claim spirits are telling him to stay away, but I think he's just damn stubborn." Clint went on say how he and Gray Wolf crossed paths from time to time. He shook his head. "I don't know why we can't do honest business with them and keep our promises. Whoever figured Indians would just peacefully move away and onto reservations? I tell ya, I'd rather work with them than make enemies of them."

"I agree," Win said. "Seems like there's room enough out here for everybody."

"I'll tell you something, Win, just between us. I am doing business with him . . . on the sly. I owe him."

"I can understand that. He saved your life. What kind of business?"

"Well, Gray Wolf don't take charity. You gotta trade square. I brought him a few small things to make their lives a little easier — you know, kettles, and some warm blankets. I came back with more furs than I knew what to do with. But I've been thinking. I got an idea that might be equally good for both of us."

"What's on your mind?"

Clint swirled the amber liquid in his glass. "Well, you know who Ben Holladay is, right?"

"The Stagecoach King? Who controls most of the stage lines and is one of the largest employers in the country? Yeah, I think I've heard of him." Win grinned.

Clint chuckled. "All right, all right, stupid question. So, he's got a monopoly on the stage and postal business. Can't do much about that. He's got money and a station at Lyonsville, and I can't do much about that either. Good spot, I'll admit. Right now, folks go through Lyonsville on their way to LaPorte, 'cause that's the route he made. But the way you came is faster — through that little Paradise place. People just don't take it 'cause Holladay's got them convinced it's safer his way. But you saw it. There's already a blacksmith, saloon, and general store sitting in the middle of a grassy, flat spot. Could be a nice route for folks who want to cut a little time off between Cheyenne and Denver."

"Beautiful country," Win said, repeating Meg's words and thinking of her.

"I'd sure like to run a private stage line through there, keeping on the flatland, of course. Cheyenne, LaPorte, Cold Springs . . ."

"Why don't you?"

Clint drained his glass. "I'm sure you know that early this year, Indians burned Julesburg to the ground. They tore down over seventy miles of telegraph line. Killed eighteen people. They stole provisions from there and from Antelope Station, about twelve miles east. Cheyenne and Sioux burned all the buildings, murdered the caretaker. Spring Hill, Beaver Creek . . . most of the stations east of LaPorte were attacked by Cheyenne, Kiowa, Pawnee,

193

Sioux — they're banding together now instead of fighting each other. They're mad as hell, and I don't blame them. Government shoves them out of their homes and promises them food but doesn't deliver. It's a goddamn mess." He got the attention of the barkeep. Another round arrived.

"Latham wasn't attacked . . . Why do you suppose that is? Fort Collins isn't any closer to it than Fort Morgan is to the other stations," Win said.

"I got a couple of theories about that. One is they've steered clear out of respect for Gray Wolf."

"What's your other theory?"

"They just haven't gotten around to it yet," Clint said. "That's why I've been slow to invest. Maybe Holladay can afford to lose thousands of dollars in supplies and materials to rebuild stations, but I can't."

Win stared into his shot glass, Clint's words slowly registering. "You're thinking you could run freight and stage lines through Paradise if you had Gray Wolf's cooperation, and what you'd trade for his cooperation would be . . ."

"Rifles."

"Hmm . . . When Gray Wolf and his party attacked Sutter, they had only bows and arrows. If they had rifles . . ."

"They'd be more powerful," Clint said. "Protect their families."

Clint cocked his head. "Hunt easier."

"Keep the road secure," Win said, following Clint's line of thinking.

They clinked their glasses together. Win mulled over the idea of supplying rifles to Indians. It was illegal, not to mention risky. It could easily get the lot of them hanged.

Clint held up his glass as an indication he was closing the subject for the time being. "I'm going to chew on it awhile, but I'm encouraged by our conversation, Win." He drained his glass. "Now, you brought up this Meg gal more than once. What's she to you?"

The mention of Meg's name brought a smile to Win's face, but all he could do was to shake his head. "I honestly don't know, Clint. Haven't had much time to reflect on it. A lot has happened these last few weeks."

"What about Jeb? He sweet on her?"

"We made a pact, Jeb and me, that she wouldn't change our friendship."

For a second time, Clint threw his head back and laughed a good belly laugh. "Good luck with that. I live with one of them, and, let me tell you, women change everything."

Win wondered if Clint ever missed his days on the trail. When they traveled together, Clint told stories that always made Win's feet itch, stories about riding through wide, open country, free of want or responsibility. Yet here he was now, managing a business and living with a woman he gave up the trail for. He had traded the open road for a responsible life and a soft, warm bed. Win wondered briefly if he'd ever feel like settling down, but brushed the thought away, impossible to imagine. His thoughts turned instead to Meg.

CHAPTER EIGHTEEN:
JEB

Dewer, Colorado Territory

After a few days' rest to give his head a chance to heal, Jeb set out with Win and a shipment to the rowdy mining town of Dewer, about ten miles into the mountains. The assignment drew no protest from Clint's other teamsters, as the town had no sheriff. No one wanted to deliver supplies there, as robbers often intercepted the delivery. Jeb took the job because his doctor received a telegram from Dewer, saying that the medical equipment he'd ordered had been delivered there by mistake. Dr. Miller hadn't the time or inclination to pick it up himself, so retrieving the misdirected equipment became in-kind payment for Jeb's medical care. Kill two birds with one stone, someone said. Jeb hoped he and Win weren't the birds.

Dewer was a depressing place — gray and muddy. Relieved to have delivered the shipment to the dry-goods store without incident, Jeb quickly cinched the last knot on a canvas covering the doctor's equipment in hopes of leaving the town as soon as possible. A man in a traveling coat and carrying a satchel exited the telegraph office and picked his way through the mud to the wagon. The man's bushy muttonchops were a sharp contrast to the thinning hair on top of his head. More notable than his impressive whiskers was the large wine-stain birthmark on the left side of his forehead and temple. The birthmark extended into his muttonchop.

"Pardon me, gentlemen, my name is Albert Rothenberg. I find I have been as misdirected as Nathan Miller's new equipment. Nathan needs to improve his penmanship, particularly his *N*s and *V*s, but that is not your problem, is it? I've heard you are taking his shipment to him. I wonder if I might ride along. Would you mind?"

Win glanced at Jeb, who shrugged to indicate he had no objection. The man didn't look dangerous, and might even be useful as an extra lookout.

"Not at all. Climb aboard." Win took Mr. Rothenberg's bag and slid it under the springboard seat.

"I'm much obliged." Rothenberg hoisted

himself up, his birthmark changing from a chokecherry red to a ripe buffalo-berry purple from the exertion.

Jeb took a seat on the crates loaded in the wagon, facing backward to have eyes in all directions, his rifle across his lap. Win hopped into the driver's seat and grabbed the reins. A sharp whistle to the mules and they were underway.

"What's your business with Doc Miller, if you don't mind my asking?"

"Not at all!" Rothenberg's spirits seemed to rise now that he was leaving the dismal hamlet. "Dr. Miller served with Ferdinand Hayden near the end of the war. Dr. Hayden is now professor of mineralogy and geology at the University of Pennsylvania and is gathering a team together for an expedition back into the upper Missouri River country." Rothenberg turned to include Jeb in the conversation. "Have you ever read *The Ancient Fauna of Nebraska*? It includes fossilized Dakota specimens that Hayden found and sent back to Professor Leidy. Vertebrate paleontology, gentlemen, right here in America! Can you imagine? Evidence of ancient camels, elephants, rhinoceri — right under our feet!"

Jeb wasn't sure he understood every word Rothenberg spoke. He didn't know what vertebrate paleontology was, but he surely knew what Win was thinking. At the mention of an expedition, Win's posture changed. He shifted in his seat restlessly, a telltale sign he was already bored with the freighting business.

"How does Dr. Miller figure into this?" Win asked.

"Ah, of course, forgive me. Dr. Hayden wants me to persuade Nathan to come along. He liked Nathan's keen attention to detail. I'm a scout, of sorts, for Hayden and other scientists. I facilitate their projects in a variety of ways."

Win said nothing, which was unusual for him. Jeb knew Win's silence probably meant he already felt conflicted between his loyalty to Clint and his desire to join an expedition, and was wrestling with his conscience. Jeb took up the slack in the conversation. "I didn't realize scientists were so interested in the West."

"It's the next big step in the name of progress, Mr. Dawson. Exploration and discovery. Our appetites whetted before the war, now science is ready to take a great leap forward, and geology will lead the way."

Rothenberg went on at length, describing the valuable materials the land hid. Jeb knew he caught Win's ear, though, when he said, "Washington wants to investigate and map our western territories. They need information about the land — what can be farmed, what natural resources we have, and so on — and that requires a survey, and surveying takes money. I am certain money will be appropriated to explore the West as part of our domestic policy. At present, universities fund expeditions into the frontier. Field research has become prestigious and popular.

"For decades, we've been gathering data about cartography, botany, zoology, and geology," Rothenberg said, "ever since Lewis and Clark's Corps of Discovery traveled up the Missouri. But there's no rhyme or reason to any of the information; no system. There's a trend now to organize, specialize, and put this information to work. We're looking for geologists, more specifically, metallurgists, to do out west what has been done in the past decade in each eastern state. Geological surveys. They want to know what resources are available in the territories."

Jeb scanned the hillside. "I can't help but wonder what the Indians think about these survey expeditions."

"Particularly when military escorts accompany them," Win said.

"Early explorers viewed Indians as part of the landscape," Rothenberg said, "more of a marvel than man. Indians were observed and classified along with the rest of the landscape. Times have changed, though. I won't deny that some of the reconnaissance now is to gain information about their fighting strength."

"That sits ill with me," Win said. Jeb was relieved to hear that Win had the same concerns.

"You sound like my friend John Mix Stanley," Rothenberg said. Jeb observed that the man had hardly taken a breath since he joined them. "He traveled all over the west with no other motive than painting the landscape and portraits of the natives."

Jeb said, "I can't help but feel uneasy about the effect the surveys will have on the Indians."

Rothenberg nodded. "I understand. But scientists can survey the land and bring our aboriginal friends no harm. Audubon traversed the country without inciting hostilities. The world would be a lesser place without his *Birds of America,* wouldn't you agree? His motives were hardly suspicious or malevolent."

Jeb had to admit that Rothenberg made it sound plausible and dispelled some of his reservations. After all, it was innocent work; scientists studying rocks and fossils, artists painting portraits, surveyors drawing maps. No military campaign, no removal of Indians. Scientists were peaceful, not political.

Judging by Win's expression, he was already miles away, riding with an expedition that had the magnitude of Lewis and Clark's Corps of Discovery.

CHAPTER NINETEEN: MEG

Clint Sanders's freight company stables,
Denver

Meg scrambled up the five-foot wall that separated Galen and Hippocrates in their straight stalls in Mr. Sanders's barn. Dangling her legs from her perch, she broke three carrots into pieces and gave the horses their treat. Biscuit snorted in the stall next to Galen.

"I'm saving some for you, Biscuit," Meg chided. "Don't worry." She hiked herself up and balanced on the ledge like a tightrope walker over to the next stall. While Biscuit crunched on carrots, Meg inspected her ears and scratched her forelock. She pressed her own forehead against Biscuit's. "No lectures. I know I've gotta find a job. I just don't know what I can do."

Win and Jeb had already left on their first freight delivery. A few days after they arrived in Denver, their boss sent them on

204

what Meg considered a risky delivery to a mining camp. She overheard Clint tell them to stay sharp on the blind curves, where bandits set traps. Clint suggested that they keep their revolvers close and told whoever rode shotgun to have his rifle in hand, loaded and ready. Meg wasn't sure what was so "exhilarating" about driving into such lawless country, but that was the word Win used as he slapped the reins to get the team of six mules going. Maybe he was joking, but, then again, he looked pretty excited.

Meg sighed and returned to her own problems. Most of the jobs open to women required skills she lacked. Jeb had a good idea about clerking at a bookshop. She inquired at the only bookshop in Denver, but the owner had just hired someone and couldn't afford any more staff.

She and Gus had always done their best thinking when they brushed down the horses together. The stable was a good place to figure things out. She found a brush and got started on Hippocrates.

"You like that, fella?" Meg said to him as she brushed his neck. "Biscuit likes it. She likes a good brushing. It makes her feel pretty. You and she have been through a lot already, haven't you? Are you and Biscuit close? Probably not as close as you and

Galen. The two of you have a lot of history together. A girl can't hardly break that bond, can she? Not that she'd want to. You know, Biscuit has a lot of respect for friendship. She'd never come between two handsome horses like you and Galen, no, sir —"

Meg heard someone clear his throat, as if to make his presence known. Clint stood in the doorway.

"Oh! Hello, Mr. Sanders. I'm just looking after the horses, not that your men wouldn't . . ." Meg said, embarrassed to be caught talking to animals. She wondered how long he'd been standing there.

"I understand, little lady. Don't worry about it; you're welcome here." Clint ambled over to the stalls. She turned back to Hippocrates and continued brushing him.

Clint picked up a brush and started on Galen. "Win says you're quite the horsewoman."

"Well, horses are easier to deal with than people, Gus would say. They each have their own personality, though, just like people."

"Ain't that the truth. I had a bay once that would only allow my saddle on her. She'd come over to me in the remuda and wait for me, and if anyone else tried to saddle her, she'd snort and paw and act all ornery."

"Well, no doubt your bay just had a simple

schoolgirl crush on you." Meg picked a burr from Hippocrates' mane. "I'll bet she pouted when you rode some other pretty filly."

Clint laughed. "Come to think of it, the day I gave her a rest and let her run with the others in the remuda, she bucked and bit and caused all sorts of commotion. After that, I figured it was better just to ride her so I could keep an eye on her."

"There you go. Is she still with you?"

"Nah, a Paiute stole her. He came out of nowhere and nearly scalped me, but after we scuffled awhile, he figured it'd be easier to steal her than to kill me. I'd like to think she turned on him somewhere in the desert, the rotten bastard." Clint stopped brushing and turned to Meg. "I heard something about you looking for work. How's that going?"

Meg sighed. "I don't know how to do anything anybody'll hire me for."

"Sorry to hear that. What can you do?"

"Not much . . . brush ponies." She waved the brush in the air. "That's why I'm here. Gus and I did our best thinking and planning in the barn. I thought if I came here and spent some time with Biscuit, I might find some answers."

"Why don't you just go home to that Gus feller?"

Meg shook her head. "I'll never go back. Gus and I belong out here. I can't explain it, but we just do."

"When I was trail boss, people used to ask me why a family would pick up and leave everything behind to make a suicidal trek across land full of dangers and hardships to an uncertain new home with no guarantees. I always responded that if you had to ask the question, you wouldn't understand the answer. I hear what you're saying, Miss Jameson."

Meg liked Clint. They brushed the horses in comfortable silence. Meg ran her hand down the back leg of Hippocrates, checking for bruises or tender spots.

Clint watched her as she lifted his foot and examined it for cuts. "Can you switch a team?"

"Yessir. I help Gus all the time at the stables." Meg boosted herself up onto the wall separating the stalls and balanced herself in the corner. "We're going to have a horse ranch out here, just as soon as we can find the right piece of land. Gus says I'll be a good trainer someday."

Clint leaned against the stall and folded his arms across his chest. "Miss Jameson,

Amanda will probably kill me for offering a man's job to a nice gal like you, but you can work for me here at the stables, if you're willing. It's hard work —"

"Oh, I don't mind! I'm used to it. I know what to do!" She jumped down to shake his hand. "Thank you, Mr. Sanders! You won't be sorry!"

Meg picked up a rake and began mucking out the stalls.

"Hold on, hold on. You gotta meet my Mandy first, so I don't get into trouble. She'll like you. C'mon. We'll find you some work clothes, too."

Chapter Twenty:
Win

*Clint Sanders's freight company stables, a
week later*

Win was so distracted by thoughts of joining an expedition that seeing Meg at work
in Clint's livery barely registered. Then she
confused him even more when she waved as
they drove past on their way to deliver the
equipment and Rothenberg to the doctor.
Joy fluttered like a little bird inside his
stomach as she ran out to greet them.

"Mr. Rothenberg!" Meg called.

Win pulled the team to a stop, hoping his
bruised ego didn't show.

"This is a surprise," Meg said, her attention aimed solely at Rothenberg. "You may
not remember me, but we've met before.
You came to my house in Council Bluffs
years ago — a decade, maybe. My father
was Charles Jameson." She extended her
hand to him.

Rothenberg climbed down and took her

hand in both of his. "Miss Jameson, what a pleasure! I apologize for not recognizing you, but you were just a little girl the last time we met. Your father and mother . . . I'm so sorry."

"Thank you," Meg said. "I recognized you because, well, my father spoke highly of you. He was very interested in science."

"The birthmark is hard to forget, as well." Mr. Rothenberg smiled and pointed to the noticeable stain on his head, causing Meg to blush. But minutes into an animated conversation, Rothenberg had invited her and any guests she wished to include to dinner. Meg accepted for Jeb and Win, Clint, and Amanda. "Excellent! Perhaps when we locate Nathan Miller, he'll be free as well. We'll have a party and get reacquainted! Shall we say seven o'clock? Nathan will find a place for us."

"That sounds lovely. We look forward to it," Meg said, as though she were standing in a garden in a pretty dress rather than outside a barn in overalls.

They deposited Rothenberg and the doctor's equipment at Miller's office and finalized the dinner plans. Two hours later, Win was seated in one of Denver's finest restaurants, clean and in fresh clothes, a bit bewildered as to how he got there.

Rothenberg sat at the head of the table. He requested that Meg sit to his left and Dr. Miller take the place on his right. Amanda sat to the right of the doctor and to the left of Clint. Win jockeyed into a position to the right of Jeb, thus securing the seat next to Meg.

Gone was any evidence that she had been working at a livery. Amanda might have had a hand in that; Meg smelled faintly like Amanda's perfume and her dress was new. She'd brushed her hair, too, and without the breeze to disrupt it, it stayed in place, with the help of a comb Win recognized as Jeb's mother's. She looked comfortable in the elegant surroundings, but ignored the glittery details, as though she were familiar with wealth and luxury, but unimpressed by it. Clint, on the other hand, craned his neck staring at the chandeliers and squinted at the tiny markings on the back of the silverware.

Mr. Rothenberg was in a jolly mood and keen to share stories about Meg. "The first time I saw Miss Jameson, she was climbing through the window of her father's library! Charles Jameson had invited me to their home for dinner. We walked into his library for a drink and caught this charming young lady trying to hoist herself up and swing her leg over the sill." He chuckled as he recalled the scene.

"Why doesn't that surprise me?" Win whispered to Jeb.

"Our young Miss Jameson was teetering half in, half out of the window. Charles ran over to catch her and pulled her in. Then we were properly introduced. Charles recommended that we forego a handshake, however. You had a handful of muddy arrowheads in your grasp," Rothenberg said, chuckling again. "You were in bare feet, your shirt was muddy, and your hair was in a bit of a mess."

"That's no surprise, either," Win again whispered to Jeb, grinning.

"Why were you meeting with my father?" Meg asked.

"Ah, yes; I was telling Mr. Avery and Mr. Dawson on the way here that my friend John Stanley went west to paint landscapes and portraits of Indians and tribal life. I helped him secure sponsors, and found an ally in your father." Mr. Rothenberg turned to the others at the table. "Charles was very supportive of Stanley, and funded much of his work. Interestingly enough, photography is beginning to replace painting as a means of documentation. It was used to document the War."

"So its horrors can be shared with all." Dr. Miller shook his head sadly.

"Maybe by sharing the horror, battles won't be so glorified," Jeb said.

Mr. Rothenberg nodded. "Indeed, but I can think of better things to photograph. So can Ferdinand Hayden. At present, his plans take him to the upper Missouri River valley, an area rich with fossils, but he'll get caught up in the geological surveys of the West, of that I'm certain. And he'll bring photographers. It will be interesting to see if photographs can capture the grandeur of these mountains the same way they capture the horrors of war." He leaned forward, turning his attention to Dr. Miller. "You know that I'm here to entice you to join the expedition, don't you, Nathan?"

Dr. Miller smiled, but shook his head. "I have a lot of respect for Dr. Hayden, you know that. He served admirably in the War. But he thinks I came west for excitement. I did not. I came seeking peace. I wrote to him three months ago, declining his offer, and to announce that I'll be moving my practice to Cold Springs soon. I'm sorry your trip was in vain, Albert."

Rothenberg dismissed his disappointment cordially and leaned back in his chair. "Nothing is ever in vain. Even that dreadful

Dewer was worth seeing. I learned it is *not* the place from which to launch an expedition. The scientists will be picked clean of their survey equipment upon arrival!"

Everyone laughed politely, familiar with Dewer's reputation.

"Why are you moving to Cold Springs, Doc?" Clint asked.

"It's a community of farmers and ranchers. Tough as nails, rural folk. I want patients who heal quickly and completely, like Mr. Dawson. I want to deliver babies rather than saw off limbs — if you'll excuse my lack of table manners — and delight in watching my patients grow from infancy to adulthood."

"That's lovely," Meg said. "Gus says there's valor in the everyday, and should be cherished."

Win watched the doctor gaze at Meg and wondered if Nathan should be added to the list of suitors.

Clint cleared his throat. "I asked because I've been thinking about running a private stage service between here and Cheyenne, taking a shorter route through Cold Springs and Paradise, rather than going Holladay's way through Lyonsville."

"Well, from the talk I hear around Denver, I think the area between here and Cheyenne will grow considerably in the future," Dr. Miller said. "It's another reason I'm moving my practice there."

"I'd be your first customer, Mr. Sanders," Rothenberg said. "A private coach service is just what I need in my line of work. Train and stage schedules never seem to align with mine. A carriage and a team would give me freedom from both timetables and the burden of driving myself. For example, I still need to locate a decent launch site for the geographical survey crews — the point where civilization ends and uncharted territory begins. That's not on any train or stage route I've seen."

Amanda turned to Clint. "What about Paradise?"

"Oh! Paradise would be perfect!" Meg's face glowed in the candlelight.

"There's already a smithy and a trading post," Amanda said, leaning forward and smiling mischievously at Meg, the way women do when they conspire with one another.

"A way station at Paradise would be a natural spot to change the team between here and Cheyenne." Meg returned her smile, her eyebrows raised expectantly as the idea gathered promise. "In fact, why don't Gus and I run it?"

The sensation of the runaway locomotive returned. Win couldn't believe what he was hearing. "Hold on, hold on —"

"Win, when we traveled through that country, I said it was perfect for Gus and me," Meg said before he got going. "I need to earn some kind of living until my inheritance is released from the trust."

"Sad business, that," Rothenberg said, shaking his head. "You'd think the law would allow for some common sense. Well, I guess it does, in a way, but the process is so —"

Win didn't want the conversation to shift to trusts, not with Meg's plan freshly revealed. "You'd run the way station?" he interrupted Rothenberg to ask Meg.

"Gus will run the livery, and I'll look after the passengers."

"How?" Win asked. "Folks arriving by stage will want something to eat."

"I know how to cook . . ." Meg straightened her back indignantly.

"A couple of weeks tending Grace Moberg's stew does not make you a cook."

"Mr. Avery, mind your manners." Amanda gave him a wink to soften her reproach. "A person can learn."

"I have plenty of books you might like, Miss Jameson," the doctor said, either

217

oblivious to the danger, or his judgment clouded by his eagerness to impress. "They are of little use to me now that I've hired a housekeeper. I have some books on cooking and running a household."

"Why, thank you, Dr. Miller. That's very kind . . . and *supportive.*" Meg stuck her chin out as she glanced at Win.

"I can't believe you're letting Meg talk you into this, Clint." Win turned to his boss, hoping to gain an ally.

"There's really no rush," Jeb said, siding with Win.

"Aw, hell, she'll be fine," Clint said. "This private coach service is a good idea. Folks want to be able to come and go as they please, and don't always own a team that can take them the distance they gotta travel. Someone like Mr. Rothenberg, who hires my coach and driver, can go wherever he wants and at whatever pace he wants, within reason. A station at Paradise is a natural spot to change the team."

"That area is still remote and unstable," Jeb said. "It could get dangerous real fast."

"Well, that Gus feller'll be up there with her." Clint glanced at Meg and gave her a reassuring nod.

"A one-handed old-timer none of us has ever even met!" Win spread his arms to show the obvious flaw in Clint's plan.

Amanda smiled calmly. "My goodness, she's certainly turned you two up on end."

"Yeah, well, she's good at that," Jeb muttered so quietly only Win heard it.

"Men think women can't do anything." Amanda lazily waved her hand as if to dispel the notion. "May I remind you that there's already one woman living up there? Besides, from what Meg told me, she's going back whether Clint gives her a job or not. If you ask me, you couldn't ask for a better arrangement. Clint will give you boys the freight route to Paradise. You'll see her regularly." She tilted her head at them and added pointedly, "Maybe you won't lose her again this way."

Win raised his hands in surrender. The conversation turned back to the books the doctor was going to give to Meg. Win leaned over to Jeb and said quietly, "We'd better inform Gray Wolf. With Meg in Paradise, and surveyors arriving, he'll want to know. I hope he'll be on our side."

Clint overheard. He leaned into their conversation and said to them privately, "Hell, he'll love the idea. See? It's all working out."

CHAPTER TWENTY-ONE:
JEB

Denver, later that evening

Jeb saw Win in a different light at Rothenberg's dinner. Usually Jeb had to pull Win back from the precipice, keep him from jumping into some foolhardy scheme. He saw now that everyone was on a sliding scale of common sense, and this time he and Win were much more aligned on the side of caution. Their pact was more than an agreement not to fight over a girl. It also cemented their mutual concern for Meg's welfare.

The dinner ended and Win and Jeb watched Meg enthusiastically shake hands with Clint and receive a warm, congratulatory embrace from Amanda. Even Rothenberg kissed her on her forehead — Charles's little girl. Both Rothenberg and Dr. Miller offered to walk Meg to the boarding house, where she'd rented a room. A bubble of envy formed inside Jeb's gut, but dissolved when Meg accepted Rothenberg's offer, saying she wanted to ask him more about her father. No flirtation, just honesty. Jeb liked that about her.

Watching them leave, Win folded his arms across his chest. "I guess we know where we stand. I feel rather abandoned, don't you?"

"Don't read too much into it. I think I'd enjoy a conversation with someone who knew my parents, too. That was quite a co-incidence, Rothenberg knowing Meg."

"Well, when you're rich like that, the social circles are small."

They started back to their own rooming house. They strolled along slowly; Win seemed in no particular hurry to get back. "Jeb, I gotta talk about something with you, and I want you to be straight."

"Look, if this is about Ma's hair comb —"

"No, no, it isn't." Win laughed quietly. "I actually have something else on my mind. If we work out a deal with Gray Wolf, what we trade needs to be as vital to him as Meg's safety is to us."

"What do you have in mind?"

"Rifles and ammunition."

"That's illegal."

"Yup. That's why we're talking about it, partner."

"You'd supply guns, illegally, to Arapaho

Indians — people the government said have to move to reservations? Sounds like something that could end badly."

Win spread out his arms, palms up. "Except Gray Wolf isn't looking for trouble. He's a peaceful man — you saw him. But he needs to protect his family and his independence. He doesn't want to live on the Wind River Reservation. He's already had to move from the plains and adapt to living in the mountains. He says if he brings his family to the reservation, they'll die. Did you know the reservation is in Shoshone country, their enemies? He thinks the Shoshone will swallow them up and they will disappear. With Gray Wolf on our side, we could have a hidden, yet powerful, ally. And we'd watch out for him, too."

Jeb gave the idea some thought. "We'd be risking a lot. I could argue that it makes no sense to keep peace by supplying guns to people marked as the enemy. You know what would happen if we get caught, don't you?"

"Well, sometimes doing the wrong thing is right because of the reasons behind it," Win said. "Besides, we've got a better chance of getting on one of those expeditions if they launch from Paradise, where they can be guaranteed a level of safety and peace."

"Ha! I figured that's been spinning in your head since we met Rothenberg."

"We can't very well leave Clint in a bind. He's already got orders piling up. But at some point, Jeb, I see us exploring the uncharted territory between here and California!"

Jeb had to admit it sounded like the kind of adventure Win longed for. He wasn't sure it was his own personal goal, but he didn't need to argue about that right now. He changed the subject back to something they could agree on. "Meg looked really happy when the idea of running a way station in Paradise came up. She's pretty determined."

"I call it pig-headed stubborn."

Once Meg and Clint shook hands on their new business partnership, there was no stopping her. Meg campaigned for Jeb and Win to bring the supplies up for the station house, and to build it, too. She said Gus was great with horses, but with only one hand, couldn't hold a hammer and nail at the same time. Clint instructed Jeb and Win to have the new Paradise way station operational in two weeks.

Less than twenty-four hours later, Win climbed up onto the seat of a freight wagon loaded to maximum weight and slapped the rumps of eight mules. The team lurched forward.

Hippocrates had to be tied to the back, while Jeb rode Galen with Meg on Biscuit, because, somehow, they'd been talked into keeping their horses in Paradise. She insisted they would get better care up at "her station," which she already called it. "They might get stolen easier, too," Win muttered to Jeb privately. Jeb figured Win was just sour because Jeb won the coin toss that determined who got to teach Meg how to shoot a revolver.

Torn between delight in seeing Meg excited and concern for her welfare, Jeb had bought an 1860 Colt revolver for her, the same handgun they both owned. Sutter might be dead, but he wasn't the only varmint — human or animal — that might wander into Paradise, he told her. And if Meg was so anxious, or pig-headed stubborn, as Win called it, to leave Denver before Gus arrived, she'd better know how to handle a gun that carried more persuasion than Carl's little derringer.

Midday, Win stopped to rest the team at a good place for a shooting lesson. He said if they made enough noise, perhaps Gray Wolf would find them. Then they could tell him about Clint's plans for a stage route and give him a gift from Clint: five repeating rifles and ammunition, hidden in the building materials.

Win set up a pile of rocks about twenty paces away and then stood in front of the mules in case they got spooked by the loud noise. In a last-ditch effort, Win pointed out to Jeb that he, Win, was the better shot, and should be giving the lesson. Jeb reminded him it was a lesson, not a contest, and he could show off later.

After Jeb gave Meg a few preliminary instructions and warnings about recoil, Meg fired her first shot. She missed. Jeb explained how the weight might drag her arm down and he stood close behind her, holding her arm up and level. She didn't flinch or move away, and her hair felt soft against his cheek. He wanted to wrap his arms around her, but backed away to give her room. She shot again and hit the bottom rock.

"You're a quick study," Win said from his spot in front of the mules. "I swear, you learn to play Twenty-One and you could become as legendary as Eleanor Dumont."

"Who's Eleanor Dumont?" Meg cocked the hammer with both thumbs. Then she leveled out her aim, closed one eye, and fired at the rocks again. She hit the ground in front of the pile.

"She's a famous lady gambler in California. One of the best card players you'll ever find." Win eyed the pile of rocks. "Her lover conned her into buying a cattle ranch, and she lost her fortune. She was quite the marksman. Unloaded both barrels of a shotgun on him. He dropped dead on the spot."

Meg took aim again. "Gus would say he had it coming. He doesn't like scammers and cheats." She fired. This time she shot too high and missed the rock pile.

"She was a character," Win said, patting the nose of one of the mules. "I saw her once in a gambling house. Folks flocked all around her, watching her play. They called her the 'Mustache Madam.'"

"Why on earth was she called that?" Meg asked as she cocked the hammer again.

"Ha! Why do you think? She had a —"

"Win, quit distracting her. This is serious." Jeb scowled at him. Turning to Meg, he said, "Make sure you look past the end of the barrel, not at the hammer." He showed her with his own gun. She nodded and aimed again, closing one eye. "And don't close your eye like you're shooting a rifle," he said. "Keep them both open."

She nodded again, took aim, and fired.

This time she hit the pile square on target. "Maybe she shot her lover 'cause he was the one who nicknamed her Mustache Madam." Meg lined up her next shot. "Having a name like that's worse than losing a fortune." Again she hit the pile square on.

Win let out a low whistle. "I'll keep that in mind."

"You seem to have the hang of it," Jeb said to Meg, "and can carry on a ridiculous conversation at the same time." He shot Win a quick scowl. "Just be mindful where the barrel is pointed. It's a lot shorter than a rifle . . . turns faster."

"I will." Meg looked up at Jeb and smiled. "Thank you for the lesson, and the gun."

"Let's hope you never have to use it," Jeb said.

Gray Wolf and Sharp Eye appeared on the hillside. Win signaled to them and they proceeded down the hill. The two Arapaho greeted them amicably. When the conversation turned to business, Win told Gray Wolf about hauling freight, Clint's stage service, and the scientific expeditions. "We want to live side-by-side with you, with no trouble between us. Clint wants to trade with you, and says rifles and ammunition will help you defend your village."

Gray Wolf closed his eyes. Jeb wondered if

he was weighing the risks to his people, considering his options, or perhaps simply praying. When he opened his eyes, Gray Wolf said, "The spirits tell me we must remain invisible to the blue-coat soldiers so they do not take us to a reservation where there is sickness and death. Blue coats come to white people when they are in trouble. If our white friends have no trouble, the blue coats stay away."

Jeb respected Gray Wolf's cunning and intelligence. He was no fool, Jeb thought, and a logical thinker. What better way to protect his village than to have an alliance of peaceful white folks act as a buffer between his people and the US cavalry? Gray Wolf's greatest fear was being discovered. In the foothills above Paradise, he could remain safely hidden.

Sharp Eye added an element of practical reality. "Rifles will make the fight equal if we need to defend ourselves."

Win said he didn't see the harm in supplying rifles to Gray Wolf's people so they could hunt and protect themselves. Jeb agreed, and felt better about Meg living in Paradise with Gray Wolf on their side.

CHAPTER TWENTY-TWO:
MEG

Paradise, September 1865

Georgia enthusiastically welcomed Meg back to Paradise. She said she hadn't realized how much she'd missed female companionship until she had it briefly, and then lost it again. Meg fell into her new friend's warm embrace, feeling like a lost child who'd just been found.

Construction of the station began immediately, everyone pitching in. Jeb and Win felled trees and used the mules to drag them to the building site. They built a small, temporary corral before starting on the main building. Meg gathered fieldstone while Mick mixed up some cement and, with help from Angus, built a respectable fireplace. Jeb laid the floor using milled lumber they brought with them. The outer walls of the building were made from hewn logs, and no one could hew logs better than the blacksmith.

Blackie wielded an adze with folklore strength and speed. He had logs squared and notched almost as fast as they could get the rough timber to him. He seemed to enjoy the task, too, and worked like a locomotive. Even Jeb, who was so strong, said he felt small working next to Blackie, and it was all he could do to keep up with him.

For the station's large main room, Jeb built a long, sturdy table and benches for travelers to rest and eat a meal. In the attached kitchen in back sat a cook stove, an unexpected luxury from the Carters, who already had one of their own. Mick had traded with a settler who needed food and clothing far more than he needed a heavy, cast-iron stove. Mick said he was happy to get it out of the way and into use. They built a washroom off the kitchen, and private quarters for Meg and Gus. It was perfect — as perfect as the land and the community for her horse ranch.

Win didn't seem to see it that way. He often looked up from his work to gaze at the horizon, as though it were calling to him. Finally, he got so antsy he rode up into the hills. Meg watched him ride away, disappointed, yet sympathetic. She knew what it felt like to yearn for something not quite within her grasp.

One of Georgia's chickens went lame, so Georgia killed it, saying it was time for a chicken dinner anyway. Meg offered to make a meal for everyone. She'd been reading Dr. Miller's household management books and was ready for the challenge, she said. Could she try? Georgia handed over the chicken and said she was going to spend the afternoon writing her sister a much overdue letter, and to call if she needed help.

Meg soon realized the task was more daunting than she'd thought. Jeb appeared in Georgia's kitchen just as Meg released a flurry of cuss words in frustration.

"What have you got there?" Jeb asked.

"Ach! More than I bargained for, I'm afraid. I've got Mrs. Beeton's *Book of Household Management,* Catherine Beecher's *Treatise on Domestic Economy,* and *The American Frugal Housewife.* I was sure I could find something in one of them that would explain what to do with this." Meg lifted up the headless chicken. All three books were open on the kitchen table.

"It's hard to read about something that's more easily shown," Jeb said, "particularly the first time."

"That's it exactly. None of these cookbooks describes it in a way that makes sense."

"Chickens are hard. Ma never handled chickens very well, so I got pretty good at cleaning and plucking them. Want to watch me? I'd be happy to show you."

"Oh, would you, Jeb? You're very kind."

"No problem. Let's take it outside." Jeb took the carcass, Meg following. They sat down on the back steps together. He showed her how to grasp the chicken so she could pluck the feathers more easily. Meg took the chicken and tried it. "You're pretty amenable to domestic work. I thought you were a girl born into privilege."

"Well, if Gus and I are going to run a ranch together, somebody has to cook. It won't be Gus, that's for sure, and who knows how long it will be before we can hire someone like Fanny."

"Who's Fanny?" Jeb asked.

"She was my aunt's housekeeper for a time. My mother had just hired her a few months before she died."

"How did your parents die?"

"My father was a banker. He was in Lawrence on business when pro-slavery men burned the Free-State Hotel and sacked the city. He was there to invest in the anti-slavery newspaper, and my mother went along to care for him, as he had not been well. I'm not even sure how they died, but Gus said knowing the details wouldn't bring them back. I imagine he was protecting me."

"I imagine so."

"Fanny stayed on for a while after my aunt and uncle moved in. I used to help her with the washing, because I preferred her company to my aunt's. When we finished, I'd read to her while she sewed or worked in the kitchen. She never learned to read, but loved to listen to stories.

"One day, my aunt came into the kitchen and found me sitting on the counter reading a silly romance novel out loud while Fanny peeled potatoes. We were having such a good time. My aunt grabbed a broom and started beating us both with it. I never understood why. But I screamed, Fanny screamed, and my aunt chased us around the kitchen, calling us all sorts of terrible things. Poor Fanny was fired immediately.

"But Fanny never let anything get her down. Gus let her stay at the stables until her beau came to fetch her from Chicago. While she waited for him, we finished reading our book together. I also taught her how to write her name." Meg stopped abruptly. "I think I'm talking too much."

Jeb smiled. "Not at all. Win says I'm too quiet."

"Maybe folks don't ask you the right questions. Tell me about you and Win growing up."

"Well, Ma used to read to Win and me all the time. We can read and write, of course. But it was real entertaining to have her read aloud. She was good at it. When we were little, she read stories about pirates and sailing the high seas. We had our own sword fights before going to bed." One of the downy feathers wafting around them landed in Meg's hair. Jeb removed it — able to manage the delicate task even with hands as strong as his.

"Your childhood sounds lovely." Meg suddenly felt shy. "Gus says there's no easy way to lose a parent. I'm sorry you lost yours, too. But they certainly raised you both well." Her voice trailed off and she busied herself by brushing away the down that had landed in her lap, feeling oddly elated.

Win came around the corner. "You two properly chaperoned?"

CHAPTER TWENTY-THREE: WIN

Paradise

Win had seen them sitting on the back step together. When Jeb reached up to remove a downy feather from Meg's hair, he was struck by a pang of jealousy for which he had no explanation. After all, it had been his choice to leave them alone.

Meg jumped in surprise, but Jeb, always annoyingly calm, just smiled. "Welcome back," Jeb said. "Do you have news for us?"

"Yes, but it can wait." Win dismounted and removed the tarp from a makeshift travois. "I'm not sure that chicken will feed seven of us for dinner. I shot an elk."

Georgia appeared, saw the elk, and announced it was time for a housewarming. The men started a fire to roast a hindquarter and began cutting much of the elk meat into strips to jerk. Angus brought over a bottle of whiskey, and Blackie brought a horseshoe to hang on the station door for good luck.

Both helped hang the meat strips on a drying rack.

Meg prepared her chicken stew anyway. Georgia baked up a sweet potato pie and biscuits. When the work was done and the hind leg roasted on a spit, Angus uncorked the whiskey. He handed glasses to everyone and they all toasted to the new way station, soon to be open for business. Meg raised her glass to Georgia in a gesture of feminine solidarity and drank the whiskey down with surprising familiarity. Win felt his jaw drop.

Georgia leaned back in her chair with a smile. "Where'd you learn to drink like that, honey?"

"My friend Gus poured me a small glass on special occasions, saying he shouldn't drink alone. He managed a stable and never had a day off, but every once in a while, he'd have a quiet night and we'd toast to better days," Meg said, adding quietly, "I think mine have arrived."

Georgia nodded appreciatively. "Usually women act scandalized if I enjoy a little libation. I swear, you are one pleasant surprise after another."

"Well, the stew isn't so pleasant. Something went wrong. I'm sorry I wasted your chicken, Georgia."

"Aw, honeybee, don't fret." She patted

Meg on the shoulder. "You'll get the hang of it."

Win decided it was time to share his news. "I ran into Sharp Eye today. He was hunting, too. He helped me dress and quarter the elk so I could pack it out. I thanked him with a shoulder."

"I was wondering if you had shot a three-legged animal, or if you had help." Jeb leaned against the new, heavy, oak table he'd built. "What did he have to say?"

"Well, I can see that our relationship with the Arapaho is going to be interesting," Win said, "because Sharp Eye wants his son to learn to read and write English."

Angus snorted. "Hell, most white folks can't do that."

"I think it's a good idea," Meg said. "They wouldn't have to sign something they couldn't read for themselves."

"Well, I'm glad you feel that way, Meggie, 'cause I told Sharp Eye you would teach Running Elk how to read and write."

"Me?" Meg furrowed her brow and folded her arms across her chest. "What made you think I could do such a thing? I don't know the first thing about teaching anybody anything!"

"Sure you do," Jeb said. "You taught Fanny; you'd be good at it."

"Why his son?" she asked. "Why not Sharp Eye himself? He already speaks a little English."

Angus snorted again and laughed out loud. Win spread his arms out and stated what he thought was obvious. "Meg, they have some pride, for God's sake. You don't really expect grown men to learn from a girl."

Everyone else seemed to think Meg teaching Running Elk to read was a good idea except Meg. She didn't stay perturbed, however — a quality Win admired in her.

The next day, as Win and Jeb prepared to leave for Denver, Meg brought warm gingerbread wrapped in a cloth out to them. Win made the mistake of hesitating slightly, and she noticed. "Oh, for heaven's sake, Win, it's fine . . . . tastes just like Georgia's. She said so."

Jeb reached down from his seat on the wagon and plucked it from Win's hands. "I'm sure it's delicious. Thank you, Meg."

"Just teasing, Meggie. Thanks." Win gave Meg a quick kiss on the cheek, in part to annoy Jeb and in part to bolster her spirits, as she looked a little nervous now that they were leaving. He jumped up next to Jeb. With a whistle to the mules, Jeb steered the team south to Denver.

"You two have a safe trip. Come back soon," she called, waving good-bye. Just before she turned to go inside her new station house, Win saw Meg touch her kissed cheek.

Once under way, Win breathed in the crisp morning air and said, "Well, my friend, this is certainly turning out to be a hell of an adventure. I never expected I'd be trading with the Arapaho. I figured there was a better chance we'd lose our hair out here."

"If you were worried about your scalp, why didn't you get a nice, safe job in Rockfield?"

" 'Cause thinking about losing my scalp makes me feel alive, and feeling alive feels good."

"Can't argue with that logic." Jeb shook his head. "You're so full of shit."

CHAPTER TWENTY-FOUR:
JEB

Cold Springs, Colorado Territory

Jeb was headed back to Paradise with Win less than a week after leaving Meg at her new way station. Mick had telegraphed an order to Clint, announcing the early arrival of an expedition crew. They were running low on essentials. Jeb asked to be assigned the job. He looked forward to surprising Meg with their early return.

They made it as far as Cold Springs before deciding to stop for the evening. Jeb and Win were on their way to find a meal when a stagecoach pulled in and emptied its passengers in front of the new Cold Springs hotel. Everyone shuffled inside except one. A man in his early sixties remained outside in the last of the evening light and watched the setting sun flare up from behind the peaks, painting the few scattered clouds overhead with brilliant red and gold. He wore a crisp, white shirt and a dark suit with a vest, but there was no mistaking him for a businessman. His barn boots and hat gave away that he was a horseman. The left sleeve of his coat was stitched to itself below the elbow to keep it from flapping about. Not as tall as either Jeb or Win, but lean and wiry, the man had no doubt spent years working hard, both in and out of the saddle. He sported a long, bushy, white mustache, which matched his eyebrows. He watched the evening sky until the red and gold faded into dusky purple.

Spirits must be at work, Jeb thought. Win was already walking over to the man. "Excuse me, sir, but are you Gus Steensland?"

The man turned sharply. "I am." His piercing blue eyes studied Win first, then Jeb. They held a flicker of amusement and youthful vigor, despite the weathered creases around them. "Only two men in this territory would give a damn who I was. You must be the wonder boys." Gus offered his hand. "From Meggie's letters, I'm guessing you're Avery," he said to Win.

"Good to meet you, Mr. Steensland," Win said as they shook hands.

"Jeb Dawson, sir." Jeb extended his hand as well. "It's a pleasure to finally meet you. Meg's told us a lot about you."

The comment produced a cock of the

head and a wry smile. "If it's half of what I've heard about you two, it's still too much." Gus looked around. "Meggie with you?"

"No, sir, she's at the st— Wait, how did you get here so fast? Meg only just sent her letter," Win said.

"Never got it. I just came 'cause it was time to come. She OK?"

"Oh yes, sir, she's fine, she's wonderful." Jeb sounded like a fool. Out of the corner of his eye, he saw Win smile. "We'll take you to her first thing tomorrow." Jeb nodded his head north toward Paradise.

"That way?" A low whistle came from Gus. "Damn glad I ran into you boys. I'd be chasing that little bird all over the territory. I was headed for Denver."

"You're the new station keeper in a town called Paradise," Win said.

"Shew, she's got me a job already?"

"Our boss just started a private coach service. She's already at a swing station," Jeb said.

This brought a chuckle out of Gus. "I'll be damned." He looked at the dark sky. "I guess it'd be foolish to travel at night." He turned back to Win and Jeb. "Let's get a drink. I'm bone dry."

"Yes, sir," Win and Jeb said in unison.

"If you two keep calling me 'sir,' you're buyin'. It's just Gus. C'mon, let's go knock ourselves off these pedestals she's got us on." Gus picked up his bag and headed for the saloon.

Inside, Gus deftly removed his jacket, loosened his tie, and motioned to the bartender to send over three glasses and a bottle — all in the time it took for them to sit down. Win uncorked the bottle and poured the drinks. Gus lifted his in a brief salute to their health, and then drained the glass with one swallow and let out a satisfied sigh.

Gus knew everything about Meg's experience with the wagon train from the letters she'd written, causing Jeb to wonder what she'd written about them — or, more specifically, *him.* Gus said in her last letter, they'd arrived safely in Denver, and he figured his little bird had landed long enough for him to catch up with her. Then he asked about his new job; Win explained about the stage route through Paradise and told him about Gray Wolf. Gus said he looked forward to meeting him, as if meeting Indians were something he did every day. Jeb poured another round.

Gus paused before he drank and said, "I can't figure out why Meggie campaigned so hard to run a station. She can't cook. I suspect she's doin' it for me." He squinted at his glass.

"She got attached to Paradise as soon as she saw it," Jeb said. "She said it was where you two were going to buy land for a ranch."

Gus blinked a few times. Jeb sensed that hearing about the ranch made him emotional. Her strong attachment to Gus was clearly reciprocated.

"She says you saved her life, Gus," Win said.

Gus shook his head. "Aw, hell, I needed her as much as she needed me — maybe more, truth be told." He swirled the whiskey around in his glass. "I wouldn't normally say this to such new acquaintances, but from all that Meggie wrote about you, I feel like I know you both. I barely tolerated the job at the stables. But then this little red-headed whirlwind blew in, with her brand new horse. Her eyes all sparkly, a grin spread ear to ear, and that hair of hers — always a mess. She was the reason I stayed on all those years. Couldn't leave once she came along; made a promise to her ma."

"You knew her mother?" Jeb asked.

Gus got a wistful look in his eye and nodded. "The last time we spoke was the day before she died." He winced, as though feeling the tug of an old scar. "She and Mr. Jameson came down to the stables to say good-bye to Meg before they caught the train to Lawrence. He was going to invest in some newspaper. She gave Meg a quick hug, one that was meant to last a couple days, not a lifetime. She didn't know. Meg scampered off, and, as she left, Elise Jameson thanked me for taking Meggie riding and making her daughter so happy. I told Miz Jameson that Meg was a natural, acted like she was born on a horse and was a real joy, sweet and funny. Her ma shook my hand real genuine-like. Just as she was about to walk out the door, she said, 'Take care of our Meggie now,' with a smile I'll never forget. She was the kind of woman that the best of men don't deserve. She was a fine person. When they didn't come back and Meggie ended up living with her aunt and sonofabitch uncle, I couldn't break my promise. So, I stayed to look after her." Gus paused to take a sip of whiskey. "Did the best I could, but an old bachelor like me . . . We managed, I guess. When she got that ranch idea in her head, I'd tell myself I was a blame fool for getting sucked into her pipe dreams, and, yet, it was contagious. She'd chatter on and on, and pretty soon, she had me believing it, too." He chuckled. "And see? Here I am. Now, who saved who?"

Jeb finally understood the kinship between them, and his jealousy of Gus dissipated. "She's mighty devoted to you," he said, feeling generous toward the old man.

"She has a powerful hold on my heart; that's a fact. She came into the stables one day . . . she was about ten, I'm guessin'. She says, 'Gus, I love you and you love me, so we gotta get married. I don't see any other way around it,' " he said, chuckling. "Damn, she was cute. She had a dirt smudge on her nose. If all love was the same, I'd have snatched her up in a minute, but, of course, it ain't. Instead, I had to sit her down and explain a few things to her about birds, bees, and men. The kind of talk that's supposed to come from a ma. Felt bad for her, especially since that goddamn aunt wasn't worth spit. The day Meg started her female business, she got scared, didn't know what was happening to her. Found her hiding in Biscuit's stall, curled up in a corner, blood on her pants. I sat down with her and she crawled up next to me. I explained what I knew about it, which wasn't much, but I guess was enough for her. Brought her back to my place to let her clean up. She was washing out her clothes and complained, kinda irritated like, that she didn't see why women couldn't just go into heat like horses."

Jeb smiled at the image of Meg as a little girl, passing the time with the old stable-man. He remembered how she put her arm around the little girl from the train, Lizzie Moberg, probably just as Gus had done with her. One thing was certain: if her gentle nature came from Gus, so did her cussing.

"We'll take you to her first thing in the morning," Win said.

"Aw, hell, I can find my way."

"We're going that way anyway; got a delivery in Paradise," Jeb said.

Gus leaned forward, eyeing them both. "So, how's it goin' — you both angling for my Meggie?"

Jeb glanced at Win, not knowing how to answer.

Gus leaned back and chuckled. "Well," he said, smoothing his mustache, "matters of the heart ain't easy. You just make sure you don't break hers, 'cause she's special."

The next morning, the wagon lumbered along far too slow for Jeb, who could only imagine it must feel slower for Gus, squashed in beside them on the bench seat.

When they crested the hill, Meg was in the yard staking out a garden plot for the following spring. She looked up when she heard the wagon. Gus removed his hat to reveal his snow-white hair. She dropped the stakes, picked up her skirts, and ran toward him.

"Gus! Gus!" She raced up the hill. Gus hopped down almost before the wagon had fully stopped. She stopped just short of him, out of breath, and stared at her friend as though checking to be sure her eyes weren't deceiving her.

Hat in his hand, he spread his one arm out and smiled. "C'mere, you."

She walked into his arms, her face screwing up with emotion as she wrapped her arms around his waist, buried her face in his neck, and began to sob. Despite all she had been through, this was the first time Jeb recalled seeing her cry. Gus brought his arm around her and they clung to each other with so much emotion that Jeb got a lump in his throat himself.

"I shouldn't have run away, but I was afraid for Biscuit."

"Protecting what you love is as natural as breathing." Gus held her close.

"I was real scared, Gus."

"Only fools are never scared." Gus pulled her back so he could look at her. "Darlin', you're the bravest person I know." He cocked his head. "When did you get so

248

pretty, too?"

"Oh, Gus!" She wiped the tears from her face. "I bet you still won't marry me, though."

Gus threw his head back and laughed. Intended to be a private joke, Win and Jeb nevertheless laughed, too, and Meg noticed. "Oh, no! You didn't tell them my growing-up stories, did you? Win'll tease me to no end."

"Not all. Saved the really good ones for when I need a favor." With their arms wrapped around each other, they strolled slowly back to the way station. Jeb and Win followed them into town.

The man Meg worshipped was back in her company, and while Jeb was happy for her, he couldn't help but wonder what it meant for Win and him. Their pact, the purpose of which was to keep their friendship intact, seemed pointless. If anyone was the focus of her attention and her life, it was Gus.

CHAPTER TWENTY-FIVE:
MEG

Paradise

Gus fit into the little Paradise community like a missing piece of a puzzle. The comfort of his presence and their plans for a future ranch completed a picture Meg had kept in her mind for a long time. Filled with joy, she hummed happily as she and Gus oiled tack together in their new barn.

"Oiling tack ain't that much fun, Meggie. From the looks of things, I'd say you got a fella." He worked the oil into the leather with one hand faster than she could with two.

"What? Me? No. Besides, Win and Jeb made a stupid pact that I wouldn't ruin their friendship."

"That don't matter. Which one of those boys caught your eye?"

Meg paused to consider the question. Both were handsome; both treated her with respect. Win was funny and charming; Jeb was kind and thoughtful. "Both."

Gus chuckled. "God help us, then."

"Have you ever been in love, Gus?"

"I have. A couple of times. It's a powerful feeling."

"What happened?"

"Well, the first time I fell in love, I asked her to marry me."

Meg stopped oiling Biscuit's bridle and looked at him in surprise. "Gus! Why didn't you ever tell me this?"

"Oh, I don't know. Maybe after you proposed to me, I figured it might make you jealous." He cocked his head and winked at her.

She laughed. "I was ten! I'm serious. Tell me what happened."

"Well, we were young and foolish. Her pa didn't think much of the idea and sent her away. Never saw her again."

"Oh, how sad!"

"Not really. When I look back, I think I dodged a bullet there."

"But then you fell in love again?"

"Yup. But she was already married. Happily, too. So, being the gentleman that I am, I left her alone. She never knew."

Gus would never say it because he was, as he said, too much of a gentleman. But Meg knew the woman who had stolen his heart the second time was her own mother. She saw it in his eyes when he talked about her. Meg knew Gus had watched over her all these years because he'd loved her mother, and Meg loved him for it.

"Gus, what does it mean if I like both Win and Jeb?"

"It means you ain't ready to settle down yet. 'Til then, you just stick by your ol' Gus."

■ ■ ■ ■

PART TWO

■ ■ ■ ■

CHAPTER TWENTY-SIX: WIN

The road to Paradise, two years later,
  Summer 1867

Win couldn't decide which bored him more, holding the reins of the stubborn, stupid mule team or riding shotgun — keeping an eye out for bandits or hostile Indians. Both tasks required enough attention to keep him from daydreaming about the expeditions Albert Rothenberg had mentioned. After nearly two years freighting for Clint, Win's feet itched.

"Can't this team go any faster?" Win fidgeted in his seat.

"Speed isn't what's annoying you, Win." Jeb slapped the reins against the rumps of the mules anyway. "You get this way every time you read a newspaper."

Jeb was right about that. Lately, the news was a pebble in his boot.

The latest irritant was from the *Montana Post,* which predicted a large emigration from the East this season along the North and Platte River routes — fortune seekers hunting for gold and silver in the mountains in Montana. Some prospectors arrived by steamboat on the Missouri River at Fort Benton. Others came overland, following the Bozeman Trail, named after John Bozeman and John Jacobs, the men who found a cheap, direct route from Fort Laramie to Virginia City, a prominent mining city in Montana. No one seemed to care that the Bozeman route cut through land between the Bighorn Mountains and the Black Hills, Indian territory by treaty. White prospectors and settlers disrupted the last remaining unspoiled, sacred hunting grounds of the northern Cheyenne, Arapaho, and Lakota Indians.

"Listen to this," Win said, reading from the newspaper. " 'There is a sickly sentimentality existing in some quarters that revolts at progress. If they prefer barbarism to civilization, and that because a race of blood-thirsty, treacherous knaves claim to have prior rights to these mountain and valleys as hunting grounds — ' "

"I read it, too, Win," Jeb said. "I swear, I'm gonna keep all newspapers away from you. You get ornery every time you pick one up, and then fuss all the way to Paradise."

" 'Claim' to have prior rights? Of course the Indians have prior rights! It's their land, for cryin' out loud," Win said. "White people are trespassing, Jeb, and they know it."

Despite his indignation, tucked inside Win's shirt was another article from the *Montana Post* about a survey expedition led by Clarence King. Congress had authorized a thorough geographical, topographical, and geological survey of the territory between the Missouri River and the California line. A strip 100 miles wide, with the 40th parallel and the Pacific railroad line as the center, was to be "put under scientific examination, and the results mapped and recorded for the benefit of all civilization," the article read.

Maybe scientists could contribute to a body of knowledge that really would benefit all mankind. Different from gold seekers, in Win's mind, scientists had motives far more noble than pure monetary profit. But even science didn't capture Win's heart. To him, exploring the unknown was far more enticing than either gold or science. Joining a scientific expedition was the more appealing way to see new territory.

A bump in the road pulled Win out of his reverie. Paradise lay just over the hill. The only part of hauling freight that appealed to Win anymore was seeing Meg at the end of the line. Pretty and full of fun, Meg brightened an otherwise dull route. Her attention toward Win and Jeb, evenly distributed and revealing no preferences, was shrewd on her part. She had made it clear she was dead set on getting her inheritance released as soon as possible, so they could buy land. She and Gus openly discussed their attempts to release her trust money before she turned twenty-one. In truth, Win liked Meg a lot, but he wasn't ready to settle down anyway, and her determination to buy land for a ranch before doing anything else helped assuage any serious rivalry that bubbled up occasionally between Win and Jeb. Her fixation on her inheritance kept his ego in check as well. Nothing did that better than when Meg would gallop out to meet their wagon, only to have her ask breathlessly if they had a letter from her Council Bluffs attorney.

The only seemingly content one of the group was Jeb. Win frequently reminded him that they were Meg's *two* best prospects in the whole territory, just to stir up and annoy his otherwise happy and satisfied disposition. Jeb was the only one who didn't act like his life had stalled; the only one who wasn't waiting impatiently for something else.

Paradise came to life when anyone passed through town, and Win and Jeb arriving with their weekly delivery was no exception. Angus and Blackie, always eager to share news, hurried over as soon as Win and Jeb pulled up to the Carters' store.

"Been over to Meg's yet?" Angus asked.

"Just got in," Jeb said. "Anything wrong?"

"Nah. Been pretty interesting, though."

"Angus, you dang Scot." Mick emerged from the store. "You always gotta be first!"

"Aw, I wasn't gonna tell the whole thing; I was just gonna get 'em curious."

"We're curious," Win said, his arms spread to show his impatience. "What happened?"

"Well, you'll be proud of your gal. She damn near stopped a massacre."

Mick sighed. "You exaggerate everything, Angus, for crying out loud."

"I can't stand this. I swear — Georgia!" Win called out. Georgia appeared at the door. "What the hell happened? Is Meg all right?"

"She's fine, honey," Georgia said. "We've had some excitement, though. Four wagons came through here. The folks were pretty grim. A big fellow named Rivers did all their talking for them, like he was running the

259

show. He said they had been attacked by Indians, yet there was no evidence to support the accusation. Mr. Rivers said they had gotten lost, and that's when the Indians swarmed them —"

"You know as well as we do that Indians, particularly 'swarming' ones, could've easily wiped them out," Mick said, "but I'd be a damned Indian-lover if I called him a liar."

"You are a damned Indian-lover, Mick." Angus seemed to enjoy arguing about anything.

"Hush, you two, and stop interrupting," Georgia said. "Meg and I were in the station with the women. We didn't believe Mr. Rivers's story either, and were asking questions when Running Elk showed up. That's when all hell broke loose. One of the women saw him and screamed. Rivers tried to shoot him, but he got away. Meg shielded him by jumping on the back of his horse and rode behind him, knowing Rivers wouldn't dare shoot a white woman, particularly in the back."

Running Elk frequented the station and was often present when Win and Jeb arrived in town. Despite Meg's early reservations about her ability to teach, she had done well. She and Sharp Eye's son had become friends. Everyone in town liked him, too.

"They met up with One Who Waits and Sharp Eye, who were painted up and ready for war." The concern in Georgia's voice was enough for Win. He dropped the sack of grain back into the wagon. Jeb was already heading for the way station.

The summer that they first arrived in Colorado Territory had been a bloody one. Lakota and Cheyenne warriors descended upon the Platte Bridge Station in July of 1865, killing twenty-nine soldiers. A month later, Brigadier General Patrick Connor led a charge on an Arapaho village on the Tongue River, killing sixty-three Arapaho — only thirty-five of whom were warriors — and burned the village.

The following summer, Colonel Henry B. Carrington of the 18th Infantry, following orders from Washington, attempted to build three forts along the Bozeman Trail to protect its citizens. Indian attacks began as soon as they arrived. The Lakota, northern Cheyenne, and northern Arapaho — banded together under Red Cloud, an Oglala Lakota chief — attacked both military and civilian wagon trains, as well as wood- and hay-cutting details sent from the forts. Relentless and skillful, Red Cloud's warriors engaged in raids all along the trail and vowed to continue as long as white people encroached on their land.

On Christmas Eve 1866, a man arrived at Fort Laramie, exhausted and half frozen from riding four days in the snow and cold. He staggered into a full-dress Christmas ball and announced in the midst of festivities that all eighty-one men under the command of Captain William Fetterman had been killed by Indians. Newspapers called it the worst military disaster ever suffered on the Great Plains. Editorials expressed growing impatience with the savages.

When Win asked Gray Wolf about it, however, Gray Wolf said Red Cloud simply fought to drive away invaders and preserve what was left of his people and their way of life. What else would you have him do? Gray Wolf had asked. He was only trying to survive.

Red Cloud's warriors did not attack Paradise. The little hamlet and the Arapaho village just behind the foothills lived peacefully next to each other. Clint operated a private stagecoach line through Paradise from Denver to Cheyenne, a town along the Union Pacific route. Wagon trains came through and stopped for supplies and to make repairs. Privately funded surveying expeditions occasionally launched or resupplied from Paradise, thanks to Albert Rothenberg. Other than that, no one paid much attention to the little town.

Gray Wolf kept his people safe in the mountains. A few young men left to fight with Red Cloud; Gray Wolf didn't stop them. Sharp Eye sent his son, Running Elk, to learn to read and write from Meg. Sharp Eye said when he was Running Elk's age, counting coup was a mark of a man, but these days, education might prove to be a more effective weapon with which to wage war against the white invaders. Now it seemed Paradise might finally be pulled into the conflict — something everyone had tried hard to prevent.

Win and Jeb found Meg pacing in the station house. She cried out with relief when she saw them. "Oh, Jeb! Win! I'm so glad you're here!" She threw her arms around Win first, then Jeb. "I've done a horrible thing. And now Gus is risking his life to fix it." Jeb kept his arms wrapped around her as she buried her face in his chest.

"I can't believe you'd do anything horrible, Meg. What happened?" Win asked.

"Running Elk's cousins were on their way here from the Tongue River." She pulled away from Jeb and wiped her eyes. "They saw the settlers and steered clear, but one of the white men had a long rifle and took

263

pot shots at them. He hit Niteesh, the nephew of One Who Waits. He died before they could get him to the village. One Who Waits was waiting for the settlers to leave Paradise to settle the score. He said he had no quarrel with us, only the man with the long rifle — Rivers.

"I asked One Who Waits to let the authorities at Fort Laramie handle Rivers. I said if he attacked the settlers, soldiers would come looking for him in the mountains and find their village. He agreed not to attack, but said the presence of the settlers in Paradise offended him. I told him I would send them away immediately.

"I rode back here and told them the only way to save their lives was to leave Paradise and turn Rivers in at Fort Laramie. Gray Wolf and the village began mourning the boy's death with their drum ceremony. We could hear the drums. The ladies panicked, believing they would be killed as soon as they left town, but I told them I had the Arapahos' word that they wouldn't. That's when Rivers flew out of control, pounded his fists on the table, and ranted about them being dirty red devils."

Meg's voice began to quiver. "So, Gus said he'd go along with them to Fort Laramie. He said it was the only way to ensure their safe passage and to see that they turned Rivers in. I'm afraid Rivers will kill Gus and go after Gray Wolf's family!" Tears welled up in her eyes again and she wrung her hands. "Sharp Eye and One Who Waits looked so fierce, painted for war. I'm afraid they'll take revenge, and everything will fall apart."

Win was already saddling Hippocrates. "Jeb, stay here with Meg. I'm going after Gus."

As Hippocrates galloped out of Paradise toward Fort Laramie, Win wondered if Jeb saw through his seemingly valiant act. In truth, he wasn't worried about Gus. For a man his age and limitations, Gus managed remarkably well. He could take care of himself. Win's real motivation was just a chance to bust loose and be part of the action.

On a stretch of trail across a wide, flat plain, two figures appeared on the horizon. Win recognized Gus immediately. He rode Neighbor, his favorite horse, and they fit together like a hand in a glove, the silhouette unmistakable. He rode unhurriedly and showed no sign of harm or distress. His companion took a little extra time to identify, primarily due to the additional feathers tied into his hair. But Win finally made out the figure to be One Who Waits. When he got close, Win marveled at how strategically placed soot on an Arapaho's face could be so threatening, as One Who Waits did indeed look fierce.

"Well, look who came to welcome us home," Gus said.

"Meg was worried about you."

Gus snorted skeptically. "So, you rode out to rescue me, did you?" He had a way of seeing through people.

Win ignored the sarcasm and fell in alongside One Who Waits. "What happened?" Win asked. "Was Rivers turned over to authorities at the fort?"

Gus shook his head. "Never got that far. About halfway to the fort, Mr. Rivers had an unfortunate accident. He lost his footing up in the rocks and fell. Hit his head and died."

To have Rivers fall to his death solved a huge dilemma. Win recognized the difficult position One Who Waits had been in. The Arapaho people believed in justice, but if they had retaliated and attacked the settlers, their hidden village might have been discovered. However, if One Who Waits had let Rivers go, he would dishonor his nephew. Rivers's accident was too convenient. Win studied the faces of both men. Their stoic expressions revealed nothing, so Win had to ask, "Who really killed him?"

Gus shook his head. "Don't rightly know. I didn't see what happened, but that was by design, I reckon." He smoothed his bristly mustache. "It changed the situation considerably. The rest of the folks said Rivers had acted alone, and without their approval. They had no quarrel with the Indians. Once we buried the sonofabitch, there didn't seem to be much point in me going all the way to Fort Laramie."

"It's just too —"

"Not my place to stir up a hornet's nest by asking a lot of fool questions, if you understand what I'm sayin'."

"Hmm . . ." Win fell silent.

"Rivers was a sorry excuse for a man, any way you slice it. Using human beings as target practice — what a goddamn idiot," Gus said. "Wouldn't surprise me a bit if one of his own didn't help him over the edge, but we'll never know."

Win turned to One Who Waits. "I'm sorry your nephew was murdered."

One Who Waits said nothing at first, but then acknowledged Win's condolences with a nod. "My nephew's spirit lives in the world we cannot see, but is among us still."

"Meg feels like she betrayed your trust,"

267

Win said to the Arapaho. "She said she had no right to promise that Rivers would be brought to justice."

"Tell her she had no part in this."

It impressed Win that One Who Waits didn't let his anger cast a wide net of blame. While fairly confident they wouldn't have attacked Paradise, it was not implausible for Gray Wolf's clan to have avenged Niteesh's death by killing the settlers. Win wasn't sure if it was shrewdness or a defeated spirit that restrained them.

One Who Waits turned to head into the foothills. As he left, he said he hoped for a winter cold enough to keep blue coats close to their own fires.

"Well, you're welcome at mine, my friend," Gus replied, "anytime."

Once One Who Waits disappeared into the trees, Win asked, "Do you think the settlers will say anything when they reach the fort?"

"I told them that reporting what happened might stir up more questions than they had answers for. They said if it was all the same to me, they'd just put the whole matter behind them. I reckon they're feeling lucky to be alive, and will leave well enough alone." Gus turned to look him in the eye. "You'd be wise to do the same. I didn't meet up with One Who Waits until I was riding home. I honestly don't know if he had a hand in what happened, and I don't care. Rivers was a dead man from the moment he shot Niteesh. The only uncertainty was whether the rest of the party died with him. I knew that, and so did they. Whoever killed Rivers did us all a favor. That is, if he really was killed, and not just unsteady on his feet."

So that was it.

Win asked no more questions. His thoughts returned to Meg. She had raced Post riders, she conspired to keep Arapaho living in freedom off the reservation, and now had put herself between Running Elk and a bullet. She was a loyal friend, devoted to the Arapaho. Or, was she bold and brave, seeking excitement — just like him?

Chapter Twenty-Seven: Jeb

Paradise way station, August 1867

The stage horn's blast, announcing the arrival of a private stage, was so loud Gus jumped and spilled his coffee. He cussed. "I gotta tell Charlie to quit blowing that horn so goddamn close." Gus wiped his shirt. "He must think I'm deaf. I can goddamn hear his squeaky springs before he blows that thing."

"I'll keep your meal warm," Meg said, reaching for his plate and taking it to the stove. Gus grumbled a few more cuss words as he left the station to change the team.

"Don't let him fool you," Meg said to Win and Jeb, who were having Sunday dinner with them. "Gus looks ten years younger than he did in Council Bluffs. He's never been happier."

"Maybe he's ornery 'cause he thinks Jeb'll eat all the peach pie before he gets back," Win said.

Jeb figured Win was trying to get a rise out of him, something Win did when he was ornery himself and restless. Or, maybe Win worried he'd miss out on a piece for himself. Meg did bake a delicious peach pie.

From the window, Jeb saw two men and their wives spill out of the stagecoach, followed by three businessmen. A private coach didn't have the strict schedule other coach runs had, so the women walked over to Georgia's store. The men headed for the station.

"Folks are on their way in, Meg."

She scooped up her pie and hid it in the cupboard. She pulled out the cornbread she always had on hand and put the coffee pot on the stove. She treated Gus, Win, and Jeb better than the stagecoach passengers.

The men walked in and accepted Meg's offerings. The two men with wives were brothers, and the three businessmen were in land purchasing and development. They asked a number of questions about the area, which Win seemed to enjoy evading.

"No problems with Indians?" one of the brothers asked.

"There are no Indians in this part of the country anymore," Win said. "They were sent to the Wind River reservation."

Meg glanced at Win, but set out a plate of

cornbread without a word.

"What about Red Cloud? We hear he's causing trouble," a businessman named Ferris asked.

"He's up north, defending the land the government gave him when the Sioux were pushed out of Minnesota." Jeb noticed how Win had trouble keeping a critical tone out of his voice when the topic of Indian land came up.

"They don't use the land. They could be taught how to farm, raise cattle, but they don't do it. They're all stubborn savages," Ferris said.

"Just fighting for their lives," Win said. Meg softly cleared her throat, her way of giving Win a gentle warning. He softened his tone. "Maybe the Indians know this land better than you think. It's too dry for farming."

The businessman named Brewer kept glancing at Meg while conversing with Win. Jeb wondered if he would try flirting with her. Lots of men did. "Irrigation, Mr. Avery," Brewer said. "New methods of farming will turn this desolate landscape into fertile cropland."

The two women came in and joined the group at the table. One of the women stared openly at Meg. "Pardon me, miss, have we met?"

Meg barely glanced at her, but busied herself pouring coffee. "No, ma'am. Unless you've been through Paradise before, I doubt we've met."

The woman squinted at her, still quizzical. "Henry, doesn't she look familiar? Where have we seen her?"

Her husband hadn't paid any attention to Meg up to this point, but a big grin now spread across his face. "Why, I'll be . . . if it isn't that little horse racer! I won a sizeable bet on account of you! Zeke, remember me telling you about that gal in a race when we were over in Bodine? Martha and me were passing through on our way to Centerville. I met a fellow setting up a contest with the locals, and he showed me your pretty little bay." He whistled appreciatively and shook his head. "What a race. Walked away with fifty bucks in silver. You still got her?"

"She's in the barn." Meg was so matter-of-fact about it that Jeb couldn't read what she was thinking, and wondered why she was so reticent.

Henry's eyes lit up. He said to his brother, "Zeke, c'mon, let's take a look before we go." He turned back to Meg. "Do you still race, Sugar?"

Meg shook her head. "No, sir."

"That's a pity; you could cut a hole in the wind. Got a kick out of you bein' a gal, too. I've never known any other female with gumption like that." He walked out of the station, but they could hear him describe the race to his brother as they headed for the stables.

"Miss, this is cold," Henry's wife said, her voice as cool as her coffee. Without a word, Meg yanked the pot from the stove.

Mr. Brewer spoke up. "I thought you looked familiar. I saw you race in a town along the Box Elder. I lost five greenbacks."

"Oh, I'm sorry." Meg's apology sounded genuine as she warmed the woman's coffee.

The gentleman shrugged affably. "Learned my lesson. Got talked into putting my money on a mustang when I should've gone with my first instinct."

"Well, I learned my lesson, too." Meg refilled Mr. Brewer's coffee. "Did you say you are from the land office? I want to buy some land out here."

Mr. Fisher, the third businessman, jumped into the conversation. "You won't be able to grow a crop. Mr. Brewer here is the most optimistic soul I've ever met. Irrigation . . . bah!"

"Surely one could keep a small herd of

horses." Meg directed her query at Mr. Brewer.

Mr. Brewer nodded. "Mr. Fisher may not agree, but I think you could."

The stage driver appeared at the doorway. "Time to go, folks."

The other passengers left the station, but Mr. Brewer lingered. "Land is pretty cheap out here, but you'd need a lot of it. It's hard to scratch out a living on the parcels the government doles out for homesteaders."

"I have more capital than just my racing profits."

"Glad to hear it. You'll need to control a water source. That's the key. If someone buys land upstream, he can divert the water and you'd be left with desert." He pulled out his card and gave it to Meg. "My company helps transfer government land to private ownership. It's a process called 'land entry.' Look me up, and I'll see that you get good acreage."

"Thank you, Mr. Brewer." Meg shook his hand. "You're very kind."

"Consider it a mea culpa for betting against you. I won't make that mistake again." He tipped his hat and walked out the door.

"You leave quite an impression, Meggie," Win said after Brewer left. "Do a lot of folks recognize you from your flimflamming days?"

"I wasn't flimflamming!" She began to clear the table. "I don't know why that woman had to get all huffy. After all, her husband won fifty dollars." She dumped the dishes into the sink less gently than usual.

"Apparently a husband's admiration is worth more." Win gathered the two extra cups left by Fisher and Brewer and placed them in the sink.

Meg held up Mr. Brewer's card. "This," she said, brightening, "is certainly worth more than a stranger's admiration. I have a good feeling about Mr. Brewer."

CHAPTER TWENTY-EIGHT: MEG

Paradise, September 1867

Jeb shouted to Meg as they drove their shipment into town. He had a letter for her. A breeze encircled her as she hurried over to their wagon parked in front of the Carters' store. If what Gray Wolf said was true about paying attention to spirit signs, it was a good omen.

The letter announced that her trust had been released early. She would not have to wait until she turned twenty-one — she and Gus could buy land.

Gus sat Meg down and suggested several other ways she could spend, save, or invest her money, but Meg insisted on buying land. Nothing would change her mind. In Denver, in Mr. Brewer's office, Meg and Gus pored over maps of the territory. With Mr. Brewer's help, they outlined an area just west of Paradise that included a complete watershed, thus securing their water supply. A great deal of acreage, it was more land than Meg ever dreamed she could afford. The area included a high mountain meadow behind the first set of foothills, a higher elevation mountain range, and the valley hidden behind it. Mr. Brewer said it gave him great pleasure to secure so many acres for an industrious young woman, although cautioned that it was really much more than she needed for a small herd of horses, and much of it was too mountainous for crops. She assured him she knew what she was doing.

When they walked out of Mr. Brewer's office into the sunshine, Gus took Meg's hand. "You add luster to my days — that's a fact." He kissed her on the cheek. "Congratulations."

"You don't think I'm a fool, do you, Gus," she asked, "buying land for Gray Wolf?"

"Darlin', you follow your heart and you will never be a fool."

With her inheritance, she purchased seven thousand acres from the United States government. The plan had been forming in the back of her mind ever since Gray Wolf shot Sutter and saved her life. She wanted to repay him with land — land no one could ever take away. On private property, he and his family could live in peace, and off the reservation.

Excited to share her news, when Meg and Gus returned home they rode into the mountains to tell Gray Wolf about their purchase. Meg was taken aback when Gray Wolf balked at the idea.

"It was not theirs to sell. No one can own the Earth or sky. Do you own the air we breathe here, too?" Gray Wolf appeared more offended than pleased.

"No, of course not."

Gray Wolf became agitated. "White men bought land at the warm springs where the Ute wintered. Now white men come from the east to camp for pleasure. They have homes in the east. Why don't they stay there and let the Ute have their home?"

"I heard about that," Gus said. "William Byers created his own little town and brings bigwigs there to show off. He has plans to make it a resort. Wants to call it 'America's Switzerland.'" Gus looked Gray Wolf in the eye. "It's a damn shame, but all the more reason to buy this acreage. If Meg didn't, someone else would."

"We're going to raise horses, Gray Wolf, not create a resort."

"Treaties are smoke from a fire. The wind blows it away and it is nothing," Gray Wolf said. "It is not wise to trust what is on paper." He looked more confused than angry, perhaps troubled. Meg's heart broke for him.

"This is not a treaty. Gus and I bought the land to live on. We want you to live here, too."

Gray Wolf looked old and tired. He closed his eyes, the way he often did when he tried to gather his thoughts. "We used to move with the seasons. We listened to our Mother Earth and followed her voice. Her cold wind blew us where the sun was warm while she replenished the north. Her hot breath pushed us north again, where she gave us the buffalo. We hear her voice, but are no longer allowed to follow her wisdom." He paused for a moment. Meg tried to control her emotions, but tears escaped and ran down her cheeks. "Our home was once where our ancestors lived. We had to leave and call a new place home. I no longer know if we will meet our ancestors when we die. How will they know where to find us?"

His words wrenched Meg's heart. "I want your grandchildren's grandchildren to live here." Her voice quavered with emotion. "They will be able to find you. This is your home for as long as you want it to be. I don't know what else to say."

Gray Wolf opened his eyes and looked at

her softly. "I believe you. That you welcome us to live here is not what saddens me. I am sad that our Mother Earth has been sold, like a slave."

"I'm sorry about that, too," Gus said, "but this way you'll never have to leave."

Even sitting, Gray Wolf appeared to grow to the size of a grizzly bear. "Guns say we never have to leave."

CHAPTER TWENTY-NINE: WIN

Denver, one year later, Autumn 1868

Win and Jeb sat in the saloon across the street from Sanders's Denver warehouse, reading a newspaper. Normally they'd be waiting for a shipment to be readied, but Clint had just informed them that he closed down his freight business. The Union Pacific Railroad had reached Cheyenne the year before. While it continued to work its way west to join the Central Pacific, feeder routes spread out everywhere. Track had been laid to Lyonsville, and soon, regular service between Cheyenne and Denver would put his freight line out of business completely. Clint's private stage still served some areas, but he decided to get out while he could. Earlier in the day, Clint finally approached them with the news — he and Amanda were headed for California. Their good-byes had been congenial, their wishes for good luck sincere.

Win couldn't have been happier. He didn't wish hard times on Clint, but this was a long overdue opportunity. Civilization encircled him, choked him. He had waited as patiently as he could while Clint tried to keep the business afloat, not wanting to add to his troubles by quitting.

Now free, and with time on their hands, Jeb and Win sat in the saloon, celebrating their unemployment with a beer. Win picked up a newspaper on the way, which Jeb warned he'd take away if Win started complaining.

Win scanned his section as Jeb announced, "We just purchased Alaska from the Russians."

"Did Meg buy it?"

Jeb laughed. "No . . . it says, 'The House approved the appropriation, which has been called Seward's Folly, in July, by a vote of 113–48.' "

"Let me see that," Win said, and held out his section of the newspaper to trade. They exchanged pages and Win found the article. "Wonder what's up there," he mumbled, his curiosity piqued.

"A bunch of states ratified the Fourteenth Amendment. Does that include Indians?" Jeb asked, reading a new article. Win didn't answer. He was calculating how long it would take to get to this new place called "Alaska."

Win felt the presence of someone else at the table. He looked over the top of his paper to find a short, wiry gentleman about a decade older than he standing next to him. He was missing his right arm.

"It is rare to see two men in a drinking establishment so engrossed in such a cerebral activity." The man removed his hat. "Please excuse the intrusion."

Win closed his paper. "What can we do for you?"

The man placed his hat on the table and stuck out his left hand to shake, which was awkward, but Win shook it anyway, as did Jeb. "The name's Powell. I'm a museum curator, natural history. I'm here studying the West with students from Illinois Wesleyan University. We are the Rocky Mountain Scientific Exploring Expedition."

A bolt of electricity shot through Win. He jumped up to pull a chair from the neighboring table and invited Mr. Powell to join them. The barkeeper brought over two beers at Powell's beckoning. Too excited to drink, Win grasped the mug tightly as Powell told them about his work. The professor and his party had amassed collections of rocks and fossils, insects, birds, and small mammals.

They were sending shipments back to Illinois for the museum. He and his wife had climbed Pike's Peak, he said proudly, modestly adding that he and a party ascended Long's Peak in August. His next project was to take an exploratory trip down the Colorado River.

Then Powell leaned forward. "Most of my students are returning to Illinois with the crates of specimens, but a few want to stay on. Jack Sumner, a guide at Byers's ranch, told me about you two. He said you might be able to help me."

"How does he know us?" Jeb asked.

"He is aware of two freighters who have unusually good luck on the route from here to a little place called Paradise. He found it curious that you never had any trouble with Indians robbing or begging. I need some able fellows who can keep my ambitious students out of harm's way while they continue their research. Guides who have sense enough to keep a peaceful watch. One of my students is convinced he'll uncover the next Stonehenge. I hate to dampen such enthusiastic curiosity, even though I must move on. He comes from wealth. He'll pay handsomely for the privilege of staying behind."

Jeb leaned back in his chair. "I would

escort your students as long as they give their word that they'll respect sacred burial grounds and steer clear of them."

Powell nodded. "I assure you, they are well indoctrinated with my views and will respect the aboriginal inhabitants of these parts. My students will give you no cause for concern."

His mind reeling, Win had heard little of the conversation after the mention of the Colorado River. "Indian and white men alike believe no one can survive a journey down the Colorado."

"So I've been told." Powell leaned back, scrutinizing Win. "But there's a large blank space on even the best Colorado maps. It's time something was done about it, don't you think?"

"How do you propose to do it?" Win asked.

"With sturdy boats and a fearless crew, I should imagine." Powell smiled, as though he knew his answer didn't address the essence of the question. "Eventually, I'll head back east to make the arrangements. I have ideas to incorporate into some custom built boats." Powell shrugged. "And, I need to locate my brother. He'll join the crew who's assembling at Green River City in the spring. But, first, I want to learn as much of the Ute language as I can, so I plan to winter at the basin. Understanding Ute would be a useful tool in Ute country, wouldn't you say?" He chuckled. "With this ambitious timeline, you can see why I need to put my procrastinating students in your care."

As Win listened to Powell, he felt like St. Elmo's fire was glowing from his fingertips. Something momentous was about to happen. "You're really going to do it, aren't you?"

Powell leaned in, his eyes locked on Win, as though he saw the blue glow, too. "Why not?"

Electricity crackled through Win again.

Glancing out the window, Powell stood up. "There's Mrs. Powell. I must go. The three students remaining behind are resupplying now. Will you guide for them?"

Half listening, Win heard Jeb agree for both of them, and through hazy window glass watched Powell walk down the street and join a woman who he assumed was Mrs. Powell, a wife who joined her husband on adventures. An intriguing thought. Win tried to imagine Meg on an expedition, riding through the mountains, but the dark-haired girl from Win's recurring dream appeared in his head, smiling and shaking her head. *What are you trying to tell me?* he asked her.

"I said that was perfect timing," Jeb said, breaking into Win's thoughts.

Win sat in silence planning his future for a long time before he drained his beer mug. He'd escort the college students as they dug for fossils and studied plants. But next spring, he would be at Green River City to join Powell's expedition.

Chapter Thirty:
Jeb

The Road between Denver and Paradise
The mules lumbered along in the late afternoon, pulling one final order for delivery at the Carters' store in Paradise. The wagon and mules were a parting gift from Clint. Embarrassed that he couldn't pay them in cash, he bought them a beer at the saloon before bequeathing the wagon and team to them.

"You aren't telling us anything new, Clint. We've been expecting this conversation for a while now," Win had said. He raised his mug and grinned. "But thanks for the beer."

"What are you going to do?" Jeb asked.

"Amanda and I are headed to California. I've got a couple of connections in Sacramento from my trail days. Interested in joining us? I'd get you work."

"I think we're set here. But thank you." Jeb had no intention of leaving Meg for an adventure in California.

"I figured I couldn't pull you two away from that pretty little hostler, and I don't mean Gus." Clint raised his eyebrows suggestively and had a good belly laugh at his own joke.

Jeb was happy to see Clint at ease. He'd provided Win and Jeb with steady income for three years, and, with few expenses, Jeb had accumulated a respectable stake. While Win made it clear he wanted to move on, Jeb had plans of his own, too.

Almost as soon as Clint left, John Wesley Powell showed up and secured the two friends as escorts for his students. Then Powell left to prepare for his trip down the Colorado River. Within an hour, their lives had completely changed. Jeb saw in Win's eyes a sparkle he hadn't seen for a while and knew Win wouldn't understand that Jeb no longer shared his yearning for adventure.

Jeb slapped the backs of the mules as their team of six labored up a steep rise before the terrain leveled out again. A buckboard wagon coming from the opposite direction appeared on the horizon.

Win talked of nothing but Powell's expedition. "That Powell fellow was something, wasn't he? We've got to sign on with him, Jeb. We'd be perfect for his crew going down the river." Win sighed happily. "Unexplored territory."

Jeb didn't respond. Win's feet were itching, that was obvious. A few years ago, Jeb had liked traveling with Win. They had been through a lot together and had some good times. But lately, Jeb had been thinking a lot more about that pretty little hostler, as Clint called her. The best times of the last few years included Meg. Crossing the plains and meeting Gray Wolf brought big changes to their lives, but she brought pleasure to his every day. He couldn't wait to get back to Paradise whenever they were away, and felt content when he was there. Meg and Gus had the land to ranch, but they couldn't run it alone. Jeb hoped Meg would stop joking that she'd never marry and consider having him.

The buckboard wagon they'd watched progress steadily closer was almost upon them. Win squinted at it curiously, and then tensed up as the driver slapped his mules into a run.

"Shit . . . Stop the wagon!" Win yelled to Jeb, clutching his own rifle while reaching for Jeb's under the seat. Two men with rifles emerged out of hiding behind the driver. Jeb slammed the brake into place. Win jumped from the wagon, Jeb following right behind him. A bullet just missed Jeb, stinging his skin as it shot through his wool coat.

They were out of the line of fire for a fleeting moment while the bandits cut in front of the wagon. With expertise that Jeb would question him about later, Win tossed Jeb his rifle and yelled at him to take cover and shoot the driver. Win remained next to the wagon wheel. As soon as the bandits drove into view, bullets rained at them. As instructed, Jeb shot the driver. A lucky hit, the driver slumped over. Win shot one of the two men with rifles and accidentally hit one of the mules. The wagon flipped as the mule fell, tossing the injured man out of the wagon like a rag doll, but the other jumped off and raised his rifle. Win and Jeb fired at the same time and he dropped to ground. All three bandits lay motionless. Win kept his rifle pointed at the fallen men as he collapsed to his knees. He'd been shot in the thigh. Blood spread onto his pant leg, soaking it.

"Win!" Jeb said and started over to him, but he waved him off.

"I'll cover you. Go make sure they're dead." Win grimaced in pain as he pulled himself up onto the wagon wheel and drew his revolver. Jeb crept over to the bandits. The dead driver still held a revolver in his hand. If Win hadn't told Jeb to shoot him, the driver would have shot him first. Jeb wondered how Win knew that. "Anything on them?" Win called over to him, grunting as he struggled to remain standing. Jeb searched their pockets; it felt strange doing so, like he was the bandit instead of them. "Check the wagon."

"Jesus, Win." Jeb straightened up. "What does it matter?" He started over to Win.

"They're robbers, Jeb. I want to see what they stole."

"No; I'm getting you home."

Ignoring Win's complaint that they might be leaving something valuable behind, Jeb tied a handkerchief tight above the wound on his thigh. It was bleeding badly. Jeb lifted Win into the wagon bed, adrenaline giving him extraordinary strength. He wrapped a blanket over him and climbed into the driver's seat, taking a quick glance at the carnage they were leaving behind. One of the mules stood, imprisoned by the harness attached to the overturned wagon. Jeb jumped down and cut the animal free, giving him a smack on his rump. The mule trotted a few paces ahead and stopped, as though freedom confused him. Jeb returned to his own wagon and headed north.

It was past sunset and snow fell lightly.

The flakes floated around lazily, not intending to gather into a storm of any significance. With clouds covering the moon, Jeb drove far too fast in the darkness, barely able to see where he was going. Win groaned whenever Jeb rolled over a bump. Jeb finally saw the light from the way station ahead. When he got close, he shouted that he needed help. Meg appeared at the door, and when she saw him, immediately called to Gus. She ran out of the station without her boots or coat.

"Win's been shot. Help me get him inside." Jeb jumped from his seat. Meg and Gus each grabbed a leg as Jeb wrapped his arms around Win's chest and backed into the way station. He eased him down on the floor next to the fire. Win's eyes were closed and his teeth were chattering. Jeb quickly cut away his pant leg, revealing the gunshot wound in his thigh. Meg brought a pan of water over to him and gasped when she saw the black hole surrounded by red swollen skin. The bullet was still lodged in his leg. Jeb glanced at Gus and knew what he was thinking — Jeb would have to dig it out.

Meg brought over a stack of clean rags while Jeb retrieved his small bundle of surgical instruments. Gus found a piece of kindling in the woodpile and rummaged around for a bottle of whiskey.

"Tie another knot on that tourniquet with this stick attached, Meg," Gus said, nodding to the rag on Win's leg. Meg did as instructed. With his one hand, Gus tied a couple of knots into one of the clean rags. Jeb sterilized a scalpel and small forceps by holding them in the fire.

Win came to and, seeing the activity, cussed. "I had a feeling it didn't go through."

"I've gotta get it out," Jeb said. "It'll get infected if I don't."

"I know. I just wish you'd stayed in school longer." Win breathed heavily.

Jeb smiled weakly at Win's attempt at humor, but in truth, he felt sick as he weighed the risks. He wasn't sure he could dig a bullet out of his friend. If he nicked an artery, Win could bleed out and die. But if the bullet stayed in his leg, no doubt with a piece of his pant leg with it, it would only fester. Gus handed Win the open bottle and suggested that he take a swig or two.

"Here's the plan —" Jeb said.

Win held up a hand. "I don't want to know. Just do it, and do it fast."

While Jeb delayed just long enough for Win to feel the whiskey, he showed Meg how to twist the stick and hold it tight.

"Meggie, this is gonna go fast when it goes . . . you stay with us, you hear me?" Gus looked as ashen as Meg, but he held her gaze until she nodded. Gus pulled his own knife from the fire, keeping it out of Win's line of sight. He turned to Jeb. "It might be faster with an extra hand. Once you get the bullet out, this'll stop the bleeding."

Jeb knew Gus was speaking from his own experience, when he had to endure his hand amputation. He was probably right — do it fast, all at once. As hard as this was, it would be best for Win, and he wasn't going to argue with Gus. He nodded.

"Let's get this over with," Gus said, putting the rag with the knots in it in Win's mouth.

Jeb hesitated. He remembered his father telling him that inflicting pain, even when necessary, was not for the fainthearted.

Gus leaned on both of Win's legs and ordered a sharp "Go" to Jeb. With scalpel and forceps, Jeb dug into Win's thigh. Win clamped down on the rag in his mouth and groaned loudly. Beads of sweat formed on his forehead and tears squeezed out of his eyes and ran down his temples. Jeb couldn't feel the bullet, but knew there was no going back. He dug deeper and Win arched his back in pain. Finally, Jeb felt the bullet. He pulled it and a small piece of cloth out with the forceps. Gus immediately sank the hot knife into the wound to cauterize it while Win was still reeling from the bullet removal. Win passed out, much to Jeb's relief. Gus removed the knotted rag from Win's mouth, and Jeb quickly put a few stitches in with a needle and thread.

Meg held the tourniquet for another minute while Jeb washed the blood off and bound it tight with clean bandages. Meg tenderly wiped the sweat from Win's pallid face, a gesture that both bothered Jeb and endeared her to him.

Win stirred. He looked down at the bandage and whispered, "My leg's on fire." Jeb handed him the whiskey bottle. They lifted Win onto a cot brought in from the bunkhouse and propped up his leg. Jeb washed off the bullet and saved it, figuring Win would want it when he was feeling better — after he forgave him for saving his life so painfully.

"What kind of mess did you leave behind?" Gus asked.

"We killed all three men." Jeb glanced at Meg. He wondered what she would think of him. "Can't say it feels good."

Gus leaned against the big oak table.

"Thieving is risky business. They know that going in. You didn't bring this on, son. You're either alive or dead at the end of a gunfight — take your pick. I'll go with you tomorrow to clean it up. We'll have to bring 'em to Cold Springs, I figure. The sheriff will have some questions. I reckon you have answers." Gus nodded at Jeb's bloody arm. "You got nicked."

"It's nothing," he said.

"Let Meggie clean it up for you."

Jeb took off his shirt. Meg filled the water basin again and washed his arm. Her hand trembled as she bandaged the scrape.

CHAPTER THIRTY-ONE: MEG

Paradise

"You did well, Meggie girl."

Meg sensed that tending to Win had taken its toll on Gus. He looked drained when he left to toss out the basin of bloody water, so she followed him. She found her old friend in the barn, resting his forehead in the bend of his elbow.

"He's going to be all right, isn't he, Gus?" Meg asked.

"I'd say so. The bullet didn't hit bone; his leg ain't broken." Gus pressed his forearm against the barn wall, as if trying to push the ache from the stub.

Poor Gus. She rubbed his shoulder gently. "You're always the one bolstering me up. I'm old enough now for you to lean on me." She sat down in the straw. "Tell me about it, Gus. What happened when they took your hand?"

With his forehead still pressed into the

299

crook of his elbow, Gus said, "I had to talk the fella through it — the one who handled the saw. Sonofabitch drank all the whiskey before I could get some to help dull the pain. Goddamn fool." Gus reached down with his good right hand and patted his thigh. He laughed sadly. "You know, I thought I felt ol' Buddy's heavy head resting on my leg there for a minute . . . and his warm breath. Funny how real memories can be." He stood up straight and rubbed the stump of his left arm. "I can still smell my burning flesh when they cauterized the bleeding; damned unpleasant."

Gus had not told her the details of losing his hand before. He'd only told the story in reference to his dog, Buddy. She wrapped her arms around her old friend. "I don't tell you enough how brave you are, Gus, and how happy I am that you're part of my life."

"Feelin's mutual, darlin'."

"We should start ranching," she said, hoping the thought would cheer him up. "There's no reason to wait."

"We're gonna need some help," Gus said. He studied her. "We can't do it alone. You should think about taking a husband."

"We can handle a ranch ourselves. Or hire some hands. I don't need a husband."

"I don't see how it could hurt. I know a

pretty girl like you gets a lot of unwanted attention, and I don't blame you for being a bit skittish around men. But you grew up fine, darlin', and you've got a lot to offer. You should think about your future, having a family."

"You're my family."

"You know what I mean. A husband, babies . . . it's just natural. Now, Jeb and Win —"

"Those two promised each other that I wouldn't interfere with their friendship! They made a pact about me!" Meg folded her arms across her chest.

"Nope, that ain't it. That's the excuse you've been using, but what are you really scared of?" Gus had a way of seeing more in a person than that person wanted to reveal, and he was especially good at reading her.

She looked away then, and felt her face burn. "I . . . don't want to disappoint him."

"Which one?"

She shrugged and dropped her head. "Either one. I don't know anything about men and what I'm supposed to do."

Gus opened his arm so she could bury her face in his shoulder. He closed it around her and said, "I wish your ma was here. A gal needs a ma at times like these." He sighed heavily. "Female talk ain't my specialty, you know that. But I'll tell you something I know is true. Every baby girl is born with sparkle. It's just a fact. And it's the job of the men in her life — her pa, her husband, or even an old geezer friend like me — to make sure the sparkle don't get scraped away. A husband is particularly called upon to see that his wife don't lose her sparkle. It's a big responsibility, and it can humble a man who has any sense in his head at all. It ain't just the wife that's fearful of disappointing, and I'd say the best marriage is the one where they figure things out together. Are you following what I'm saying?"

Her questions were answered in the one simple sentence she'd heard before. The furrow in her brow relaxed. "Yes, I do, Gus."

CHAPTER THIRTY-TWO:
WIN

Paradise

Win woke to the smell of coffee and found himself alone with Meg. She draped a towel over a bowl of bread dough and set it next to the pot of simmering stew. She opened the oven door to check the gingerbread, a favorite of Win's. He smiled slightly, feeling the joy of being cared for, even though his leg hurt like hell. They spent the morning quietly together, Meg in the kitchen and Win resting in front of the fire. He tried to read, but the pain made concentrating difficult. From behind his book, Win watched her work.

Meg moved through her chores as though preoccupied, too. Win wondered what she was thinking about — if she was bored at the station, or worried about him, or dreaming about something else. He wondered what she would say about Powell and the Colorado. Would she wait for him? What if he invited her along on the expedition? She'd be fun to have along. If Meg joined them on the expedition, he'd even be doing Jeb a favor.

He put his book aside and said, "Are you and Gus really going to ranch out here? You sure that'll make you happy? Are you sure Gray Wolf will let you?"

Meg laughed and looked up briefly from scrubbing a pot. "We've been planning this for a long time. Of course we're going to be happy ranching. Gray Wolf didn't understand at first, but he does now."

"And you never second-guess yourself? Are you sure it's enough?"

"Ha! I know *you* need more excitement."

"My feet get itchy, I admit." Win rubbed his leg. "And even though Wyoming is now a territory, there's still some wilderness left to explore. Jeb and I met someone forming an expedition party. He plans to map some rivers. It sounds like quite the adventure."

Meg's smile faded, but she didn't speak.

"You know, the man's wife is going along. She climbed Pike's Peak."

"Hmmm . . . She sounds formidable."

"Maybe you should come along, too."

Meg stopped scrubbing the pot. She froze, like people do when so much is flying through their heads that their bodies can't cope with extra activity. But then she started scrubbing again and shook her head. "You and Jeb are the adventurers, Win, not me."

Win scoffed. "Right. Someone who rides her horse across the Nebraska Territory all alone has no spirit of adventure at all!" When that didn't bring a smile, Win changed his tactics. "You and I are more alike than you think, Meg. I've always seen the daring side of you. I should've stopped that day you raced me; that day you proved you were as fast as a Post rider. If I had met you properly back then, I'd have whisked you away. Hell, we might have traveled the globe, you and me."

"I was twelve!" she said, laughing. "You can be so outrageous, Win." But she looked at him for a moment, and the tenderness in her eyes stirred his heart. He wondered if she were imagining what it would be like to do just that, travel the world together.

"Come over and keep me company." Win stretched to reach a chair. He pulled it closer to him.

"Looks like you want to drink and play cards." She eyed the bottle of whiskey and the deck of cards on the table next to him.

"C'mon, sit with me. My leg's aching. Let's play a few hands of gin rummy to take my mind off it."

The fire was warm, the stew was off the stove, and the bread was rising. Other chores could wait — he wanted to be alone with her. She took two glasses from the shelf and dropped into the chair. He pulled a little table up and poured them both a shot. A collegial bond sparked between them as they toasted and took a sip. The warmth rushed into his chest as he dealt the cards. They played a few hands; Meg won the first, but he won the next two. She leaned back in the chair and sighed with a laziness that comes from drinking in the middle of the day. He shuffled the deck.

"Do you miss racing?" The effects of the drink allowed the question to escape his lips. He dealt the cards, hoping she wouldn't take offense. At least he hadn't called it "flimflamming."

She picked up her hand. "Biscuit prefers this life. She could have been hurt . . . stepped in a hole . . ."

"I didn't ask if she missed it. I asked if you did."

Meg held his gaze. "Sometimes." Maybe the whiskey was talking, but he liked the candor it produced. A distant memory fell across her face. "There was something about racing. It was scary, but thrilling at the same time. It was a little dangerous, and yet I loved it. There was something about it . . ." she repeated, and looked at him as if to seek confirmation that he understood.

Maybe there's a chance she'll come with me, Win thought. He nodded encouragingly. "Spoken like a trailblazer. You've got . . . gumption. I think that's what they call it." Win put down his cards. "Think of the vistas we'd see, Meggie. Gus could come. Powell lost a hand, too; if he can manage, you know Gus can. Gus is ten times stronger than Powell, he'd —"

"Stop, Win." Meg shook her head. She rose a bit unsteadily to check the ginger-bread and pulled it from the oven. When she returned, she poured them both another drink. "I'm not the girl you think I am, and I doubt it's gumption you see. I've been so confused lately."

Win's heart sank, but didn't press the idea of Powell's expedition. Instead, he asked, "What are you confused about?"

She shrugged and shook her head. "I was so content a few months ago; now I feel unsettled about almost everything. I want all this to stay just as it is." She opened her arms. "But I want to move forward, too. I feel caught between two worlds. Gus and I have the money to start our ranch now, but I don't want this to end." She tossed her

307

cards on the table. "Ach, I'm not making any sense."

"There's no way to move ahead without leaving something behind."

She stared at the fire, her brow furrowed. He could tell she'd heard him by the look in her eyes. He'd been moving forward and leaving behind all of his life. "It hurts, though."

Her honesty seduced him. It was damned inconvenient that his leg throbbed every time he moved, otherwise he might have taken her hand and pulled her into his bed. But he was kidding himself. He would lose everything. She'd never forgive him if she gave herself away to him like this, and it would hurt Jeb deeply. He'd ruin any chance of friendship with either of them. *Jeb had better appreciate what a goddamn gentleman I am,* he thought.

Intimacy sparked between them, however, the whiskey was doing its job. Win poured them another drink and they began to talk, a cerebral form of lovemaking that kept propriety in the foreground and regret at bay. Win told Meg that when his job as a Post rider ended, he was too embarrassed to return to the Dawsons penniless, so he broke into a library and lived in the basement for a while until he met Clint. Meg confessed that she, too, spent a few weeks in the Council Bluffs reading room when she was expelled from school and thought Gus would be disappointed if he found out. Win asked why she had been expelled. She got in a fight, Meg replied. What was the fight about? She said another girl called her a tomboy, so she decked her. Win started laughing and she joined in until tears rolled down their cheeks and their sides ached. Another drink later, Win confessed how the color of certain sunsets reminded him of her hair. She pretended to scoff and said that he never looked more handsome than when he gazed out at the horizon. "Wilderness beckons you like a lover," she said. He replied he was undoubtedly looking at one of those reddish-gold sunsets. She blushed. Win nearly professed his love a couple of times, but, even drunk, he held back. And, though for a brief afternoon it was nice to pretend that Meg loved him and that she was his, another lover called.

CHAPTER THIRTY-THREE: JEB

Paradise

Jeb didn't know what to think when he and Gus walked through the door in the late afternoon and found Win and Meg sound asleep next to a fire of only glowing embers. Win was passed out in his cot and Meg was curled up in a chair, her face buried in her arms. The half-empty bottle of whiskey and the scattered cards told a story he wasn't sure he wanted to hear.

Win stirred and rubbed his head. "Aw, damn. What time is it?"

"Late," Gus growled as he picked up the bottle and showed it to him. "What the hell were you thinking?"

"Sorry, Gus." Win winced in pain when he tried to move. "We just got to talking."

"She's gonna wake up feeling mighty poorly." Gus sounded as gruff as any father would. "You oughta know better."

"You're right." Win rubbed his head. "We

had a damned good time, though."

Jeb wondered what he meant by a "damned good time" as Gus went to the stove to start some coffee. Jeb built up the fire. The noise woke Meg. She raised her head, her hair falling in her face. She squinted. "What happened?"

"Apparently, a 'damned good time' with Win." Jeb stirred the embers and tossed a log on top; it quickly caught fire.

She rubbed her face with both hands. "I feel terrible."

"You look terrible." Win grunted as he tried to stand up. "C'mon, let's sit up at the table. Gus is fixing you some coffee, and if I'm real polite, he might pour me some, too."

"I'd rather just shoot you." Gus banged around in the kitchen, retrieving coffee mugs. Meg pulled herself out of the chair with a groan and staggered over to the table, leaning on every support she could find along the way. She sat down with a thud and held her head in her hands. Win hobbled over as well. No one asked, so Jeb decided to fill them in on the men they shot. "We brought the bodies to Cold Springs."

"That was decent of you," Win said, combing his hair with his fingers.

"Something in short supply around here."

"Gus, be nice. Win didn't force it down my throat, for heaven's sake." Meg spoke to the table, holding her head in her hands. Win smiled a half-feeble, half-smug grin. Jeb couldn't remember a time when he felt angrier at Win, yet less inclined to say anything about it.

Gus sighed roughly. "You two are a god-damn piece of work, you know that? Time to sober up." He pounded two tin cups down in front of them and poured hot coffee into each. "Goddamn piece of work," he muttered to himself. The anger within Jeb eased a bit, since Gus was covering it pretty well for the both of them.

Whatever happened between Win and Meg that afternoon changed the angles and sides of the triangle that formed their friendship with Jeb. Within a few days, Win was up and around, feeling restless and getting underfoot. He limped around the kitchen when Meg was trying to cook, getting in her way and causing a fair amount of noise and disruption. Instead of getting irritated, however, she just laughed. The bottle of whiskey they shared seemed to have brought them closer together. Win tested his patience, but Jeb remained silent. He believed jealousy made a man look small.

In addition to the question of what went on between Meg and Win, the question of how Win knew he and Jeb were about to be attacked remained unanswered. Jeb didn't say it out loud, but he wondered if Win always did everything he could to avoid trouble. Once, when they were kids, the weather had been so cold that the pond next to the Blankenships' farm froze over. He and Win were warned that the ice was too thin to support them, but Win had to see for himself. He kept going farther and farther out onto the frozen pond, despite Jeb standing on shore telling him he was a fool. Sure enough, the ice cracked open beneath him and he disappeared into the water. Jeb grabbed a rope, tied it to a fallen tree branch, and slid it out over the ice to Win, who was flailing about, trying to pull himself out on to the ice. Jeb eventually got his shivering friend to shore, but not before Jeb nearly risked falling in himself trying to rescue him. Win managed a grin and, with his teeth chattering uncontrollably, said the infamous words, "Sometimes you gotta do somethin' bad, Jeb, just to know you're alive."

So, when Jeb asked Win why he stayed out in the open and how he knew that the driver of the wagon was carrying a gun, he expected a half-fabricated, outlandish story. Win began to tell Jeb how he'd got mixed up with some undesirables coming back from his first trek with Clint. He didn't know they were thieves at first, he said. In fact, they were good company. Jeb braced himself to once again hear Win's stupid-ass motto when Win caught him completely off guard.

"I was riding along with them, unaware of the evil inside them. We came upon a single wagon traveling alone. With no warning or cause, they shot the driver dead. Then they ransacked his wagon. I couldn't believe it." Win shook his head, as though, years later, he still felt remorse. "I was going to report them to the sheriff — the most naïve idea I've ever had. They had no intention of letting me get close to a town, or a sheriff. They were going to force me to go along on the next robbery, though. They told me I would be the driver and hide my revolver in my lap, just like those other fellows did to us." Win paused and looked so miserable Jeb couldn't help but feel sympathy for him. "Jeb, I told them what they had done was wrong. I sounded like a schoolboy. They just laughed at me. Said I could either go along or die right there. I couldn't believe what I'd gotten myself into. I started arguing with them and well, like Gus said, at the end of a gunfight, you're either alive or dead."

"You killed them?" Jeb stared at Win.

Win shrugged. "It wasn't one of my proudest moments."

Reckless or brave, Win had taken a bullet for him. He stayed out in the open so the men would shoot at him, a deliberate act that saved Jeb's life. Now his unbridled excitement about the prospect of joining Powell, and his assumption that Jeb would come with him, made it hard for Jeb to tell Win he'd decided to stay behind. He had to tell him soon, he just didn't know how. When the first of Powell's students arrived in Paradise, he knew time was running out.

John Caldwell, a college student with wealthy parents, arrived ahead of the others. He had decided to take up photography, in addition to archeology. He purchased his own wagon — a photography van, he called it — which not only carried his equipment, but also served as a darkroom. He had hired an assistant, and while they waited for the other students, Caldwell asked if anyone in Paradise would like a portrait taken, as his assistant needed practice and Caldwell wanted to test his new darkroom. Georgia enthusiastically accepted and organized the whole town. She and Mick had their portrait taken in front of their store. Blackie and Angus also stood proudly next to their businesses for their photographs. Mr. Caldwell used a Sutton for those pictures, the panoramic camera he would use to capture the grandeur of the western landscape, he said. For portraits, he had a different, wet-plate style camera with a bellows and a Petzval lens. He arranged a table and chair in front of a backdrop he hung in the way station. Georgia insisted that Meg, Win, Jeb, and Gus all have their portraits taken individually, and then together. While Caldwell fussed with his camera and Georgia argued with the men, who groused about changing their shirts and sitting still, Meg brought out Biscuit and spent more time brushing her coat than she did fixing her own hair. She asked Mr. Caldwell if he would take Biscuit's photograph, too. He agreed. What young man would refuse a request from Meg?

Caldwell and his assistant soon had an assortment of albumen prints and tintype photographs spread out on the big oak table to show everyone.

"These turned out fine, Mr. Caldwell," Jeb said, looking them over. "I'm impressed."

"Thank you, Mr. Dawson," the student

photographer replied. He held up the formal portrait of Meg. The image was clear and sharp. "She is a beauty, that one."

"Actually, I think Miss Jameson will prefer this one." Jeb held up the photograph of her taken with Biscuit. The bright sunlight made her squint, and strands of hair blew across her face, but she had her arm wrapped around Biscuit's neck and grinned happily at the camera. He smiled back at her image.

Mr. Caldwell shook his head in disappointment. "That one, I'm afraid, did not turn out well. I shouldn't have had her looking into the sun. Not at all flattering."

Jeb disagreed. It captured Meg perfectly.

Meg walked in and, seeing the photographs, rushed over to the table. "Oh! You have them finished already!" She scrutinized the images. "These are lovely." She held up the one of her and Biscuit. "Oh, my precious Biscuit," she said to the photograph. "This is my favorite."

Ha, Jeb thought to himself. *I got that right.*

"Miss Jameson, you are stunning in this portrait. Surely you'd prefer an image that captures your striking features —"

"Beauty fades over time, Mr. Caldwell." She stared at the photograph of Biscuit and herself. "Everyone marvels at a rose while in bloom, and discards it as soon as its petals drop. But this . . ." she said, holding up the picture of Biscuit. "Friendship and loyalty are currency far more precious than beauty."

Mr. Caldwell shrugged his shoulders. "It's yours, if you want it."

"Why, thank you! I'll buy some others from you, too." Georgia appeared, and Meg motioned her over to the table. "Georgia, come see! Look at us, all together." She held up the portrait of the whole town. The formal portrait of her that Mr. Caldwell had admired lay ignored on the table.

"Friendship and loyalty." The words rang in Jeb's ears with every swing of the axe. His stomach churned. He and Win were splitting wood behind the shed for the coming winter. The supply of firewood was a parting gift for Meg and Gus, except Jeb hoped to be warming himself by their fire.

"You're quiet. What's on your mind?" Win balanced a log on end.

"Nothing," Jeb said. "Well, actually, a lot. I'm . . . thinking I'd rather stick around here."

Win stopped, holding his axe in mid-air. He stared at Jeb. "What are you saying? It's the Colorado River, Jeb! We'd be the first men down an uncharted river. Don't you want to be part of it?"

"I can see how you would, but there are different kinds of adventures, Win."

"Yeah, and this one will make history!"

"It sounds exciting to you, I know. I think I'm headed on a different path."

Win stared at Jeb. "Jesus Christ, what's the matter with you?"

"Nothing's the matter —"

It didn't take long for Win to guess. "You're going after Meg."

"Been thinking about it. I haven't said anything to her yet."

"I can't believe this! You'd rather settle down than go exploring?"

Jeb was tired of Win's incredulity. "I don't need to live my life so near the edge all of the time. You're looking for something, and you don't even know what it is. I've found what I want." He hoped they wouldn't fight, but he didn't like the betrayed look in Win's eye.

"Well, this is just great." Win spread his arms out, as if he was hearing the most unbelievable news ever. Sarcasm rang in his voice. "You want to marry Meg . . . And have a passel of kids!"

"Win —"

"You're a sonofabitch, you know that?

You're a goddamn sonofabitch." He split the log in front of him, sending the pieces flying in opposite directions.

"And why is that?" Jeb leaned on the long handle of his axe. "We just want different things, Win."

"We don't want different things."

"What do you mean by that?"

Win spread his arms out again. "Are you blind?"

"I'm not blind to Meg! Don't you think she deserves a little consideration? You think she's gonna wait around while we drift through life?"

"Is that what you think I'm doing? Drifting?"

Jeb couldn't reply, because gunshots and loud whooping came from the stage in the distance. John Caldwell came out of the station and shot off his gun into the air and whooped as well.

Apparently, the last student had arrived. They could leave now. When Jeb turned around, Win had disappeared.

CHAPTER THIRTY-FOUR: MEG

Paradise

Meg hung the laundry, her thoughts everywhere but on the task at hand. She had always wondered why Gus never poured her more than a half shot of whiskey, but now she knew. Her head had ached and her stomach had churned for hours after she and Win shared the bottle together. She wouldn't make that mistake again. But she and Win shared more than a bottle. She felt like they had reached an understanding.

So why was Win acting irritable? He picked a fight no matter what anybody said. When Meg mentioned that Powell wintering with the Ute Indians sounded dangerous, Win argued that Lewis and Clark got all the way to the Pacific with the help of Indians. He seemed to miss her point deliberately.

Everything was different, and it unsettled Meg. Unlike the times other expeditions gathered in Paradise, the presence of Powell's students left her feeling restless. Restless like Win? She wondered. She couldn't quite put her finger on what was eating at her, but Win's words kept ringing in her ears: "You can't move forward without leaving something behind." He'd invited her along. If she didn't go, were they leaving her behind?

Tension between Win and Jeb was palpable. What was going on? As sad and worried as she was to see them go, part of her wished they would just leave before someone's simmering pot boiled over.

"Meggie, you're hangin' dirty clothes on the line." Gus came up behind her, startling her out of her thoughts.

"Oh, dammit." She yanked the clothespins off the line, letting the laundry fall.

"You're not yourself. What's the matter?"

"I'm not sure."

"You've got those two men spinning like tops."

"Good. Maybe they'll spin some sense into themselves."

"Don't count on it. But whatever happens, darlin', I'm on your side," Gus said. "You can count on that."

CHAPTER THIRTY-FIVE: WIN

Paradise

Win saw Gus slip behind the barn. The aroma of a cigar filled the air moments later. With the commotion caused by the arrival of Powell's students, who were all over at Angus's saloon, this was the first opportunity Win had to talk to Gus alone. He limped over and sat down next to him. Gus gave him one of his cigars. They puffed on them in silence for a while.

"Women are strange creatures, aren't they, Gus?"

"Depends. Got any particular one in mind?"

"Meg sure has a lot going on in that head of hers."

"Well, she's intelligent and thoughtful. I'd expect something to be goin' on up there."

"Yeah, she's got a lot on her mind, that's for sure."

Gus sighed. "How 'bout you tell me

what's on yours."

Win paused. Saying it out loud made it seem definite, no turning back. "I'm gonna get hired to do something on Powell's trip down the Colorado, even if I have to learn how to steer a boat."

"It sounds momentous."

"But doing something momentous usually means giving up something else that's . . . important."

"Matters of the heart are rarely straightforward." Gus watched the smoke from his cigar dissipate in the moonlight. "I'll skewer you if you hurt Meggie."

How Meg might get hurt was tricky. He could hurt her by leaving, but he'd do more damage staying. "This was bound to happen. Jeb and I are so different, yet, the day we met Meg, I could've told you we'd both get stuck on her."

Gus puffed on his cigar. "You got a complicated mess, that's a fact."

"To be honest, I'm surprised peace between us lasted this long. Give Jeb credit for that. He's so goddamn true blue, I can't even get mad at him . . . the sonofabitch."

"Let her go, Win."

The words hung in the air, silencing Win. Gus was right. Something called to Win in the mist of the unknown, and he had to answer. He had to see what was out there. He couldn't have both.

"Once we get Powell's students squared away, I'm headed for Green River City."

Gus nodded thoughtfully. "I told Gray Wolf about that river trip with Powell. Said you might be headed that way. He suggested Loud Crow go with you. He speaks Ute, and that might come in handy."

"So you agree this opportunity is too good to pass up."

"Nope, it ain't that at all. Gray Wolf says you got no business going down that damn river. Says it'll kill you quicker than a Ute will. Be prepared for Loud Crow to try to talk you out of it. To be honest, I hope you'll listen to him."

"I thought you wanted me to leave, for Meg's sake."

Gus turned to study Win. "I didn't say you should commit suicide on some foolhardy caper. Mourning your death ain't the way to make Meggie happy."

CHAPTER THIRTY-SIX: JEB

Two months later, November 1868

Jeb and Galen loped back to Paradise from the Cheyenne train depot, where he'd left the last of Powell's students in charge of five crates of carefully packed plant specimens. Win had left a week earlier, headed for Green River City to meet some of Powell's crew members, who planned to winter there and prepare for the upcoming launch in the spring.

Saying good-bye to Win had been hard. Jeb chastised himself for falling into a second outrageous pact with him, but, in truth, it was the only way for them to remain friends. He couldn't let the tension continue between them any longer.

The day they left Paradise with Powell's student in tow, Jeb said good-bye to Meg and rode ahead, not wanting to watch Win and Meg say their good-byes to each other. He pointed out the direction they were headed to the first student and lingered at the back of the mule train, letting the students lead the way. Win rode up beside him.

"This is stupid, Win. We can't have this anger between us. That was the whole point of the pact. Look, I've always put up with your wild ideas, now I deserve a little support."

Win grinned viciously. "So, you admit going after Meg is a wild idea —"

"You know that's not what I meant."

"All right, all right." Win held his hands up as a sign of truce. "I'll admit that at first I was just . . . surprised — no . . . jealous, maybe." He sighed. "Aw, hell, I was disappointed you weren't coming. I felt like I'd just lost you both."

"You haven't lost either one of us, Win."

Win looked westward and didn't speak. What he was pondering, Jeb could only imagine.

"I have to go," Win said finally.

Jeb nodded. "I know." Win couldn't pass up a trip down the Colorado River, but Jeb knew the trip wasn't all he was referring to. He wouldn't stick around to watch Jeb take Meg from him. As much as he needed to move on, it was hard. "You ok?"

"Aw, hell, I'm terrific. I got so much

jealousy boiling up inside of me I'm doing my best not to knock you off your horse." Win shook his head. "You know, it's mighty strange thinking of you with a wife and children, Jeb. Damn, are you sure you're ready to be a father?"

"I haven't even asked her to marry me yet. She might say no."

"She won't say no. We're the only two men in this whole goddamn territory who could possibly put up with that complicated creature, and she knows it. Since I just bowed out of the competition, you're her last hope. Ha! Meg's babies! God help you if they inherit her stubbornness."

Jeb had laughed because he wanted good-will between them. He needed Win's friendship as much as he needed Meg, and didn't want to argue. But, in truth, he neither agreed that she was stubborn, nor thought of himself as her last hope.

Riding back to Paradise, that worry now occupied Jeb. While he spent considerable time imagining what it would be like to be married to Meg, he had given very little thought to what would happen when he first arrived back in town alone. He wasn't sure how, or if, he should court Meg.

When they used to deliver supplies to Paradise, Jeb would look for Meg as soon as he and Win crested the hill. When the sun stayed up late at the end of the long summer days, she'd ride out to meet them, smiling and waving. She and Biscuit stirred up the grasshoppers as they rushed toward them, sending a spray of flying insects into the air. The setting sun made her hair sparkle in the golden light of the late afternoon. Maybe she was happy to see them, or maybe she was just happy riding. At other times, they might find her in her garden, hanging laundry, or tending to the chickens. Regardless of where she was or what she was doing, they could always tell when she first spotted them. Her hand would fly up and she'd wave to them enthusiastically. The sight of her was as thrilling as it was comforting, but now Jeb wondered if she'd been waving to just one of them, to both of them, or was just exuberant from her own contentedness.

Even before their night drinking whiskey, Win and Meg had always had a curious relationship. He'd tease her incessantly and she'd take off after him. He'd flee out the door, she'd follow, and soon Jeb would hear them laughing outside together. One time, Gus caught Jeb squinting thoughtfully at the door, listening to them carry on.

"That ain't love you're hearing, Jeb. That

out there is just foolishness."

Jeb scoffed, embarrassed. "Aw, hell, I know." But he didn't really know, not for sure. Win was talkative and entertaining; he was not. There was never an awkward silence around Win. Jeb wondered if Meg would be angry that Win left — blame him perhaps. Maybe she saw them only as a set, not as individual men. Jeb didn't want to make the foolish assumption that just because he agreed to ranch with them, she'd just fly into his arms. He began to feel queasy.

He crested the hill and Paradise came into view. Galen loped down the hill and into the vacant yard. No one came out to greet them. He brought Galen to the barn and unsaddled him. Trudging to the quiet station house, he had second thoughts about coming home.

Gus was hovering over Meg when Jeb opened the door. They both looked up, and their expressions changed from concern to relief. "Oh, Jeb! Thank goodness!" Meg cried. "We're having quite a time!"

Gus held a blood-soaked towel to Meg's hand.

"What happened?" Jeb dropped his saddlebags at the door.

"I saw you coming and wanted to pull the

pie from the oven before coming out to greet you." Meg nodded at the knife on the counter. "I pushed that aside to make room for the pie, but the knife got caught and stayed right where it was." She showed him the deep cut in the palm of her hand. "I feel stupid."

The cut bled badly, despite their efforts to stop it. With the use of only one hand apiece, she and Gus had been trying to get a washbasin filled, and were having a clumsy time of it. Jeb pumped water into the basin and set it on the table.

"Let's take a look." Jeb held her hand over the basin. Blood dripped steadily into the water, at first spreading out like pink smoke before the water turned red. He rinsed the cut carefully and gently.

Meg glanced up at him. "I'm sure this wasn't the homecoming you'd hoped for. I'm sorry."

"I don't mind." He smiled slightly. "It's good to be home. I think you need a couple of stitches. It'll heal faster if we can get it closed up a little. Are you up to it?"

"Do what you think is best." Her face lost its color.

"Hold this on the cut, then. Press as hard as you can." Jeb hadn't been forgotten after all, he realized as he gathered what he needed. He found the thinnest sewing needle he could in Meg's sewing box, and good thread. Gus poured Meg a glass of whiskey, which she turned down. She put her hand up on the table and turned her head away. Jeb stroked the back of her hand — a trick he learned from his father to shift sensation from one part of the body to another. Even with her head turned away from him, he could see her flush.

Gus sat down in front of Meg. "Did I ever tell you the story of the two-headed goat?"

"Yes, but tell me again."

Gus started spinning a yarn so outrageous Jeb wanted to set down the needle to listen, but it was clear the intent was to distract Meg, so Jeb worked as quickly and gently as he could. Just about the time Jeb tied his last knot, Gus wrapped up his tall tale.

"You change that story every time you tell it." Meg squeezed Gus's hand with her free one and laughed. She turned to discover three neat stitches in the palm of her hand. She looked up in surprise. "I barely felt it. Thank you, Jeb."

Jeb shrugged modestly, pleased that he had not inflicted pain. He wrapped up her hand with a clean bandage. "Thank Gus. He was a good distraction."

Gus slapped him on the shoulder. "Welcome back. Get those college boys off?"

"Yep, they'll have plenty of cataloging to do in Illinois." He decided against mentioning Win, and neither of them asked.

With a large, clean bandage tied to the palm of her hand, Meg returned to her dinner preparations.

When they sat down to dinner, Jeb moved purposely to sit next to Meg. He'd never paid much attention to where any of them sat before. Across the table, Gus watched them both.

"It's time to start breeding," he said. His declaration startled Meg; her knife clattered on her plate. With a half smile, Gus continued. "Jeb, remember that fair-haired reinsman, Davis? His brother's got a stallion in Cheyenne. I got a couple of fillies almost ready. I'd like you to come with me; see if you agree that the stud's worthy."

Jeb nodded as he bit into a warm biscuit. "Be glad to," he said with his mouth full. "Fine meal, Meg."

Out of the corner of his eye, he saw Meg smile.

An early winter storm blew in, postponing the trip to Cheyenne and catching everyone in Paradise off guard. Blackie worked inside only in the dead of winter, and had his outside furnaces going full strength when the temperature dropped suddenly and it started to snow. Meg quickly cut back her herbs and covered her garden with straw. She was in the middle of bundling the cuttings to hang when a stage arrived unexpectedly.

Nine passengers burst into the way station, stamping their frozen feet and blowing into their cold hands. Jeb came in with them.

The driver removed his hat. "Miss, I am sorry to impose, but there's quite a storm on its way. Had to come this way; drifts are blocking the road to Lyonsville. I'd like to keep my passengers here overnight, if you don't mind."

She glanced at Jeb, who waited for her answer. After an unruly passenger had backed her into a corner, Gus, Win, and Jeb took up the habit of always making sure one of them came in with the travelers. Meg scanned the group of seven men and two women. "Of course we don't mind. You're all welcome." She nodded to Jeb, who then left to help Gus.

In the barn, Jeb unhitched the team from the snow-covered stagecoach. One of the stranded passengers unloaded a fiddle from the luggage rack. No doubt there would be music later that evening — a chance to dance with Meg. Jeb had to collect his thoughts. He told Gus to go on ahead. He fetched a clean shirt from the bunkhouse and took a few minutes to wash up while he searched his memory.

In Denver a few years earlier, while driving freight for Clint, Win sat down next to Jeb at a poker table with a gleam in his eye. Jeb was having a run of good cards, but as much as Jeb tried, Win wouldn't be ignored.

"Jeb, old friend, I got someone set up for you upstairs. You go find Carla; she's got something for you."

"Nah, not tonight. I've got luck on my side right here." Jeb tossed a card. The dealer drew another for him.

Win wouldn't relent. He'd already talked to Carla, he said, who'd agreed to spend time with Jeb. He had already paid her. She was leaving in the morning. "You've gotta do this tonight," he said.

"Win, drop it. And shut up — I'm trying to play out this hand." But Jeb lost track of what the others had bet. He folded and excused himself from the table. He and Win stood at the bar. "Thanks a lot. How am I supposed to keep track of the cards with you buzzing in my ear?"

Win was undeterred. "She's upstairs, Jeb.

My treat."

"Jesus, Win."

"You'll thank me. Now go." Win jerked his head toward the stairs.

Jeb glared at his friend. Win could be a real pain in the ass sometimes, but he was also right annoyingly often. Jeb walked up to the room where Carla was waiting.

Carla was a midget — a third of the size of Jeb. She was plump and about ten years older than he, although it was a little hard to tell. She wore only a lace robe, through which Jeb could see her dark areolas and pubic hair. The room smelled of soap and perfume; she had her own little bathtub, which she had just used. Jeb couldn't have fit in it even if he curled up in a ball. She saw him looking at it and smiled.

"When was your last bath, honey? I don't let no dirty fellas touch this jewel," she said in a high, squeaky voice. She leaned back in her bed and stroked her breasts seductively. Jeb did not find her appealing. That goddamn Win.

Jeb wanted to leave, but didn't want to offend. "Uh, today . . . when we got in . . . but I'm not . . . I mean . . . I don't think . . ."

"Well, good." Carla sat up, apparently understanding his hesitation. She poured two shots of whiskey from a bottle at her bedside. "Your friend and I sat up here talking for most of his hour. He paid me good and asked if he could send you up for a little chat, as he put it. I said as long as I get paid, it don't make no difference which end does the work, and my lower half could use a rest."

Jeb smiled slightly, relieved. Win thought whores were fascinating creatures, although Jeb had never found them particularly intriguing. He removed his hat, and as there was no place to sit except for the bed, took off his boots so he wouldn't get the linens dirty. As he sat down gingerly on the edge of the bed, Carla handed him his glass of whiskey and stroked the inside of his thigh with her tiny hand. It looked so much like a child's, he almost recoiled. But an idea came to him — one that surprised even Carla.

"You sure you're leaving tomorrow?"

"I'm sure." Carla grinned wickedly, doing her job. "You wanna have some nasty fun with Carla? Something you don't want your friend to know about? I do most anything, but you're gonna have to pay extra."

Jeb had less interest in the nasty fun Carla was referring to and more interest in something else he thought she might be able to teach him. Would she teach him to dance? She asked if he was joking at first, but after he convinced her he was sincere, she spent the hour showing him what she knew.

Now the opportunity to dance with Meg arrived and he wanted to practice what Carla had taught him. In the chilly barn, he closed his eyes and tried to remember her instructions. He imagined her standing in front of him.

"I could show you quadrilles or reels, but they ain't as much fun as this here dance. A gentleman showed me this once — very genteel. Listen to the tune and count the beats. If you can count a 1-2-3, 1-2-3, you're in good shape. Here's how you start . . ." Carla showed Jeb the steps. "Nope, start with your other foot." He tried again. "That's it, you've got it." They waltzed around her room for a while, Carla counting and humming. "Anytime you can count to three like that, do this and you'll be fine. Say, you're pretty smooth. You're gonna do just fine."

Jeb checked the barn door to make sure it was closed. He counted slowly and stepped deliberately until he moved easily around the floor. When he felt confident, he ran his fingers through his hair to comb it and walked up to the way station. It was snow-ing heavily now, and the wind plastered the snow against the side of the station.

He walked into a crowd of people. Blackie, Angus, and Mick had come over. Georgia was helping Meg in the kitchen, and the two women passengers were bundling the rest of Meg's herbs and tying them to a drying rack. Blackie was stacking extra firewood by the fireplace. Meg looked up from her work when Jeb walked in and smiled. He hoped he didn't look like he had just been dancing in the barn, as ridiculous as that sounded.

As Jeb predicted, after dinner, the music began. After a couple of foot-stomping tunes, the large table was pushed aside. Gus took Meg by the hand and led her into the center of the room. Georgia and Mick followed. The couples from the stagecoach got up, too.

The fiddlers played a quadrille — at least that's what Jeb figured, since the four couples squared up into two groups. Gus and Meg looked like they were having fun. Gus's jaunty step reminded him of Bill Foster from the wagon train.

When the dance ended, the squares dissolved and the musicians began to play a slow waltz. It was obvious that Meg and Gus had waltzed together before, because

Meg grasped the cuff of his left sleeve and held it with her hand in the right position. Anyone who didn't know them would have to look carefully to see that Gus wasn't holding his dance partner's hand in his own.

Gathering his courage, when Gus and Meg came around, he tapped Gus on the shoulder. Gus turned over his partner so promptly Jeb was startled to find himself holding Meg in his arms. His heart beat so fast he feared it would mess with his counting, but somehow he managed to spin her onto the makeshift dance floor and they were on their way. The next tune was also a waltz and Meg happily agreed to remain his partner. This time, Jeb relaxed enough to enjoy the experience. He wondered if he would appear too forward if he proposed.

After the second waltz ended, Jeb escorted Meg to Gus, who had two glasses of punch waiting for them with a warning to be careful, as Angus had concocted it.

A gentleman passenger appeared in front of them and requested that Meg join him in the next dance. She politely accepted. From the side of the room, Jeb and Gus watched her form a square with an older couple.

"I can't believe you turned her down when she asked you to marry her," Jeb joked.

"It was a child's yearning to cling to the only love she could count on . . . I think she's growin' out of that, don't you?" When Jeb didn't answer, Gus nudged him with his elbow. "What are you waitin' for?"

"She comes from wealth. She may have expectations beyond my means. And, to be honest, I don't know how I stack up. She and Win got along pretty well."

"Interesting group, rich people. A lot of them act like they're better than the rest of us." Gus watched the dancers. "Meggie takes after her ma, though. Her ma was never the snooty type. She saw qualities in people that were far richer than their bank accounts."

"You thought a lot of her mother, didn't you?"

"Yep, she was fine," Gus said. He smoothed his mustache. "Now, about this business with Win. He's is a fine fellow and a good friend, Jeb. But he takes the long way home. Meggie deserves someone who's content right where he is."

"So, you think she'd say yes if I asked her to marry me?"

Gus chuckled. "I'd say your chances are pretty good. Just don't screw it up."

The storm passed and the passengers left.

Two nights later in the barn, Jeb sanded a chair leg he'd just turned on the lathe. Working with wood gave him time to mull over everything on his mind. Despite Gus's vote of confidence, he wondered about Meg's feelings for Win. They always seemed happy around each other. It bothered him.

Meg appeared at the barn door. She boosted herself up on the wall of Biscuit's stall and watched him work awhile. She said she was thinking she might make a pie, and asked if Jeb preferred one made from canned peaches or dried apples.

"The mention of any pie of yours makes my mouth water, but, if it makes no difference to you, I guess I'm partial to peach."

"Peach it is." She jumped down, but leaned against a support beam, apparently in no hurry to leave. She picked up a piece of sandpaper and began rubbing it on one of the legs.

"Here, use this." Jeb handed her a rougher textured paper. "I start with the rougher paper, then, as the wood gets smoother, I switch to this finer stuff." He showed her the difference between the papers.

Meg took the rougher paper and tried it. "Oh, I see. How do you know all of this? Did your father teach you?"

"He taught me the basics, and helped me

get started." He returned to his own work.

"Hmmm . . . I'll bet you'll be able to teach a lot to your own children someday."

Jeb stopped sanding as images of making love to Meg raced through his mind so fast that his fingers forgot to work. He felt his face burn. He resumed sanding, not knowing what else to do.

Meg turned to him, tilted her head, and sighed. "Jeb, when are you going to ask me to marry you?"

Disappointed in himself for stalling too long, Jeb put down his sandpaper and turned to face her. "I was trying to come up with something special to say. Aren't men supposed to have some poetic speech ready?"

"I think you should just ask me."

"Will you marry me, Meg?"

"Yes, I will." She smiled.

Jeb smiled back. "Well, that's good news." He thought of the question he had wanted to know the answer to before he proposed, although it was a little late now. "This is a bit backward, 'cause I should have asked you this first, but . . ."

"You want to ask me about Win."

"You're a step ahead of me, today. But yes, I do." Jeb ran his hand through his hair and leaned awkwardly against a support

343

beam. "I can deal with Win having feelings for you. Hell, I don't see how he could help himself, you being you. I can't do anything about it, but there's no point in pretending I don't see it." He looked her in the eye. "But if you have feelings for him —"

Meg held up her hand to stop him. "Win has always been in your life, and I want him to continue to be. He's a part of my life, too, just like Gus is a part of yours. Win won't come between you and me any more than Gus will. We made a pact."

"Who? You and Win?"

"The day you two left. You rode off, leaving me to say good-bye to him alone. I was a little hurt at first. I had wanted to tell you I'd be waiting for you, if you ever came to your senses, but you didn't give me a chance. Win asked me if I'd be happy married to you. I told him I would, if you ever got around to asking me."

Jeb thought back to the day he and Win parted. That sonofabitch already knew. "Am I the only one who doesn't know what's going on around here?"

"So it seems." She smiled.

"What was the pact about?"

"Just foolishness — you know Win. He made me promise to be happy; I made him promise to not be angry at you — that sort of thing. Things people say when they part ways and want no ill will between them."

Jeb nodded. He and Win had done the same thing.

"You're the one I want to marry, Jeb." Meg moved closer.

Jeb wrapped his arms around her. She responded when he kissed her and he wondered why he'd waited so long to ask for her hand.

"I'll be right proud to call you Mrs. John Edward Dawson, Jr."

Meg pulled away, her eyes opened wide. "That's your real name? John Edward?"

"Yep. Jeb is just a nickname, from my initials."

Meg furrowed her brow. "Well, then, shouldn't it be 'Jed'?"

He paused. "Yes, of course." He hadn't thought about it in years. "There's a story there. It involves Win." He waited for her reaction.

"I suspect you have a million great stories and fond memories of Win. You don't have to keep those to yourself." She grinned and spread her arms out impatiently, exactly the way Win would do. "Let's hear it!"

Meg showed no embarrassment talking about marriage — or about Win. He curbed his desire to lay her down right there in the barn. Instead, he motioned for her to sit down next to him. "My folks started calling me Jed because they'd named me after my father, and two Johns got confusing — something to keep in mind, I reckon." Meg smiled. Jeb cleared his throat and continued. "Ma didn't like 'John Junior' or 'Johnny,' so they agreed to use my initials. Win lived on the farm next to ours and before his ma died, she'd come over to visit. Win and I played together, and he just started calling me Jeb. Maybe it was easier for a little kid to say, I'm not sure. Ma liked it and started calling me Jeb, too, and it just stuck. If you ask Win, he'll take full credit."

"He would; I'm sure of it," Meg said, laughing. "I always thought it was short for Jebediah."

"Most people do." He moved close to Meg and put his arms around her.

"This is nice." She put her head on his shoulder. "You need some time to get used to the idea of being married?"

"I've given the idea considerable thought. We could go to the county courthouse in Piedmont this Friday, if you're ready."

"Sounds perfect."

Jeb laughed out loud, delighted with her candor. He promised to see that she never regretted her answer. Meg smiled, shook

her head, and replied that she hoped he'd never regret asking.

Jeb thought that was unlikely as he imagined making love to her.

her head, and he sped that she hoped he'd
never come back...

Jeb thought that was unlikely as he smiled,
tried making love to her.

CHAPTER THIRTY-SEVEN:
MEG

Dawson ranch, April 1869

"This is the most perfect and lovely porch I've ever seen," Meg said. "It's exactly right."

Meg walked back and forth across the solid flooring. The only part of their new home that she'd asked for specifically was a porch. She left the rest of the design to Jeb.

He displayed extraordinary craftsmanship and ingenuity building their home in the high meadow. The footings and load-bearing walls of stone gave strength to the core foundation upon which the rest of the structure sat. Pilings were sunk deep, extra thick planks were used for the puncheon floor and structural supports, and the roof was shingled with good cedar, laid in a pattern that ensured years of protection from leaks.

Their friends from Paradise and the hidden Arapaho village helped with construc-

tion. Blackie hewed logs for them again, stacking them like firewood for when they were ready to build the barn. Running Elk visited one day and asked Jeb to show him how to use some of the building tools. He came frequently after that and learned to lay brick straight and true, cutting the time required to build the main house in half. One by one, other members of Gray Wolf's tribe showed up to help. One Who Waits and Mick built a fine stone fireplace with good draw. When it was finished, their home was as solid as a structure could be.

Meg fell more deeply in love with her new husband every day. She loved his steady manner, and he and Gus worked well together. Jeb was strong, capable, and dependable. She trusted the man in whose arms she lay every night. From their wedding night on, he'd been more tender than she'd thought possible. She felt a burst of butterflies in her stomach at the thought of their lovemaking. And then she felt a new sensation — one Georgia had told her to expect. *Quickening,* she had called it. Meg was four months pregnant.

CHAPTER THIRTY-EIGHT: WIN

Green River City

May 25, 1869

Dear Jeb, Gus, and lovely Meg,
Yesterday, Wesley Powell and his expe-
dition left to voyage down the Green River.
I was among the well-wishers gathered at
the shore as three impressive oak vessels
launched behind one swift, pine boat, car-
rying Powell himself. Supplies and sur-
veyor instruments had been divided be-
tween the crafts so that if one should be
lost, the expedition could continue. They
have provisions for ten months; the
amount will be cut by a third each time
one of their boats succumbs to the rapids,
if such a tragedy occurs.
Major Powell has an interesting crew:
his brother accompanies him, along with
another set of brothers, the Howlands, a
few mountain men, and an Englishman. I

never learned his purpose for going along, but never asked, either, for, as Clint used to say, "If you have to ask why a man does what he does, you won't understand the answer." I think I feel most akin to a young fellow named Andy Hall. At 19 years, he is quite an oarsman — a skill that will prove vital, I am certain.

I am impressed with Wesley Powell. He has a keen scientific mind; I daresay his mind stays on task with little distraction over what most men favor, namely, fighting, drinking, and women. I do not doubt the Powell expedition will make history, should they survive, and you may wonder, since I was so driven to journey down the mighty Colorado, why I am not among those brave souls.

While wintering at the banks of the Green River, I became acquainted with a French mountain man by the name of Gabricl Bouchard. Bouchard has a Crow wife, whose name I can neither pronounce nor spell, but that means "Birds Protect Her." Bouchard calls her "Birdy." He speaks enough Crow to get by and Birdy understands French, but there is no word in any language for the anguish in her eyes when Bouchard translated the news from the telegraph office that the Union Pacific and

Central Pacific Railroads had linked at Promontory Summit. As the only other soul in town who did not whoop with joy and who despaired that a transcontinental railroad would trigger a flood of humanity pouring into the remaining open spaces, Bouchard invited me to join them traveling into Crow country. Birdy seeks the comfort of her family and Bouchard, though outwardly rough and burly, is smitten and seeks to please Birdy.

Allowing Fate to steer my ship, my course has been changed toward an adventure I believe holds greater interest for me. We are heading to the Yellowstone River valley. Bouchard told me there is nothing on Earth so beautiful, so it is obvious that he has never been to Paradise when the evening sun casts a glow of golden light on Meggie's hair, but I have decided to judge that for myself. If it is as grand as he claims, I would like to see Yellowstone Falls myself before someone tries to mine the gold from it — or charge admission, like I have heard they do at Niagara. Bouchard believes that as the gold dries up in Montana, it is only a matter of time before prospectors head south, and, once discovered, that will be the end of the Yellowstone.

If you think of me, know that I heeded Gray Wolf's warning and declined a spot on Powell's ambitious quest. Without Jeb and his trusty rope to pull me from certain death, I felt it was best to avoid water travel. Instead, I post this letter and, with a Frenchman and a Crow, head north on Hippocrates, with whom I could not have parted in any case.

It is my sincere wish that you — Jeb, Meg, and Gus — are well and happy. I think of you daily.

Win

CHAPTER THIRTY-NINE:
JEB

Dawson ranch, July 1869

From the barn, Jeb watched Meg pull onions from her garden with an introspective composure Jeb had not seen in her before. Perhaps she had come to terms with the events of the last week.

A week ago, Jeb had been walking on clouds. He was proud of how well the main house had turned out. No temporary dwelling, this sturdy brick structure would stand the test of time and see many generations raised in it. Meg was handling the pregnancy well. She glowed with good health and happiness. And, lastly, they'd acquired stud service from a fine stallion in Cheyenne. Two mares would foal in the spring. Meg declared that she had never been so content.

Their idyllic life turned dark, however.

One morning, Gus discovered Biscuit was gone from the corral. She hadn't gone far, straying to a spot under a single piñon tree on a hill not far from the meadow. They found her at the piñon tree again a few days later. This time, Jeb walked up to get her. Meg insisted on coming along. The view was spectacular.

"Well, Biscuit girl, I can see why you like it up here. It's a beautiful spot." Meg patted her neck. Biscuit tossed her head as if to agree. A breeze swirled around them, carrying a subtle scent of pine. Meg breathed deeply. The slope just above them was covered in alpine wildflowers. "I know how much you like to run, my precious Biscuit, but you know I can't ride you in my condition, don't you? Running Elk likes to ride you, though."

"He says he's never ridden a smoother animal." Jeb stroked her nose.

"Aw, you hear that, Biscuit? Running Elk loves you, too. Come on, girl, let's go get some breakfast," Meg said. They walked back to the ranch together.

A day later, Biscuit lay in her stall, and, despite their efforts, was either unable or unwilling to get up. Meg sat down with her, resting Biscuit's head on her lap. She stayed with her all day, stroking her neck. Gus and Jeb let them be, as there was no point in trying to separate the two.

In the late afternoon, when the sun's blaze

colored the air golden, Biscuit suddenly stirred. Teetering a bit, but steady enough to walk, she began to scale the hill to the lone piñon tree. Meg followed her, letting Biscuit lead. At the piñon tree, as Meg caressed her neck, Biscuit collapsed and died. In grief, Meg dropped to the ground next to her. She cradled Biscuit's head in her arms, rocking back and forth, sobbing until Jeb spotted her and ran up the hill. Gus and several Arapaho gathered around Biscuit and Meg.

The Arapaho began to chant prayers. Running Elk told Jeb that chanting creates a bridge between this world and the next. Later, when the news of Biscuit's death reached the village, Jeb heard the sound of drums.

"The drum is like a heartbeat, connecting creatures to their Creator," Running Elk had said. "It helps the departed pass into the spirit world. Those who have been loved on Earth have strong spirits. They can be heard in the wind as long as they are felt in our hearts."

The Arapaho death chant moved Jeb in a way he had never anticipated. He had to admit there was something comforting about it — something he couldn't find words to explain. He and Gus dug a grave for Biscuit under the piñon tree at Meg's request.

"What do you think about what Running Elk said . . . about the spirits in the wind and all that?" Jeb asked Gus as he drove the spade into the ground.

"I think Running Elk was able to comfort Meggie. That's all that matters."

"Do you believe it?"

"I've seen some strange things in my day; today was one of the strangest. It isn't for me to say what is and what isn't. Frankly, it brings me comfort, too, to imagine that Biscuit might have a spirit and still be with us somehow. Damn hard to say good-bye." Gus choked on his tears. He had cared for Meg's horse for years, and he undoubtedly felt the loss as much as she. Jeb gently squeezed the old man's shoulder.

Biscuit's death rubbed away some of Meg's sparkle, as Gus called it, but she said she heard the thunder of hooves in the wind, a declaration made as a matter of fact. Neither surprised nor afraid, she conceded that Gray Wolf and Running Elk opened her mind to the idea that the spirits of loved ones never leave.

Now, as Jeb watched Meg move from harvesting onions in the garden to pulling a few weeds, he wondered if marriage, pregnancy, horse ranching, or Biscuit's spirit should be given credit for the quietude in her expression.

Gus drove the buckboard wagon into the yard and straight to the barn. He pulled an envelope from his back pocket after Jeb took hold of the reins. "A letter from Win," Gus said, with the same tempered enthusiasm that Jeb felt. The supplies in the back were forgotten.

"Read it to us, will you, Jeb?" Meg said when she saw Jeb open it. She sat down on one of the porch chairs as if to make an occasion of it — as though a friend had come by to visit.

Gus joined them on the porch. Jeb lifted himself on to the porch railing and unfolded the letter. "It's two months old," Jeb said, "from May 25th." He began reading the letter.

Jeb read about Powell and his crew launching their boats, the crowd cheering and waving good-bye. Meg sighed with relief when he read that Win had decided to venture on horseback into the mountains instead of navigating the boiling river rapids. When Jeb read Win's reported description of the Yellowstone, however, he was taken aback.

". . . it is obvious that he has never been

358

to Paradise when the evening sun casts a glow of golden light on Meggie's hair . . ."

Jeb paused and cast a glance at Meg. She seemed to read his mind and had no patience for it.

"You are my husband, Jeb. If you think Win's flattery is going to turn my head and make me change my mind about you, you don't know me very well. If there's anyone who should be worried, it should be me. It sounds like he's having quite an adventure. Maybe you'll just up and leave me in this condition and go off to the Yellowstone." With an indignant huff, she folded her arms over her enlarged belly.

Jeb turned to Gus for support. Gus raised his hand in a gesture that indicated it was their argument, and to keep him out of it. Without looking at Meg, Jeb continued reading.

When he finished, they all sat in silence.

Finally, Gus slapped his hand on his thigh and stood up. "I'm glad he wrote. Good to know he didn't go down that damn fool river." He ambled off to the barn.

Meg said it was nice to hear from Win and tried to stand up, but her center of gravity had shifted and she struggled to get out of her chair. Jeb jumped down and helped her up. Once on her feet, Meg disappeared into the house without another word.

Win's letter didn't cheer up Meg as much as Jeb thought it would, and she didn't bring it up in conversation. A few weeks later, when he was working on a cradle in the barn, he broached the subject with Gus. "Meg seems a bit out of sorts." Jeb focused his attention on the detailed design he was carving on the headboard.

"That she does."

"I had hoped the baby might help ease her loss."

Without the use of both hands, woodworking had never been something Gus enjoyed, he'd told Jeb. Still, he pinned one of the cradle pieces on his lap with his stub and sanded it with care. "Meggie was always protective and nurturing with Biscuit. It's in her nature to be a good ma."

"Biscuit gave her freedom, though. She might be feeling a bit tethered right now."

Gus nodded. "It's gotta be something, carrying life inside you like that. Bound to give any intelligent creature pause. It's something to watch, a woman's belly growin' to such unnatural proportions. I imagine it feels mighty peculiar, too."

"Maybe Win's letter made her feel even more weighed down."

"I wondered if that was the thorn in your

side." Gus put his work down. "You might be interested to know that I was privy to a conversation Meggie had with Georgia last week. They were sittin' on the porch; Georgia was trying to show Meg how to knit. It didn't come easily for Meg, as you might expect. She dropped her hands to her lap in exasperation and told Georgia she felt clumsy and impatient. She said she couldn't knit, could barely cook, and didn't know a thing about babies. Georgia said some reassuring words to her, but then Meg started bawling and said something about you wanting to go off with Win because his life sounded so exciting . . ."

"I've never given her cause to think that."

"I figured so, but it's not my business what you two fight about. Georgia defended you, and said Meggie hadn't been paying attention if she thought you felt stuck. Georgia said you were a family man, not a wanderer." Gus shifted in his seat. "Meggie may not be feeling confident about her mothering skills, and she may wish she could be delivered from the load she's carrying, but that don't mean she isn't happy to be married and having your baby. She's fiercely loyal and protective, a mama bear if there ever was one. She's that kind of horse owner, that kind of friend, and that kind of wife."

Gus knew how to reassure without being condescending, and Jeb was grateful. "I guess we're all a bit nervous. I hope child-bearing comes easy for her. It isn't always."

"It's unsettling to watch, that's a fact. Mares get kind of a wild look in their eye. You ever see a woman give birth? With your pa, maybe?"

Jeb shook his head. "Sometimes Pa took me on house calls. I helped him set a broken leg and watched him stitch up plenty of wounds, but when it came to delivering babies, a wide-eyed boy wasn't welcome in the birthing room."

Gus chuckled softly. "No, I don't reckon so." He blew away the dust from the piece he was sanding and ran his hand along the smooth edge. "I've helped plenty of mares foal, but can't say that's a comforting thought for Meg. Damn glad Georgia's around."

"Amen to that."

The days passed. Late one September evening, Jeb came into the house from the barn, stamping his feet dry; the autumn rains soaked everything. Gus had gone to bed. Meg sat staring into the fire, deep in thought, a book resting on her enormous belly. Jeb noted how pretty she looked. The baby would come soon. Jeb didn't see how she could get much bigger. The thought was thrilling and terrifying at the same time.

"You look far away, Meggie."

"Come sit with me." She extended her hand out to him. He took it as he pulled up a chair and waited for her to speak. "I have a confession," she said.

Jeb hoped she wasn't about to confess something about Win. He didn't want to know if something had gone on between them. He braced himself.

"I don't think I loved you as much as I should have when we got married. I didn't love you nearly as much as I do now. Does that hurt your feelings? I don't mean it to. I'm trying to say that I feel much closer to you now."

Jeb took her hand and kissed it. "I've had those same thoughts. I look back and marvel at the leap of faith we took. It's been working out, though. I think attachment is supposed to grow over time. It's hard to imagine loving you even more than I do right now, but I think I will."

Meg brought his hand to her cheek, holding it in her two hands. He leaned over and kissed her temple. She didn't let go of his hand, and he sensed she had more to say. "If something goes wrong when I have the baby . . . I want to be buried up on the hill under the piñon tree where we buried Biscuit." She looked at him with so much disquiet, he felt a little guilty for feeling relieved to hear she was worried about dying and not confessing secrets. He'd rather soothe her fears than listen to her clear her conscience about Win.

"Meg, you're going to deliver this baby just fine." He sounded more confident than he had a right to be.

"Just promise me, please?" she asked. "I love it up there. It's so beautiful, and it would make me happy to be close to my precious Biscuit. Under the piñon tree . . . Promise?"

There was no point in arguing with her about a burial place. He looked at her solemnly. "I promise."

Meg sat back and sighed. In the middle of that cool September night, she went into labor.

It turned out that Meg's fears about dying in childbirth were unfounded. By the time she realized what was happening, it was too late for either Jeb or Gus to ride to town to fetch Georgia — not that she would have let either of them leave her in any case. Jeb watched her labor progress quickly, forced to turn the pages of the book on childbirth he'd borrowed from Dr. Miller much faster than he would have liked. Then, for a moment, Meg seemed to take on an essence for which Jeb had no words, but felt with inner clarity what others describe as a miracle. Once the baby's head appeared, Jeb helped his shoulder to slip out, and he found himself holding his newborn son. James Gustav entered the world in the late morning with little fuss, but with much relief to all adults present.

Meg said she liked Jeb's idea for a name. James was a variant of Jameson, Meg's maiden name, and Gustav just seemed right. Mother and child were tired, but fine.

Georgia arrived a few hours later for her daily visit. She walked in to find Meg with her newborn baby latched to her breast. Jeb and Gus stood by like proud sentries.

"My, but don't you two look mighty pleased with yourselves," Georgia *tsk*ed at them. "Like you're the ones who had a baby." Jeb was too elated to be hurt by Georgia's comments and attributed her harshness to disappointment that she missed the excitement.

"They deserve some credit, Georgia. I

couldn't have managed without them." Meg smiled gratefully. Jeb felt overwhelmed with strange new pride. "I'm glad you're here now, though, Georgia. I need you," Meg said, causing Georgia to shoo the men away. From the porch, Jeb heard the rustle of Georgia changing the linens while Meg asked her if James looked all right, if she was holding him right and feeding him right.

Georgia chuckled. "Honeybee, you're a natural. Look at him . . . I'd swear you both had done this before. You're doing just fine."

"You want to hold —"

"Just for a second," Georgia said before Meg finished asking the question. Jeb heard the pile of linens drop to the floor. "My, he's a handsome critter. Just look at him . . . My goodness, you and Jeb do fine work, yes-sir."

Blackie, Angus, and Mick arrived a few hours later. Angus brought a bottle of good whiskey to share and Mick brought the cap, booties, and sweater Georgia had ready to give to Meg. Blackie shyly presented Meg with a cleverly crafted toy for her baby — a gourd with dried seeds inside and covered with soft leather. Once they all caught a peek at the new baby, Georgia again shooed them away from the sleepy new mother and child.

Out on the porch, bets were settled. Blackie predicted a boy, as had Georgia, but he also won the bet that the baby would be born in early morning. He seemed particularly pleased with himself as he collected coins from everyone. All the men toasted each other with Angus's whiskey, prompting Georgia to ask out loud why men acted so victorious when it was women who deserved the credit.

"Aw, hell, Georgia, let us strut a bit. It's the closest we get to being part of a miracle." Mick sweetly pulled her into his arms and kissed her in front of the other men.

"Oh, you old coot," she chided him, blushing with pleasure. She gently and playfully slapped him on his arm. The men laughed, knowing Mick was right. Hearing the word "miracle" made them peer in through the open window to get another look at the newest one, but found both baby and mother had drifted off to sleep. Georgia whispered that they should all go home. She told Jeb she'd be back later with dinner.

After everyone left, Jeb brought the finished cradle to their bedroom. He placed it next to their bed and gently lifted sleeping James from Meg's arms. Instead of putting him directly in the cradle, he held him for a while, studying his face and watching him breathe. It was a marvel to behold — a newborn baby. Jeb wondered how he could feel so attached to something only hours old.

"You don't look like a man who'd rather be on an expedition." Meg had awakened and smiled sleepily at him. Then she noticed the cradle. "Oh, Jeb, it's beautiful." She reached down and rocked it. Perfectly balanced, it rocked smoothly back and forth.

Gus stood in the doorway. "Meggie, darlin', this is a happy day. Well done. Congratulations to you both." He came in, leaned over, and kissed Meg on the forehead.

"Having a baby is as easy as riding a horse," she joked drowsily.

"I suspect you'll be just as sore from it." Gus stroked her forehead. "You take it easy. Georgia's coming back with dinner. She'll be handy to have around for a while. You let her take care of you."

Meg nodded and fell asleep again. Gus motioned to Jeb to follow him into the kitchen, out of earshot from Meg.

"I don't want to put a mark on the day, Jeb, but I think you ought to see this." Gus pulled a page of a newspaper out of his pocket. "Mick brought this with him." He handed the newsprint to Jeb. Dated July 8, 1869, the headline read:

TWO WHITE MEN KILLED BY CROW INDIANS ON THE YELLOWSTONE

CHAPTER FORTY:
MEG

Dawson ranch, 1870–1871

Meg had not expected her world to become so small and focused with the arrival of a baby. She didn't object. James captured her heart in a way she couldn't have imagined. Even ranching held new meaning — the purpose of work no longer done for personal gratification, but to secure a good life for her child. Her new role brought surprising joy and satisfaction.

Her preoccupation with James and the ranch isolated her from the outside world, however, which was filled with turmoil. Reports from Running Elk, who visited the ranch regularly, often brought news that seemed farther away than it actually was.

The Fort Laramie Treaty of 1868, which gave back land to the Indians that had always belonged to them anyway, was no better than any other treaty. It still did not keep white people away. Prospectors tres-

370

passed into the Black Hills searching for gold. Cattlemen drove herds through land on which the buffalo were being slaughtered by the tens of thousands. Indians of all nations, living in every part of the country, were either killed or sent to reservations, where many died from malnutrition or disease. Red Cloud's supposed victory had not brought lasting peace, nor improved life.

Running Elk's older brother could not adapt to living in the mountains like the rest of Gray Wolf's clan. He took the name Warrior Who Travels Far, because he frequently left the tribe to fight with Crazy Horse, who fought in scattered raids and skirmishes, trying in vain to keep the white man out of Indian land. Sometimes Warrior Who Travels Far was gone for weeks at a time. When he returned, his stories of what was happening in the Dakotas and Wyoming unsettled Meg. His anger was hard to appease and impossible to ignore. Nor was he alone. Increasing numbers of infuriated warriors joined together.

Dissimilar worlds converged and collided as the winds of change blew. Similar views could not be found even among members of the same race. White men like John Wesley Powell wanted to study and preserve Indian culture, while others, like General

George Armstrong Custer, led campaigns to eliminate the Indian along with the buffalo. Conflict lived within the Indian community, too. Men like Gray Wolf, Sharp Eye, and Running Elk were willing to accept their white neighbors, while Warrior Who Travels Far and Crazy Horse vowed to fight to the death before conceding more land or surrendering their ways.

Not completely oblivious to the gathering political storm clouds, Meg kept an eye on the horizon for Win. They had not heard from him for some time.

Finally, Mick rode up to the ranch to deliver what they had been anxiously waiting for: a letter from Win. All work stopped as Jeb, Meg, and Gus gathered on the porch to hear the news. Mick invited himself to stay, saying he promised to report back to Georgia, Angus, and Blackie. Jeb unfolded the pages and looked at the date.

"This is seven months old, dated October 7. James was born." Jeb and Gus exchanged glances.

Meg noticed the lines on their faces relax. "What's going on? Why is that important?"

"We saw a newspaper article that said there was some trouble in Yellowstone." Gus reached over to James, sitting in Meg's lap, and squeezed his little toe. James smiled.

"What kind of trouble?" Meg asked.

Gus waved his hand to dismiss the matter. Eager to hear Win's letter, Meg didn't press.

Jeb began reading.

Dear Jeb, Gus, and lovely Meg,

Today is October 7, 1869.

I am writing this in a town that once claimed to have 67 residents, according to a badly painted sign, but now holds fewer than Paradise, if that is possible. I believe the folks who populated Lucky Strike lived in canvas homes, which they simply rolled up and took with them when they realized the town's name applied to only the initial prospector. There is one wooden structure remaining, and Bouchard, Birdy, and I are in it. It is a dismal day of steady rain, but Birdy has made a fire to dry us out. Bouchard is sound asleep and I am making use of a table and chair to write some words to you while Birdy skins a rabbit for dinner.

Do not think the bleak description above reflects my general mood. I have had an extraordinary few months. The three of us entered the Yellowstone River Valley and soon met Birdy's people. They do not have the same peaceful nature as Gray Wolf, and, at first, I was not welcome. My mistake was speaking Arapaho, thinking they would appreciate my efforts to communicate in any native tongue. I quickly learned that being white was not as serious a crime as speaking the language of their enemy. The Crow were pushed into the Yellowstone by the Lakota, who are allies of the Arapaho. Apparently, it didn't matter that white settlers are to blame for the displacement of the Lakota, who, in turn, displaced the Crow. Decades of stealing each other's horses preclude banding together against the White Invaders, as Bouchard calls us. Regardless, in the end, Birdy came to my rescue. Women hold higher status among the Crow than they do in other tribes. That she married a white man did not send her away from her people in shame, but rather forced them to accept Bouchard, and, by extension, me.

Once we gained their acceptance, we explored such places as I've never seen elsewhere. Bubbling mud pots, water spouts shooting into the air from underground, and hot springs are unusual and spectacular phenomena, but what I have seen before of trees, rock formations, waterfalls, and wildlife are put together in such a way that inspires awe and leaves me without words to do justice to its beauty. I cannot imagine how anyone who sees such splendor can remain unmoved by the experience.

We came upon a trio of explorers mapping the area. Two are boyhood friends, and the other is a Dane they met in Diamond City. You would think the Dane — Peterson by name — would be the odd man out, but he had the right combination of good sense and good humor to be excellent company for them both.

While they were fine fellows, it worries me greatly that this magnificent country will be so advertised that soon it will be overrun by crowds of visitors, who will trample down the very vistas they hope to see. At any rate, they returned to Diamond City and, once we had parted, I regretted not taking time to write so I could send a letter with them. As it is, I must entrust this letter to a gentleman who calls himself Theed (or Seed, or possibly Teed — it is difficult to understand the poor fellow, as he has no teeth). He assures me he is headed for civilization, however, and will post this when he can.

I am not sure what the winter months hold for me. Be assured that I am in good *company and have good health. I will write again when I have the opportunity, although mail service among the Crow is a humorous image to hold in one's mind. If this letter does reach you, please know that my adventures come second to the affection I hold for you all,*

Win

"Well, I'll be," Mick said. "That Win, he's an interesting fella, making friends with the Crow. I always thought they were an ornery bunch. Well, if you don't think me rude, I'd better git. Georgia'll tan my hide if I don't get back with the news. For once, Angus'll be the last one to know!"

"Good seein' you, Mick." Gus rose and stepped off the porch with him. "You tell Georgia to come along next time. We don't want to lose you to her wrath." Gus and Mick exchanged pleasantries as Mick tightened his cinch strap and mounted his horse.

Alone with Meg, Jeb stared at the letter. "The man is still in love with you, Meg. I thought he'd have moved on by now."

"Oh, for heaven's sake, are we going to argue every time we hear from Win?" Meg sighed in exasperation.

"Well, he and I sure never used the word 'affection' in reference to *each other*!"

"Jeb, Win closed his letter with kind words to us all. Can't you hear it? He wants to be in the Yellowstone, not here. But he also wants to share it with us. He doesn't love me the way we love each other. I don't love him the way I love you." She reached for his hand. "You have to believe that, or every time he writes, we're going to fight! I expect you to rise above this silly jealousy. He needs you, Jeb, far more than he needs me." Meg leaned back in her chair. "I suspect you're more annoyed with him because he's caused you so much worry. You didn't tell me about the news story you and Gus saw."

Jeb swept James into his arms and tossed him gently in the air. James giggled. Cradling their son, Jeb turned to Meg. "Jealousy is not becoming in a man. I apologize."

"Particularly when there are no grounds for it." She smiled. "You are forgiven."

Two weeks later, Georgia and Mick rode up to the ranch together. Meg's new icebox had arrived, so instead of waiting for Jeb to come by and get it, they thought they would take a pleasant drive up to visit and bring it along. Besides, they were eager to hear more news. They pulled their wagon into the yard, smiling from ear to ear. Georgia waved another letter from Win.

Once settled on the porch, Georgia took

James from Meg and covered him with kisses.

"When was this one written, Jeb?" Meg asked and then turned to Georgia. "His last one was seven months old!"

"See? I told you!" Mick pointed his finger at Georgia. "She didn't believe me!"

"Oh, for heaven's sake. It's ridiculous for a letter to take so long in this day and age." She bounced James on her knee and his delighted gurgle carried away her grumpiness.

"This one's dated April 10th," Jeb said, "only two months ago. Win must have found a more reliable postal courier."

He seated himself on the porch railing and read the letter aloud:

Dear Jeb, Gus, and lovely Meg,
Today is April 10, 1870.
I hope this letter finds you in good health.
Over the winter, we had the pleasure of running into our friend Albert Rothenberg. He was very happy to see us because when Bouchard and I found him he was bound to a tree, looking mighty miserable. He was a prisoner at a Crow village, unable to convey to them that he had come in peace. You can just imagine the look of surprise on his face when Bouchard and I

378

arrived. He immediately called out to me and nearly wept with relief when we asked that his life be spared and the Crow reluctantly slit his bindings.

The Crow soon forgot their aggression toward him and instead became intrigued with his wine-stain birthmark, which they saw once he removed his hat to wipe away the nervous sweat from his forehead. It made for an interesting communal experience; one of Birdy's uncles had a similar birthmark on his stomach, and her family considered him to have special gifts because of it. I cannot say what gifts he supposedly had, as the word for "magic" has a variety of meanings, but Rothenberg's status was elevated to a white person unsuitable to slay, and we left it at that.

When it appeared that Rothenberg would live through dinner after all, he calmed down considerably and was finally able to ask, "How is our Miss Jameson? I half expected to see her walk into camp as well." To his pleasure, I produced ~~your~~ Meg's photograph. He was overjoyed upon seeing it and said, "Ah, Miss Jameson, what a delightful creature." He got no argument from me.

Finding Rothenberg turned out to be invaluable for us. He was on his way to

Helena when he was detained by the Crow. The three men we met last year — Bill Peterson, Charley Cook, and Dave Folsom — generated interest in the area, as predicted. General Henry Washburn, the Surveyor General for Montana Territory, is gathering support for a second expedition into the Yellowstone using maps and information from Cook and Folsom, who works in Washburn's office. With a good word from Rothenberg, I feel I might find a spot on this crew. Albert and I send our kindest regards to all, as does Gabriel Bouchard. After listening to the two of us talk about the residents of Paradise, he feels kinship toward you as well.

Win

Gus slapped his knee contentedly. "Good for him. He sure had an itch when that Rothenberg fella came through here. I hope he gets a spot."

"Some of his stories sound like close calls," Meg said. "I worry sometimes."

"Win's been living off his wits and charm all his life. Believe me, he's fine." Jeb sounded a bit perturbed. No one mentioned that Rothenberg had referred to Meg as Miss Jameson and not Mrs. Dawson, and that, apparently, Win hadn't bothered to

380

correct him. She wondered if there was any other reason for Jeb's crankiness.

"James, you are growing like a weed." Georgia bounced James on her lap while the others looked on. "How've you been feeling, honeybee?" she asked Meg, who was pregnant again.

Meg said she was tired, but otherwise fine. As they all turned their attention to James, Meg's thoughts turned to Win, and she imagined him on that warm summer evening, making camp with the Crow.

The Dawsons had another good harvest in the fall and the following February, Charles Winston was born. Meg delivered so quickly that again, Georgia missed the birth, but came anyway to help with James and see the new baby. Jeb wanted to name him after Meg's father and give him "Winston" for a middle name. Meg hesitated, asking if Jeb wouldn't prefer to give his son a name from his side of the family. He reminded her that they were already Dawsons, which gave him more pride and satisfaction than he'd ever imagined possible. Since he seemed to have resolved whatever jealousy he felt toward Win, she agreed.

In mid-June, Gus delivered two saddle-ready geldings to a nearby rancher and returned with a mysterious sack. He was grinning ear to ear as he dismounted and gently pulled the big burlap sack off the back of his saddle.

"Got a surprise for you, James." Gus laid the wiggling, yipping bundle gently on the ground. Two yellow pups tumbled out. "Got one for you, and one for your brother. You're gonna have to take care of 'em both 'til Charlie's old enough. Can you do it?"

James wasn't yet two years old and stared blankly at Gus. Meg, holding Charlie in her arms, raised her eyebrows in doubt. Gus looked at the child's mother with pleading eyes.

"I'll help him a little. Their names are Billy and Buddy. Is it a deal?"

Meg laughed. "How can I say no to that?"

Gus pulled a wad of cash from the horse sale from his pocket and handed it to Meg as he sat down with James and the pups. They all scrambled over to him, vying for his lap. Jeb came over from the barn and knelt down to play with the pups as well. Gus reached into his back pocket and pulled out a letter from Win. Meg cried out in surprise; it had been almost a full year since they had heard anything. Jeb opened it and scanned it quickly.

"He's all right," Jeb said. Meg sighed with

relief. "He wrote it only two weeks ago."

Dear Jeb, Gus, and lovely Meg,

Today is June 1, 1871.

I hope this letter finds my dear family in good health and prosperity.

You will undoubtedly read about the Hayden expedition in the news, the first federally funded geological survey of the Yellowstone. While the man in charge gets the recognition by having the expedition named after him, you should know that he is one soul among thirty-two who are along to facilitate the operation. I am one of those souls as well.

Our purpose is to further survey and document features of the region. Along on this expedition are a couple of well-known names — Wm. Jackson, the photographer, and Thomas Moran, artist. Lieutenant Doane, who I met last year, is heading our military escort. While the presence of the military often attracts the very problems they are hired to protect the surveyors from, he is a fine chap. He grew up out here and possesses natural frontiersman qualities. A superb horseman and excellent shot, he won over the Crow guides with his capabilities. There is a botanist, a topographer, a meteorologist, an ornitholo-

gist and mineralogist, and an entomologist and physician. Nearly all of them have at least one assistant. I counted twenty-seven horses and twenty-one mules in the remuda, and five wagons and two ambulances are packed and ready with food, tents, and stoves to keep us comfortable. There is also a good supply of instruments — I learned how to use a clinometer, which measures the angle of a slope, and there are enough sextants and compasses with which to circumnavigate the world.

The whole operation is directed by Jim Stevenson, a fine fellow, as is the wagon master, Ben Hovey. Jeb, you would like them both. In my experience, good trail bosses tend to be the most down-to-earth folks around. Their judicious minds and steady demeanors serve a traveling party well, and these gentlemen are fine examples. Their objectives are transparent and straightforward, something I cannot say about a handful of the participants accompanying Dr. Hayden. Scientific research is the overt objective, but now that I have spent some time with some of Dr. Hayden's associates, I wonder to what end the research is for. So far, Hayden believes there is nothing in Yellowstone of any practical value, such as extractable minerals or usable timber. He maintains the only value is esthetic. Someone in the party said the area should be kept from human access in order that it remains in its pristine, untouched state. Another mentioned he hoped to find a good spot for a hotel, as the area would soon boom with tourism. The first fellow made me laugh, since numerous tribes have lived here for centuries, but the second fellow made my heart ache with loss and sadness. I wonder what conclusions will be drawn from this endeavor and what will become of Yellowstone once it has been thoroughly studied. While admittedly eager for the adventure, I am keeping a cautious eye on what comes from it all.

I am signed on as a guide and hunter. The other hunter, José, and I are in the good graces of both cooks, knowing from experience that they can be some of the most important, yet unrecognized, contributors to a successful mission. In addition to hunting, I was told I will be called upon to communicate with Indians if necessary. I am becoming more proficient in Crow and French, but I pray any conversation does not become too sophisticated. By the way, Bouchard found he had no patience for scientists, preferring sensual rather

385

than cerebral company. He and Birdy have disappeared, as I expected. I understand and even envy him to a certain extent. We parted amicably and I hope we will meet again.

We are stopped at an outpost not unlike Paradise to assemble before heading into the Yellowstone River valley. Due to the terrain, I imagine we will set up a base camp where our wagons can rest on level ground and the scientists will venture on foot to complete their work. If there is opportunity to write again, I will. There is good traffic back and forth, as specimens are sent back regularly. I should dearly love to send an order for one of Meg's peach pies. It would be a welcome surprise to emerge from one of the resupply crates, but, as it is, I must simply savor the memory.

I think of you all every day and hope you are well,

Win

Meg waited for Jeb to meet her gaze. She then smiled and said, "We are . . . well and happy."

CHAPTER FORTY-ONE: WIN

En route to Dawson ranch, 1873

Win rode south. Hippocrates stepped lively, with renewed energy, as though he recognized his surroundings.

It had been four years since Win and Jeb escorted Major Powell into the mountains; four years since Win had asked Meg if she would be happy married to Jeb. Much had happened.

Win had written to announce he was coming for a visit, asking if they would welcome a weary traveler. He made his letter sound lighthearted, but, in truth, he had been away far too long and needed to replenish his soul. He needed Meg. He wanted to see Jeb, too, and to be around people who loved and accepted him.

During the four years Win had been gone, Powell had taken his crew down the Colorado River and not only lived to tell about it, but was famous for it. Passing interest in the American West had turned to obsession by many, with competing interests. As Rothenberg had predicted, exploration of the territory became a government priority. By 1872, Yellowstone became a national park, and four large, federally funded surveys were being simultaneously conducted.

Powell obtained funds from both the Smithsonian Institution and the government to lead a second expedition, the Geographical and Topographical Survey of the Colorado River of the West. Primarily interested in geology and ethnology, he investigated the problem of aridity and human adaption in desert lands. Win still believed Powell to be the most sympathetic to the native inhabitants, and acutely aware of long-standing cultures disappearing.

Clarence King continued to lead the 40th Parallel Survey, the survey Win first read about in the newspaper while still driving freight. King's crew examined the geological features and natural resources across a band of land between the 105th and the 120th meridians.

Congress granted George Montague Wheeler $75,000 to map the area west of the 100th meridian on a scale of eight miles to the inch, a task expected to take fifteen years to complete. Wheeler's purpose was pragmatic, as his maps would be used for settlement. They would aid the first steps toward building roads and railroads for transportation, and dams and irrigation that would enhance agricultural development. The quietest, least talked about of the four giants, Wheeler's survey was supported by the war department, which made Win increasingly uneasy.

Ferdinand Hayden, geologist-in-charge of the United States Geographical and Geological Survey of the Western Territories, searched for deposits of oils, coals, clay marls, and other mineral substances. His reports of his expeditions to Nebraska and adjacent territories — southern and eastern Utah, southern and eastern Wyoming, the upper Yellowstone, and eastern Montana — opened the Great Plains in a way no militia could. But Win wondered at the price being paid. Yellowstone National Park was an example of the dilemma.

While Win approved of preserving Yellowstone from development, he was appalled to discover it meant preserving it for the recreation of white Americans only. Indians were not allowed to live within the park's borders. *Can you believe the irony?* Win had written in one of his letters. *I am so frustrated and torn between the marvels of discovery and the subsequent exploitation that comes from it. I find myself increasingly at odds with those I initially held in high regard.*

He was equally enraged by Hayden's Nebraska report, in which Hayden advised that the Great Plains were not the "Great American Desert," but a richly endowed region, in which even the Sandhills of Nebraska would "yet become a fine pasture ground for herds of sheep, cattle, and horses." *Then why not let the buffalo graze and the Indians hunt on it, then?* Win wrote with derision.

Win became increasingly critical of the people and politics shaping the country. The appointment of Francis Walker to the position of superintendent of Indian affairs disappointed him deeply. When he discovered that Walker agreed with President Grant that all Indians should be secured on barren reservation land that had no mineral or agricultural value, an enraged Win wrote to Jeb:

How can a man who is so deluded as to call the Indian "lazy and cowardly in battle" be qualified to address their needs with the judiciousness they deserve? If Crazy Horse decides to challenge this ludicrous directive, I will be with them. Those with whom I felt initial alliance, those whose purpose I thought was to protect the wilderness from exploitation, have now become my enemies. I should have known that even scientists, though they understand the natural world far better than the average person, are naïve when it comes to politics and are coldly indifferent to the impact their research has had on the peoples originally living here.

Win and Hippocrates loped past the entrance to a farm lined with a row of lilac bushes. He hadn't seen lilacs in years, but remembered them from Rockfield. Every farm had them and their scent filled the air. He rode up to the house; a middle-aged woman came out and stood on the porch, wiping her hands on her apron.

"What can I do for you, mister? There's no job for you here."

Aware that his wild appearance might frighten her, Win held up his hand. "Not looking for one. I just stopped to admire your lilacs, ma'am. They remind me of home."

"That's why we planted them. They smell pretty, at least when in bloom, and are as tenacious as weeds."

"I wonder if I might buy one from you.

I'm going home to visit my family. Lilacs would be a nice addition to their garden. I'll dig it up myself and promise to be careful."

She sized him up from top to bottom, looking wary, but decided in his favor. "Tell you what, if you dig up both of those on that end, and these two here, they're yours." She pointed to bushes that, if culled, would clean up her hedgerow nicely. "I'll give you some burlap to wrap the roots. Just dunk the bag every time you pass a stream and they should make it. You going far?"

"Paradise."

"Oh, they'll make it just fine. Plenty of streams, and, like I said, they're tenacious. Can't hardly kill 'em."

Several hours later, Win was back on the road, dragging a makeshift travois with more lilac bushes than he had intended. But it was worth the extra work. After he thinned her lilacs, she asked if he would climb up on her roof and patch a spot that leaked last time it rained. He agreed, and when he climbed down from the repaired roof, she handed him a bar of soap and a razor and suggested that he scrape some of that wilderness off him and spruce himself up before his visit. She even gave him a haircut and a new shirt as payment for his help, saying that if he was going home, he should arrive presentable.

Win bypassed the town of Paradise itself. He'd see everyone eventually. He found Jeb in a high meadow at the corner of their property, constructing a stone pillar to mark the boundary. Hippocrates whinnied at the sight of Galen. Jeb looked up as Win picked his way down a steep slope.

Jeb greeted him the same way he had years ago when Win returned after his parents' deaths. Jeb's inability to hold a grudge was one of his better qualities, yet it still surprised Win to be greeted so warmly.

"Win, you old outlaw." Jeb's handshake turned into a bear hug. "By God, it's good to see you."

"Likewise, partner. It's good to be home."

"I'm glad you let us know you were coming. We've all been higher than kites since we got your letter. It's been far too long."

"I was beginning to wonder if I could find my way back." Win looked around.

"I never doubted you could. You've been making love to my wife through those damn letters of yours for years. You were probably hoping I'd be out of the picture by now. I should break your jaw right here."

Win threw his head back and laughed. "My letters annoyed you, eh? All written

393

with innocent good humor in mind, my friend. Hell, look what I brought — lilac bushes! What does that tell you? I've accepted the fact that you two are an old married couple. Why, a row of lilac bushes is as domestic as you can get!"

Jed looked at the bundles. "She'll love them."

"Will she forgive me for staying away for so long?"

"You're talking about Meg. What do you think?"

"The Meg I knew was a forgiving woman."

"She still is," Jeb said as he scraped the remaining cement from the bucket and tossed the trowel back in it. "C'mon. Let's celebrate you home." With bucket in hand, Jeb jumped on Galen and they started for the ranch.

As they rode to the house, Win felt the years fall away. Jeb asked him how long he could stay. Win replied he could probably stay a fortnight, if they could tolerate him that long. Jeb said they'd have plenty of time to ride up and see Gray Wolf. Win thought that was a grand idea. Win saw the piñon tree up on the hill and grave marker for Biscuit and for the baby Meg lost — a girl. Win had had a vision of Meg sitting on the porch with a teenaged girl. He'd had the vision several times, and wondered if he had seen the future. He thought about telling Jeb about it, as a way to offer comfort.

"Meg says she wants to be buried under that piñon tree," Jeb said.

"Hmm . . . I'm sorry about the baby. I know this sounds strange, but I think you're going to have a girl yet, I really do."

Jeb smiled. "Are the spirits telling you that? Do you hear them, too? Meg swears she hears things up here."

Win raised his eyebrows and looked around. "Maybe. You never know."

They came around a corner and stopped to take in the view of the Dawson homestead below. Their sturdy brick home, two stories tall and positioned perfectly in the meadow, looked like it had always been there. It fit. Smoke rose from the stone fireplace in the kitchen at the back of the house. Meg chased a little blond-headed boy through the garden in front. He squealed with delight as she swept him up in her arms and spun around. A breeze carried his giggle up the hill to them.

Win stared, taking it all in. From Jeb's letters — written with faithful regularity to the Diamond City post office, where Win passed through when he could — he knew Meg was a mother, the mother of Jeb's two boys. But until now, it hadn't completely registered. How long had he been gone? Gus came out of the barn and saw the men. He must have said something to Meg, because she turned then and eased the boy gently down to the ground, peering up the hill. Win could tell the moment she recognized him. Just as she had done years ago when they first brought Gus to the old way station in Paradise, she picked up her skirts and ran full speed toward them, shouting his name with such excitement it made his heart pound. Years and children had slowed her a little, but she was still surprisingly fast. And typical for her, she was covered in dirt, having just wrestled a toddler out of a garden. Win jumped down and Meg flew into his arms. He held her tightly, finally experiencing what he'd dreamt about since the day he left. He longed to kiss her passionately and for her to kiss him with equal fervor, but he knew it wouldn't happen. She was happy to see him, but she was happily married. She kissed him quickly on his lips with the same affection she showed Gus. Then she tucked her head into his chest and hugged him tightly.

Jeb looked on, a man at peace, a man without envy. As they walked to the house, Win held her hand. He felt the wedding ring on her finger and his heart broke just a little. He squeezed her hand, privately, wondering if she would pull it away. She smiled at him, openly took his hand in both of hers, and squeezed back. There was nothing secretive about being happy to see him. His heart sank — unwarranted, but it sank nonetheless.

Gus strode over as they entered the yard, two little boys and two dogs in a jumbled mess behind him. "Damn good to see you, Win." Gus stuck his hand out and slapped Win on the shoulder with his stump.

"Same here, Gus." Win shook hands with the old man warmly. Then Win knelt down to be eye level with Meg's boys. James was four years old and had Jeb's sand-colored hair and build. He would be tall and strong someday. Charlie had Jeb's build, too, but Meg's coloring. He had his mother's playful eyes, and they sparkled. Win pushed his hat back and took a long look at them both.

"You boys know who I am?" He wondered if he should have asked the question. He might have set himself up for disappointment if they had never heard of him.

"Sure we do." James stood next to Charlie, who only stared in silence. "You're our Uncle Win." Charlie nodded his head in agreement, not taking his eyes off Win.

Win's eyes stung, moved by the warm reception. To regain his composure, he stuck his hand out to shake with James, who shook it as hard as the four-year-old was capable. "C'mon, Charlie, do like I did," James said to his brother, who shyly held out a sticky little hand. "We's best friends, too, Charlie and me." James put a protective arm over his brother's shoulder.

"Well done, boys. Now, before we get to celebrating, we've got a job to do. Your Uncle Win brought your ma some lilac bushes, and we've got to figure out a place for them. C'mon." Jeb led the horses to the barn. Gus and the boys — plus the dogs — trailed after him, leaving Win and Meg standing alone together.

He turned to her and grinned. "Look at you, all grown up with a passel of kids." He kept a teasing tone in his voice, but in truth, he wanted to tell her that he thought about her all the time, that he regretted giving her up so easily to Jeb, and that there wasn't a day that went by that he didn't dream about riding up to their ranch and having her run out to greet him like she had just done.

"They are my life, Win. Life changes when babies come."

"I expect so." He looked at her carefully. "Motherhood suits you. You look wonderful, Meg."

She brushed the dirt from her apron and tried to tame the loose strands blowing about her face, but succeeded only in bringing the dirt from her apron up to her hair. "Oh, Win." She sounded as though she doubted his words. Then she lifted her chin to look him in the eye. "Why did you stay away so long?"

Much had happened in the few years he'd been away. Meg looked the same, but she was indeed a completely different person now, with children and Jeb and Gus to look after. He couldn't help but feel a little ache remembering the carefree days from their past, when she would ride out to greet them as they drove their freight wagon into Paradise. He saw her in his mind's eye — Biscuit loping toward them, Meg smiling broadly. He cleared his throat. "Didn't want to come back a failure."

"You think your success is all we care about?"

Before Win could answer, Jeb had already emerged from the barn. He held up a lilac bush and called to Win good-naturedly, "Are you going to help us plant these or just stare at my pretty wife?" James dragged a shovel across the yard following Gus, who had Charlie in tow. The dogs romped and barked alongside, excited by all the activity.

Win spread his arms out. "Stare at your pretty wife, of course!" But Meg started to walk toward Jeb, so he followed.

After some discussion as to their best location, they planted the lilac bushes at the sunny southeast corner of the house, in a fertile garden bed next to the porch. As they dug the holes and dropped the bushes in them, Meg held Charlie against her like a shield. He eventually squirmed, however, when it was time to water the plants, as he could see mud in his future and didn't want to miss it. Meg let him go, but crossed her arms over her chest as though protecting her heart. At least, Win imagined that was what she was doing.

After dinner and the boys were in bed, the adults sat on the porch well into the night, enjoying the comfortable evening air. Meg asked Win to tell them about his travels.

"The West is so filled with surveyors that they're bumping into each other. This last summer, Hayden and Wheeler met at the Arkansas River. Can you imagine? Congress is funding King, Hayden, Powell, and Wheeler — all of them! I wonder who is keeping track of it all. There's a fair amount of overlap." Win stretched comfortably. "I had the interesting experience of meeting Clarence King, the geologist exploring along the 40th parallel. He's younger than Hayden or Powell, and dresses rather impractically, but was a great storyteller for the two nights I stayed in their camp. He and his best friend, James Gardiner, struck out much the same way the two of us did a few years ago, Jeb. They made their way to San Francisco, where King was able to convince someone to make him an unpaid assistant geologist on the California State Geological Survey. His rose up the ranks quickly, obviously."

"Are you rising up in the ranks?" Jeb leaned on the porch railing.

Win laughed. "Nah. I'm too irritating."

"The paper said that the 3rd US Cavalry escorts Wheeler's bunch. You ever have Indian trouble?" Gus asked.

"Well, the cavalry can be a comforting presence to some, but truthfully, I think they bring more harm than good. It causes Indians to wonder about the motives of the expedition. Too many uniforms and it starts to look like a military campaign. And there have been plenty of those."

"I read General Custer was sent into the Yellowstone to clear out the Indians. Have you ever seen him?" Gus asked.

Win shook his head. "Been able to avoid him. Can't say what I'd do if I ran into him, to be honest. The man carries out orders with voracity beyond mere obedience. His life will not end well."

"You know that if you fight with the Indians against the military, it will be considered treason, and they'll hang you, don't you?" Jeb leaned forward, being practical as always.

Resting comfortably on the chair, Win raised both hands as if to surrender. "I have no wish for death, or bloodlust. Last time I faced my own mortality, I was face to face with a Shoshone with a knife in his hand —"

"Oh!" Meg cried. "Maybe I don't want to hear your stories, Win! I can't bear to hear about hangings or knife fights."

"My apologies, Meggie. Not another word on the subject."

"I worry about you enough as it is. When Jeb reads your letters to us, you sometimes sound so angry and frustrated."

"Maybe it's Jeb who's angry and frustrated reading them." Win grinned at Jeb.

Meg shook her head. "You know what I mean. We sympathize with you, but . . ."

"Your opinions are getting more and more radical," Jeb said.

"A man starts leaning so hard to one side, he's likely to tip over," Gus said.

Win chuckled. "That's why I came home, Gus. I needed some of your philosophy — and Meg's peach pie — to bring me back to center." With that, he reached over to the pie plate and helped himself to the last slice. As he did, the amulet he wore around his neck, which was given to him by a northern Arapaho chief named Black Coal, fell out of hiding beneath his shirt. He tucked it away without a word about it, and instead complimented Meg on her baking skills.

The next morning, Win slept in and shuffled sleepily into an empty kitchen. He peered out the window. The dogs were sitting attentively outside the hen house, so Win figured Gus must be inside collecting eggs. James was undoubtedly with him. From the side window and through the open barn door, he caught a glimpse of Meg's skirt. She must be milking the cow. A few bits of hay fell out of the hayloft above. Jeb must be up there. A bucolic scene — white settlers living their lives in peace. How different it looked through the eyes of the Indian, who watched helplessly as their land disappeared. How different from the point of view of the railroad men, who wanted to conquer nature as an enemy, or fleshy, pasty politicians, who drew lines on a map to declare what was theirs. Win poured himself a cup of coffee, sat down at the kitchen table, and pondered the complicated mess. Charlie appeared at the doorway.

The boy padded in and climbed up on a chair at the head of the table without a word. He looked as if he had dressed himself. Barefoot, his pants were held up by only one button, and his shirt was buttoned wrong, so that his collar was askew. He yawned, but focused his attention on the bread and preserves on the table.

"Mornin'," Win said when Charlie glanced up briefly, rubbing the sleep from his eyes.

Charlie reached across the table and pulled closer the plate of fresh bread and the bowl of preserves. He took a slice of bread and laid it on the table. Grabbing a spoon tightly, he clumsily scooped out a big dollop of preserves. It landed on the table, so he pushed the preserves back into the spoon with his hands. Once the sticky mess was finally on the bread, he abandoned the spoon and spread the preserves with his fingers. Then he folded the bread and took a large bite, chewing thoughtfully. A glob of preserves dripped out the end of the folded bread, landing on the table. Charlie put his lips to the table and sucked up the preserves with a loud slurp. Then he grinned broadly at Win, who couldn't hold back a chuckle.

Charlie finished off his breakfast and then, face and hands covered with preserves, climbed down from his chair and disappeared outside.

Moments later, Gus opened the door for James, who carried a basket of eggs to the sink and ran back outside. Gus grabbed the back of the chair where Charlie had just eaten. His hand landed in the smear of preserves. He swore quietly under his breath.

"I reckon Charlie's up." Gus wet a rag and calmly wiped up the sticky mess. "Takes after his ma," Gus said, giving him a resigned but knowing look. Win could not suppress his laughter. Gus then asked a question that sobered him quickly. "That talisman around your neck . . . where'd it come from?"

"It's a long story."

"Is the short version that you've taken sides?"

"I'm no fool, Gus."

Gus squinted at Win, unconvinced.

CHAPTER FORTY-TWO:
JEB

Dawson ranch, during Win's visit, 1873

The sun was barely brightening the eastern sky when Meg whispered into Jeb's ear. He smiled at her suggestion before even fully awake. When he opened his eyes, he saw her smiling back at him in the dim light. Silently they dressed and slipped out of the house and climbed into the hayloft, where they made love. Afterward, they lay wrapped in each other's arms and listened to the first stirrings of the morning.

"That was a nice surprise." Jeb smoothed Meg's hair.

"I wanted you to know where my heart is."

"I know where your heart is, Meggie."

"Good." She looked up at him, grinning. "Just so we're clear."

"You made it crystal clear, although if you'd like to reassure me again —"

The barn door opened, startling them

both. They jumped up, rustling the hay. "I hope that's you two up there and not some varmint I gotta shoot," Gus said. "Don't mind me; I'm just lettin' the horses out."

Meg laughed. "We're coming down, Gus. I'll milk Sadie." They dressed quickly and, with one more kiss, separated to do their daily chores.

Meg's soft skin and her bold act lingered in Jeb's thoughts, alleviating any concern that her heart could ever be wooed away from the life they'd built together at their ranch. She was content.

He finished his chores quickly when he saw Gus with a basket of eggs. Breakfast would be ready soon, and he was starving.

CHAPTER FORTY-THREE: MEG

Dawson ranch, during Win's visit, 1873

Meg finished milking and breezed into the kitchen with a full pail, an area on her bloomers wet with sex and sticking to the inside of her thigh. She surprised Gus and Win sitting at the table, deep in conversation.

When Gus saw her, he stood up abruptly. "Charlie's up . . . got breakfast himself."

Meg sighed, deposited the pail on the table, and left, glad for an excuse to leave. She wondered if her romp in the hay with Jeb would show on her face. She didn't know if Win would feel free to tease her about marital relations.

She found Charlie playing in the dirt. He allowed himself to be swept up and carried into the kitchen. Holding the boy over the sink, she rinsed him off, an action routine for them both.

"Charlie, honey, next time offer something

to eat to our guest first." She dried his hands with her apron and buttoned his shirt properly, smiling at her beautiful boy.

Charlie furrowed his brow and looked at Win, crinkling his nose in confusion. He pointed to Win. "Fammy."

"That's right, partner. I am family. You remind your ma." Win chuckled.

Charlie got a kiss on his forehead from his mother and a sigh. "You're right; I stand corrected."

Gus plucked a piece of straw from Meg's hair before he took the boy's hand. "C'mon, Charlie boy . . . let's go find James and your pa and tell 'em breakfast is about ready." He walked out the door, leaving Meg alone with Win in the kitchen.

Only then did it register that she'd interrupted their conversation. "What were you and Gus — ?"

"Your boys are great, Meg. The younger one's a little sticky, but great."

"They are my life." She watched out the window as her boys trailed after Gus, headed for the barn. "I lost one, Win; a little girl." She wasn't sure why she revealed something so painful and personal.

"Jeb told me. I'm sorry."

Meg looked past the barn to the piñon tree on the hill. "There are pieces of my

409

heart buried up there, under that piñon tree. Someday, all of me will be up there, too. I told Jeb that's where I want to be buried, next to my baby girl and Biscuit."

"Maybe you'll have a girl yet."

Meg wondered if she and Jeb had just made a baby. The idea made her smile. "Maybe so." She turned from the window. "Will you slice more bread while I fry the eggs?"

"Absolutely! Holding something soft and warm will remind me of holding you."

Meg shook her head in exasperation, but laughed. She broke the eggs into the frying pan. "Those lilac bushes are so beautiful, Win. They're just perfect for that side of the house. Thank you so much."

"Well, what can I say? I see something beautiful, and it reminds me of you."

"Win . . ." she said, this time adding a warning tone to her voice.

"Aw, hell, Meggie, don't fret. Jeb knows I'm madly in love with you — it's no secret."

Before she could respond, the family descended upon them and another conversation ended unfinished. It seemed to be the case with Win. Meg served the crew with the efficiency of a station keeper while Win told the boys the story of the time she was recognized from her racing days.

"Wow . . ." James whispered, with awe and admiration in equal parts. Charlie whispered an identical exclamation, although Meg doubted he understood the story — he often mimicked his brother.

"It was a long time ago, James," his mother said.

"Not that long," Gus and Win said in unison. Only Jeb seemed to understand how long ago it really was.

Chapter Forty-Four: Win

Dawson ranch

The day's work complete, Meg sat next to Win on the porch. James and Charlie played at her feet. A breeze swirled around them, and for a moment, Win imagined himself married to Meg and felt at peace. "This is heaven," he said to no one in particular.

"Agreed," Jeb said. He and Meg looked at each other and smiled.

His fantasy shattered, Win closed his eyes to hide his jealousy. "I think I'll run up to see Gray Wolf tomorrow."

"Want company?" Jeb asked. "We could all go — make a day of it."

"Nah. I need a break from this infuriating happiness." Win opened his eyes, picked up Charlie, and held him upside down and face to face. He grinned and Charlie giggled, obviously delighted to be infuriatingly happy.

Meg sent fresh gingerbread with Win the

next day, along with an invitation to come for a visit soon to see the new foals. It was a romantic ideal that such different cultures could live peacefully side by side. It would stagger the mind of someone like General Custer to see the warm relations between the two families. Sadly, just months earlier, Custer led a campaign to hunt down Sioux in the Yellowstone and exterminate them. Win didn't know how to stop the madness.

Gray Wolf welcomed Win with pleasure. He motioned for Win to join him at his fire while he produced and lit a pipe. He smoked his pipe first, and then passed it to Win. When they had smoked a while, he pointed to the amulet. "My runners tell me you twice warned our people of soldiers coming. Tell me the story behind the markings. Some are new to me."

"I rode into Powder River country, once to a Lakota village in the area you call the Greasy Grass, and later to a small Arapaho camp on the Yellowstone, to warn the people that soldiers were coming. The first warning came with enough time for everyone to disappear into the canyon, but, the second time, the soldiers were close and the people barely made it across the river, which was high from the spring melt.

"Two children had wandered off before

the frenzied escape. Their mothers couldn't find them. I stayed behind, unsaddled Hippocrates, and stoked up the fire. The children came back to camp to find me waiting for them, but there was no time to flee. I hid them in a pile of furs the Arapaho left behind and started roasting their freshly caught rabbit. When the soldiers rode into camp, I told them I had come hoping to trade, and wondered what spooked my customers, but reckoned it was the 7th Cavalry, by the looks of things.

"Custer, in his eagerness to fight Indians, had no patience for my repeated attempts to sell my furs to him and rode off in frustration, his men trailing after him. The two Arapaho boys stayed hidden until the last cavalryman disappeared over the hill. Then the three of us high-tailed it across the river. I put the boys on Hippocrates and we swam together, me holding onto his mane. We caught up to the camp late that evening."

Gray Wolf nodded. "It was a brave and honorable deed."

"Anyone would have done the same thing. It was nothing."

"To the boys' mothers, it was everything."

Win shrugged and thought of Meg and her devotion to her boys. Perhaps Gray Wolf was right. He pointed to the *hiiteni,* symbols representing abundance, prosperity, and the life force. "This, as you know, is a prayer for good health and fortune. This wavy line and the two circles represent the river and the two boys. The mother who made it for me said wearing it will protect me from drowning. If I'd had this a few years ago, I might have chanced the Colorado River." Win looked at the beadwork for a moment before he tucked it inside his shirt. "Gray Wolf, Gus worries that my anger at the white government clouds my thinking and is making me reckless. I'd like to know what you think."

The graying Arapaho closed his eyes, suspending time. Win waited.

Finally, Gray Wolf opened his eyes. "We all must follow where our hearts tell us to go. I am grateful for your friendship." He didn't say anymore, but offered his pipe to smoke.

As Win prepared to leave, Gray Wolf summoned one of the women, who brought a supply of aspen bark, dried sumac berries and leaves, and piñon seeds and pine nuts for Meg, who had learned from the Arapaho how to use them for medicine and tea.

Win stayed for two weeks at the Dawson ranch. Meg became weepy near the end of his stay, saying it was hard on a heart to say good-bye so much. Win said he agreed, but, in truth, it was even harder to stay.

Jeb rode with Win to the edge of their property. They rode in silence for a while, giving the emotions that surfaced during the farewell a chance to settle again.

After a bit, Win said, "You've got yourself a fine family, Jeb."

"What about you? Have you met a woman that could settle you down? Is there anyone out there who could tame that wandering spirit of yours?"

On the tip of Win's tongue was *You already took her,* but he knew it was inappropriate and didn't want his visit to end badly. Instead, he just laughed. "There have been a few women who wanted to share their blanket with me, but I managed to escape unscathed. I think I'm destined to wander awhile."

And wander he did. Whether he sensed truth in the old prediction that the frontier would be closed in his lifetime, or was simply brokenhearted that he'd lost Meg, Win disappeared into the wilderness.

CHAPTER FORTY-FIVE:
JEB

Dawson ranch, three years later, 1876
Deep in the woods, Jeb and Gus wrapped a chain around a fallen black walnut tree to drag back to the ranch. Black walnut made fine wood for furniture.

"This ain't gonna be another cradle by any chance, is it?"

"No such luck, Gus. I wish we knew what the trouble was. She just can't keep them. No, I thought Meg might like a writing desk."

"That's a tough road. You have my sympathy."

The gunshot blast interrupted him. A second report three seconds later signaled trouble.

"Something's wrong." Gus dropped the heavy chain and grabbed the rifle he'd propped against a tree. Jeb abandoned the mule and headed for Galen.

Racing around the corner on the trail back

x

417

to the house, Jeb saw Meg thrash through the brush and emerge onto the trail directly in front of an Indian on horseback. He had five of their horses in tow. The Indian's horse — which was actually one of theirs — reared up in surprise, and in the close quarters of the thick forest, a tree branch knocked the rider from his mount. He lay motionless on the ground.

Meg rushed over to him.

"Meg, don't!" Jeb shouted, but he wasn't quick enough with his warning. She had gotten too close. The Indian jumped up and grabbed her, pulling her in front of him for protection. Her rifle fell from her grasp. He held a knife to her throat. Jeb and Gus rode up and Jeb raised his rifle, aimed at the horse thief's head.

"Let her go," Jeb demanded, but the Indian only held on to Meg more tightly.

"You speak English?" Gus asked.

"I speak English." The Indian sounded more nervous than angry.

"Then you understand me. Let her go." Jeb anchored the rifle butt into his shoulder, ready to shoot. The Indian tightened his grip.

Gus held up his hand. "Think about this. You stole our horses, and horse thieves hang. If you hurt her, we aren't going to

418

care why you stole 'em; we're just going to kill you. If you let her go, we'll let you live. You give that some thought."

Jeb could see that the Indian was giving quite a lot of thought to his situation. He probably hadn't expected Meg to chase after him when he stole their horses, not knowing the ferocity of her protective nature. And, he certainly couldn't have predicted that he'd run into two armed men on his escape route.

"I am already dead," the Indian said. Meg struggled. Loose strands of her hair blew in his face.

Jeb felt a trickle of sweat run down his back. "Easy, Meg."

"Meg, don't try to get free. Give this man a chance to do the right thing." Gus spoke calmly.

The Indian furrowed his brow, confused. "What is your name?" The Indian turned his attention toward her.

"Meg Dawson. Please don't hurt me. I have children . . ." she whispered.

"I will let her go," the man announced, sounding urgent. "You do not shoot me." He lessened his grip on her, but kept her in front of him.

Jeb lowered his rifle an inch as a gesture of trust.

419

The Indian let go of Meg and raised his hands. Meg slipped away and ran over to Jeb and Galen. "Do not shoot me," the Indian said. "I know this woman with fire for hair. She is May-g. I did not recognize her, and I should have. I am Washaneeko-mosema."

Meg gasped and peered at him.

The Indian nodded in response to her unspoken question. "I am boy with broken feet."

"Well, I'll be . . ." Gus said under his breath. Jeb lowered his rifle.

"You stole our horses." Meg put her hands on her hips.

"They stand still for me." He whistled the tune Gus taught Meg. All the horses rotated their ears toward him.

"Why so many? Are there more of you?" Jeb asked.

"They are hiding in the mountains, waiting for horses. Soldiers chase us. They are coming."

Meg looked up at Jeb in a panic. "Gray Wolf."

"You go," Gus said to Jeb. "We'll get back to the house. I'll take care of this fellow."

"Stall them as long as you can," Jeb said. He turned Galen toward Gray Wolf's village.

■ ■ ■ ■

Jeb shouted the warning as he got close to their camp. By the time he arrived, Standing Horse was already handing rifles to the women, as most of the men were away from camp, fighting with Crazy Horse. Standing Horse had seen the cavalry, too, and knew they were coming.

"I'll steer the soldiers away if I can get to them," Jeb told his Arapaho friend. Standing Horse nodded and grabbed a box of ammunition.

Jeb headed down the mountain to intercept the cavalry, but the blue coats turned suddenly and headed straight up the mountain on another path. They must have seen the Indians with Washaneekomosema, Jeb thought. He heard gunfire and rode toward the fighting.

For years, Gray Wolf had tried to stay out of the fight and protect his family. He found a new home when his was taken away, he learned English, and he even lived as peaceful neighbors next to a white community. He had remained free of bitterness. His only crime had been his desire to live off the reservation. Now, finally, he and his people had to fight. When they heard the rumble of horses approaching, they took cover and raised their rifles.

Jeb rode into the battle. He saw Gray Wolf, One Who Waits, Standing Horse, and Sharp Eye standing in front to protect the older women and children. Several young women stood bravely next to them, including Running Elk's new young wife. She was a good shot, and even when a bullet nicked her shoulder, she did not flinch, but stood her ground. Those too old to handle a rifle huddled over the young to protect them. The battle was brief, but fierce.

In the end, all the men in the small cavalry detail lay dead. Running Elk shot the last soldier just after the soldier shot his wife. The soldier fell from his horse and landed next to her. The tenacious Arapaho were victorious, but not without cost. Over half the tribe had been killed. Sharp Eye and One Who Waits were among the fallen.

Jeb had never seen such carnage. Through the smoke, he saw an old woman clutching a baby tightly in her arms and realized she had died that way. The baby was alive, protected from harm by Sharp Eye's wife, the baby's grandmother. Mercifully, only one wounded Arapaho suffered for any length of time; life slowly ebbed from him as he lay in the arms of his sobbing wife.

The Arapaho began to chant their death song.

A breeze blew through the battlefield, swirling the smoke from the gunfire like ancestral spirits coming to escort the newly departed across the bridge they built with their song. He watched Gray Wolf chant, his eyes closed. Jeb wanted Gray Wolf to open his eyes so he could see the spirits at work, but guessed Gray Wolf didn't need visual confirmation.

Gus arrived and, together with Jeb, helped the Arapaho honor their dead and prepare them for burial. Then they set about removing the dead soldiers.

Gray Wolf appeared as Jeb and Gus loaded a wagon with bodies. "I will help you." The Arapaho leader looked old.

"There's no need. You've suffered a great loss."

"That is why I must help you. It will keep my heart from turning black. I must remember that I killed a mother's son today, too," Gray Wolf said.

"I'm sorry we couldn't stop it."

"We all hoped this day would not come." Gray Wolf stared at the dead soldiers. "You will bring the dead soldiers to the fort?"

"More soldiers will come looking for them if I don't."

■ ■ ■ ■

What to do with Washaneekomosema presented a problem Jeb didn't know how to handle. He was Pawnee, and an enemy of the Arapaho. His people scouted for the cavalry, so it was a mystery why he was running from them. Gus left him alone with Meg because she said he was her friend. Jeb, Gus, and Gray Wolf followed the path back to the house, encountering the three dead Cheyenne Washaneekomosema was stealing horses for. They had been gunned down by the cavalry.

When Washaneekomosema saw Gray Wolf, he explained how he knew Meg, how she helped him bind his injured ankles and let him ride her horse years ago. He said his father let her go because his mother had a vision that a woman with a head of fire would save his life. The vision frightened his mother, and his father feared Meg's presence in their village would cause trouble. Having heard Meg's version of the story, it intrigued Jeb to hear the Pawnee's perspective.

Gray Wolf asked why a Pawnee was so far from home. Washaneekomosema said he no longer had a home. His people were among the first to move to a reservation and, even as peaceful farmers, had not fared well. One by one, all of his family died from smallpox, including his wife and child. In his despair, he left the reservation. Cheyenne found him wandering the prairie. He fought them without fear. He was not afraid to die, he said. He released his anguish as wrath upon them until only one remained. He fought, knowing it would be to the death. For hours they fought, but neither one would die. He finally passed out from exhaustion and woke only when another party of Cheyenne stood over him. A warrior was about to put a knife into his heart when the warrior he had fought stopped him. "He told his brothers it would dishonor him to kill me," Washaneekomosema said. "I was his to kill. But he was too weak to fight, so they brought us back to their camp, where a Cheyenne woman cared for my wounds and then asked for my life. I married her and learned Cheyenne ways."

Washaneekomosema said that even though he became Cheyenne, he still had to prove his loyalty and had joined the gathering forces under Crazy Horse, a Lakota warrior.

Gray Wolf asked Washaneekomosema a question in language Jeb didn't recognize.

The Pawnee replied. Neither offered to translate.

Washaneekomosema then said in English that he'd fought in a battle against the blue coat named Custer. He said he was proud to fight alongside men who had once been his enemy. Jeb told him the newspapers called it the battle of the Little Bighorn.

The Pawnee turned to Meg then and said he never forgot her act of kindness, and although he hadn't seen many white women, those he had seen reminded him of her. He said with earnestness that he'd never raided white settlers, and had fought only soldiers.

In a move that surprised Jeb, Gray Wolf invited the Pawnee to live at the Arapaho village. He said a wandering man who had no place to return to, no tribe to call his own, and no family waiting for his return needed a home. Jeb thought Gray Wolf admired, maybe even envied, his resilient spirit and ability to survive change. Maybe spirits were at work, but Gray Wolf said there was little point in holding on to prejudices from a disappearing world.

Washaneekomosema stayed, but not at the Arapaho village; Jeb hired him as a ranch hand. When Running Elk told Jeb that, with his wife dead, he saw no future for himself in the old world, Jeb hired Running Elk, too.

The two Indians built a bunkhouse between the house and the barn and made it their home. Occasionally, Running Elk disappeared into the mountains to visit his mother, unable to give up his old life completely. Running Elk and Washaneekomosema were not instant friends; prejudices die hard, and arguments were settled with a wrestling match, but, eventually, Washaneekomosema went along with Running Elk when he visited his family.

Both Indians transformed, perhaps because they saw change as the only way to survive. Washaneekomosema and Running Elk accepted white ways. They wore hats and boots like white ranch hands, they learned to ride with saddles, and spoke only in English, even to each other. Jeb couldn't tell whether they were truly changing, or playing the role of a white person. Meg said it seemed like they were giving in, accepting defeat. But Running Elk said they could remain Indian and be hunted, or adapt to white men's ways and live, perhaps even prosper. Jeb saw wisdom in their actions, as sad as it was to witness.

Washaneekomosema even changed his

name. He brought it up one day during the noon meal. He and Running Elk were sitting at the kitchen table with Jeb and Gus and the boys. Meg dished up their plates.

"I have respect for those who gave me my name, but it is long for you to say."

"What does it mean? I've always wondered," Meg asked.

He and Running Elk talked to each other briefly, figuring out the best translation. "It means 'He brings happiness to his mother and fills her soul with laughter.' "

"Oh, that's lovely," Meg said. "It suits you."

"But impractical." Gus never could get the Pawnee's name right and seemed eager not to have to struggle with it. "How 'bout we shorten it to just Wash? You keep what was given to you, but it'll be easier on all of us."

"But I want a new name — an English name," Washaneekomosema said.

"Wash could be short for Washington, too. That was our first president." James entered the conversation. He rarely spoke words that weren't worth listening to.

The Pawnee broke into a huge smile. "Ai, ai, that is good."

Meg was concerned that they would lose their connection to their heritage, citing examples of lost language and customs from Win's accounts in his letters. She asked Wash about the stories he learned as a child. She asked Running Elk to teach her the chant that was used by his people to connect with the spirit world. Jeb knew that she heard the sound of hooves in the wind, thundering across the plains. He was intrigued by everyone's behavior. The farther the Indians moved away from their culture, the more Meg seemed drawn to it.

CHAPTER FORTY-SIX:
MEG

Dawson ranch, 1876–1881

Custer's battle at the Little Bighorn River was only one of many the US cavalry fought against the Lakota and Cheyenne. Troops from Fort Robinson in Nebraska attacked Cheyenne at Warbonnet Creek, as other fighting continued in the Bighorn Mountains along the Powder River at Bates Creek and Ash Creek. The cavalry clashed with Indians throughout Montana and in the Dakotas. Crazy Horse died at Fort Robinson — some said because he resisted arrest; others said it was a misunderstanding. As he was led to a guardhouse, a soldier stabbed him with his bayonet.

When Meg learned of his death, she slipped quietly into the forest to sing a death chant in private.

Win wrote sporadically. His letters often included news clippings describing the savagery of the Indian massacres and the elevation of Custer to heroic levels. He would circle passages and write "Lies!" across the newsprint. Meg worried that he'd drift so far from their lives that he couldn't return.

However, with her worry came respect. There was satisfaction in knowing that even though they led far different lives, they were aligned in their sympathies. They were on the same side. Meg understood the irony better than anyone when he wrote about the new job he had with Wes Powell and the Smithsonian Institute:

A chance meeting with Powell has once again caused the winds of Fate to shift and my ship is sailing to new horizons. He confirmed a long-standing concern of mine: that equally destructive to the American Indian as white man's military power and diseases is our industrial culture. Once modern conveniences are in anyone's possession, it is difficult to do without them, and so it is with tribal communities who have so far survived the more transparent destructive forces. Powell claims those cultures that are not already extinct have been altered and diluted as they mix with one another and white civilization. It is not my belief that tools for comfort and

*survival should be kept from anyone —
their existence merely hastens our efforts
to record dying languages and preserve
tribal lore. I will be among several crews
recording and cataloging such treasures,
as it is indeed like a treasure hunt. The
only difference is the limited time we have
before civilization eats away the cache.*

Wash and Running Elk were perfect examples of the dilemma the American Indian faced, so the urgency to preserve a dying world struck Meg at her core. Jeb was not unsympathetic; he had done more than most just by keeping Gray Wolf's secret. But he also accepted people for who they were, and if two Indians chose to work and dress like ranchers, it was not up to him to judge.

As peace and progress flourished in Colorado Territory, evidence of its original inhabitants disappeared. The year Custer was defeated at the Little Bighorn, Colorado became a state. Railroads already crisscrossed in a complex network and agricultural communities sprang up everywhere. Each new town seemed to have a newspaper. The Colorado School of Mines was established in Golden, and Colorado College was founded in Colorado Springs. A year after Colorado became a state, the

University of Colorado held classes in Boulder. Opera houses opened. Soon, the first telephones operated in Denver.

Land was parceled out and sold. Ranchers flooded into the area and settled around Paradise. The town grew; a boarding house popped up, someone took over the livery, and the Carters took on extra help. The town soon had enough residents to support a church and a school. When James was eleven and Charlie turned nine, Meg no longer had to school them at the kitchen table. The town hired their first teacher, Mr. Holgrum, and built a schoolhouse in a central location halfway between Paradise and Lyonsville. He lasted only a year and moved on. A young, single woman was hired next, but, within two months she married a widowed rancher with three children and resigned. Etta Sinclair was hired in October of 1881 to replace her. She was the only part of the quickly changing world that Meg liked.

Etta was a forty-five-year-old widow with a mysterious past. It was rumored that she was widowed young. Folks who found it entertaining to talk about people heard that she had married an outlaw, who was jailed and later got shot while trying to escape. Most people were too polite to bring it up in conversation in front of her, but wondered aloud to each other why she called herself "Miss." Some who couldn't help themselves hinted at the rumors to her face to watch her reaction. She never took the bait and always kept conversation at a higher level, preferring to talk about literature, philosophy, and history rather than gossip. She carried herself well, with her back straight and her chin up, as if to guard herself against the stories that seemed to follow her from one teaching position to the next. She was fodder for gossip, and many parents did not like her for that reason. But James and Charlie chattered away at the dinner table every night about what she'd taught them in school. Meg loved her.

Miss Sinclair arrived at the Dawson ranch driving her own carriage late one afternoon. Gus came out of the barn as she pulled up, the dogs trailing after him.

"Oh, hello," she said gaily as he arrived at the side of her carriage. The dogs were unusually excited and curious about the visitor and created a churning sea of wagging tails, barking, and general enthusiasm below the carriage.

"Buddy, Billy! Get down, now. Give this lady some room." The dogs quieted and lay down by the porch steps. "Ma'am." Gus offered his hand to her as she climbed down.

"Thank you." She smiled at the obedient dogs. "Goodness, I wish my students listened as well! I rather miss having dogs around. I grew up with them." Billy and Buddy lifted their heads, encouraged by the lilt in her voice, but Gus pointed his finger at them and they put their heads back down on the ground and sulked.

"They have joyful souls; that's a fact. It's hard for a dog to have a bad day."

Miss Sinclair laughed appreciatively as Jeb came around the corner. Meg stepped out of the house at the same time. Meg glanced at Jeb, wondering if he heard the playful sound in Gus's voice, but Jeb was striding over to the teacher with his hand extended.

"You must be Miss Sinclair. I'm Jeb Dawson, and this is my wife. I see you've met Gus Steensland."

"No, actually, not formally." Miss Sinclair smiled cheerfully and extended her hand to him again. "Etta Sinclair, schoolteacher and dog lover." She winked and Gus grinned.

Miss Sinclair was invited inside, but she motioned to the chairs outside and asked if they could sit on the porch, as it was such a pleasant evening. Meg readily agreed; she preferred the porch over any room in the house. Instead of returning to the barn, Gus

435

joined them.

Miss Sinclair wore her thick, dark, auburn hair piled on top of her head. Although full-figured, she was not heavy. She was telling the adults how much she enjoyed her new teaching post when she caught a glimpse of the boys peeking through the window.

She tilted her head, peering back at them. "Oh! Here I am, chattering away, when I've neglected to state my purpose for visiting." She pulled out a primer from her book satchel. "Charlie left this at school. Since I gave an assignment from it, I thought he might need it."

"Charlie, come out to the porch," Meg called. Charlie emerged from the house looking sheepish. "Miss Sinclair was very kind to bring you your book. Do you have anything to say to her?"

"Yes, ma'am; thank you, ma'am." Charlie took the primer from her.

"Charlie, I'm rather glad you forgot your primer." Miss Sinclair tilted her head again. "Now I've had the chance to meet Billy and Buddy and the rest of your family. This is the most beautiful spot in the whole county."

The boy dropped his reserve. "Yes, ma'am; I think so, too!"

She leaned forward, as though sharing a

secret. "I know this primer isn't very interesting. But I hope you'll learn from it so you can read much more interesting books, literature, philosophy, science —"

"We've got a bunch of those books! Wanna see 'em?" Charlie jerked his thumb at the window, indicating the books were just inside.

"If your mother doesn't mind, I'd love to." Miss Sinclair glanced at Meg.

"By all means, Charlie can show you. You are welcome to borrow some if you'd like," Meg said.

Charlie grabbed Miss Sinclair's hand and dragged her into the house. They could hear her by the bookcase exclaiming delight at seeing familiar titles. James joined them. Jeb, Meg, and Gus just looked at each other, eyebrows raised in pleasant surprise. When she came back out, she was alone.

"Well, this was well planned on my part." Miss Sinclair held up three books and laughed. "In exchange for one dull primer, I found three extraordinary tomes. I hope you don't mind."

"Not at all. What did you find?" Jeb asked.

"Well, I believe books should feed the heart, mind, and soul. So, for my mind, I chose Emerson's *Essays;* for my soul, Henry Thoreau's *Walden* . . . and, for my heart, this Wilkie Collins novel looks delight-ful!"

"Oh, it is!" Meg liked Miss Sinclair; she was fun.

"You are very generous to let me borrow all three. I will return them soon, I promise."

"I'll be going into Paradise next Tuesday. I could stop by . . . save you a trip," Gus said.

"That would be just fine, Mr. Steensland. I appreciate it. My goodness, you've all made me feel so welcome, I have completely abused your kindness. I must be going now and let you get on with your day." Miss Sinclair stood up to leave. Gus jumped up faster than Meg had ever seen him move. Before he helped her back into her carriage, she reached down and scratched Billy and Buddy behind the ears and praised them for their exemplary behavior. They remained planted at their spots, but their tails wagged furiously. "I look forward to seeing you on Tuesday, Mr. Steensland." With a slap to the rump of the livery horse, she was gone. Meg watched Gus's eyes follow her out of sight.

"I'll bet she was a firecracker in her youth. She's a pleasant addition to the town, that's a fact." As he returned to the barn, Meg noticed a spring in his step.

■ ■ ■ ■

The bell over the door into the Carters' store announced Meg's arrival. Georgia poked her head out from the back room and let out an excited chirp.

"Meg, dear, you have time for a visit, don't you?" Georgia gave her a significant look as she swept across the room to her. "Of course you do. Mick, watch the store. I'm going home."

Mick blinked, stunned, as Georgia linked arms with Meg and escorted her next door to their home. So clean and quiet compared to the ranch, Meg could actually hear the clock tick on the mantle. She sat down on the love seat. Georgia dropped into the seat next to her, smiling mischievously.

"Georgia, what on earth is going on?"

"Love. That's what's going on." Georgia looked behind her to confirm that no one was listening. Then she leaned toward Meg. "Last Tuesday, I came from the back room and saw Gus out in front of the store, pacing and looking as nervous as a bridegroom. He had on a clean shirt, had combed his hair, and carried two books with him. I was about to go out and visit with him when Miss Sinclair came around the corner. Well,

439

you know I wouldn't normally be so impolite as to eavesdrop, but when I saw the look on his face when she appeared, I couldn't help myself.

" 'Oh, Mr. Steensland, there you are,' Miss Sinclair said. 'I hate to trouble you with these books.'

" 'It's no trouble at all,' Gus replied. 'In fact, I brought a couple of others I thought you might enjoy.'

"They started a discussion about philosophy that wove its way into literature and then into poetry. I had no idea Gus knew so much. Finally, after quite a long discussion — all the while I dearly hoped Mick wouldn't show up and catch me hiding behind the door listening — Miss Sinclair said: 'Your daughter is lovely. I hope she and I can be friends.'

" 'Meggie's not my daughter,' Gus said. 'I took her under my wing when her folks died. Over the years, she's brought a lot of joy to my life.'

"Through the crack in the door, I could see Miss Sinclair break into a big smile and say, 'That's the second time you've used the word *joy* in the two conversations we've had, Mr. Steensland. You are a most unusual man.' Then she tilted her head the way women do to let men know they've just

440

been given a compliment. You know men —
usually they're too thick to notice — but
Gus picked up on it right away.

" 'Well, thank you, ma'am,' he said. 'Most
folks don't look hard enough for it — joy, I
mean. They think it's supposed to land in
their laps. I figure you gotta dig for it a little.
You find it in surprising places, sometimes.'
He smiled at her so sweetly she blushed and
smiled, too. Then he said, 'If I'm not too
forward in saying so, I think we may have
stumbled upon a little joy right here. I'd
feel right special if you'd call me Gus.'

"And then *she* said, 'Only if you call me
Etta.' "

Meg gasped and grabbed Georgia's hand
as they giggled together like schoolgirls.
Georgia said she had no idea that old buzzard could be so charming.

Meg squeezed Georgia's hand. "Oh, Georgia! This is wonderful!"

The following Saturday, Miss Sinclair
released the children early. When James and
Charlie rode into the yard, Gus announced
that he was going into town to play a little
poker and wouldn't be home for dinner.
Meg noted with a half-smile that he angled
Neighbor in the direction of the schoolteacher's little house. The next morning, as
he sat at breakfast, Meg asked Gus if the

441

cards were good to him. He looked puzzled for an instant before he fabricated a response. Meg allowed him his privacy and said nothing, but placed her hand reassuringly on his shoulder as she poured his coffee. Gus started going to town regularly to "play poker."

Finally, one evening, Jeb pulled Meg close. Wrapped in his arms, Jeb told Meg that Gus had come into the barn bright and early, whistling away, more chipper than he'd ever seen him. "I asked him if he had a good poker night, and all he said was, 'It's a fine day,' but chuckled to himself most of the morning."

"I've never seen those blue eyes of his twinkle quite so bright. Jeb, he's in love."

"You're right about that. I told him I knew he was seeing Etta. He said she was concerned that folks would start talking about her. They can fire her for cavorting."

"I don't have any problem with Etta and Gus seeing each other."

"I told him that. I said we were mighty glad she'd come along and that she was something special. Then Gus said he thought so, too. He asked her to marry him, Meg, and she said yes. They'll marry at the end of the school year."

Meg sat up in bed. "That's wonderful news!"

Jeb grinned. "I agree. But there's more. Gus was marveling at the power of love and its ability to stir a man's soul. He was under Sadie milking her and I had my back to the barn door, so we didn't see the boys come in."

"Oh, dear," Meg said. If the boys overheard and talked about it with anyone, Miss Sinclair's reputation and career would be ruined. "Jeb, what did you do?"

"I said, 'Mornin' boys,' as casually as I could, but loud enough to warn Gus. He jumped up in surprise, kicked the milk bucket over, and cussed. The commotion in the corner of the barn caused our two wide-eyed boys to turn in unison toward the noise. I said, 'You two looked a bit stunned. What did you hear that's making you look like a couple of owls?'

"James was speechless, but Charlie — who you know has trouble hiding anything — scratched his head and said 'Geez, I can't figure out how grownups find out about so much stuff. How'd you know poor James got kissed by Olivia Dean? She only got him last Friday!' "

Meg gasped, half surprised, half relieved.

"What? Olivia Dean? James kissed Olivia Dean?"

Jeb held up his hand. "Not exactly. Hang on. Gus stood up and leaned over Sadie and asked, 'What exactly did you hear me say, boys?'

"Charlie said, 'Somethin' about kissin' girls.' James turned crimson. Charlie then turned to James and promised that he hadn't squealed, that someone else must have. James told Charlie it was OK and that he was going to talk to me about it anyway. He looked miserable.

" 'So, I guess you heard about Olivia,' James said. 'She started it . . . honest. I was coming in from recess and she just cornered me over by the coat hooks and . . . and kissed me.' He wiped his mouth with his sleeve, as though he was reliving the horrible experience and said, 'I guess you know the rest.' "

Jeb sat up and leaned forward. "Apparently the boys thought we were talking about James and his trouble with girls, not Etta Sinclair. Gus ducked back under Sadie to finish the milking. All I could think to say was, 'James, whatever I heard doesn't matter. I'd like to hear your side of it.' "

"Oh, that was clever." Meg tucked her legs up under her nightgown and sat on the bed

444

like a child hearing a bedtime story.

"James explained — with Charlie's help — that all he did was wipe his mouth after Olivia kissed him. Olivia asked why he did that, and wasn't he gonna kiss her back? It must have been the way he answered no that made her hand fly across his cheek. 'So I guess Olivia's mad at me,' he said. He added 'She's perplexing' and a chuckle escaped from Gus, which he disguised as a cough. Then James said that Miss Sinclair pulled him aside and observed that it was the first time she'd seen a fellow get slapped for what he *didn't* do rather than what he did, which produced another chortle from behind the cow. I agreed and said that, someday, girls would occupy more of his thoughts than they do now, and they'd get more enjoyable to be around, to trust me on that. I said girls go through a tough time at this age and they can be perplexing.

"Charlie said, 'I'll say! They whisper and giggle all the time . . . I can't figure out what's so funny!'

"I recommended steering clear for a few years, until girls grow up and calm down a bit. That's when James grumbled that he bet you were never perplexing."

"Aw, James is always so sweet." Meg caressed Jeb's arm. "What did you say?"

"I said that was a question for Gus because, when I met you, you were a lot older than Olivia is now."

"Oh, for heaven's sake. That sounds like something Win would say."

"Hang on, don't tar and feather me yet. Gus stood up and said, 'You are correct, son, your ma was never silly. She wasn't no giggly, boy-chasing fool; that's a fact. She was a fine young girl who grew up into a fine young lady, just like her own ma, and just like Miss Sinclair. Good advice your pa just gave you. Steer clear of perplexing girls for a while. You deserve better, and better ones will come along.' "

Meg smiled wistfully. "You and Gus, you're a couple of old romantics. And our sweet boys are growing up." She reached over and caressed his cheek.

Jeb pulled her over to him and unbuttoned her nightgown.

CHAPTER FORTY-SEVEN:
JEB

Dawson ranch, May 1882

Jeb woke with a start. Someone had just ridden into the yard. He pulled on his trousers and grabbed his shotgun, but put it down when he saw Etta jumping down from Neighbor. Even in the moonlight, he could see the schoolteacher's grim expression.

Meg woke, too, put on her robe, and followed Jeb out on to the porch, brushing her tousled hair from her eyes.

"Mr. Dawson, Mrs. Dawson, I need your help!" Miss Sinclair whispered.

Meg grabbed Jeb's arm. "What's going on?"

"Gus . . . I mean, Mr. Steensland, he . . . he was . . . returning a book. He collapsed and . . . said I should get you. I think he's having a heart attack . . ." She stopped then, put her hands to her face and started to sob.

Jeb was already halfway to the barn to saddle Galen, his heart sinking. Moments later, he emerged and rode over to the women. "Meggie, stay here. I'll bring Gus home." Etta turned Neighbor around and rode back to her house with Jeb.

The moon was so full and bright that it cast shadows. A warm, gentle breeze stirred the scents of the prairie in new bloom. Every Saturday since they'd met, Gus had bathed, put on clean clothes, and left for town in the late afternoon. He'd have dinner in town, he'd say. He was always in the barn the next morning, whistling cheerfully as he cleaned the stalls. He kept his horse in the old barn next to her house — hidden from anyone passing by — in order to protect her reputation. But no one ever came by. No one gave the spinster schoolteacher a second thought once school let out for the week. No one except Gus.

Etta and Jeb rode up to her house. Hiding the horses was unnecessary at three o'clock in the morning. Jeb followed Miss Sinclair inside. Gus had tried to dress himself, but hadn't gotten far.

"Jeb's gonna bring me home, Etta . . . keep your reputation intact." Gus whispered the words and allowed Jeb to help him with this shirt.

Miss Sinclair glanced at Jeb but said nothing. Together, they dressed the old cowboy and carefully helped Gus into his saddle. He slumped over, his face twisted in pain. Sheer willpower seemed to keep him conscious. Dying in the schoolteacher's bed, creating a scandal, was not Gus's way. They slowly rode home. Meg was waiting for them on the porch and helped Gus out of his saddle. Jeb and Meg carried him into the house and put him in his bed. He said he preferred to sit, so they propped him up.

"You're a good man," Gus whispered when they had him settled.

Jeb rested his hand on Gus's shoulder. "So are you." He felt a lump form in his throat. Jeb knew he had just said good-bye to his old friend.

Meg began to cry softly. "Gus, what can I do?"

"Come here and let me hold you, darlin'. 'Cept I can't move my arm, so you'll have to put it around yourself."

She climbed in next to him and wrapped his right arm around her like she was a little girl. She rested her head on his chest.

His breathing was shallow. Tears spilled down her cheeks. Gus looked up at the ceiling and said, "You know, Meggie, I've lived my life backwards. Back when I was young, I lost my hand and started living like an old man. Then you came along and I became the father of a young lady. Then I got to bounce your babies on my knee, just like a new young papa . . . and now, now that I'm really, finally old, I've fallen in love again like a seventeen-year-old boy." He closed his eyes. Jeb could tell he labored to breathe.

Meg held on to him tight, as though to keep death from grabbing him away from her. "You're everything to me." Her voice trembled. "I wouldn't be here if it weren't for you. I love you so."

"You were part of all my good days, darlin'; that's a fact. I'm mighty glad I could . . ." He cringed again and whispered urgently. ". . . glad I could see you all grown up, with a family . . . tell Etta I'm sorry we didn't marry, will you? The boys, too, they're fine boys . . ." Gus gasped for a breath, then, and grabbed her hand.

"Gus! Don't leave me!"

"Never, Meggie . . ." he whispered. Those were his last words.

Jeb sat down next to Meg and gathered her into his arms as she sobbed. "I'm so sorry, Meggie."

"My heart is breaking, Jeb. It hurts so much."

Jeb nodded. "I know."

Running Elk and Wash dug a grave at the

piñon tree as Gray Wolf chanted and the boys stood by. Jeb sat on the porch with Meg, who quietly chanted along. Together they built a bridge to the next world for Gus, creating a passage for him, connecting the two worlds, she said. Finally, she walked up the hill, holding Jeb's arm. She gently took the shovel from Wash and dug up a few shovels of dirt.

"Did I ever tell you boys that the first time I met your pa, I was digging a grave? He was so kind to me. Your pa helped me dig a grave for a couple of settlers neither one of us knew, but who had died and deserved a proper burial. So there we were. Do you know who I wrote to that very week, telling him all about meeting your pa and Uncle Win? Gus. Gus has been watching over us from the very beginning, and he's going to keep on doing just that. His spirit is in the wind, all around us."

When their friends from town arrived, they buried Gus under the piñon tree. It was the official family cemetery — where their babies were buried, and Meg's beloved horse. Now her oldest and dearest friend rested there, too.

That evening, Jeb and Meg and the boys sat out on the porch together. Off in the distance, they heard drums. Running Elk and Wash had ridden back with Gray Wolf with the news. The Arapaho honored Gus, a white man, as they would their own. The drumbeat was like a heartbeat, connecting creatures and Creator. The Dawson family sat silently on the porch well into the night, listening to the drums beat like the Earth's pulse.

Jeb startled Miss Sinclair when he stopped in at the schoolhouse. The children had been dismissed for the day and she was washing the blackboards. Jeb knew from the change in her expression exactly what she was thinking . . . and hoping. For a brief moment when she heard him, she thought Gus had walked in. It was hard for Jeb to believe he was gone, too.

"Miss Sinclair, I apologize for the intrusion." Jeb removed his hat.

"Nonsense," she said, without the firm tone the word usually carried with it. "Please come in."

Jeb stood in the center of her classroom, hat in hand. If he acted embarrassed, she would just feel ashamed, he thought. He stood tall and looked her in the eye. "I'm sorry Gus was taken from you, Miss Sinclair." There was nothing in his voice that held any judgment. She accepted his condo-

452

lences. He took a deep breath and said, "I could use your help, ma'am. Meg is having a tough time. She's . . . drifting."

"She doesn't want to move forward because it means leaving Gus behind." Miss Sinclair seemed to be familiar with the feeling.

"Yes, ma'am. I didn't know how to say it, but that's it exactly. It's different from grief. It's a little like having no wind to fill the sails, or a broken rudder."

"That's interesting imagery from a man born and raised in a landlocked prairie," she said with a sad smile.

Jeb nodded and returned a faint smile. "It's all those pirate stories from my youth, I guess. Win and I were sailors in our imaginations long before we came out here." Jeb cleared his throat and said, "Whatever it is, I just know she misses Gus, and so do you. You two have a lot in common . . . your love of books, children, and Gus. Meg can't quite bring herself to reach out to you, so I'm asking you to do what she can't."

"You don't think I'll bring more pain to her? Be a reminder?"

"I think your company is exactly what she needs."

"I'll give it some thought," she said. Jeb

turned to leave. "Thank you, Mr. Dawson, for . . . for everything." She didn't say it out loud, but Jeb figured she was thanking him for not judging her, for helping Gus get home, for not spreading gossip, and for being kind.

"Love is powerful, ma'am. You may not feel this way right now, but we're the lucky ones — the ones who can love and be loved." He put on his hat and left.

On the ride home, a breeze circled around him and he thought he heard Gus whistling.

CHAPTER FORTY-EIGHT: MEG

Dawson Ranch, Summer 1882

"Would you show me your barn?" Etta surprised Meg with the unusual request.

"Why, of course." Meg and the teacher rose from the porch swing they shared and strolled across the yard. Jeb signaled from the edge of the meadow that he and the boys were headed for their fishing spot by raising a pole over his head. Buddy and Billy lingered at Miss Sinclair's side just long enough to receive a scratch behind the ear before Jeb whistled to them and they bounded off in his direction. Charlie, always full of life, waved to the women like the stand of quaking aspen into which he disappeared.

Etta called on the Dawsons regularly. The first time she visited was painful for both women, but the persistent schoolteacher and Meg eventually discovered they had more in common than their shared loss.

Meg felt Gus's presence whenever Etta was around, and was comforted by it, but she also liked Etta's company.

Meg swung open the door and they stepped inside.

Etta breathed deeply. "I like the smell of fresh straw." She looked around. "You keep your barn very clean."

"Well, the boys just mucked the stalls. You came at a good time." Meg tried to be lighthearted, but saw Etta wistfully stroke the tack hanging neatly on the wall and knew her friend must be missing Gus terribly. "Gus taught me how to clean and oil tack when I was just a little girl, and to keep the stable clean. You'd think someone so fastidious would be stern and strict, but he wasn't at all. Much like the way you teach, Etta — you have high expectations, yet you show nothing but warmth and kindness."

"Thank you for those sweet words, dear. I think he and I were alike in many ways."

Etta's fingers lingered on the tack for a moment. "Well . . ." She sighed heavily. "You might find it strange, but I just missed his smell. Gus always smelled of soap and newly laundered shirts, but what I liked most was the subtle hint of fresh straw and the oil he used on the tack. Am I becoming . . . peculiar, as Georgia calls it?"

"Not at all." Meg loved Etta's candor. "I come out here often for that very reason."

"I wouldn't wonder if you spent every waking moment out here. I feel him here, don't you? It feels good. I should become a horsewoman like you if I were a few years younger!" Etta smiled broadly, a woman who had found peace.

The teacher's words lingered on Meg's mind, even into the next day as she swept the floors, the broom heavy in her hands. Cleaning sapped Meg's energy in a way that working in the barn or riding never did. She stayed away from horseback riding for fear of damaging any fragile new life growing inside her, and, yet, despite all the precautions taken, she had not been able to bear more children.

Meg peered out the bedroom window. The boys had come home from school and were hanging on the corral fence, watching Jeb work with a young colt. *I wouldn't wonder if you spent every waking moment out here . . . a horsewoman like you.* Etta's words rang in her head. On impulse, she abandoned her broom and searched through the chest and found her old breeches. The buttery soft feel stirred a long dormant energy inside her.

To the boys' surprise, she arrived at the

barn wearing her old boots, jacket, and riding breeches. She announced she was taking Neighbor for a ride.

"Want company?" Jeb gave her a curious look.

Meg shook her head and saddled Gus's favorite horse. She climbed into the saddle and rode out of the barn, excitement building inside her.

Neighbor had a fluid gait, much like Biscuit's. She steered him to where the terrain flattened out and gave him the signal. He took off as though he read her mind.

Meg leaned forward and held on. She still had good balance. Her hat blew off and dangled behind her, the leather tie abrasive against her neck. The sun warmed her face and the wind pressed her jacket against her body. Every step Neighbor took jolted and jarred her older body. She hadn't bound her breasts and she didn't have the same strength she had with younger legs, but she felt intoxicated by the thrill of riding again. She closed her eyes briefly. In the wind, she thought she heard Gus whooping with delight. Exhilaration washed over her.

The boys jumped off the fence when she rode back into the yard. "Ma, I didn't know you could ride like that!" James said. Charlie's face was washed with awe.

Jeb's eyes met hers. Jeb always understood.

That evening, after the boys were asleep, he pulled her close and she responded like she used to before Gus died. She lay in his arms afterward and said it was good to feel alive again.

"You haven't ridden like that for years. I know it's because you've wanted another baby." Jeb said the words softly, undoubtedly because the subject of babies usually made Meg cry. He kissed the top of her head as she rested her head on his shoulder. "When I saw you ride today, it made me think. We have two healthy sons. I think we should count our blessings and figure this is going to be our family. We've lost two, maybe three babies, counting that time last year. I'd rather see you riding again, if that's what you want. I know how much you wanted more children, but you've been so careful, and it just hasn't worked."

Meg wanted more children, but her attempts to stay pregnant left her too cautious to live the life she already had. Maybe it was time to move on.

"We do have two fine boys, don't we? James will be twelve soon . . . Can you believe how fast the time has gone? I've been thinking about it, too, Jeb. I so wanted a little girl, but you're right. I've been treating my body like it was made of glass, trying to keep the babies safe and growing inside me with no luck. I'd rather spend my time with you and the boys training the horses. We're going to need help, now that Gus is gone. Frankly, I'd rather hire a woman to work in the house than take on another ranch hand. What do you think about that?"

True to his nature, Jeb said it was worth a try, because a content and satisfied man is a generous man. He added that they might have trouble finding ranch hands who would work with Running Elk and Wash anyway. Training horses wasn't typical woman's work, but hiring an Arapaho and a Pawnee wasn't typical, either. Besides, she knew better than anyone how to get a little filly to behave.

"Will you promise me something, though?" His voice sounded happy. "You still make the pies, ok? There's no one who can make peach pie better than you."

Anne Wallace responded to the notice Jeb posted outside the general store in Cheyenne. A capable young woman, Anne was hired to cook meals and clean house. She was the oldest of twelve children, which meant she had been cooking, washing, and caring for her younger siblings for as long as she could remember. It soured her to the idea of doing it all over again with a husband, she told Meg candidly at her interview. Instead of marriage providing her with financial security, she hoped a job with the Dawsons would.

Meg liked the fact that Anne took charge. Efficient and thorough, Anne preferred to work alone and decide her daily schedule for herself. She didn't live on the ranch, but rented a room at the new boarding house in town. Every day except Sunday, she arrived after breakfast, which Meg still prepared. Anne cleaned, washed clothes, and cooked the noon dinner and evening supper. She emerged from the kitchen at the end of each day with fresh bread cooling on the counter and supper ready to be served. Anne would ask perfunctorily if there were anything else Meg needed, and without more than a few pleasant exchanges, she'd be off in her carriage. Anne freed Meg from the burden of domestic chores. Meg adored her for it.

The arrangement allowed Meg to work with Jeb and the horses. Now, after breakfast, Anne arrived to clean up, the boys left for school, and she headed to the barn with Jeb. Wash and Running Elk had a little trouble adjusting at first. Gus could tell a good off-color joke and was easy to be around. But after they saw the way she handled the yearlings and the way she coaxed a bridle on the two year olds, they had a change of heart. They also seemed to prefer Anne's cooking over hers, their increased appetites and frequent compliments as evidence.

It didn't take long for Meg to return to the familiar routine she had known years earlier. She preferred oiling tack to washing pots. Meg and Jeb went riding nearly every day in the mountains. Jeb would ride one of the newly trained horses to put him through his paces before selling to the livery. She rode Neighbor.

A letter arrived from Win in early July. Everyone gathered together on the porch to listen. Even Anne joined them, which surprised Meg, as she was not inclined to intrude in family business. As was their custom, Jeb sat on the railing and read the letter to everyone. Meg closed her eyes to listen.

June 7, 1882

Dear Jeb and Meg, James and Charlie, Wash and Running Elk,
  There are no words to express my sadness when I received Jeb's letter and

learned that we lost our beloved Gus. I can only imagine your sorrow in particular, dearest Meggie. He was truly one of the best men I've ever known. I will miss his wisdom and his company. I will be unable to write this letter if I continue, so although I write of other news, please know we are together in our grief. There is no easy way to lose a loved one. When the love is great, the loss is, too.

Mentioning Gus stirred a mixture of happy memories and sad emptiness in Meg that she figured would never go away completely. She realized Jeb had stopped reading. She opened her eyes to discover him watching her. "I'm all right, Jeb." She smiled weakly. He turned his attention back to the letter and found his place.

I am grateful and honored to be kept abreast of the events in your lives, both the good and the tragic. As Gus related to us once, joy is doubled and sorrow is halved when it is shared. I am reminded of that adage every time I find a letter for me at whatever headquarters I work from. For that reason, I hope that relaying my news will bring you some happiness in the midst of your sorrow.

I had the unexpected surprise and enor-

463

mous pleasure of running into some old friends in the bustling train depot of Chicago. I rounded a corner and collided with the most charming young woman, knocking her hat askew. Pushing her hat back in place, her eyes immediately grew as large as saucers and she cried out with enthusiasm, "Mr. Avery! I can't believe it!" If you haven't guessed by now, I will reveal that it was our own Lizzie Moberg, all grown up. She had been east for the summer visiting relatives and had just arrived in the city herself. She was waiting for her parents to arrive from Milwaukee so they could all travel back to Oregon together. As I had the evening free, I sat with Lizzie while she waited for her folks to arrive. You can just imagine the look on their faces when Glenn and Grace saw their daughter with an old scout from trail days. After receiving more embraces from the female sex than a man deserves in one day, we all had dinner together and I filled them in about the Dawson family. Grace was so happy, she wept tears of joy. She sends everyone her love, but especially you, Meg. She said she always knew life would turn out well for you, as long as you married either Jeb or me. Actually, I made up that last part just to annoy Jeb. What *she really said was that she was most happy for you. I would agree; even as we ache in our hearts and say good-bye to Gus, you must see the joy you've brought to all of our lives, and I hope you find some peace in that.*

The Mobergs are well and happy. Years ago, they ended their journey by prairie schooner close to a little town of Oakdale, where they purchased land and started farming. The farm next to theirs happened to be owned by a family with four sons, and Lizzie is in love with the second eldest, Stephen. He has proposed marriage and she has accepted. They plan to wed after harvest.

I have more news to share, but instead of writing, I think I will give you all the details in person. I have decided to come "home," if you'll allow me to call it that. I have some time before I'm needed at my next assignment, and I should prefer to spend it with all of you, if you don't mind. I plan to arrive in early August. I hope this letter reaches you before I do, so Meg can start on one of her peach pies.

Fondly,
Win

"Uncle Win's coming? Yippee!" Charlie

465

jumped off the porch and started dancing a Pawnee dance Wash had been teaching him.

The young are so resilient, Meg thought. "I'm glad he's coming," she said. "It will be good to see him."

Jeb nodded and folded the letter. "He has a way of cheering people up."

It was late afternoon in mid-August when Win appeared on the hill. James and Charlie jumped on their ponies and rode out to meet him. They took their time coming in. Always eager to share stories, Charlie gestured broadly, telling Win something Meg couldn't quite hear. But when he spread his arms and tilted his head back like he'd seen his mother do while riding, she knew he was telling Win about the new arrangements at the ranch. Meg and Jeb turned to each other and smiled when they heard Win laugh out loud. It sounded like comfortable old times.

The dogs, as despondent as the rest of them without Gus, bounded out to greet the friendly voice. Win rode into the yard and dismounted in the center of a small whirlwind of boys and dogs.

"Oh, Win!" Meg ran down the porch steps and hugged him. "We've missed you so."

"I'm so sorry about Gus, Meggie, so

sorry," he whispered in her ear, causing her eyes to mist. She wondered how long it would take before her heart didn't break at the thought or mention of Gus. She mustered her strength, however, and smiled through her tears.

"Gus would want us to go on living and be happy." She took a deep breath. "And that's just what we're doing."

"Good to hear it. I was concerned about you."

Jeb and Win greeted each other with their traditional bear hug and slap on the back. Charlie grabbed his saddlebag as James brought his horse to the barn. The men disappeared into the house to get settled. Meg heard the sound of glasses being pulled from the shelf and sat back down on the porch swing to wait for them to return. No more work today; they would celebrate Win's return. A gentle breeze swirled around her. She smiled and whispered, "There you are. I knew you'd join us. He looks good, doesn't he, Gus?"

■ ■ ■ ■

PART THREE

■ ■ ■ ■

PART THREE

CHAPTER FORTY-NINE: WIN

Dawson ranch, mid-August 1882

Win realized he'd been away too long when he crested the hill to the Dawson ranch. Two figures rode out to meet him, and he was taken aback when he finally recognized James and Charlie.

He knew the reason for his extended absence. The joy and anguish of seeing Meg were so intertwined he denied himself one to avoid the other. When she had appeared at the door and skipped down the steps to embrace him, his heart fluttered. "Oh, Win!" she'd cried. "We've missed you so!" He loved hearing her voice, even though she said "we." When he whispered in her ear that he was sorry about Gus, he felt her arms tighten around him appreciatively.

Inside, Win met Anne, who was leaving for the day. Jeb fished around for the bottle of whiskey that didn't get much use these days, he said, but they had to properly

471

celebrate Win home. Win grabbed three glasses and stole a glance at Meg sitting on the porch swing. She was smiling. Her lips moved as though she was talking to someone.

They toasted to each other's health on the porch and Win shared his news. He told them everything he'd learned from the Mobergs about Lizzie growing up next door to her beau, Stephen. She had become quite an accomplished horsewoman. Glenn gave Meg credit for piquing her interest. Win paused his account long enough to squint at Meg.

"I hear you can still cut a hole in the wind."

"I was so sore! I could barely move the next day."

"Nobody else's ma can ride like that." James made no attempt to disguise his admiration. "It was something to see. After that, Miss Anne came to do the housework for Ma so she could work with the horses."

Win noticed Jeb and Meg glance at each other. Meg had grown even lovelier over the years, as her physical beauty had always radiated from a natural inner sparkle. Jeb had himself a sweet and satisfied wife, that was apparent. It was the painful part of coming back, seeing them love each other.

When he was away, he could imagine Meg wishing for him to return, wanting him. Returning was always bittersweet. Obviously, she was doing just fine without him.

"Well, it looks as though my new neighbors run a successful operation," Win said, attempting to brush away the sting. He waited for his comment to register. Jeb and Meg turned to him in surprise.

"Neighbors? What are you talking about?" Meg asked.

"I wrote to our friend Mr. Brewer awhile back. I bought that mountain." Win pointed to the nearest peak. "Just got word it's all settled." He pulled a telegram from his pocket and held it up as proof.

"Win!" The delight in Meg's voice made his heart pound.

"What the hell are you going to do with a mountain?" Jeb seemed unaware, after all these years, of the effect his wife still had on Win. Perhaps he chose to ignore it.

"I'm not doing anything with it. It protects the canyon where Gray Wolf winters, though."

Meg sighed with gratitude and reached over to grasp Win's hand. "Oh, Win."

"The pay isn't good on expeditions, but I've had very few expenses over the years." Win squeezed Meg's hand, strong from hard ranch work, but still surprisingly soft. "I socked some money away and jumped on the opportunity. Got it real cheap, too. When the land was surveyed, they found no precious metals, so no one wants to mine it. It's too steep to farm or graze cattle. I got to name some landmarks on the map when we drew the boundaries. C'mon, I'll show you." Still holding her hand, Win plucked Meg from her seat, but then let go first before she could pull her hand away.

Everyone scrambled off the porch and into the yard, where they had a clear view of the mountain range. Between the ridge and their ranch were the valleys and forests where Gray Wolf and his family lived, secluded and well protected by rough terrain. Gray Wolf's people had tried to escape into the canyon when the cavalry discovered their camp. Had they made it, they would have been impossible to find.

"See the ridge that runs from over there to there?" Win asked, pointing at the mountains. "I named that Dawson Ridge. Just below it is Gray Wolf Canyon."

Jeb laughed. "Let me guess. You named that highest point up there Avery's Peak."

"Ha! No; actually, I named it Steensland Peak."

Meg put both her hands to her mouth to

stifle a sob, but it came out anyway. Jeb put his arm around her and kissed her temple, a comforting gesture Win wished was his to give.

That night, while Jeb and the boys milked the cow and fed the horses, Win dried the dishes as Meg washed them. Win thought they might use the time to talk privately, but Wash and Running Elk arrived unexpectedly and lingered. Meg excitedly told them about Win's land purchase. They shared the news that two mares were almost ready to foal. By the time they ran through the condition of the whole herd, the dishes were put away and Jeb was back. Later, when they sat on the porch in the dark and watched the moon rise over the plains, Win saw Jeb take Meg's hand and squeeze it affectionately. An old scar pulled open. He wondered if longing for Meg was keeping him from enjoying other life pleasures. Maybe it was time to let her go — really let her go — so he could think about settling down himself and be happy with someone.

Win had met a singer on the riverboat that brought him as far as Omaha. What inspired him to take the riverboat instead of the train, he couldn't say; the winds of Fate, maybe. The singer, Jeannette Bordeaux, was pretty and fun. She had a voice like a songbird and alluring eyes. She lived on the riverboat, traveling up and down the Missouri, entertaining passengers between St. Louis and Omaha. He liked her and apparently, she liked him, because she invited him into her bed. He told her he was on his way to the mountains and that he wouldn't be able to stay, but she said she didn't care. She accepted his wanderlust, she told him, leading an independent life herself. Unfortunately, they quarreled before he left. But most of their time together had been enjoyable and, oddly enough, he missed her.

Win told Jeb about Jeannette the next day when they rode into town.

"You are full of surprises, you old drifter." Jeb looked at him sideways. "I thought it was buying land that made you seem different, but I guess love is the reason. It's about time a woman caught your heart. You gonna bring her here to live on your mountain?"

Win figured Jeb could have easily said it was finally time a woman *other than Meg* caught his heart, but he didn't, so Win didn't joke, either. Meg and Jeb seemed closer than ever, and immune to the jabs of jealousy he'd been able to inflict in the past. "I don't know if Jeannette caught enough of my heart. I'm not sure she'd like living on a mountain, anyway." He decided to change the subject. "Meg looks good. I expected her to be in quite a state, losing Gus."

"She was at first. She was pretty low, but the schoolteacher, Etta Sinclair, helped her out of it. So did taking on some of what Gus used to do. Working with the stock helps her feel close to him, I think. She grew up in the stables, so it makes sense that she feels comfortable there. She only learned to cook so they could run that way station together. She sure wanted Gus to live out his life out here. You know how devoted she was to him." A breeze swirled around them, kicking up a little dust. "That was a mighty thoughtful thing to do, Win, naming the peak after Gus. How did you really get the money to pay for the land?"

"Ha! What makes you think I didn't just save my wages?"

"Because I know you, and this seems like one of those times where you say that stupid motto of yours."

Win grinned. "Well, I didn't want to brag in front of Meggie and the boys, but, Jeb, old friend, you are looking at one hell of a lucky poker player. In Washington, DC, I finagled my way into an inner circle of men with too much money and too little common sense." He shook his head. "That group of shifty bastards had been murdering Indians for years with their damn treaties and policies, starving those who stayed on the reservations and hunting down those who didn't. I spent a painful month with those pigs, trying to change their minds. In the end, I finally just played poker with them, quietly taking their money. I felt justified funding a land purchase for Gray Wolf from their personal bank accounts."

Jeb whistled. "Do they know what you did with their money?"

"Nah. I was tempted to throw it in their faces, believe me. Brewer had wired me the cost of the acreage, so I knew exactly what I was playing for. I resisted gloating and walked away as soon as I had enough to buy what I needed."

"Shows good restraint to quit while you're ahead."

"Once I won their money, they wanted to win it back, of course. I've gotta make myself scarce in Washington for a while. I wasn't doing a lick of good there anyway. There's a woman, Mrs. Jackson, who published a book last year about the government's treatment of the Indian. It's called *A Century of Dishonor*. She sent a copy to every member of Congress. I heard she wrote a quote from Benjamin Franklin in each copy . . . something about looking at your own hands stained with blood. Even she couldn't change policy."

"Maybe people will see the light someday."

"You're optimistic."

"Sometimes it's hard to see the effect of someone right away. Just like that riverboat singer."

"Hell, Jeb, I tell you about one gal who turned my head, and you're already marrying us."

"Ha! You're right; sorry."

"I just became a goddamn land owner; that's a big enough bone to chew on for a while."

Jeb and Win arrived at the Carters' store and Georgia created quite a stir greeting Win. She fussed over him like a mother while Mick scolded her for fussing, but then behaved the same way. After the news was shared and business tended to, however, Georgia got a sad look in her eye and pulled a package out from under the counter. It was addressed to Gus.

"I'm not sure what to do with it," she said. "I don't want to upset Meg or Etta . . ."

"Etta?" Win asked.

"Gus's sweetheart, the schoolteacher." Georgia spoke in a whisper, although no one else was in the store. Win raised his eyebrows, causing Georgia's finger to wag at him. "Don't you say a word, Win Avery. Miss Sinclair is a very private person and would be horrified to know I knew about Gus and her. But Gus came in just days before he died, looking for something special for her. He saw these hair combs, but the Smith boy had knocked the case over and one was chipped, so he ordered a set from our catalog. I'm sure that's what is in the package."

"Gus always told Meg how pretty she looked when she wore the combs I gave her. The ones Ma had, remember?" Jeb stared at the package.

"I remember." The image of Sarah Dawson, sitting in front of a mirror and putting the combs in her hair, popped into his head. Jeannette would hold an earring to her ear as she looked at her reflection. What was it about women and pretty things? He wondered if Meg had earrings. He had never seen her wear them. Combs for her wild hair seemed better suited for her. He brushed all three women from his thoughts as Jeb opened the package. Two matching combs were neatly packed in a box.

"What do I owe you for them, Georgia?"

"We're square, Jeb." Mick dismissed the offer with a wave of his hand.

Jeb carefully returned the combs to the

box. "Well, it's obvious he bought them for Miss Sinclair. I'll deliver them to her."

"Thank you, Jeb. You handle things so well and I . . ." She pulled out her handkerchief and dabbed her nose. "I just get emotional. Poor woman . . . with those rumors that follow her around and now Gus . . ." She didn't finish, but only shook her head.

As they rode toward the schoolhouse, Win pressed Jeb with questions until he finally spilled the beans about Gus and Miss Sinclair. Gus had told Jeb it had been a long time since he had been in the company of a woman who inspired him in such a way.

Win laughed out loud. "Jeb, you amaze me. You're the most moral and decent person I know and yet you condoned this amorous union."

"Aw, hell, Win, you make me sound boring."

"So old Gus swept a schoolteacher off her feet and had a heart attack while they were —" The image rendered him momentarily speechless. "It's just not fair."

"Not fair, perhaps, but don't pity him. They had been seeing each other for months. He spent every Saturday night at her place. He'd come home just ahead of the sun, whistling and smiling. In fact, I cautioned him that their secret wouldn't stay a secret if he wasn't careful. He was concerned about Miss Sinclair's reputation, but . . ." Jeb smiled. "It was hard to keep him from floating off the ground."

Win laughed. "See? That's what I'm talking about. Most people would say they oughtn't have been carrying on . . . Why don't you?"

"What's right and what's wrong is measured by a rule stick I've come to question." Jeb shook his head. "I say as long as it isn't hurting anyone, let people be. There were rumors Miss Sinclair was married to an outlaw who was killed busting out of jail, yet she is one of the most charming women I've ever met. The boys get excited about schoolwork — can you believe it? I don't care if she kept company with Gus. She gave him some of the best months of his life."

"Amen, brother," Win said. "I should be so lucky."

When Win and Jeb arrived at the schoolhouse to give Etta her package, the ponies James and Charlie rode were still tied up outside. The boys and Miss Sinclair were bunched together, hovering over her desk. They turned their inquisitive expressions toward the door when the two men blocked the sunlight streaming in.

Miss Sinclair straightened up. "Mr. Dawson, please come in. We've become quite absorbed by a walking stick." Her eyes held amusement, the way Gus's used to.

Win took off his hat as he strode over to the teacher and extended his hand. "Winston Avery, ma'am."

"Of course you are! I'm Etta Sinclair." She shook his hand. "What I've heard about you could fill a book."

Win wanted to say that he had heard the same about her, but held back, not wanting to start off on the wrong foot. Besides, the boys had torn shirts and dirty faces. James had a bloody lip.

Miss Sinclair turned to Jeb. "It's not as bad as it looks."

"Looks like a fight. What happened, boys?" Jeb touched James's swollen cheek.

"Billy Smith called Anne a squaw. Said only Indians work at our ranch, so she must be a squaw and cooks squaw food. Said we ate dog. So I punched him," Charlie said.

"How come James looks worse than you, then?"

"Cuz he jumped in before Billy could punch me back. Billy grabbed my shirt and tore it, but James was quick! Got a couple a good licks in before Billy knew what was up!" Recounting his version of the story, a wound-up Charlie began reenacting the fight until James scowled at him, uncoiling his wire spring.

"James and Charlie know I don't approve of fighting in the schoolyard, but honestly, the Smith boy had it coming. He taunts everyone. I've reprimanded him many times, and finally had to speak to his parents. I'm afraid the apple doesn't fall too far from the tree in this case. I can hardly blame James for something I'm tempted to do myself."

"So, they aren't being kept after school as punishment?"

"Oh, heaven's no! When we dismissed for the day, I spotted a walking stick on the window ledge. We just got to looking at it." Miss Sinclair tilted her head in a way that indicated all was well.

"I figured I'd give Billy a chance to get on home." James scratched his cheek. "No sense rehashing the same fight. He's a pretty sore loser."

"That was wise, James. You OK?" Jeb rested his hand on his son's shoulder.

James nodded. "I reckon."

James looked so much like Jeb at his age and Jeb reminded Win of Dr. Dawson. Calmness and understatement certainly ran in their bloodline. For a moment, Win was transported back in time to Miss Palmer's classroom, after he and Jeb had committed some minor crime. He glanced at Charlie who, although he had Meg's coloring, could have easily been a young Winston.

"How does Billy look?" Win asked Charlie, barely able to suppress a smile.

"Worse than James, that's for sure!" Charlie was eager to share more details, but James just shrugged and said Billy would be fine — he hadn't hit him that hard. Miss Sinclair suggested the boys run along home, which they did, but not before one last wave of thanks to their teacher as they disappeared out the door.

Once the boys were out of earshot, a shadow fell across the teacher's face. "Jeb, I should warn you. Billy Smith was just echoing the hateful talk he hears at home and in town. Please be careful."

"I'm sorry you had to deal with this, Etta." Jeb and the teacher relaxed formalities now that the boys were gone. "I appreciate your understanding about the fight."

Miss Sinclair dismissed his thanks with the wave of her hand and a smile. She gently picked up the walking stick and placed it back on the windowsill. "Your boys are such a treasure. It warms my heart to see the way they look out for one another." She remained at the window, watching them ride away. "I should have liked boys, if I'd been lucky enough to have children."

Jeb handed the package he'd been holding to her. "I believe this was intended for you."

She sat down at her desk and carefully opened the box. She sighed when she saw the combs. "Oh, Gus, how thoughtful of you. I miss you so."

Gus often described women in terms of how much sparkle life had scraped from them. None of the sparkle had been scraped from Miss Sinclair, despite her history. Win stared quizzically at the woman who had captured Gus's heart, wondering how Jeannette would behave in this situation.

Miss Sinclair glanced at Win, a sad but gentle smile on her lips. "Jeb and I have shared experiences that allow candor between us. Don't judge me too harshly."

"Oh, no, ma'am, I don't. Actually, I was thinking about how lucky Gus was to have known you."

"I'm the lucky one. He brought me a lot of joy, even if briefly. I'm not sorry about it. 'Better to have loved and lost, than never to have loved at all.' " She held her head high.

"Tennyson."

"I see you've had access to the Dawson's library as well! Gus loved poetry."

Win wondered if Jeannette would be so

486

kind when she talked about him, if at all, and if she would still refuse to see him if he looked her up.

Etta came to the Dawson ranch for Sunday dinner. When Meg learned of the fight at school, she rode over to the teacher's cottage to thank her and to invite her to join their family for the day. Miss Sinclair arrived in her carriage with a small wooden box in the seat next to her, covered with a dish towel.

"Hello!" The teacher pulled to a stop in front of the porch. Win took the reins as Jeb helped her down from her carriage with the box in hand. Meg stepped out of the house and the two women greeted each other with a kiss on the cheek. "I brought nothing to contribute to your meal, Meg, dear, as I refuse to compete in arenas in which I have no chance of winning." She laughed gaily. "I do, however, have a project for James and Charlie." She turned her attention to the boys. "This poor thing caught sight of his reflection in my window and bashed into the glass just as I was leaving." She gingerly removed the dish towel to reveal a sparrow, unwilling, or unable, to fly away. "I was hoping you two had some ideas as to how we could help the poor chap."

James and Charlie peered into the box. James said, "How 'bout you put some hay in the box to make it softer, Charlie? I'll make a little cup out of a leaf and put some water in it. Then we can get some seeds. I think sparrows eat seeds."

Charlie ran off to the barn.

"Maybe the bird just got the wind knocked out of him. He might need a little time to clear his head." James spoke to his teacher as though she were a concerned relative. Miss Sinclair nodded soberly, but her eyes danced.

James walked away slowly, carefully carrying the box. Miss Sinclair sighed and once again wished aloud for boys of her own. She turned and found a seat on the porch. The dogs, preferring Etta even to the mysterious box she had handed to James, crowded around her feet for attention. "Oh, my darlings, such devotion!" She put her forehead against each as she scratched their ears. "My goodness, coming out here is a tonic, Meg, darling. I so appreciate it."

"You are a tonic for us as well, Etta." Meg patted her friend gently on her back. "Thank you again for understanding about the boys."

" 'Protecting what you love is as natural as breathing,' someone once told me." Etta winked at Meg before turning her attention to Win. "Mr. Avery, Meg tells me you've had quite a lot of contact with the Indians. Have you seen some progress toward assimilation?"

"They're being forced into schools where they have to wear white men's clothes and speak only English. We've taken everything away from them." Win paced across the porch. "We've taken their land, their means for survival, and now even their language and culture."

"Wash and Running Elk changed voluntarily, with no pressure from us." Jeb sounded defensive.

Win raised his hand. "I'm not talking about them. Even Gray Wolf wanted his people to learn English. He thought it would show that they were willing to cooperate at some level. You didn't force him to give up his culture. I'm talking about Indian children on the reservations. You should see them. The schools are poorly managed, with few supplies or books. And the children look ridiculous in their suits and dresses. Generations are now divided by language, and it's killing their traditions. Grandparents are no longer able to pass down their history through stories because of a language barrier, if you can believe it."

"My heart breaks to hear you talk, Mr. Avery." Etta leaned forward. "But education is important. To lose their culture in the process is wrong, but without education, they will never assimilate into our world."

"Why should they have to?" Win spread his arms out in exasperation. "We should be the ones learning their language. After all, we came to their country."

"You make a valid point, Mr. Avery, but you are being impractical. Their world has changed, like it or not. It disturbs me greatly to hear that their education is substandard to what white children receive. If they are expected to adopt white customs, they should be given the best opportunity to do so. How would you propose we fix the problem?"

"I don't know. I wish we could have found a way to live side by side with the Indians. But what should have been simple got complicated, and people don't behave well when things get complicated. I wonder how different their world might be if our government had honored even one of the treaties they made." Win nodded to Jeb. "Gray Wolf and Jeb figured out how to live next to each other — we should ask them."

"Working out an arrangement on a small scale — on private property, I should add

— is different from managing a whole country." Jeb eased himself into a chair. "At one time, I was naïve enough to believe there was plenty of land to share."

"We were all naïve. It was hard to see what was happening until it happened. By then, we were too late. It's been frustrating." Win leaned against a support beam and stared at the horizon.

"I assure you, an Indian from any tribe would be welcome in my classroom," Etta said with sincerity that Win believed. She tilted her head. "Tell us some good news . . . surely there must be some. What are you doing next?"

Win turned to Etta, not wanting to meet Meg's eyes. "There are some good things happening. Our old friend Wes Powell is directing something called the Bureau of Ethnology. Congress created it. With a pen stroke, everything pertaining to the Indian culture was swept from the Department of the Interior and dumped into his lap at the Smithsonian."

"I read about his work. It's a growing field of research," Etta said. "I understand that he holds a higher opinion of the Indian than most."

"If you mean that he's never questioned their right to exist, yes. It is not a common belief, but one I hold, too. Powell's going to study the language and culture of Indians before it disappears, if you can believe the irony. It sounds far more appealing to me than the survey expeditions I've been on. I was offered a job on another survey into the Sierra Nevada, but I turned it down. The job meant living with geologists and entomologists, and I've grown tired of their scientific, unemotional minds! They spend their lives identifying rocks and bugs. I have never seen such attention given to such dull objects. They hold up a rock and confer with one another for hours, using words that sound like a foreign language. They're so engrossed in their work they don't see the splendor around them."

"Don't you like science?" Etta looked at him with amusement.

"Win doesn't care for scien*tists,*" Jeb said. "They don't drink enough or play enough poker for his taste."

"Ha! You're only half right, Jeb. It's true that they don't drink much, but their real problem is that they understand probability too well, and without the aid of whiskey to muddle their judgment, they stay too sharp and never become reckless. Takes all the fun out of it. To answer your question, Miss Sinclair, I don't dislike them, but they have disappointed me. I may not see eye to eye with gold seekers or railroad men, but at least their motives are easy to spot. I can fight an enemy that I can see. Scientists are scarier because I don't understand their motives and the purpose of their studies, or know if the knowledge they gain will be put to good use or ill."

"Are there others who share your romantic view of the world?" Miss Sinclair asked.

"There's a photographer who lives in the Sierra Nevada, name of John Muir. He's been photographing the vistas. They say his pictures are astounding. He sounds like someone who sees land as more than mining potential."

Jeb and Meg glanced at each other — one of those looks married couples give each other that says their minds are so aligned that whatever they think must be true; no divergent, only espousal, points of view. Win found it annoying, though he had to admit to himself that they were on to him. He *had* avoided answering Miss Sinclair's original question, which was to ask what he was doing next. He knew it would upset Meg, or maybe, in his muddled mind, he hoped it would.

"So, you're no longer with any geological survey teams. What is next for you, then?"

Jeb asked.

"Ha!" Win spread his arms. "Jeb, would you believe it? I'm conferring with one agency director on Tuesday, and, by Wednesday, another is offering me an opportunity too good to pass up."

Jeb shook his head amicably at his friend. "Ha, yourself! You dance with every eligible prospect and then beguile the prettiest one into thinking they need you." Win just shrugged, pleased with the image Jeb created because it sounded like he was in control of his own future.

"You still haven't said what you were doing." Meg looked concerned.

Win braced himself. "First I'm going to the Idaho Territory. I'm taking a team to a tribe near the Canadian border . . . We're going to record their language."

"And you somehow convinced Powell that you knew where to go," Jeb said.

Win grinned. "You are correct. I have an extraordinarily keen sense of direction." Win pretended he was getting away with something. "Powell is known for picking up locals to hire, and since we've crossed paths over the years, he considers me a native. He and Hayden don't get along, but he didn't hold that against me. In fact, he seemed to enjoy hiring me away from him."

"You said 'first.' Do you have plans after that?" Etta asked.

Win had had enough of his own divertive banter. "Yes, after that, I'm headed for Alaska."

"Alaska!" Meg slumped in her chair.

"I'm not going yet, Meggie. I'll be in the mountains of Idaho for a while."

"Working for the Smithsonian," Jeb said. His voice held reassurance, as though being connected to the institute brought a level of safety to it.

"It could be awhile before I actually get to Alaska. Hell, it'll probably be crisscrossed with railroads by then. I hope I can see it while it's still a frontier." Win shifted restlessly. Just saying the words made him feel as if he might miss the opportunity.

"Mr. Avery could do some very important work there." Etta surprised him with her alliance. "His devotion to the Indian is admirable. While I hold to my belief that education and assimilation is the key to their survival, preserving their culture is important. It is noble of you to be on their side."

"Well, I see I have some support." Win tossed an indignant glance in Meg's direction.

"Oh, Win, you know we support you. We'll just miss you. It's so far away." Meg folded her arms across her chest.

"I'll miss you all, too, Meggie." Win felt pulled in so many directions he had to physically move. He rose from his chair and paced slowly back and forth across the porch, half listening as Etta told Jeb and Meg about some of the policies regarding the education of Indians. He thought about the week he'd spent with Jeannette. She was the first woman other than Meg who had held his interest. The ladies he met in Washington loved his exotic company, but knew nothing about the man he was. His opinions were often met with puzzled stares. Bouchard had encouraged him to take a Crow woman, but they regarded him with bewilderment as well. Jeannette seemed to understand him — at least until she got angry and threw him out. She was the one who had said it first, that he *needed* to see Alaska. It was territory purchased from the Russians. Who lived there, and why? How did they survive in a climate so harsh? He had to see it and find out. Maybe he truly could be influential; do some good. His heart beat faster. He wasn't sure if it was from his eagerness to get there, or his anguish at leaving behind people he cared about.

His thoughts were interrupted by a yelp

from Charlie. The adults on the porch all turned to see him fallen backward in the dirt as the recuperating bird flapped his wings about in the box. The two boys had been hunched over the bird all afternoon. It flapped its wings again and then suddenly took flight, landing on the fence post of the corral. Everyone clapped and cheered.

Miss Sinclair declared the Dawson boys to be her smartest students. Meg glowed with pride. Although both were no stranger to sadness or pain, still, the sparkle hadn't been scraped from either of them. He thought about Jeannette. Maybe he should write to her. Maybe she'd be willing to change her mind and see him again. It was hard to imagine her sitting here with two proper women, though. Jeb's mother could sit with them; so could Grace Moberg and Georgia Carter. They were proper women. Jeannette wasn't, but she sure could sing, and her skin was so soft . . . . He jumped off the porch and trotted over to the boys to brush away the conflicting thoughts swirling around in his head.

CHAPTER FIFTY: JEB

October 1882

Jeb wasn't sure what he'd done to deserve the little piece of heaven right here on Earth, as Meg called it. He'd wondered if she would feel differently about laying with him now that they'd given up trying to have more children. He worried that sex would remind her of their failures, and she would turn away from him in bed. But the opposite turned out to be the case. Happy in her role as a horse-training partner, Meg was full of sexual energy. Jeb collapsed in breathless satisfaction next to her, their bodies glistening from exertion. His arms still around her, he pulled her over to him so her head rested on his shoulder, her breasts pressed against his rib cage, and her legs tangled with his and the bed sheets.

"I'm the luckiest woman on Earth."

Jeb acknowledged that he felt the same way with a kiss on the top of her head. A loving wife and two fine boys — no dream of his had gone unrealized.

Meg never seemed drawn to luxuries, but Jeb wondered if she worried that their modest business would never grow into much more than it was now. "Does it bother you that our profit margin will always be thin?" he asked.

"If we can't do better because our neighboring ranchers don't like Running Elk and Wash working for us, then I will trade profit for friendship any day of the week; you know that." Meg nestled closer. "What we have is all I've ever wanted."

"I'll keep that in mind next time I balance the books."

"Joke all you want. You have no idea how happy I am."

"Actually, I do, Meggie." He caressed her thigh.

"I wish Win would find someone. I'd like to see him happier."

"I believe he has. He told me about a woman he met on a riverboat."

"He never said anything to me about her."

"Well, of course not. Then he couldn't flirt with you."

"Oh, for heaven's sake — Win and I don't flirt!"

"You don't, but Win can't help himself.

499

He loves women — he loves you, anyway, and maybe this other woman."

"But not like he loves adventure."

"He can't seem to settle down; that's true. Since you're taken, maybe this Jeannette will finally rope him."

"Such talk! I can't believe you're saying these things!" Meg pretended to be indignant. "You men are mysterious creatures."

Jeb laughed. "Not really."

A letter from Win arrived shortly after his visit.

September 30, 1882

Dear Jeb and Meg, James and Charlie,
 I hope this letter finds the Dawson family well and thriving. I am delayed in Beaver Creek and decided to use the extra time to thank you again for your delightful hospitality.
 I was unaware, when I was James and Charlie's ages, that boys grow so incredibly fast at a certain point that it is almost unsettling to watch. It is as though boys that age become mystical creatures who transform at a different rate than the rest of the world. It gives youth a certain power — something they are unaware of, much

like a beautiful woman who does not know the influence she holds over men captivated by her beauty. Equal to the awe parents experience while watching their children grow so exponentially appears to be the exasperation those same creatures generate. The daily mischief of an eleven-year-old boy can produce a level of vexation I am only now coming to appreciate. I should write to our Miss Palmer, Jeb, and apologize for my classroom transgressions during those trying years. This all comes to my mind because, as I write this, I am witness to an Indian mother furiously scolding her adolescent son. What crimes he committed I do not know — all I can say is that I hope you boys know how lucky you are to have parents —"

"You're makin' that up!" Charlie interrupted Jeb, who was reading Win's letter aloud on the shady side of the porch. Jeb raised his eyebrows at the boy and held the page so he could see for himself.

"Hmmm . . . I think you owe your father an apology," Meg said.

"I'm sorry, Pa." Charlie sighed deeply.

Jeb knew it had been a difficult week for the eleven-year-old. James got to help Jeb get one of their new horses saddle ready, and he caught two more fish than Charlie that morning. When Charlie went to town with Jeb, Mrs. Carter had given him a big hug at the store, which he said he didn't mind, but Penny Smith, Billy's little sister, had seen him and smiled evilly. Jeb knew that on Monday Billy would have something to say about it. Now Win was talking about some mystical power. Jeb figured that Charlie might draw comfort from the fact that somewhere, an Indian boy was having as hard a day as he was. "May I continue?"

Jeb got a sullen nod from the boy.

"Let's see . . ."

. . . how lucky you are to have parents who have high expectations of you, but who are kind and fair as well.

I am waiting for the rest of my party in a town that has seen much over the decades in spite of being so isolated. Although it seems like I am at the edge of the world, the fur trade had a route through this area for generations. Gold seekers worked claims nearby as recently as a decade ago. A Jesuit priest lived here, as evidenced by a small chapel built from logs and stone, but he isn't around anymore, and no one seems to know what happened to him. I met an old Indian woman wearing modern eyeglasses who was creating a beautiful pair of beaded moccasins for her granddaughter. She spoke crude French, so we could communicate a bit, but I was unable to discern if she was senile or merely playing with me when I asked her where the beads came from. She answered "la Chine," which I assumed to be China. I asked her how long she had had the beads, and she answered that her grandmother made moccasins for her with the same beads when she was young. I looked at her design and realized they were letters from an odd-looking alphabet that the Russians use, which is quite different from our own. Bouchard and I met a Russian once who carried a book written in his language. I remembered the letters, as they were so unusual looking. I asked her if she knew Russian, but she just laughed at me with a toothless grin and said she thought they were pretty designs. I made the mistake of asking her what tribe she was from. She got angry then and shooed me away, although why it was wrong of me to ask, I cannot say. Perhaps all of my questions simply became annoying.

Before I become annoying to my dear family as well, I will end this missive. It is

*my hope that I have more news to share
soon. Although I am eager to see the next
horizon, I am even more certain that buying the land adjacent to the Dawson ranch
was prudent for this old wanderer.*

Win

"Did the old Indian really have beads
from China?" Charlie asked his father.
"How'd she get them?"

Jeb started to explain how furs were
traded for other things all over the world
when Meg rose from her chair suddenly and
wrapped her arms around him.

"I'm so glad you're here with me, Jeb. I'm
so glad . . ." She buried her face in his neck.

He leaned into her embrace, her wild hair
soft on his neck. After all their years of marriage, her touch still felt like coming home
— every time.

Shortly after Win's letter arrived, Mick galloped up the trail from town, waving a
telegram, shouting for Jeb and Meg.

Meg, working with a yearling inside the
corral, ran to the fence. "Mick, my goodness, what's wrong?"

Mick handed the message to Jeb, who'd
hustled out of the barn and over to their
friend.

504

Jeb stared at the words, panic in his throat. He read aloud:

BEAVER CREEK, IDAHO TERRITORY AVERY ATTACKED BY BEAR stop JEB COME IMMEDIATELY stop

Meg gasped; her hand flew to cover her mouth. Jeb turned to Meg. "The boys can handle things here. I'll ask Wash to stay close until I come back."

"No!" Meg glanced uncomfortably at Mick.

A married man, Mick needed no more signal that the couple required privacy. "I'll let you two alone to figure this out. Let us know if we can help." He turned his horse and rode out of the yard.

"He needs me, Meg," Jeb said as Mick disappeared.

"I need you, too, right here."

Jeb tilted his head. "This isn't like you. What's going on?"

"He's God knows where, in some remote corner of the world —"

"It's settled enough for a telegraph office."

"There! Exactly. He probably has plenty of help."

"But he's asking for me. That's concerning."

"Well, I'm concerned about you!"

Jeb gathered his thoughts for a moment, searching for the right words to reassure her. "Don't let a bad dream cloud your judgment, Meg. I know it scared you, but sometimes a nightmare is just a nightmare . . . nothing more."

Days earlier, Jeb woke to Meg whimpering in her sleep next to him. He gently shook her awake, repeatedly assuring her she was safe until she emerged from sleep and recognized him. She clung to him, saying she hadn't been in danger in her dream — Jeb had. Since Gray Wolf believed spirits spoke to him in his dreams, she worried she was receiving a message. Jeb had replied that while he would never dismiss Gray Wolf's beliefs, he'd had plenty of nightmares during his lifetime that never materialized into anything real.

"But you were in danger . . ." she said now, covering her face with her hands. A desperate sob escaped.

"Meg," he said softly, pulling her close. She wrapped her arms around his waist and buried her face in his chest. "We're all he has. How can I not go?"

Meg held on to him for a long time. When she released her grip, her brow was furrowed. "I'll get some food together for you."

■ ■ ■ ■

Four days later, Jeb rode into Beaver Creek, a muddy, gloomy little place — perhaps because it was raining, although he couldn't imagine how the sun shining on it would improve it much. He found Win asleep, lying face down and naked from the waist up on a dingy cot in a dimly lit back room of the town saloon. Jeb learned from the saloonkeeper, Dal Peyton, that a mountain man found him barely alive and half buried in pine needles in the Bitterroot. He brought him down the mountain to Peyton because his wife was a healer.

Win's fever broke just the day before, Peyton said, and he had had a good night's rest.

Jeb dozed in the chair next to Win's bed, listening to his friend talk in his sleep. When Win finally stirred, he cursed in pain.

"Drink this." Jeb held a cup to Win's lips.

Win recoiled. "What is it? Peyton's squaw concocted something that gave me visions. I couldn't feel my face for two days." He rubbed his cheek as though reliving the experience.

"Willow bark tea. Meg's recipe."

"Meg's? Oh, God, this will probably kill

me." But he drank, swallowing noisily. He lay his head back down. Jeb felt his ailing friend's forehead, relieved that it was cool. Win wasn't fighting a fever and had already made a joke. Convinced he wasn't going to die, Jeb leaned back in his chair. "You were talking in your sleep."

"Hmmm . . ." Win furrowed his brow. "Can't remember my dream."

"No matter. What the hell happened to you?"

"You want the tall tale I've been working on, or the truth?" His voice was hoarse.

"The truth, if you remember how to tell it."

Although fuzzy with the details, Win told Jeb that he was a hundred yards ahead of his party on a well-traveled Indian path when he surprised a grizzly. His horse reared in a panic, threw him, and bolted. The grizzly chased him through the woods. He could hear his party shouting at him, and even heard someone fire a rifle, but the bear was relentless and pursued him to an outcropping next to a waterfall. Win stumbled and landed on the precipice. The grizzly took a swipe at him, ripping open the flesh on his back. He rolled off the edge and fell twenty feet into the icy, rushing water. He banged himself up on the rocks as he was swept downstream. Barely able to pull himself up on to the riverbank where the river finally slowed, Win lay there all night, unable to move. How he got to the bed he was in he couldn't say.

Jeb stretched his long legs out and folded his arms across his chest. "You're gettin' old. You used to be able to outrun a grizzly."

"Well, goddamn, don't get all sappy and sentimental on me."

"Goddamn yourself. That telegram scared the hell out of me. I thought you were a goner. You could at least still be shivering with a fever or something."

"Sorry I can't be sicker for you! I felt someone go through my pockets to see if they could find out who to notify. *That* scared the hell out of *me*!"

Win kept Jeb's name and address in his vest pocket. The military escorts on his expeditions had made this a habit during the war, saying it gave them comfort to know their loved ones would be notified if they were killed. Jeb admitted that having someone fish on his person for next of kin information would scare him, too.

"I can't believe you came all this way." The banter ended. Win sounded grateful.

"Well, I've always admired that rifle of

yours. Figured now was my chance to get it."

Win chuckled, but grimaced again. "Damn, my back hurts. How's it look?"

Jeb lifted the bandage loosely covering the oozing wounds. Win had four long, deep scrapes on his right shoulder and several other smaller scratches and bruises all over his back. Two of the deeper cuts had been crudely sewn to close them. His whole back was covered with some kind of greasy salve. "Someone sewed a chunk of skin back together. That's probably what's bothering you — the stitches pulling, I mean. They put something on the scrapes, looks like Indian medicine."

"The bartender's squaw put something on my back. I hope it isn't moose shit. Smells like it."

"Nah, I think that's just you."

"The rest of the team went on without me." Win sounded disappointed.

"I thought you were their guide."

"Hell, they don't need me. Damn maps."

Win had spent years with surveyors making maps of uncharted territory. There was hardly a stream or mountain that hadn't been marked on paper. Jeb leaned back and pondered the irony as Win drifted back to sleep.

Jeb stayed ten days in Beaver Creek, tending to Win. It was a peaceful village, and the people living there were used to traders and mountain men. Jeb saw the old woman Win wrote about in his letter who had made the moccasins for her granddaughter, but saw no young woman wearing them. Miners came into the saloon; Indians came and went — Win said he still didn't know what tribe they were from.

When Win was feeling better, they went fishing. Jeb found a spot where Win could sit comfortably. It was a sunny day, and although the golden aspen leaves shivered, it was unseasonably warm for late October.

"This is beautiful country." Jeb breathed deeply and gazed at the green and gold hills.

"It's prettier when a bear isn't chasing you down."

"I imagine so. How's the back?"

Win leaned forward and grimaced. "The scabs itch. That tea helps, though. Takes the edge off."

They were quiet for a while. Win watched a trout take a look at his bait and snap at it. He pulled up on his line so quickly he let out a sharp cry of pain, but held on to the fish nonetheless. "Ach, I think I broke something open."

"Here, let me." Jeb reached for the line

and grabbed the flapping fish. He unhooked it and tossed their dinner up on the bank. "You ever think your luck might run out someday?"

"I spent the last week thinking of nothing else." Win shrugged. "Buying that mountain next to yours got me thinking. When I signed my name on that deed, I realized it was the only place my name was written somewhere permanent. It was the only record of me ever being here."

The bear attack had brought about a level of introspection Jeb had not seen in Win since their youthful pact years earlier. "The world is a better place for you being in it, my friend."

"Not sure you'd get complete agreement on that, but thanks." Win was quiet for a moment. "You ever feel burdened, tied down by that ranch?"

Jeb wasn't sure whether Win was changing the subject or about to make a point. In either case, it was an easy question to answer. "Well, the work never ends, but it is satisfying. Meg and the boys . . . they're all I need, or have ever wanted. I am . . . fully content." He glanced at Win, wondering if he'd think Jeb was bragging, but he didn't seem to notice.

"The government sends threats: assimilation or annihilation. Church groups send aid, expecting converted souls for their trouble. You and Powell are among the few who make no demands on these people. I wish they could all live like Gray Wolf." Win squinted at the sun. "And I don't mean hiding in the mountains. I mean able to decide their own future."

"He's had to compromise, too. He's had to watch his way of life fade away, no matter how much he tries to isolate himself. We all have to live in a changing world, like it or not. Hell, I took the train halfway here! I remember when Ma and Pa died. You sat at their kitchen table and said I had to get out here and see this country before it filled with people. You saw it coming."

"You make me sound like a shaman. But it is true that I've watched progress come with a price, and with great uneasiness on my part. I bought that mountain next to yours so I could control what happened to it. I wanted to keep the government, the railroads, miners — hell, even the scientists, away." He picked up a pebble and tossed it into the stream. Unlike a lake, where ripples form in widening circles, the pebble simply disappeared. "Jeb, I think in our lifetime, Indians will be given citizenship. There's been talk. When I bought that mountain, I told Brewer what I wanted to do with it eventually. The disclosure was a little risky, but he was really great when Meg and Gus bought your land, and I felt I could trust him. He advised me to get a good lawyer in a reputable law firm to draft the documents I needed."

"What do you want to do?"

"I want to leave it to Gray Wolf. The laws won't allow it right now, but I think they will in time. Meanwhile, a safe alternative was to leave the property to you. If I die, the mountain is all yours. That's all legal. But I'm hoping you'll honor my wishes and see it through when it is possible and make it legal for the mountain to belong to Gray Wolf and any of his descendants. Permanently."

"No wonder you've been so sober and serious," Jeb said. "You thought you might die without anyone knowing of this? Of course I'll honor your wishes. Does Gray Wolf know?"

"That old Indian believes in spirits more easily than he believes in land ownership. Just wait 'til they pass legislation that makes Indians citizens! He'll either laugh at the irony, or he'll be so confused his head will explode. He knows I bought the land; he doesn't know I want him to have it. I figured

514

I'd let you tell him."

"Ha! Thanks a lot. You tell him yourself. That's the hardest part about all of this — explaining your generosity to that man."

"I can't be sure Gray Wolf will see it as generous. Land ownership is touchy with him already. He may be offended by the idea of me giving it to his family." He settled in; now that his wishes were known, he looked ready to enjoy the day. "I'm doing it for myself, really. Maybe you can help him see it that way."

"Was Gray Wolf the real reason you bought it? I thought you might be getting tired of all this roaming and would settle down with the riverboat singer, Jeannette."

"Nah . . . didn't work out. She's too much of a free spirit. Sent a telegram to the *Missouri Star* in Omaha — that's the riverboat she was on. Telegram came back from the captain saying Miss Bordeaux had moved on. No forwarding address."

"I'm sorry."

"Hell, we had some fun, but it wasn't like you and Meg." He pretended to focus his attention on luring another fish to his bait.

When Win had recovered and was ready to rejoin his crew, Jeb came home. He got off the train at Big Bend. He had done business with the livery there and knew the owner would let him borrow a horse to get the rest of the way home. He wasn't sure he'd get the same reception in Lyonsville. The folks in Lyonsville didn't like the fact that an Arapaho and a Pawnee worked for him. The last time he tried to sell some horses there, he was told they had plenty, even though he could see for himself that the stables were nearly empty. So he got off at Big Bend and rode twenty extra miles cross-country, but at least he rode on a horse he had trained himself and no one gave him trouble about it.

It was rejuvenating to ride through open country. If he looked in the opposite direction of the railroad tracks and telegraph poles, it still looked like the plains they had crossed with the wagon train. What a twist of fate it had been to find Meg out on the prairie. What a life he had made with her. As he crested the last hill, his home came into view. Meg came out of the barn leading a young colt and when she saw him, she dropped the reins and climbed over the corral fence with such urgency Jeb thought surely she would hurt herself. She rushed toward him, waving excitedly. It was a splendid sight.

Jeb sat with Meg on the porch and enjoyed

a quiet evening alone. It was Saturday; Anne had left for the day and Etta had requested the help of the boys to unload a shipment of books. Running Elk and Wash had plans of their own.

"So this is what it will be like when the boys are married and gone." Jeb sighed contentedly and stretched his long frame.

"It's too peaceful and quiet. Besides, they are far too young to be marrying!"

"You weren't much older than they are now when we got married."

"True enough, but you were! Men should be older when they marry, have some experience."

Jeb reached over and held Meg's hand, already thinking about how he would make love to her that night. "Win left his mountain to us in his will, Meggie. But if something happens to him, we're supposed to make sure Gray Wolf eventually owns it. He thinks the laws will change and Indians will be able to live wherever they want to someday."

"He thought he was going to die, didn't he?" Meg shivered and pulled her shawl closer around her.

"He had a pretty close call. He said something interesting. He said when he signed the deed, he realized it was the only indication that he'd ever been on this earth, and that knowledge troubled him."

Meg furrowed her brow. "That makes me sad. Here we are, so lucky to have two beautiful boys." She squeezed Jeb's hand. "I'm sorry I was so silly before you left. I just felt like something terrible was going to happen."

CHAPTER FIFTY-ONE: MEG

Dawson Ranch, Summer 1886

Meg hung the freshly oiled tack neatly on the wall, a habit learned from Gus. She heard the sound of the wagon. Charlie and Jeb were back from town.

"Ma! James!" She and James exited the barn just as Charlie jumped from the wagon, waving a letter. Only a letter from Win could generate such excitement. It had been over a year since he'd written to announce his departure for Alaska. James and Charlie had grown into young men. She and Jeb planned to give James a brand new rifle for his seventeenth birthday. He and Charlie had been at the Carters' store picking it up.

Jeb waited for everyone to gather on the porch, another habit they'd developed over the years. Meg swore she felt Gus join them for Win's letter readings. It couldn't be a coincidence that, although no one ever sat in his favorite chair, it rocked ever so slightly whenever they gathered. Jeb explained that the chair moved from the vibration when everyone clambered up the porch steps, but Meg preferred believing that Gus had joined them.

Jeb began:

July 1885

Dear family,

Alaska is as muddy and ugly as any part of the world I've ever seen, and, at the same time, is more breathtaking than any vista in my memory. The stench from the fish cannery in Sitka burns the inside of my nose, yet, I make a trek inland and ache to share the splendor with all of you. It is mid-summer and the sky stays light almost continuously. The night is extremely short and I am filled with both energy and exhaustion.

While the weather is mild, I have journeyed to stinking Sitka to mail a package to you. It contains Athabascan artwork made by a woman from a tribe who has readily taken me in, and to whom I will return when my business in Sitka is finished. I thought her work was particularly skilled and traded with her. We both believe we got the better trade. I am living near Talkeetna, a place where three rivers meet and where tribes hunt, trade, and gather together seasonally. I enjoy living with these friendly people, who are as eager to bring me along on a caribou hunt as they are to teach me their language.

Our conversation with Miss Sinclair lingers in my head and I continue the debate within myself. Education appears to benefit the youth, if for no other reason than to communicate our differences with clearer understanding. Also, there is no doubt that those who learn English are far more likely to prosper in the new order. Defiance at change, while noble and even understandable, seems to bring nothing positive. Economic self-sufficiency will play an integral role in their success if one accepts Miss Sinclair's pragmatic viewpoint that the native's world has forever changed, like it or not. It seems economic independence is something they should have, at the very least. Finding a way to move forward peacefully is essential, as the native people are ill equipped to fight against the advanced weaponry and machinery we bring to their world.

I feel confused about my purpose here. I want to protect what can be protected and preserve what can be preserved, yet my very presence brings changes that cannot be undone. A few of the Athabascan youth seek me out to hear stories of the land to the south and express interest in traveling with me when I return. Why I worry about their restlessness and not my own keeps me awake at night, along with the persistent daylight.

We both turn forty this year, brother Jeb. Why round numbers stir introspection more than their neighbors just 12 months ahead or behind, I cannot say. There have been times when I never thought I'd make it this far, both in years and in distance. Although I feel welcome here, the only place where I have felt complete peace is the place where I send this letter. With it comes my wish for your good health and happiness.

Win

Jeb pulled a package out from hiding. "This arrived with the letter. What do you think we should do?"

James gasped in surprise.

"Open it!" Charlie shouted, who knew about the package and had been waiting patiently. James nodded in agreement.

"I figured so." Jeb broke the string that held the oilcloth wrapped around a piece of deerskin. Tucked inside was a note and elaborately decorated gifts: a knife and sheath, two pouches, and a necklace. The note indicated that the knife was for Jeb and the sheath was made from the hide of a caribou, an animal similar to an elk, but with different antlers and which ran in large herds. The necklace for Meg, made of abalone shells and colorful beads, was backed with deer hide softer than velvet against her skin. The two pouches for the boys were fashioned from caribou hide and decorated with porcupine quills and hundreds of beads.

"Wow!" Charlie exclaimed, carefully running his hand over the beadwork. James whistled softly in amazement.

"Those are fine gifts, boys. Your Uncle Win was very thoughtful," Meg said. She put the necklace around her neck and looked to Jeb for his opinion.

"It looks very pretty on you," he said, smiling.

"He sounds tired and alone," she said, removing the necklace and looking carefully at it.

" 'Move forward peacefully,' he says. It seems unlikely, doesn't it?"

The fight James and Charlie had with Billy

in the schoolyard years earlier was just the beginning of a problem that continued to grow in the area. Prejudice smoldered, never igniting fully, yet it could never be fully extinguished, either. Folks who hired Indians found they were limited by who would do business with them. Running Elk and Wash had been working at the Dawson ranch for so long they were considered more like family than ranch hands, but others who settled in the area were shocked when the Arapaho and the Pawnee brought horses to the livery and handled the business transactions. Why were Indians allowed to live among the white settlers when General Custer, a war hero, had been slaughtered by these savages only a few years earlier? How can anyone trust that they won't turn on an unsuspecting white citizen? Meg grew more and more impatient with every ignorant remark.

When Running Elk tried to pick up the new reaper-binder Jeb had ordered at the Lyonsville train depot, the machinery sat on the loading dock while Running Elk sat in jail, accused of attempted thievery. Prohibited from telegraphing a message or speaking to anyone, Running Elk was stuck until his absence worried Meg and Jeb left to search for him. Jeb returned with Running

Elk and the machinery, saying he had to pay a hefty fine for his release. She asked what he'd done wrong and Running Elk replied, "Being Indian." After that, either Jeb went himself to pick up orders, or they paid for extra shipping to have it sent to Paradise.

Even Paradise was not free from ugliness. Anne was stopped in the street by a worker from a nearby ranch who asked her why she worked for Indian-lovers. Was she Indian, too? If so, was she from a tribe who ate human flesh, or murdered babies? Luckily, Angus was in the Carters' store and overheard. He came to her defense and the ranch hand was sent on his way duly reprimanded, but not before warning Angus that Paradise would never prosper like Lyonsville if they continued to allow Indians in town.

Tension mounted; the Dawsons stood their ground, along with other Paradise residents. The town grew, but erratically. Businesses opened and failed. One surprise success was Mrs. Finnegan's bakery. The Irishwoman arrived by stage and declared she was opening a bakery next to the saloon. "Over my dead body," was Angus's initial reaction, until he tasted her potato bread and declared it a national treasure. He talked up her breads and pastries with every drink he poured. Soon her shop was busy and profitable. Angus persuaded Mrs. Finnegan to collaborate with him and together they produced their first batch of moonshine from a handmade still in back of their establishments. She welcomed any and all business; it made no difference to her whether her customers were ranchers, farmers, or Indian. She was the exception, however. Most businesses found better success in Lyonsville, which flourished as its residents enjoyed the presence of the railroad and the absence of people different from them — particularly Indians.

Meg did not understand white resentment against Indians. Crazy Horse, their unifying leader, had been killed at Fort Robinson five years earlier. Settlers had flocked into the sacred land of the Black Hills. Chief Joseph of the Nez Percé tried to leave the country, but had to surrender forty miles from the Canadian border. It wasn't only in battle that the Indians were defeated; seemingly well-meaning social reformers tried to mainstream the Indian, resulting in the near destruction of their culture. Outnumbered and poorly armed, prevented from self-sufficient living and with no place to go, the Indian race was brought to its knees. Even Gray Wolf and his small band of Arapaho were caught between two worlds. Conflict rose between Running Elk and his tribe; they didn't think it was safe for him to live in the white man's world, but he saw no other way to survive.

Smoldering tension finally ignited one late-summer day in 1886 when Burton Cauley, Darryl Smith, and Phil Jenkins, three ranch hands at a neighboring spread to the south, walked into Mrs. Finnegan's bakery. Wash and Running Elk had been hired to build a second brick oven for her. Meg heard voices rise and left the Carters' store to investigate. She and Georgia heard Cauley complain that the baker should have given the job to white men, saying that Indians could dress white but would never be white — they were only dirty savages.

Running Elk threw a punch at Cauley. Wash caught a blow when he got between them to try to stop the fight. Mrs. Finnegan screamed for help; Angus burst out of his saloon with a shotgun in hand and fired it into the air. "Hold on there! What are you fools doin'?"

"We have as much right to be here as them." Running Elk rubbed his knuckles.

"You ain't the fool I was talkin' to." Angus nodded in the direction of the three white men. "They're the goddamn idiots

527

who ain't got a lick of brains between 'em. Did your mama drop you on your head when you was a baby, Cauley? Why would Miz Finnegan hire numbskulls to build her oven when she can hire two fellers who can get the job done? It's a free country, or have you forgotten?"

Cauley, Smith, and Jenkins glared at Angus and left without a word. Mrs. Finnegan threw her arms around Angus after they left, causing his face to blush bright red.

"Oh, Mr. McPherson, aren't you a brave lad!" Her Irish accent always got thicker when she spoke to him. "For a Scot, you're quite the fine fellow!"

"Ah, Mrs. Finnegan, those lugs oughta learn a thing or two from a Scotsman and a bonny Irish lass livin' and workin' side by side. 'Tain't so hard." He stole a kiss and she blushed, too.

Meg smiled at the two, stumbling upon joy, as Gus would've called it. Still, the tension she'd just witnessed blocked the sun, chilling the air.

Jeb and Meg were up late delivering a new foal when they saw a red glow coming from town. Jeb called to the bunkhouse for Running Elk and Wash. She heard the two hustle to get dressed; the urgency in his voice required no questions. They emerged moments later and, seeing that fire had broken out in town, headed for the barn to saddle horses.

James appeared on the porch. "I'll come, too, Pa."

"You stay here with your ma, son." Meg helped them get saddled and on their way. Jeb kissed her before he jumped on his horse and said they'd be back as soon as the fire was out. Meg stood in the middle of the yard and watched Jeb, Running Elk, and Wash ride away.

She returned to the house, but smelled smoke. She thought it was from Paradise until Charlie shouted that the barn was on fire. Meg ran out, horrified to see flames lick the side of the barn. She ran toward the fire, not seeing the stranger before he grabbed her.

"Your dirty Indians shoulda stayed home. Then you woulda only lost some worthless savages, and not your whole ranch," he said, his face inches from hers. She shoved the man away with strength she didn't know she had. He fell back, but regained his balance and started toward her. James fired his shotgun, blasting the man off his feet. Meg was momentarily paralyzed, the shock closing her ears to nothing but a rushing sound.

As though looking through distorted glass, Meg watched another man turn and run. He was forgotten as smoke began to billow out from under the barn door. A panicked whinny from one of the horses brought her sharply back to the crisis at hand. She raced to the barn behind James and Charlie.

They were able to get the horses, including the new foal, out of their stalls and outside. Their milk cow got a wild look in her eye and tried to jump out of her stall in a panic. Her front hooves became stuck and she was thrashing in all directions to try to free herself. James kicked at the stall until it broke. Sadie freed herself and mooed loudly as she trotted from the burning barn.

"Ma! Watch out!" Charlie shouted as her skirt brushed over burning straw. She jumped away and grabbed a bucket. The three began the futile task of fighting the flames by tossing buckets of water on them.

Meg didn't know exactly when Gray Wolf and Standing Horse arrived. They materialized and fought the fire alongside them throughout the night. It was endless, exhausting work. With the help of the wind, which shifted in direction and kept the flames away from the other buildings, they were able to save everything except the barn. They watched the fire consume the last of it.

Smoke filled the air as the sky lightened. The charred remains of the barn collapsed. Gray Wolf told her they had run into a white man escaping into the night. He now lay on the forest floor, he said, his throat slit from ear to ear. Meg stared at the other man lying dead in their yard and wondered how James would carry the burden of taking a life. Jeb would have reassuring words. He'd know what to say. Standing Horse dragged the body out of sight.

She stood in the yard with her sons — both of whom towered over her — her mind already calculating how long it would take to rebuild the barn. A couple of no-good vandals couldn't stop them. With that on her mind, she did not comprehend at first why Georgia and Etta, in Etta's carriage, arrived at the ranch just ahead of Mick and Blackie, who drove a wagon with Wash sitting in the back holding two bodies.

Blackie climbed down, reached into the wagon bed, and took Jeb's body from Wash. The giant of a man began to cry when he saw the look on Meg's face. Her mind wouldn't accept what she was seeing, even as her body reacted. She sank to the ground, her legs unable to support her. Blackie laid Jeb gently in her arms.

Etta stepped out of her carriage and put her arms around the boys. Standing Horse and Gray Wolf lay Running Elk on the ground. Everyone stood helplessly by, rendered speechless by grief, shock, and exhaustion.

Mick tried to find words. "They set fire to the saloon and the bakery. Miz Finnegan got out all right, thanks to Angus." His voice broke. "But someone shot him, right there in the middle of the street." He wiped his eyes and reached for Georgia, who buried her face in his shirt, crying. "He shot Running Elk, too, when he tried to save Angus. Jeb and I, we were able to find where the bastard was holed up, but there were two of them. And —" He couldn't finish.

"Jeb didn't know what hit him," Blackie managed to blurt out. "He didn't suffer. I promise you, he didn't suffer."

Meg stared at Jeb's lifeless face. He looked asleep. He said he'd be back when the fire was out. He was supposed to talk to James. His chest was covered with a dish towel Meg recognized as Georgia's. She didn't remove it.

The sun was up. As it rose higher, she expected Jeb to wake at the blinding rays, to blink, squint, and then squeeze his eyes shut. But his serene expression didn't

532

change. She shaded his face nevertheless, putting her hand between him and the harsh, uncomfortable light. She stared at the shadow and watched it move as the Earth turned — and would continue to turn without Jeb. Meg felt a cold hand reach into her chest and squeeze her heart. It hurt so much, tears fell from her cheeks onto Jeb's. He didn't flinch.

Gray Wolf and Standing Horse began to chant the sacred song that connected creatures to their Creator, creating a bridge between this world and the next.

Chapter Fifty-Two: Win

Athabascan Village, Alaska, September 1886
Win woke with a start, and before completely conscious, his dream was more real than the bedding of hides he lay on. He'd had the dream many times before — the dark-haired girl smiling at him.

He sat up and ran his fingers through his hair. He opened the flap of his newly built winter home. The day before, he'd covered the wood frame with birch bark, then moss, and finally topped it with dirt. Like all the other dwellings in camp, his was now covered with the first snowfall. From his doorway, he could see smoke curling out of the centers of several white-colored mounds. He closed the flap door, stirred the fire, and pulled a log from the woodpile against the wall. He tossed it into the embers and watched it crackle to life. He thought of Gray Wolf and their conversation just before he left the Dawson ranch. How many years now? He scratched his long, heavy beard. Four years, he figured.

The last time Win visited the Dawsons, he'd ridden up the mountain to visit his old Arapaho friend. He'd brought Charlie with him. Together, they told Gray Wolf about the land Win had purchased, and, once again, Win struggled to explain the meaning of lines drawn on a map. The Indian humored his friend for a while and then let the matter drop. Gray Wolf had summered in the mountains and wintered in the canyon for years. He had defended his right to do so by maintaining a peaceful friendship with people he could trust, and with rifles against people he didn't. Something written on paper didn't change anything. Win wanted him to know, nonetheless. Gray Wolf accepted this with a nod of his head; the matter was as settled as it would ever be.

"Where will you go next, my friend?" Gray Wolf asked. "You are the wind, blowing over the Earth and never resting."

"It is called Alaska. A territory far away. I want to see it." Win suddenly had an idea. "You should come with me. It will be safe if we travel together. Wouldn't you like to see what's beyond the mountains?"

"You are truthful and noble. You and I will always be friends; I know this. But while your spirit has wings and flies over great distances, my spirit stays on the ground, like a wolf." The aging Arapaho gave Win a wry smile. "Just as your heart tells you to go, my heart tells me to stay and protect my den. It is wise to listen to our hearts."

Win had reached into his shirt then and pulled out the wolf's tooth that he always wore around his neck. He showed it to Charlie. "See this? Gray Wolf gave this to me when I left on my first expedition. I have kept it with me all these years. It helps me be a good hunter, strong and swift, like the wolf it came from."

Charlie looked at it carefully. "Is it magic?"

"It does have magic. When I wear it, Gray Wolf, your ma and pa, you, and James are with me, like a wolf pack, and I am not alone."

Charlie studied the tooth carefully while Gray Wolf studied Win. "You are more like a wolf than you know. A wolf has hunting skill and speed, but he also has strong family devotion. Your heart remains divided, my friend. It flies away searching, but always returns home." He pulled a carving from his pouch. "I made this for you." He handed it to Win. Two complete circles, carved from a single piece of wood, intertwined with no breaks in either piece. On one was carved the footprint of a wolf, on the other, the wing of an eagle.

"Oh!" Charlie whispered. "Would you look at that! How'd you do that?"

"I will show you." Gray Wolf smiled at the boy.

"I am honored to wear it," Win said. It was a magnificent piece. He untied the thin leather strip that held the wolf's tooth and threaded both wooden circles onto it. Then he retied the end and pulled it back over his head. "Thank you, my friend. It will protect me until I find my way home."

In his Alaskan lodge, Win gathered paper and pencil. His task this winter was to record the stories of the Athabascan. He would start with the chief, a fine fellow who reminded him of Gray Wolf.

CHAPTER FIFTY-THREE:
MEG

Dawson Ranch, October 1886

Meg sat at her desk in the library and stared out into the bright sun through the open window. A sudden breeze picked up the piece of paper in front of her and tossed it into the middle of the room. She hadn't written anything, so she simply took another from the drawer and let the first lie on the floor. This time she moved a paperweight over to trap the page on the desk. Blackie had made the paperweight for Jeb two years earlier. Business was slow and he had started experimenting with designs. This was one of his first. It had a flat, heavy piece of iron on the bottom with an elegant swirl attached to it as a handle. The swirl looked like the blowing wind. Meg stared at it, wondering if Blackie designed it with that in mind — a depiction of the very thing that made the paperweight necessary. She considered this for a long time. It kept her from thinking about the letter she had to write.

She had to tell Win that Jeb was gone. It was the right thing to do. She didn't want to, however, for a number of reasons. The biggest reason was that it hurt too much. Writing it down somehow made it more real, a truth she didn't want to face. She also knew her letter would bring Win home, and she didn't want him to come. Having him visit was always a little bittersweet; she loved seeing him because Jeb enjoyed his company so much. The friendship they shared had the same comfortable familiarity that she saw in James and Charlie, and knew it was precious to them both. But he always left, which always hurt. She couldn't bear any more hurt.

Her mind drifted back to one of his visits years ago. It was early spring, a few years before Gus died, so James must have been about nine, she guessed. The boys had been fishing at the stream and were walking back with a stringer of trout. Win showed up unannounced, riding in ahead of a thunderstorm, looking like a mountain man. He hadn't shaved in a year, or bathed in nearly as long. With a full beard and hair to his shoulders, he was barely recognizable. He wore an enormous bear hide as a coat and a buckskin shirt underneath. His head was covered with a fur hat. He rode up behind the boys as they carried the stringer and their fishing poles home.

"Hey boys, what's for supper?" Win called out as his horse splashed across the stream.

They both turned and saw what looked like a grizzly on horseback. Win said he could tell the moment they recognized him under the beard and furs. Grins spread across their faces.

"Uncle Win!" Charlie shouted. "Wow, you're a sight to behold!"

James held up the stringer and said, "You look like a bear. You don't mind if we cook these first, do you, Mr. Grizzly?"

Win threw his head back and laughed. Jeb and Gus came around from the side of the house, curious at the commotion. Meg appeared at the back kitchen door.

"What on earth?" Meg cried when she saw him. "You need a bar of soap and a razor, stranger." She smiled broadly. "But it's good to see you, Win."

"I do apologize for my appearance, Mrs. Dawson. Transportation is so efficient these days. I had no opportunity to clean up first, or to warn you I was coming." He told them he had arrived in Bozeman just in time to hear the eastbound train whistle announce its departure. Without thinking, he jumped on board and just a day later found himself at the Big Bend railroad depot. The town had little more than a livery, so all he could do was secure a mount. .

The wind suddenly shifted and the smell of rain filled the air.

"The storm followed you. Let's get inside." Jeb slapped Win on the back.

James and Charlie dropped the fish at the back door so they could take Win's horse to the barn, but Gus simply pointed at the fish and took the reins himself. With no more protest than a sigh, the boys picked the stringer up and headed off to clean them.

"I'll get some bathwater heated." Meg turned to go inside. Before she was out of earshot, she heard a piece of their conversation.

"You OK?" Jeb asked. They stood in the yard as the wind picked up. A few drops of rain fell. Win had replied, "I am now."

The rain beat steadily on the roof of the brand new laundry room Jeb built just off the kitchen. It was large enough to hold a full-sized bathtub, plus a place to hang laundry. Meg filled the washtub as soon as Win's bath was ready. She put up a sheet for privacy. Jeb handed Win's clothes to Meg as Win lowered himself into the steaming tub with a gasp.

"She gets the water plenty hot," Jeb warned Win too late.

"No fooling," Win replied sarcastically.

"Well, it just cools down so fast," Meg said, defending herself. "Win, you see that brush? I expect you to use it."

"Meggie, I'm not eight." Win sounded pestered. "When did you get so clean? You're usually the one with grit in your hair."

She let out an indignant cry. "Winston Avery, I can't believe you said that!"

"Now, now, you two," Jeb said, laughing. "Stop your bickering."

"She started it!" Win sounded like the eight-year-old he claimed he wasn't. Meg heard the amusement in his voice.

"Oh, now you're asking for it." She picked up a pail and pitched cold water over the privacy sheet and into Win's bath. He let out a yelp, causing James and Charlie to double over in laughter.

Her smile faded along with the memory as she picked up her pen. Her chest ached. She didn't think her heart could take any more hurt. Biscuit, then Gus. Every lost pregnancy had chipped away at her heart, and now Jeb. She put her hand on her chest, surprised to feel it beating. Finally, she began to write.

October 11, 1886

Dearest Win,

I know of no other way to write this devastating news but to state it simply and quickly. Please know that with this letter comes my regret that we can't be together as we grieve. I am with you in spirit, however, and my heart aches for us both.

Jeb was killed. I am barely able to put the words down on paper as the writing of it makes it too real. I am proud to write that he died fighting for what he believed in, but those words ring hollow when I think of the senselessness of it. He did not deserve this fate. Running Elk was killed, too, as was our dear Angus. I take no satisfaction in saying that those responsible were brought to justice, since Jeb is still gone and nothing can change that.

We will persevere, however. Jeb would have wanted us to, so the Dawson ranch will continue on as it has been. Wash and the boys, Anne, and I are able to get done what needs doing. I will not deny that our hearts are broken, but all of us will find the strength from somewhere to carry on.

Win, my dear friend, I hope there is someone where you are that will under-stand the depth of your sorrow and will

*console your grieving heart. Please know I
am with you in mine.*

Love, Meg

It was done. She sealed the letter and put
it aside for Anne to mail.

Exhausted, Meg went to bed, but slept for
only an hour. Then she woke and, as usual,
tossed and turned until finally she got up,
pulled the blanket from the bed, and went
out on to the porch. There she sat until the
sun came up, just like she had done every
night since Jeb died.

The night when her beloved Jeb, Running
Elk, and Angus died, chanting and beating
drums had lasted until daybreak. Meg and
the boys, with Etta there for support, sat on
the porch listening to the rhythmic, earthy
beat as the Arapaho built a bridge to ease
their passing, linking creatures to their
Creator. Now at night it was quiet. It was
so dark; no moon to light the yard. It was
better with no moon. She couldn't see the
charred remains of their barn that way.

⦁ Life continued, but everything felt wrong.
The days just kept coming, whether Meg
wanted them to or not. She often sat on the
porch swing all night with a thick wool
blanket around her, unable to sleep. There
she'd sit until Wash emerged from the

544

bunkhouse to care for the stock and Anne arrived with either Etta or Georgia.

Anne came every day. She said she would do so until Mrs. Dawson could manage by herself on Sundays again. Etta and Georgia took turns visiting Meg; each brought different forms of comfort. Meg wanted to slip away and not feel anything.

They both came with Anne the day Burton Cauley was brought to justice. The trial was short, and he was sentenced to hang. When Meg heard the sentence had been carried out, she made no comment, just went to her room. Etta sat with the boys at the kitchen table with Wash. Georgia followed Meg into her room, sat with her arms around her, and let her cry.

Georgia came with Anne the day after Meg wrote to Win. They pulled into the yard as Wash finished milking Sadie. He handed the pail to Anne, who turned the reins over to him and went into the house to start breakfast. Georgia sat down next to Meg.

"Couldn't sleep again?"

Meg shook her head. "I'm waiting for something."

"I'm glad you wrote to Win. He deserves to know."

"I know. I just couldn't put it into words before."

"That's understandable."

Meg squinted at the mountains. "Thank you for being here, Georgia. You're a good friend."

"In good times and bad," Georgia assured her, squeezing her hand. She heard the boys talking to Anne in the kitchen. Georgia didn't ask Meg if she wanted breakfast. Georgia didn't ask silly questions. She sat with Meg, holding her hand.

Meg wasn't sure exactly what was supposed to happen, or how, but she was unable to move forward until it did. Every night she sat on the porch swing, wrapped in a blanket. She couldn't sleep. She couldn't work. Her mind floated in mist, seeing and hearing nothing.

Finally, what she'd been waiting for arrived. She felt Jeb sit down next to her and put his arm around her.

Meggie, rest easy. You need to sleep. All these nights sitting out here are going to make you sick.

"I need to know that you're all right, Jeb."

Don't worry about me. You've got the boys to look after, and Wash and Anne. They all need you to be strong. They're counting on you. I'm counting on you.

"I miss you so much. How can I go on without you?"

546

You just do, Meggie. You just get up and go on. What gives you strength is my love. It is with you always. It will never die.

When the sun rose that morning, James and Charlie came out and found their mother sound asleep on the porch, wrapped in her blanket. When she woke and saw them, she smiled for the first time in weeks. Everything was going to be all right now, she said.

CHAPTER FIFTY-FOUR: WIN

Alaska, late Autumn, 1886

Win was recording an Athabascan fable as told by the village elder when Meg's letter was delivered. The courier, attached to Henry Allen's Alaskan expedition, drove his sled a half day out of his way for Win, one of the few other white men in the area. The expedition team knew of Winston Avery and that he lived in the Athabascan village. They had invited him along on their mission to explore and chart the Copper River, but he declined, saying he wanted to document the language of these people before the village children were sent to an English school.

As soon as Win saw Meg's handwriting, dread washed over him. He hesitated before opening the letter, but not breaking the seal would not prevent whatever had happened. He opened it and confirmed with his eyes what his pounding heart and churning stomach already seemed to know.

As effortlessly as a weathervane turns when the wind shifts, as smoothly as a scale tips toward the side holding more weight, Win started to pack his things. A young tribesman who assisted Win asked what had happened. Where was he going?

Win replied in the Athabascan language, "I must go home. My family needs me. I need to go home." He had never felt so trapped by the wilderness and in a rush to leave it.

"The last ship has sailed. No ships until spring; you know that," the Athabascan said.

"Maybe the winds have kept the harbor free of ice." Win shuffled his papers together.

The chief, who had the spirit of the wolf, presented him with a gift for Gray Wolf, his kindred brother who lived in the mountains in the southern lands. Win had shared many stories during his stay, and the chief gave him a necklace to give to Gray Wolf so that when they entered the next world, he would recognize him. Then he took Win's hands in his and said that they would meet again, and wished him a safe journey.

When Win left the chief's lodge, he found three young tribesmen waiting for him with two sleds and teams of dogs to escort him to the port. They had adventure in their eyes, eager for a reason to travel and explore worlds they'd never seen. Two of them had never been to Sitka; this was their chance. Win remembered feeling like that, long ago, when he was young. Now all he wanted was to get home. If he were the eagle Gray Wolf thought he was, he'd fly. A mere human, he accepted their offer. The dog sleds were fast, but he was too late. The harbor was frozen.

CHAPTER FIFTY-FIVE: MEG

Dawson ranch, Autumn and Winter, 1886–87
The fire and the deaths of Jeb, Running Elk, and Angus were the beginning of the end for the little town of Paradise. The folks who didn't want to live side by side with Indians had been doing business in Lyonsville for some time. Some of the old mountain men with Indian wives still came into Paradise once or twice a year to resupply, and ranchers who had hired Indians or people of mixed blood also brought their business to Paradise. Unfortunately, those few ranchers and mountain men couldn't keep an entire town going. Mrs. Finnegan did not rebuild. She closed her shop and moved away, brokenhearted over Angus. The hotel sat empty, except for Anne. Blackie stayed, but only because he didn't like change and because he knew how to fend for himself. Etta chose to stay in her little house. When James and Charlie started back at school,

they rode the extra distance with her to a new schoolhouse that had been built closer to Lyonsville. The town of Lyonsville kept her on, since she was the only schoolteacher willing to come to the area, but they made it clear they were looking for a new one.

Deep in thought, Meg sat at her desk in the library and pondered the future of her ranch. Without Gus or Jeb, it was her responsibility now. Anne appeared at the doorway.

"Mrs. Dawson, I thought you should know that Wash is planning to leave."

"No. He can't leave. We need him. Where is he?" Meg rushed out and found him at the woodshed splitting wood. Men always chop at wood when they have something on their minds, she thought, and noted the significant pile. "Wash, you've split enough wood to last through next July."

Wash paused for a moment to catch his breath. "All this will be burned by spring. It will be a very cold winter. The squirrels are gathering early; woodpeckers share that tree." He pointed to a tall tree at the edge of the clearing. "Have you not seen the rings around the moon? The season ahead will be a very cold one. You will be glad to have wood to burn."

"Then perhaps you should move into the

552

big house. That bunkhouse must be awfully big and empty without Running Elk. We'd save on fuel, too, with one less stove to heat."

"You are good friend, May-g." Wash drew out her name when he talked to her as a friend, not as his employer. It usually made Meg smile, remembering their chance meeting so long ago on the grassy plains of Nebraska. But not this time, because she knew what was coming next.

"I must leave," he said, "so people will not shun you. I only bring you trouble. I will chop enough wood to last a long time, and then —"

"No! You can't leave, Wash. Please don't go."

"People saw only Running Elk the Arapaho, not the rancher, and they killed him. I stay here, and those same people come after me. You will get in the way and get hurt. You gave me much. Leaving is what I can give to you . . . and firewood."

"If you leave, not only will we lose our friend, but those horrible people will have won. We can't ranch without you, and you will let small-minded people dictate how we live. What's the point of any of this? Jeb will have died for nothing. This ranch has to work. I'm never going to leave it . . . not ever. I am connected to this place by love. It is in the air I breathe. I will suffocate if forced to live anywhere else."

Wash leaned on the axe handle. "You sound like an Indian."

She stood a little taller and stuck out her chin. "I consider that a compliment."

"You sound like a stubborn one, and most of those are dead."

She dropped her shoulders and sighed. "I need you. James and Charlie need you."

"If I leave, you can hire white ranch hands and white men will do business with you."

Meg shuddered and held her arms, cold with fear over Wash leaving. They argued back and forth. She wouldn't relent until he promised to stay.

The barn was rebuilt. Blackie put his grief over losing his three friends into hewing logs and built the new structure almost single-handedly. Mick and Georgia assisted, however, as did Gray Wolf and Standing Horse. Etta arrived wearing a new pair of leather work gloves and a scarf tied around her head. She said nothing about her attachment to the old barn, where she'd lovingly felt the well-cared-for tack hanging on the wall and remarked how the smell of fresh hay reminded her of Gus. She faced each day boldly. Meg tried to emulate her, but the responsibility of the ranch weighed heavily on her. When she felt especially burdened and alone, she walked up the hill to Jeb's grave and talked to him. She heard him speak to her in the breeze.

Meg and James took a gamble and drove a small herd of horses to the military fort before winter. They needed to reduce their herd in order to have enough food for the rest of them. Meg wouldn't sell a horse younger than four, but that meant giving up two good broodmares. Their herd would be thin for a couple of years.

Negotiating with a sergeant at the fort, Meg discovered that James handled business affairs with the same quiet confidence Jeb had. She heard Jeb's voice inside her head say, *Good for you, James. Don't take less than they're worth. No one will respect you if you do that.* She felt Jeb next to her; his presence comforted her.

The weather had already begun to turn cold as they headed home with cash in pocket. Meg turned up the collar of her big wool coat. "I'm so proud of you. You handled that just like your pa. Oh, James, I miss him so much."

James reached over and touched her arm. "I think he'd be pleased with how we're managing. You aren't alone, Ma. I can wait to finish school . . ."

"No, no. Wash is staying. Miss Sinclair says you are almost finished. I don't want you to delay your education."

The worried lines on his face softened. He loved school and had mentioned once how he'd like to go to college. "For now, let's just get home. It's starting to snow."

They spurred the horses into a lope.

The winter brought the harshest storms and coldest temperatures Paradise had ever seen. The first storm caught everyone by surprise, so the second time temperatures began to plummet, folks scurried into action. Anne was given a choice whether to stay at the ranch or remain in town, since traveling back and forth was too dangerous. She chose to stay in town so she could be close to Georgia. Etta accepted an invitation from James and Charlie to stay with the Dawsons, saying the walls of her tiny cottage closed in around her the last time, and she would love the company. No one knew how long this next storm would last.

James and Charlie left school with their teacher and waited outside her home while she quickly packed a bag. She handed them bundles of flour, sugar, and coffee to tie on the mules' backs, not knowing if Meg would be caught short of supplies with an extra mouth to feed. Snow was already blowing into drifts as they helped Etta climb on to the back of their mule. They made it back to the ranch just in time. Wash and Meg were standing in the yard wrapped in buffalo robes, watching for them and swinging lanterns to guide them home. A half hour later, they couldn't see the barn from the house. Wash moved into the big house at Meg's insistence.

It made for an odd arrangement for Meg to have the boys, Wash, and Etta all snow-bound together under one roof. Unable to get outside because of the sub-zero temperatures, Etta read nightly to the cooped-up, attentive audience. Daytime activities included Etta giving dance instruction to the boys in the front-room library. She counted out beats as their heavy feet moved out of rhythm. When they were babies, Meg had bathed them in a washtub in that same spot next to the stone fireplace. Years ago, Jeb attached the kitchen to the rest of the house and had added a washroom, so now the front room was a cozy reading room. Wash kept the fireplace blazing while the wind howled outside. He sat hunched over an adventure book he'd pulled from the shelf, his finger moving across the page as he read each word. In the room together, they looked like a happy little family. Meg couldn't bear it and retreated to the kitchen.

She stared out the window at a scrub oak anchored to a bare rock outcropping, its twisted black branches reaching into the gray winter sky like witch's fingers. She shuddered and gasped for breath, her soul underwater, the weight of her sadness pulling her down, drowning her.

Left with too much time to think, she couldn't even get up the hill to talk things through with Jeb. She hated feeling afraid, but everything seemed to frighten her. The world had turned cold and cruel. When everyone said good night and the house was quiet, Meg cried quietly in her room. Even with a house full of people, she had never felt so alone or so lonely.

Wolves bawled in the darkness just beyond the edge of the meadow. Billy and Buddy, two young pups Jeb brought home after the original Billy and Buddy died, were normally outside in all kinds of weather, but now were granted permission to stay inside. The horses in the corral snorted and danced about nervously. Wash and James worried the wolves would attack their livestock, or, at the very least, cause a stampede. James said they couldn't afford to lose any livestock and lifted his rifle from the rack by the back door.

"No!" Charlie protested with ferocity that surprised Meg. Protecting their livestock from predators was part of ranching, and not new to Charlie.

James looked puzzled, too. "What is it, Charlie? You know it's our job to protect the horses."

Charlie squared himself opposite James and said, "Gray Wolf and Uncle Win told me about the wolf spirit. The wolf is smart and loyal. Gray Wolf has the spirit of the wolf. I know we have to protect the herd, but we can't kill the wolf."

"What do you have in mind, then?" James asked.

"What if we kept the horses in the barn? If the wolves can't get to them, maybe they will give up and go away. Then we wouldn't have to shoot them." He spoke quietly.

Charlie has seen so much death in his young life, Meg thought. Surely his idea was worth a try.

They crowded the animals into the barn every night for safety. During the day, they built a fire in an old barrel so one member of the family could stand guard at the corral while the horses got out for some exercise, and while the others quickly cleaned the barn. The wolves didn't attack. One night, someone noticed the wolves had stopped howling. The pack had moved on. They continued to crowd the horses into the barn at night, however. Meg wanted everyone and everything safely inside by the time the sun went down.

Spring finally arrived. The longer, warmer days brought hope and pulled Meg out of her darkness. Win's lilac bushes bloomed, as they had every year since he'd brought them to her. Their soft scent wafted through the house and yard, lifting her spirits.

Meg was in the barn mucking the stalls when Quinn Parker, a rancher with a large spread to the south, rode up. He and his wife were new to the area and were decent people; they went about their business quietly. They had several children, all younger than Charlie. A couple of the older ones attended school. Mr. Parker stood in the doorway of the barn.

"Mr. Parker! You startled me." Meg felt self-conscious in work pants and Jeb's old barn coat, even though it was far more practical than wearing a skirt.

"Pardon the intrusion, ma'am," he said. "I wonder if I might have a word with you."

He removed his hat.

Meg stopped her work and leaned the hayfork against a support beam. "Of course. What can I do for you? How's Mrs. Parker?"

"Well, that's what I've come about." He shifted his weight and looked uneasy. He rubbed the rim of his hat with his fingers. His hands looked quite clean, as if he had spent a lot of time scrubbing them. "Nora died last winter; caught a fever."

"I'm so sorry," Meg said. She studied him. He looked as uncomfortable and sad and overwhelmed as she felt.

Mr. Parker cleared his throat. "I guess I might as well get right to the point. I heard that you are a widow — my sympathies — and now with my Nora passing, it appears we are both in a similar bind. No disrespect, but it looks like you could use some extra help, and I sure could use a hand with my young ones. By combining our ranches, there might be considerable benefit to both."

"What do you mean by that exactly?"

"Well, I know this may be sudden, and it is certainly very forward of me, but my children need a mother, and you could probably use some dependable help with the horses."

Still confused, Meg asked, "Mr. Parker, are you proposing marriage?"

He looked uneasy, but straightened up as if to rally his courage. "Yes, ma'am. With all due respect to your late husband and my Nora, I am proposing marriage . . . for our mutual economic survival. I don't get to town much, but Nora expressed admiration for the way your boys conduct themselves. I figure she'd approve of you taking over the raising of our youngsters, seeing how she approved of yours."

Meg was stunned. It was not at all uncommon for women to marry men for security — men they barely knew. It happened all the time. He had said nothing that should offend her; in fact, he was very straightforward and polite. "Mr. Parker, thank you for the compliment about my sons. You've caught me quite off guard, however. I don't know what to say."

"Yes, ma'am. I apologize if I have made you uncomfortable. I just saw no point in beating around the bush. I don't expect an answer right away. If I may make some arguments in my favor, I'd like to say that I would take care of you and your boys, although they are pretty-well grown already. I have a good cattle business, and I am a God-fearing man. I would see to it that my children treat you with respect, as would I."

Meg wasn't sure what the last part meant, exactly, but didn't ask for clarification.

"I don't expect an answer right now," he repeated. "Pray about it, and God will lead you to the right answer."

He did have a nice family and a good cattle operation, and he would bring financial security to their struggling horse business. He was polite and kind, and his children always behaved wherever she saw them. Nora had seemed happy.

Meg nodded, agreeing to think about it. He put on his hat, tipped it respectfully, and left. She stood in the barn for a long time, lost in thought.

CHAPTER FIFTY-SIX:
WIN

Alaska, May 1887
Mail arrived on the first ship to break through the ice at Sitka. Win was among a handful of white people standing outside the post office, hoping for another letter from Meg. Finally, the postmaster called his name. He tore open the letter — two months old.

March 2, 1887

Dear Uncle Win,
We have had a bad time lately, and we need your help. We had a mighty cold winter. We made it through all right, but Mr. Parker lost his wife and wants Ma to marry him. I know you are far away, but you've got to come home and marry Ma instead. Please come home.

Charlie

"Winston Avery!" He looked up. The

postmaster was waving two more letters. He grabbed them and ripped open the one with Meg's handwriting.

April 6, 1887

Dearest Win,

We had quite an adventure this winter; nothing equal to the kind you're having, but it was all the excitement we require. A cold snap shut down some of the cattle ranches. We, however, were lucky and fared extremely well. Wash predicted a cold season, so James and I sold half the herd to the fort in order to properly feed the rest of them. You would have been pleased to see how well James handled the negotiations. As a result, we snuggled in for a very cozy few weeks here in the big house, joined by our dear Miss Sinclair and our faithful Wash. With a nice buck to add to the pantry, Wash saved us from a dull diet of potatoes and gingerbread.

The boys are doing very well in school. Miss Sinclair suggested James take his exams early. I am so proud of them both.

Although we miss Jeb more than words can express, we are persevering and are fine. We hope you are faring as well as we are. Just as your lovely lilacs bloom every spring, we, too, continue on.

Love, Meg

No mention of the struggles Charlie wrote of, but that didn't surprise Win. Meg hated looking weak. He opened the second letter.

April 6, 1887

Dear Uncle Win,

I wasn't supposed to ask you to come home in my last letter. You're supposed to think that we're all doing fine. Mr. Parker really did ask Ma to marry him, just like I said, but I wasn't supposed to tell you about it because Ma doesn't want you to come back on account of any obligation to us. She says we're going to figure something out, but James and I don't rightly know what she means by that. I can't tell if Mr. Parker still wants to marry Ma. I saw him riding out to talk with her, but then he rode off and Ma was in a bad mood when she came home.

We've got a few mares expecting to foal and just as many three-year-olds to train. So, if you can, I still think it would be really great if you came home. Please don't tell Ma that I wrote to you, though, because she'd be mighty angry with me.

Charlie

CHAPTER FIFTY-SEVEN:
MEG

Dawson ranch, Spring 1887

Meg stood over Jeb's grave, a gentle breeze circling around. She closed her eyes and breathed deeply, certain that Jeb stirred the air around her.

"I feel like a fool," she said to him. "Quinn Parker just retracted his proposal of marriage, and I feel insulted. Just my bruised ego, I suppose. I never would have married him. I'm actually relieved. He just went about it so awfully, and I was embarrassed." She laughed suddenly through the tears that welled up in her eyes. "He said that once we married, I wouldn't have to muck stalls or rely on Indians. I said I liked mucking stalls, and that Wash was part of our family." Meg shook her head. "The conversation became heated after that. He said he might have been too hasty when he proposed, but that desperation had driven him to it. Of course, I agreed. It was the only

567

thing we agreed on." She crossed her arms and sighed.

We figured things out together.

"Yes, we did. And will continue to. You and I, Jeb. We aren't in such bad shape. No one will hire on with us, but Etta says James can graduate early, and then he can take over selling our stock to the liveries. A lot of liverymen don't like dealing with women, and won't deal with Indians. But, no matter. We'll be fine."

James will still be able to go to college someday.

"Yes, of course he will."

The boys were waiting for Meg when she finally pulled herself away from the hill and Jeb.

"You OK, Ma?" James asked.

She dragged a chair over to the warm side of the house near the lilacs and sat down. "Boys, come over here. I want to talk over something with you." She leaned forward. "We're going to have to do things differently around here if we want to stay in business. We own the land outright, but we still have expenses, and we need money." She sighed. "I'll never leave this place. I won't sell it; I promise you. But if we don't make any money, life could get pretty grim."

"I could find work in Denver, Ma," James said.

"I'll work, too, Ma. Just don't marry Mr. Parker!" Charlie blurted out the words.

"What are you talking about?" Meg was shocked that her boys knew of Mr. Parker's proposal. "Hold on. First, James, you are not going to Denver to work. And second, how do you know about Mr. Parker?"

James threw Charlie a scowl.

Meg folded her arms. "I know how you know," she said. "You shouldn't listen in on private conversations. They can be very misleading."

"So, you aren't gonna marry him?" James asked.

"Don't marry Mr. Parker, Ma. You should marry Uncle Win!"

Meg groaned and put her hands to her face. "Charlie! Now, listen, we are getting way off track here."

"Just write him and tell him we need him." Charlie spread his arms, a gesture he'd learned from Win. "He'll come."

"We'll do no such thing!" Meg barked. She jumped from her seat and stood in front of the boys with hands on her hips. "I will not have him think we are his responsibility! Is that clear?"

"Yes'm."

Meg stared at Charlie for a moment while she measured his sincerity and gathered her thoughts. "Now, back to the issue at hand." She sat down. "Miss Sinclair has agreed to let you take your exams early, James, so you can graduate. I need you to do business with the liveries in the area, at least temporarily. Your pa was able to work with some of them, but a lot of folks turned their backs on us. I can't send Wash, and they may not want to deal with me, either."

"James gets to finish school early?" Charlie rolled his eyes and sighed.

"Miss Sinclair seems to think he'll do fine on the exams."

"I'll do my best, Ma," James said. He was so earnest, she wanted to gather him up in her arms.

Concerned that Win might draw assumptions similar to the boys, Meg wrote him another letter that night, assuring him that all was well at their ranch. She hoped it would keep him from feeling obligated to come back. Charlie offered to post her letter when they went by the Carters' store on the way to school.

Chapter Fifty-Eight:
Win

Sitka, Alaska, May 1887

Win left the telegraph office and pounded his fist against the support beam with such force that the icicles hanging from the roof all broke away and shattered on the frozen ground below.

Another telegraph line was down. A crew was working its way along the line looking for the break, but progress was slow. Win had spent the winter reading and rereading Meg's letter telling him of Jeb's death, folding and unfolding the paper so many times he could see through where the creases made the paper thin and fragile. Ice-bound in Alaska, there was no way out. Unable to communicate and unable to leave, Win nearly went mad waiting for the thaw.

The first ship to break through the ice had brought the letters from Charlie and Meg. He saw through her attempt to appear self-sufficient and solvent. If only he could get to her before she did something desperate, like marry Parker. Who was he, anyway? Frustration and the cold made Win's eyes water. He hit the post again.

More icicles fell and skidded in all directions as they broke, reminding Win of the shooting contest between Jeb and him one cold winter morning when they were kids. They each had a slingshot and five stones of equal weight and size. The challenge was to see who could knock off the most icicles from the chicken coop. Jeb went first and knocked off one icicle. Then Win aimed and took his shot. He hit the thickest part of the ice, so that the entire frozen shelf came crashing down. All twelve icicles smashed and skittered across the frozen ground. Jeb's face didn't hide a single emotion. He was surprised at first, dismayed next, and then perturbed, but accepted defeat in the evenly keeled manner that was Jeb. Win laughed so hard, he started to hiccup. He held a twelve to one lead that Jeb could never overcome. Win never confessed that he really missed the shot and that he didn't mean for the whole thing to come down. He wished he could tell him now. Win could hardly breathe, being stranded so far away. He wanted to be with Meg. No one else would understand.

The ship signaled its departure. Win grabbed his gear and headed for the dock. No chance to send a telegraph until he landed in Seattle. He hoped Meg wouldn't be foolish enough to marry Parker. He couldn't lose her a second time. He'd never sailed on a slower moving vessel.

CHAPTER FIFTY-NINE: MEG

Dawson ranch, June 1887

James and Meg stood in the Cold Springs livery talking with the owner, Paul Stevens, who appeared distracted as James told him that their herd was strong and healthy.

"You still got Indians working for ya?" he blurted out suddenly.

It was the same question Meg encountered everywhere. She drew her breath to speak, but James beat her to it.

"Mr. Stevens, we all have our reasons for what we do. You can tell anyone who bothers to ask that your horses come from the best ranch in the county. If they disagree because we have Wash working for us, then we can't help you."

"Mrs. Dawson!" Nathan Miller, the town doctor, stood in the doorway. "I thought that was you. I was just walking by and . . . It's been so long." He strode over to her.

"Dr. Miller, what a surprise! James, this is

Dr. Nathan Miller, an old family friend."

"Yes, we've met. It's a pleasure to see you, again, Dr. Miller." James shook his hand.

"Likewise. Are you here doing a bit of horse trading?"

"Yes, sir. We hope to, anyway. Mr. Stevens is considering our offer."

"Paul, you're a fool if you don't buy your stock from the Dawsons. Their horses are the most responsive creatures I've ever ridden." Dr. Miller turned to Meg. "Please stop by my office before you leave town, will you?"

"Of course," she said. Dr. Miller tipped his hat and disappeared down the street.

Stevens coughed and spat. "I guess I cain't argue with the doc. I lost a couple of good horses a few months ago. I could use another supplier. Sometimes Timmons don't have nothin' to sell me."

James shook his hand firmly. "You've got yourself a reliable backup, Mr. Stevens. You won't regret it."

Jeb had remained in contact with Dr. Miller ever since he and Win hauled freight. They had even stayed with him a couple of times when they were low on cash, or the hotel was full. After Meg and Jeb were married and started raising horses, Jeb occasionally had business in Cold Springs.

The last few times, he brought James with him. She didn't realize Jeb had introduced James to Nathan.

She barely recognized the street where the doctor's office stood. The office itself had changed, too. It was twice its original size and noticeably neat, clean, and well organized. Dr. Miller had married years ago, and his wife managed the office.

Mrs. Miller emerged from the back room when they entered the front door. "Hello, Mrs. Dawson, I'm Elizabeth Miller, Nathan's wife." She smiled shyly. "Dr. Miller was called away briefly. He asked if you would wait. It won't be long." She turned to James. "Hello, James, dear."

James removed his hat. "Ma'am."

"I hope you won't think I'm rude, but Nathan asked me to wire a telegraph to his colleague in Chicago. I do apologize, but if you'll please excuse me . . ."

"Of course. I understand. We'll just wait here," Meg said. Mrs. Miller disappeared.

James strolled absently around the office, browsing the bookshelves. He pulled down a large volume and opened it. The room was quiet, except for the ticking clock. Meg gently rubbed the palm of her hand where Jeb had stitched up the deep cut long ago before they were married. "I didn't know your father had introduced you to the Millers. Your pa was in medical school for a while, did you know that?"

"Yes, he said he was going to follow his father into medicine, but it just wasn't what he wanted to do. Then Uncle Win showed up and took Pa west with him. Pa said it was a good example of how something good can happen even when something tragic sets it in motion. He said he might never have come west and met you. He really loved it out here . . . and you." James looked up from the book to smile warmly at his mother. "Do you know what these are?" He held the book open to a page filled with circles colored bright orange. Curious, Meg peered at the beautiful illustrations and shook her head. "They're drawings of the inside of an eye. You use an ophthalmoscope to see the back of the eye. You can tell a lot about a person's health that way."

James set the book down and brought out a contraption from behind the doctor's desk. Before Meg could protest her son's forwardness, he explained how the instrument worked.

"My goodness. When did you learn all of this?"

"Pa taught me a little, 'cause I asked him a lot of questions. Miss Sinclair gave me a couple of old medical texts, and when Pa and I came to town last spring, he introduced me to Dr. Miller."

Meg stared at him. "Do you want to become a doctor?"

James shrugged. "Maybe, someday. Not yet. Not while we're getting the ranch back on its feet."

"Oh, James. I didn't know. We've got to see that you continue with school."

"It's expensive, and we can't afford it right now."

"We'll find a way."

"Not if it means marrying Mr. Parker."

"Mr. Parker, again! I won't marry him, I promise. It wouldn't solve anything. Please don't worry about that."

Dr. Miller came through the front door with a pretty girl about Charlie's age. "Thank goodness you waited! I'm so glad. Suzanne, this is James's mother, Mrs. Dawson. This is Suzanne, my daughter." They greeted each other politely. Then Dr. Miller asked James to help Suzanne bring the boxes they left out front around to the back of the office. "My, but he's the image of his father if I ever saw one," he said when they disappeared. Dr. Miller took Meg's hands in his. "Mrs. Dawson, forgive me for my delay in saying this. I wanted to extend my

578

deepest sympathy to you, but didn't want to interrupt your business at the livery. Poor Mr. Stevens can handle only one topic at a time, and I knew I would be a distraction if I said something there. Jeb and I saw each other a fair amount over the years. I considered him a good friend." He squeezed her hand, then offered her a seat and sat down at his desk. Apparently, he had something else on his mind. "Mrs. Dawson, James has a keen mind, and he seems quite interested in medicine."

"Yes, I'm beginning to see that. I didn't realize until today that Jeb had already introduced you."

He nodded. "What do you think about James going to medical school?"

"I think a person should follow his heart. If James wants to become a doctor, I fully support him. We can't afford medical school right now, however."

"Hmmm . . ." Dr. Miller leaned back in his chair. "I could use an assistant. Elizabeth is a tremendous help keeping the books and the office orderly, but I could use an extra set of hands with patients, and she does not enjoy that part of the work. Suzanne can help, but she's still in school. Would you consider allowing James to apprentice with me? With some practical experience with me and some formal training in Boulder, he'd make a fine doctor."

"That is incredibly generous."

"Well, it isn't charity. Here's the catch," he said. "The idea would be that once he finishes his training, he'd come back here and be my partner. I'm investing in the future of my practice."

Dr. Miller's offer was a wonderful opportunity, if that was what James truly wanted. Meg's heart ached a little. She knew he would leave someday, but so soon after losing Jeb, she wasn't sure if she could let go of her firstborn. She had to get home and talk it over with Jeb. Gus would probably have some wise words, too. She couldn't say that out loud, though. Nathan would think something was wrong with her head if she said she had to talk it over with her dead husband. She spotted James standing in the doorway, listening to their conversation.

"Is this what you want, James?"

"Yes, but only when the ranch has enough help. I won't leave until we're ready."

She shook her head. "What if that never happens? This is a wonderful opportunity. Dr. Miller is so generous, but he can't wait forever. He'll have to hire a different assistant."

"I can hold off for a while, Meg," Nathan said, abandoning formal address. "Take some time to get back on your feet. But think about it, both of you."

As soon as they arrived home, Meg raced to the piñon tree.

"Jeb, James may be able to go to medical school and become a doctor."

Ah, Meggie, that would make him happy.

"Nathan is being awfully generous. He says it isn't charity. I couldn't bear charity. It makes me feel weak, and I have to stay strong."

Nathan needs a partner; the town is growing. For him to offer James a partnership in his practice is a wonderful opportunity for James, but it's good for Nathan, too. He wouldn't offer something like that just to be charitable. Something mutually beneficial isn't charity.

"You're right, Jeb. You always see things so clearly. Do you ever regret not finishing medical school?"

What did James tell you in Dr. Miller's office?

"That you felt something good came from something tragic. If your parents hadn't been killed, you may have never come out west. We may have never met. Oh, Jeb, I love you. I miss you so much."

581

I'm right here, Meggie.

Tragic events set in motion new beginnings. It happened to Jeb when he came west and started a new life. Now, a second tragedy would be the beginning of a new life for his son. James would follow his grandfather and go to medical school. He would honor his father by following his own path. Meg relaxed and leaned back on the bench Wash had placed there for her. A breeze swirled around her.

CHAPTER SIXTY: WIN

Seattle, June 1887

Win jumped from the ship in Seattle the moment the boarding ramp was in place. He bolted to the train station, leaping onto the eastbound Northern Pacific car as it pulled out. Completed four years earlier, the railroad connected the isolated northwest to civilized points east, reducing travel time from weeks to days, one benefit of progress that Win favored in his current situation.

He sat in a passenger car and reread the letters. He glanced up to see the woman sitting across from him wrinkling her nose as though he were spoiled fish. He hadn't bathed all winter, his beard was long and scraggly, and his odor undoubtedly offensive.

"Pardon my appearance, ma'am. Just off the boat from Alaska. Didn't have time to clean up."

"Indeed," she sniffed, turning away from him. "Let's hope you find time soon."

He nodded politely and removed himself from the car. As impatient as he was to get home, the woman had good advice. He got off in Chéyenne and sent a telegram to Meg that said he was coming home. Then he bought a hot bath, a shave, and a haircut. He bought new clothes and bundled his old buckskins and furs on the back of a handsome bay that reminded him of Hippocrates. Only then did he continue on his journey home.

CHAPTER SIXTY-ONE:
MEG

Dawson ranch

Meg paced back and forth at the piñon tree, agitated and irritated. She'd received a telegram from Win.

"Win is coming! I don't want him to come!" she told Jeb.

You know he's just worried about you; he's always cared for you.

"He's coming back because he feels obligated!"

He just wants to be sure you are all right.

"I can take care of myself."

I know. But we always knew he considered this place his home.

"He will see that we're struggling and feel like he has to stay and take care of us."

Isn't life sweeter when we share it with those we love?

"He'll feel trapped. Then he'll leave. He always leaves." Meg flopped down on the bench and caught sight of Charlie and

James watching her from the porch. They turned away, but remained on the porch and occasionally looked up the hill at her. She knew they worried about her. She had overheard them talking to Wash.

Wash had tried to relieve their concerns. He told them that a week earlier, he chased a young colt who had escaped into the woods. He slipped on a pile of wet leaves and fell into a ravine. His foot was stuck in a mass of exposed roots and he couldn't climb out. He was there for an hour when their mother suddenly peered over the edge. He asked her how she found him and she said she heard the wind talking. Some people have that gift, he had told the boys. "Some people see and hear with their hearts better than we see and hear with our eyes and ears," he said.

"You're sure we shouldn't get Doc Miller to take a look at her?" Charlie had asked.

Wash shrugged. "If she lived with my people, she would be considered holy."

"Nothing else she does is strange, Charlie," James said. "Talking to Pa and Gus doesn't upset her; in fact, I think it makes her feel better. If she starts spending too much time up there, I'll talk to her."

Dear James, Meg thought. Dear Charlie. Still on the porch, Charlie ran his fingers through his hair, a telltale sign he was worried. She'd better not spend too much time up here. She couldn't stop Win from coming at this point anyway. She rose and made her way down the hill.

Charlie met her in the yard. "I worry about you sometimes, talking to Pa up there like that."

"When I was your age, I would have worried, too, Charlie," she said, rubbing his back gently. "Don't you fret. I'm fine, I promise. Everyone has his or her own way of searching for answers. We're all just trying to make sense out of the world. Miss Sinclair reads poetry. I think Mr. Parker prays. Your pa built furniture when he needed to think, and Gus brushed down the horses and talked to me. I did the same until Biscuit showed me that peaceful spot up on the hill. Now, sitting up there . . . I don't know . . . it quiets my mind, lifts my spirit, brings me peace, and gives me strength. I'm all right, Charlie."

"Don't be mad at Uncle Win," Charlie said. "He's just coming to make sure we're all right."

A sob escaped Meg, part laughter, part tears. Jeb had said that, too. She wrapped her arms around her boy. "I know, darlin'."

■ ■ ■ ■

On a warm summer night, Meg sat out on the porch swing. Earlier in the evening, she'd balanced the books. If they had another harsh winter, they might not recover. She worried about making ends meet, and that James would never get to follow his own dreams. On these sorts of nights, her mind would start to spin and she couldn't sleep. Feeling restless, she'd left her bed and wandered out to the porch. A breeze swirled around her, bringing the scents of the mountains and the plains together in a symphony of memories. The moon was full, casting shadows on the landscape before her. The crickets chirped loudly, an owl hooted. Before Jeb died, Meg never understood owls, why they called so mournfully into the night. Now she did.

A lone rider made his way slowly down the hill in the bright moonlight. Meg recognized the shadow as Win, but wasn't sure if he was real. She'd imagined him riding into the yard so many times, she wondered if she hadn't conjured up an apparition from all the magic in the heavy night air. She stayed on the porch swing, wrapped in her shawl. He rode in and quietly dismounted.

"Are you a ghost?" she whispered.

He paused halfway up the porch steps. "No, it's me," he whispered back, and continued up the steps. He sat down next to her on the swing and put his arm around her. They sat in silence. Meg could feel his warmth through her clothes.

She laid her head on his shoulder.

CHAPTER SIXTY-TWO:
WIN

Dawson ranch, a week later

From the kitchen window, Win watched Meg pace back and forth at the piñon tree.

"Does she do that a lot?" he asked Charlie. This was the third time she'd been up there in the week since he'd returned.

Charlie peered out of the window at his mother up on the hill. "Yeah, but if you ask her about it, she doesn't sound crazy. She says it calms her."

"Apparently my return has upset her."

"Oh, I didn't mean —"

"Relax, Charlie. I understand."

Since Win's arrival, all had not gone smoothly. Meg withdrew after her initial welcome. The night he rode in by moonlight, they sat out on the porch together all night. She let him hold her in his arms and they talked as though he'd never left, like he'd always been there. In some ways, he had.

They watched the sky lighten. Meg said at the time that she didn't want the day to start, it was so peaceful and quiet, and it felt so good to have Win's arms around her. For Win, it was bittersweet. He had often imagined sitting with her like this, but it was possible now only because Jeb was gone. He kept expecting Jeb to come up behind him and slap him on the back.

"The Arapaho have it right, you know," Meg told him that night. "When someone they love dies, they chant a song that builds a bridge into the next world, to make the passage easier. Running Elk taught it to me. People who have strong spirits on Earth keep their strength. He said if we listen carefully, we can hear them in the wind. I've heard them."

"I'm back for good, Meg. I'm here to look after you."

She stiffened. "We can take care of ourselves."

James had stepped out onto the porch then. In the few short years since Win had last seen him, James had grown considerably. Win was taken aback by how much he looked like Jeb, although taller. He felt a rush of guilt, as though Jeb had caught him with his arm around his wife. But James welcomed him with a bear-hug greeting.

591

"James, I'm so sorry."

"You have our sympathy as well, Uncle Win."

Meg walked into the house without a word to start breakfast.

A full week passed. Now, from the kitchen window, Charlie and Win watched her pace back and forth at the family cemetery. Eyes on his mother, Charlie said, "By the way, I appreciate you keeping quiet about those letters I sent. I was just worried Ma was going to do something she'd regret."

"Protecting what you love is as natural as breathing, son. Marrying that Parker fellow would have been a mistake. I won't say anything about your letters, but I do want her to talk about it if James wants to study medicine anytime soon."

Meg suddenly started down from the piñon tree. The two hustled away from the window and pretended to be busy with breakfast. James came in with a pail of milk, followed by Meg, who apologized for delaying breakfast. She broke eggs into the skillet.

Win sliced some bread and casually started a conversation. "James, I hear you want to study medicine."

"Yes, sir. I plan to once we get the ranch back on its feet."

"What would you consider to be 'back on its feet'? Did you have to take out a loan? Do you have creditors knocking on your door?"

"We are doing just fine." Meg sounded mildly defensive. James and Charlie glanced at each other as she brusquely stirred the eggs. "We just can't afford to pay someone to take James's place right now."

"What if I were the extra pair of hands you needed? Would you let James start working for Dr. Miller this fall? I bet I could get the hang of this ranching thing. I know a little about horses. They have a head and a tail, right?"

Charlie laughed. "Pa told us that you and he raised two colts together, trained them and everything."

"We did. Galen and Hippocrates came west with us. I miss them. You know what's amazing? The month Jeb wrote to say that Galen died was the same month Hippocrates got shot in a skirmish. He saved my life. He reared up and took a bullet meant for me." Win had finished slicing the bread and peered out the window. "It was strange that Galen left us at nearly the same exact time."

"It isn't strange at all. Animals have spirits just like humans." Meg busied herself at the

593

stove, beating the eggs with the same conviction as her words. "Their spirits were connected. One just followed the other into the spirit world to keep him company."

Win glanced at James and Charlie. Just like Jeb would have done, James raised his eyebrows and shook his head ever so slightly to suggest Win not challenge her.

Heeding James's advice, he said, "Jeb's father was smart to put us in charge of their care. We learned a lot. We learned a lot from Gus, too. You boys have had the best teachers — Gus, Jeb . . . your ma. It shows. You are fine young men, young men who should be pursuing your own dreams." Win circled back around to the point he wanted to make. "The ranch could operate without James if I took his place," he said.

"You'll get restless." Meg made the declaration as she removed the pan from the stove.

"You'll have to trust me that I won't." Win stood in the middle of the kitchen, taking a stand, this time willing to challenge her. But she busied herself serving up the plates and didn't respond. Win glanced quickly at Charlie. "Besides, it's the weakened calf that the wolves go after. I don't want some rancher sniffing around here, making some fool marriage proposal, looking to expand

594

his operation —"

Meg spun around so quickly egg flew off the wooden spoon and onto the floor. Buddy bolted and slurped it up. "I'm no weakened calf! Mr. Parker needed *me* more than I needed him!"

"What are you talking about? Who's Parker? Good Lord, you mean it's already happened? Someone already proposed?"

Thinking she'd just given away her secret, she stuck out her chin indignantly and briefly before her shoulders dropped and she returned the pan to the stove with a heavy, tired hand. With no more wayward eggs coming, Buddy slumped back onto the floor and sighed, mirroring Meg.

Now that the topic was finally in the open, Charlie was keen to talk about it. "Mr. Parker asked Ma to marry him earlier this spring."

"Charlie!"

"Oh, Ma, Win already guessed," James said. "It's not that unusual."

"I'm sorry you were put in that situation." Win wanted to hold her — a bird grounded by a broken wing.

"I never seriously considered his offer." Her voice quavered, as though she were battling a lump in her throat. She straightened her back. "I don't need to raise someone

595

else's children, thank you very much, especially all those Parkers. I wouldn't have the patience after raising my perfect James and my perfect Charlie."

She turned away, but Win could see her close her eyes briefly to regain her composure. He didn't point out the flaw in her argument. Gus had raised someone else's child and loved her with the patience of a saint. She was living proof.

James, acutely focused on the subject they'd strayed from, spoke kindly to his mother. "If Uncle Win took my place, I could start working for Dr. Miller this fall. By next year, I could probably enroll in medical school."

She turned around to see all three men staring at her in anticipation, waiting for her approval. "Oh, for heaven's sake. I don't know how you'd stand living here, Winston Avery. We're a mighty dull lot compared to your Alaska."

"It wasn't 'my' Alaska. And it's time I lived in the same place as my heart." Win wasn't sure how Meg would respond to a comment like that. She might argue that she'd never have his whole heart, only half. The other half would always be restlessly searching for new adventures. At another time in his life, she'd have been right. Not anymore.

She said nothing. Wash walked in looking for breakfast and the conversation changed.

Wash announced that he saw a fresh footprint of a mountain lion. He was going to ride up the mountain to hunt.

Meg agreed. "We don't need a cougar adding to our problems," she said as she placed the plates on the table.

Win winced, taking her comment personally. "I'd like to come along," he said. "It's been years since I checked my property."

Wash glanced at Meg, who simply shrugged. "Suit yourself."

A ride through the mountains was as restorative as any tonic. The aspen quivered as though excited by their presence, while the ponderosa pine stood stoic as chickadees and jays chattered and flittered about, cradled in their arms. The sun warmed the pine branches and the scent wafted through the air. Win recalled the day he rode with Jeb and Meg through the foothills for the first time and napped on a flat rock while they caught a fish dinner for them. Why such contentment wasn't recognized at the time and why he let it slip away, only to search for years to find it again, he couldn't say. Gray Wolf once told him that everything had its own time. Win didn't grasp the Arapaho's message then, but he was beginning to understand it now.

Wash wanted to turn back before they reached the farthest corner of their boundary, but Win saw the rock pillar marking the property line and insisted on riding to it. Wash reluctantly followed. A second pillar had been erected. On the first, inscribed in the cement, Jeb had written: *NW corner boundary Dawson ranch.* On the second he'd written: *NE corner boundary Avery property.* Evidence of Jeb's thorough and attentive nature.

Win dismounted on the grassy hilltop. Something wasn't right. The spot where Jeb had put the side-by-side markers was off by twenty or so feet. "Wash, these markers are wrong."

"No, the boundary is correct."

Win lined himself up with the original landmarks he used when he first bought the land. Jeb had placed the markers inside. An insignificant detail, considering the amount of acreage, but it was an error so unlike Jeb, Win knew he must have done it on purpose. "C'mon, Wash. What's going on?"

Wash shifted in his saddle. "He did it for Meg."

"What does that mean?"

Wash hesitated. "You ask a lot of questions. Maybe you should not ask them."

Win spread his arms. "Answer them and I'll stop. Wash, why did Meg want the boundary markers moved?"

"Carl Pitts is buried over there." Wash pointed to an area outside of the markers.

The shock buckled Win's legs. He caught himself and dropped onto a boulder.

"You remember the man, then," Wash said.

"Only the name. From a long time ago." Win searched his memory. Meg and Jeb were sitting with him on blankets at a town festival in LaPorte, eating pie. Win pressed her to tell them about the gambling man they saw her with. She told them how she raced Biscuit and Pitts took the wagers. She regretted ever meeting him and never mentioned him again. "What happened?" Win asked.

"Pitts showed up from time to time when she and Gus managed the way station. The first time he came, he said he'd heard there was a pretty hostler with red hair in Paradise and wanted to see for himself if it was his old partner. She wanted nothing to do with him. Gus sent him on his way. But he kept coming back."

"I remember her getting upset once when

she was recognized by some folks passing through," Win said. "I didn't see why. Her racing seemed fairly innocent to me."

"Pitts was not as innocent," Wash said. "He would come and cause trouble."

"What kind of trouble?"

"He wanted money. When Meg refused, he suggested another way she could help him. But Gus protected her. Pitts was a nuisance, but then he came to their ranch. James was just a few months old. Meg went out to pull a few vegetables from the garden and when she came back inside, Pitts was in the kitchen, holding the baby. He wanted money, and this time he threatened to tell her secret."

"She must have been terrified. But what secret? What could a scoundrel like Pitts blackmail Meg about?"

"He said he knew Indians were living on her land. He said he'd accept payment for his silence; otherwise, he would tell the soldiers at Fort Laramie. They argued, and James began to cry. Jeb came in to see why the baby was crying for so long and saw Pitts on the kitchen floor bleeding from the head with an iron skillet next to him. Meg stood over him, clutching James."

"Good God!" Win took a moment to let the story sink in. Protecting what you love is as natural as breathing. She protected Gray Wolf. Jeb protected her. "So Jeb buried Pitts up here."

"They did it together, making sure he was buried outside of their boundary. But when you bought your land, his grave was on your property. Meg was afraid to dig him up, but didn't want him on your land, either."

"So Jeb changed the boundary line."

Wash nodded. "Pitts was bad medicine."

Win wondered what else he didn't know about Meg. But the argument they'd had two days after he'd arrived made more sense now. He'd been in the library, looking at the photographs taken by Powell's student so many years ago. He felt her presence in the doorway.

"It seems like yesterday," he said, staring at the faces. "Yet, we look so young."

"We were." She strolled into the room, her arms folded across her chest.

"You sure could cut a hole in the wind, Meggie."

"Well, I'm all grown up now. I'm not the little girl you raced as a Post rider, and I'm not the girl you found on the prairie. I'm a mother of two grown boys and manage a ranch. This is who I am now."

At the time, Win hadn't fully understood her irritation. But now he realized what she meant. She'd made sacrifices for what she had. It had changed her.

Wash broke into Win's thoughts. "I tell you Meg's secret about Pitts because I am very fond of Meg. I am very grateful for the life I have at the ranch. I think you deserve to know this about her. You are good for her, and I think you love her."

Win cocked his head at the Pawnee. "You sound a bit in love yourself."

Wash shook his head, but tapped his chest with his fist. "Meg and I are adopted Arapaho brother and sister. You need to make no pact with me." A grin spread across his face.

Win furrowed his brow. "Is there anything you *don't* know about?"

The revelation about Pitts did indeed help Win to understand the woman Meg had become. But he had changed, too. When they returned from their cougar hunt, Win sought out Meg and found her in the library, studying her ledger. She looked up, but didn't smile.

"Wash shot one male mountain lion. He's pretty sure it was the one prowling around," Win said.

"Good. We have to protect the livestock. I don't like mountain lions. They're solitary and sneaky. You never know when they might turn up."

Like Carl Pitts, Win thought. But he just nodded and wandered over to the photographs where they'd argued. He stared at his own photograph, a young man with big plans for adventure and excitement. He flexed the muscles in his back and felt the scar tissue tug. "How do the books look? Are you managing?"

"I can handle it."

"You are extremely capable and responsible." Win was determined to avoid an argument.

"I don't need to be rescued."

Win almost said maybe she could rescue him, then, but didn't. He turned to look her in the eye. "But it might be easier if you shared the load with someone." He pulled her photograph out of his pocket. It was worn and crumpled. He had carried it with him all these years. He held it up so she could see. "You made some of my hard times bearable."

The hard lines on her face softened. She had a look in her eye that he couldn't read.

He propped her photograph against one of the frames on the mantel. "You don't have to be so strong, Meg. I'm here to help carry the weight."

"Until when? Another expedition party

forms? Your thirst for adventure is unquenchable."

"Maybe when you have to take what's second best, it's hard to get enough. Those days are over."

"You sound disappointed."

"You aren't listening carefully."

"We can manage just fine if you want to leave."

"Of course I don't want to leave."

"I never asked you to come back."

Win spread his arms out, exasperated. "I know you didn't. I came back because I wanted to. I want to be here with you."

"You're so used to leaving, you don't know how to stay! Jeb stayed and built this place with me! We built it together!" Her words stung. She stormed from the room.

He wondered if he had indeed made a mistake coming back. He wasn't Jeb. He would never be able to take his place.

Win took his troubles to Georgia, who encouraged him to persevere. He ran his fingers through his hair in frustration. "She can vex a person, Georgia. How the hell Jeb put up with her, I will never know!"

"Oh, honey, you just bring out a different side of her than Jeb did. Not better, not worse."

"I don't think she sees it that way. I really

don't think she wants me around."

Georgia sighed. "Of course she wants you around. Trust me on that."

"You didn't hear her."

"No, but I know her. Give her time. And don't give up."

Chapter Sixty-Three: Meg

Paradise

Meg stood at the door to the schoolhouse and watched Etta return a book to its place on her bookshelf. The teacher held the book in her hand briefly. By the expression on her face, Meg knew it was one she and Gus had read together. When Etta heard her and looked up, her face instantly brightened.

"Meg, dear, do come in," she said with a smile. "It's been too long since we've visited."

Meg stepped inside. "Charlie said you needed to speak to me. Is everything all right?"

"Oh, of course! That dear boy, he must have misunderstood me. I simply said I hadn't seen you in a while and that we must talk soon. He's doing just fine! He'll graduate this spring. I'm so proud of him." She tilted her head. "How about you, though? How's my dear friend?"

Meg slumped into the front desk. "Well, frankly, I could use some advice." The schoolteacher pulled her chair from around her desk and sat down, ready to give Meg her full attention. Meg sighed. "I loved Jeb so much. He's still so much a part of my life. But . . ." She stopped and looked down at her hands.

"I heard Win came back. You've known him forever, and he's someone who can hold you in his arms. You love him — you always have, to some degree — but you're wondering if you could love him the way you loved Jeb."

Meg stared at her friend. "Are you a mind reader? How do you know all this?"

Etta laughed. "Well, I haven't lived my whole life in this schoolhouse, first of all. And second, Gus told me about the strange triangle between you. When I first met Win, it was pretty easy to see how he felt about you."

"What should I do, Etta? I feel like I'm betraying Jeb."

Etta leaned forward. "Don't be silly. Jeb told Gus that when love comes around, it's best to grab it and hang on tight."

Meg squinted at Etta, a smile forming. "Jeb said that?" Talking about Jeb with Etta brought him back to her, like Etta enjoyed the smell of tack oil and straw.

Etta leaned back and nodded. "Best advice Gus ever took, and I loved your husband for it." Her eyes sparkled. "Jeb also said that we were the lucky ones, he and I, because we could love and be loved. He would want that for you, Meggie. And Win, too, don't you think?"

"How do you do it, Etta? Stay so happy when . . ." She couldn't finish the sentence.

Etta smiled sadly. "When I've lost so much? Maybe I'm a fool, but I'd rather take the risk and feel the joy love brings, even it's for a short time. But that's just me."

The day was gloomy, overcast with intermittent rain. James and Charlie had retreated to the bunkhouse once chores were done to play poker with Wash. Anne disappeared into the pantry to take inventory before canning season. Meg curled up in Biscuit's old stall and sobbed.

Etta had warned her a day like this would sneak up without warning. Something would trigger a memory and she'd find herself aching so deeply there'd be no way around it. Meg cried for Biscuit, for Gus, and for Jeb, but most of all, for herself. She knew it was selfish to want them back, but she missed them. She wondered for the mil-

lionth time how a broken heart kept beating.

Exhausted, she fell into dreamless sleep.

When she woke, she wasn't alone. Win sat
quietly next to her, letting her rest. She sat
up, wiping her face with her sleeve. He offered her his handkerchief. She accepted it
and wiped her eyes and nose. "I'm sorry
about what I said, Win. It was cruel."

"I'm sorry Jeb was killed, Meggie. He was
taken from you, and you have a right to be
angry."

"Yes, but I shouldn't have taken it out on
you. Forgive me."

"Of course."

"I miss him, Win."

"So do I."

"Do you think it's peculiar that I talk to
Jeb up at the piñon tree?"

Win didn't answer right away. He
scratched his cheek. "It's not for me to say.
Some people see and hear things I can't,
but just because I can't hear them doesn't
mean they aren't there."

"I'm afraid Jeb will go away if I stop needing him." There, she'd said it. Tears spilled
down her cheeks. Perhaps speaking the
truth out loud would stop it from rubbing
like sandpaper on her heart. "I couldn't bear
not hearing him talk to me anymore."

Win didn't say anything. Maybe she'd simply handed the sandpaper to him, and now his heart was raw and in pain. I've hurt him again, she thought. But he wrapped his arms around her, his warmth like sun on her back.

"I gave you up for Jeb once," Win said, "and now it seems he and I are still vying for you. It's hard to compete with a memory, so I'm going to play the only card I have. I don't know how that all works — you hearing Jeb, I mean — so I'm not going to speak to it. All I know is that I'm right here, in the flesh. I want to stay, not out of a sense of duty to Jeb or you or the boys, but because I love you, and always have."

She looked up at him and he kissed her. Her heart fluttered to life, a broken bird awkwardly stretching its wings. "I need more time," she said, afraid for the fragile creature.

Win relaxed his hold on her.

Reluctantly, she pulled away.

CHAPTER SIXTY-FOUR: WIN

Dawson ranch, September 1887

Haying season. If Win were on a surveying expedition in higher elevations, the crew would be wrapping up their fieldwork to head for civilization, where they'd spend the winter analyzing collected data and writing up their observations. If he were in Alaska, the Athabascans would have left their tents at the fish camps weeks ago and settled into their permanent winter homes near the caribou fence. But Win was in a section of meadow, turning the freshly cut grass so it would dry evenly. He was where he wanted to be.

Win paused to gaze at the ranch. Late afternoon — the mountains would soon block the sun and turn the land purple, but for now, the sun painted everything it touched a rich gold color. The house stood tall and proud; the porch stretched out like arms welcoming a long-lost friend. The rebuilt barn, weathered to nearly match the color of the bunkhouse next to it, maintained a defiant appearance, if it were possible for a barn to look defiant. James and Wash were in a large hay wagon, lifting the dry grass onto a conveyor belt that brought it up to Charlie and Meg in the loft. The sight of her soothed him in a way no breathtaking vista ever could.

"You deserve this, Jeb, not me," he said.

Win turned toward a sound, almost believing he'd see his old friend. But another old pal, Gray Wolf, was there instead. He looked amused. "My friend speaks to spirits."

"You and Meg . . . you're the ones who hear voices in the wind."

Gray Wolf shrugged. They both watched the work going on below them. "Why do you say you do not deserve this?"

"Jeb should be standing here, watching his wife and children."

"We each travel a path that is ours, and ours alone."

"It isn't fair."

"Our friend was content and his spirit is strong. He is at peace. If you could hear him, you would know he is happy that you are here watching over his family."

Win thought back to the day he'd left to join Powell's expedition. He and Jeb had argued again about Jeb returning to Paradise. Whose idea had it been to make a pact about Meg? Had Jeb asked him to look after Meg if something happened to him, or had Win confessed to Jeb that he also loved Meg? Maybe Jeb agreed to the arrangement because he thought he might never see Win again. It was so long ago, all Win could remember was the handshake and the feeling of relief that he would still be part of their lives.

"I've always loved her," Win said. "But Jeb loved her, too, and deserved her more than me. He made a better husband. I wasn't ready to give her what she needed, so I let her go." He took a deep breath. "Can't tell you how many times I regretted it."

"Everything has its own time."

"I hope Meg will let me share what's ahead."

"She worries you feel obligated to be here."

"Ach, my intentions aren't that noble. I wish she'd just love me for the incorrigible bastard that I am. I can't replace Jeb. I wish she'd see that I'm not trying to."

Gray Wolf leaned on the stick he used now to walk the trails. "The wind brought a vision to me as I slept. Perhaps if I tell you about it, it will comfort you."

Win turned to him.

"You were talking to white people," Gray Wolf said. "You were standing in front of them, and they were listening to what you were saying."

"What was I saying?"

Gray Wolf shook his head. "I could not hear you." He nodded in the direction of the ranch. "She was there. She was happy."

"Were you seeing the future? Meg was with me?"

"It is what the wind brought."

"You're going to make a believer out of me, my friend, with visions like those."

Gray Wolf smiled slightly and nodded toward Meg again. "She listens to the wind, too. It speaks to her."

I wish it would tell her to believe me, Win thought.

From the loft, Meg looked up in the direction of Win and Gray Wolf. She raised her hand to shield the sun. Win realized this only after he raised his own hand, thinking she was waving to him. Embarrassed, like an eager schoolboy hoping to be noticed, he dropped his arm, but Meg raised hers again and waved in response to his aborted greeting.

Gray Wolf smiled. "When we first met years ago, you did not speak our words very well, but I admired your brave effort, even though you sounded foolish. Winning the heart of a woman requires a similar kind of bravery — the risk of looking foolish. The reward is great, however, don't you think?"

A breeze swirled around them. Gray Wolf smiled as though it had told him a secret.

CHAPTER SIXTY-FIVE: MEG

Dawson ranch

Meg tapped on Win's bedroom door and peeked in. He was stretched out in a chair with his feet up on the windowsill, staring at the full moon shining in on him. "May I come in?" she asked in a quiet voice, almost immediately second-guessing herself. She'd stood in the middle of her own room for half an hour, mustering up the courage. Maybe she should have waited until morning.

"Of course," Win said and started to stand, but she motioned for him to sit back down. She sat on the edge of his bed, not sure how to begin. Then her whispered confession just slipped out.

"I'm lonely."

Win left his chair and sat next to her, her heart sparking like flint against stone when he put his arms around her. Then it began to pound as she raised her lips to him, and feelings deep inside stirred as Win kissed her. But then he surprised her by pulling back.

"What's wrong?" Meg asked, although she knew.

"I wonder if this is a good idea. I wonder if it's possible for us to be alone together . . . just the two of us."

Meg felt like she was seventeen again, stewing over the feelings she had for both Jeb and Win. This time there was no pact to hide behind.

"I don't honestly know either." Meg faced him. "But we've been friends a long time; we should be able to speak plainly to one another. So, if three of us are here, why not four? Jeb told me you were in love with a woman once. Whatever happened to her? What was her name . . . Jeannette?"

"Jeannette," Win said, furrowing his brow. He pushed himself back against the bed's headboard and motioned to Meg to join him. She climbed in next to him and rested her head on his chest, reminding her of how she and Jeb used to talk together.

"Jeannette was the riverboat singer I met on my way here once."

"I know. Jeb told me about her. He thought she might have stolen your heart."

Win laughed quietly. "She was a good

person, but life had been hard on her. When I met her, she was trying to change, to correct some of the mistakes she had made. But she didn't know how to straighten out on her own, and didn't have people around her to help her. I've often wondered how each of us might have turned out — you, Gus, Jeb, and I — if we hadn't had each other."

"We've all leaned on each other at different times for different reasons. I can't imagine where I'd be without all of you. What happened to Jeannette? Why didn't you stay with her?"

Win sighed. "Well, I might have, if . . ." He paused.

"If what?"

"If she hadn't found your picture in my things. Why she was going through my things in the first place, I never found out. We had a fight. She had quite a temper and demanded that I get rid of your photograph. I wouldn't, of course. Couldn't. It was the most precious thing I carried with me. I kept that photograph safe through storms and fights and everything else I encountered. I wasn't about to give it up. She became furious and threw me out. Told me she never wanted to see me again."

"It sounds like she was jealous and wanted

you all to herself."

"Well, stupid bastard that I am, I believed her and left. I wrote her a couple of letters, but I never heard back from her."

"I'm sorry."

Win shrugged. "I liked her, perhaps even loved her, but, it just wasn't right. I can't explain it any other way. She and I were alike in many ways, but they weren't good ways, and our differences were significant. Jeb always kept me out of trouble. Jeannette seemed to pull me into it."

"Jeb was good that way."

"Jeb was a goddamn saint."

Meg laughed. "I don't know about that. He gained as much from knowing you as you did from him."

Win pulled her close. "Marry me, Meg. We've been part of each other's lives for twenty years. You and your sons are my family. Let me love you."

James threw his bag into the back of the wagon, his face flushed with excitement. Charlie held the reins, waiting to drive him to Cold Springs so he could start his apprenticeship with Dr. Miller. James hugged Meg, who squeezed him tightly, unable to hold back her tears. She said that she knew they would see each other fairly often, it was just the idea that he was all grown-up and moving on with his own life that made her emotional. It was the truth. She was happy for him.

Win shook his hand. "We're real proud of you, James. Study hard."

"I will. Come visit soon, and bring your pretty new wife," James said. He smiled and winked at Meg. He's so much like Jeb, she thought, smiling at him proudly through her tears.

"That sounds good."

"Bye, Ma."

"I love you, James. Always."

Charlie waved and slapped the reins. Win stood next to Meg with his arm around her. She wondered if he was thinking about Jeb, too. They both waved as they watched the wagon disappear over the hill.

"So this is what it feels like to be on this side of a good-bye," Win said. "How did you do this over and over again? It feels terrible."

"When someone I love leaves the ranch, like the boys right now, a piece of my heart gets pulled with them and stretches, like taffy, into a long, thin string. It never breaks. No matter how far away they go, it never breaks. That's how I do it." Meg looked up at Win. *I'm so glad you're here with me,* she thought. Out loud she asked, "Now, tell me the truth — would you rather be James right now?"

Win squeezed her shoulders and kissed her on the temple. "No, Meggie. I am content right here."

Charlie graduated that next spring and began ranching full time. He loved the ranch and the horses, and it was what he wanted to do, he said. Etta stayed at the school only until he graduated. She submitted her resignation the same day she issued diplomas to Charlie's class of two boys and three girls.

It was not the last Meg saw of her close friend, however, as she was hired to teach at the Broadbent Academy for Young Women in Boulder, near where James attended medical school. Charlie secured the business of a livery in Boulder and made regular trips there. He visited Miss Sinclair often and she occasionally requested his attendance at social functions at the school, as proper young men were scarce at the all girls' school.

It was at the annual Christmas dance that Charlie fell in love, according to the story he told his mother. Introduced by Miss Sinclair, Charlie took a shine to one of her students, Elizabeth Walker, the third of six daughters.

James and Charlie were both married within a year of each other. James married Suzanne and went into partnership with her father. They built a small home next door to the office he and his father-in-law shared. Charlie married Elizabeth, whom he called Leezie, and who quickly adapted to living at the Dawson ranch. She wasn't a horse-woman like Meg, nor did she replace quiet Anne, who stayed on as their cook and housekeeper. But having grown up with five sisters, Leezie brought unbridled energy and a feeling of sorority to the women of the ranch. Handy with a needle and thread and possessing a lively, talkative personality, Leezie brought her sense of humor and happy nature to the family. She fit right in.

Living in the wild for so much of his life, Meg wondered if a bustling, noisy house-hold would wear on Win, but he never showed signs of discontent, nor claimed the itch to roam ever returned. He didn't gaze longingly at the horizon like he had years earlier. She saw warmth in his eyes when he looked at her, though. He stirred her soul, like letting go of the reins while Biscuit gal-loped free across a stretch of flat land.

Their marriage opened a new chapter —

and a new world — for Meg. Sharing their days and a bed, Win added texture to her tapestry. The years seemed to pass in a blink of an eye, because happiness speeds up time. She hardly felt herself grow older.

The only matter that raised Win's ire was the continued injustice shown toward the Indian people. Win openly criticized a group calling itself "The Friends of the Indian," because the well-meaning members caused more destruction to Indian culture with their aid than any military campaign had with force. He also disapproved of the Dawes Severalty Act of 1887, because it imposed private land ownership on a culture that had followed a centuries-old practice of seasonal movement and had the belief that the Earth cannot be owned. Meg didn't like the Dawes Act, either, yet couldn't resist teasing him about the ironic collision of principles and practicality, since he remained resolute in his desire to have his own property pass to Gray Wolf and his heirs.

All the same, she was sympathetic and loyal and allowed him to rant when President Harrison opened up Indian territory for settlement. At noon on April 22, 1889, eager settlers raced into unoccupied lands. Nine hours later, almost two million acres of tribal land had been lost in the Oklahoma land rush. When Win finally quieted and sank onto a porch chair with a sigh, Meg took the newspaper from his lap and slid into its place, slipping her arm around the back of his neck.

"It's maddening," she said. "How do we fight against it?"

"I don't know," Win said, taking her hand. "But I like you on my side."

"Always."

In January 1891, news reached them of the massacre at Wounded Knee a month earlier. It was the only time Meg ever saw Win break down. Even as a hundred Arapaho lived in relative safety in the shadows of Steensland Peak, he felt he should do more, he said.

Eventually, and with Meg's encouragement, he found a way.

At a dinner party Etta held for friends in Boulder, Win responded to casual inquiries by the wife of a history professor about his surveying days with a colorful tale, and soon had captured everyone's attention. As the evening ended, someone invited him to lecture to his political-science students.

In the hotel room that night, Meg mentioned that speaking to a large forum might be cathartic.

"I hope you accept the invitation, Win." She brushed her thick hair as he undressed for bed.

"We have a ranch to run."

"They can manage — Charlie and Wash. This is important, and you tell wonderful stories."

"I don't want to entertain," he said, yanking off the tie he'd been forced by convention to wear. "I want to change opinion."

"Well, every conversation around you paused as you told Mrs. Bennington about hunting caribou with the Athabascan. Once you have their attention, sharing the challenges Indians face would engender sympathy — I'm sure of it."

"What if I'd told them about Albert Rothenberg's scare with the Crow?"

Meg laughed. "You're incorrigible." She put down her brush and crawled into bed. "I'm serious, Win. Educated ears are influential ones. Take advantage and speak your mind — judiciously, of course."

" 'Judicious' has never been one of my better traits."

"Thank goodness!" She pulled him into bed with her. His initial surprise turned to a grin as Win realized what she was suggesting.

In his embrace after their lovemaking,

Meg continued campaigning on the professor's behalf. "Tell your stories and share what you know, Win," she said, tugging at the disheveled sheet. "I believe you could change opinion."

Win pulled the bed linens up to cover her bare shoulder, his warmth penetrating through the covers. "Gray Wolf once said that everything has its own time."

"Are you saying you agree it's time to speak?"

"Maybe so. You're very convincing. You aren't trying to get rid of me, are you?"

"Not a chance!"

He accepted the professor's invitation. More began to arrive as his reputation for giving engaging lectures grew.

Win carried his message to anyone who would listen, cautioning against short-sighted, simple answers — even exposing the problems frequently caused by well-intentioned policies. Some conservationists were surprised to learn their noble plans to preserve large tracts of land from exploitative developers often meant that Indians living within the borders of protected land became trespassers, and their hunting practices were considered poaching. Becoming aware of the risk of alienating important allies, he learned to use his affable nature and enthralling stories to mollify stubborn minds before he criticized misguided policies. Folks loved listening to him.

Win became known in political circles. Some encouraged him to run for office, but he declined, modestly citing lack of legal knowledge. Privately, he told Meg that he disliked politicians too much ever to become one, and he'd surely cause fistfights on the floor of Congress. He preferred his life at home, anyway. Meg didn't argue with that.

In 1898, Win was speaking at the newly established Colorado Chautauqua Association in Boulder when their lives, once again, turned up on end.

Charlie rushed into the barn, where Meg was saddling a stock horse. "Ma, you've got to come to town with me, right now. Hurry."

"Charlie, don't scare me. What's going on?" But she cinched the strap and mounted.

"Everything's OK. Believe me. But I can't say any more. Please, just come."

Meg and Charlie's horses loped into Paradise. Georgia, Mick, and a teenaged girl emerged from their store. Meg gasped and dismounted.

Without a word, the girl handed her an

old, tattered letter. It read:

May 5, 1882

Dear Mrs. Dawson,
  The child with this letter belongs to Winston Avery. He does not know he has a brought a baby girl into this world, but this is not his fault. I did not tell him I was carrying his child, and left the riverboat before he returned. I have no doubt he would have made me an honorable woman, but it appears that I must meet my Maker on different terms. I delivered at the Sisters of Mercy convent. They promised me they would bring the baby to you. I named her Virginia, after Win's mother, but please call her Ginny. I like that name better.
  I was jealous of you because of the way Win talked about you. You fairly walk on water in his eyes, and it made me angry that he loved you when he could have loved me. I have confessed to the priest here, as I lay dying, that I lured Win into my bed with the intention of making him forget you. All it did was produce this little life you see here. I know Win will show up at your door someday, and thought he should know his own flesh and blood. I know you will care for the child. The way he talked about you and your husband and

your boys, it sounded like a better place for my baby than drifting through life on a riverboat.

I regret many things in my life, but bringing his daughter into the world is not one of them. When she is old enough, please tell her that her mother tried to be a good person and do the right thing.

These were the last words of Miss Jeannette Bordeaux, singer on the Missouri Star riverboat, as dictated to Sister Mary Margaret of the Sisters of Mercy convent, Omaha, Nebraska.

Stunned, Meg stared at the date: May 1882. What happened the year before that? Win had come from Washington, said he took the riverboat, and met Jeannette. He told Jeb about her. Win and Meg talked about her before they married. *May 1882.* She looked up. "This letter is sixteen years old. This woman is writing to me about a baby just born."

"I'm the baby in the letter, ma'am. I'm Winston Avery's daughter."

Her beautiful brown hair, the cut of her chin — of course she was. She looked just like him. Meg wanted to rush to her, a wave of love washing over her. Her eyes filled with tears, at which point Georgia stepped in.

"Well, now that the initial shock is over, let's go in and talk this out. Ginny, I told you she was going to be happy to meet you." Georgia put her arms around both of them and ushered them into the house. "You men stay out here. We women have a lot to talk about in private."

Meg could hardly breathe as Ginny explained how it happened that so many years would pass before even she knew her true identity. "According to Sister Mary Margaret's account, she intended on bringing me to you right away. But after my mother — this Miss Bordeaux — died, our town was hit by a storm and a tornado ripped across the county. It caused so much damage that every person was called on to help with the injured. The sisters at the convent were needed, and it just wasn't practical to leave right away. I was temporarily placed with a mother who lost her own baby in the storm. By the time the town had picked itself up and the sisters could leave, my new mother wouldn't give me up. She'd lost her only child. They didn't have the heart to take me away."

"Why now?" Meg asked, but she already knew the answer. She saw it in the girl's eyes.

"Mama and Poppy passed on. I found the

letter in Mama's things."

"I'm so sorry, honey." Meg reached over to squeeze her hand.

"Thank you, but I'm managing. When I found the letter, I went to the convent to confirm with Sister Mary Margaret that I was the child in the letter. She confessed she'd always been torn between not honoring Miss Bordeaux's wishes and knowing I had a good home. I remember her looking in on me growing up."

"You've been through so much."

"Not really, ma'am. I've had a good life. Better, I think, than a life on a riverboat."

"Still, you are very brave to come way out here to find me. I hope you like it here —"

"Oh, I'm not staying, Mrs. Dawson. I don't expect anything from you. The letter just made me curious. Mama and Poppy didn't have any other children, so I'm obligated to no one. I figured, why not have a little adventure?" Ginny spread her arms out in a gesture so familiar that Meg's own hand flew to her mouth. She was her father's daughter. "What? Have I done something wrong?"

Georgia answered for them both. "No, honeybee, you're just the spittin' image of your father, that's all. You don't need some letter to tell us who you are. I can see right —"

"Wait," Meg interrupted. "Ginny, you called me Mrs. Dawson. Georgia, didn't you tell her?"

"Heavens, no. I'm no gossip. That's your story to tell."

"You picked a fine time to reform." Meg smiled at her friend before turning to Ginny. "Mr. Dawson died ten years ago. I'm Mrs. Avery now. I'm married to your father."

"Oh, my." Ginny's eyes grew wide with either pleasant surprise or shock, Meg wasn't sure. "I wasn't expecting this. Look, I came out here just to see this part of the country. I didn't think he'd actually be here. I was just going to wander by the Dawson ranch, but when I asked for directions, Mrs. Carter here got all excited, and then that Charlie fellow walked in and got all excited . . . I didn't mean to stir everybody up. I best be going . . . This is getting complicated." Ginny rose.

"Oh, no! Don't go, please!" Meg tried not to sound desperate. Ginny had to stay, at least until Win came home. He'd be back in just a couple of days, Meg said. Ginny could stay at the ranch and meet everyone.

It took Georgia, Mick, Charlie, and Meg

632

to convince Ginny to come back to the ranch, but, in the end, she accepted their offer, all the while insisting she had no intention of staying.

"Ginny, honey, this is Charlie's wife, Leezie, and their son, John," Meg said when they walked into the kitchen. Leezie shifted John to her other hip and looked curious, but nodded politely. "Anne Wallace is the best cook in the county. And this is Wash. He's a member of our family, too." Meg turned to everyone. "This is Ginny, Win's daughter."

While everyone uttered surprise, Ginny looked quizzically at Wash.

"I'm Pawnee. Do I frighten you?"

"No. Pleased to meet you." She held out her hand.

Charlie saved Ginny from the onslaught of questions and told everyone her story.

"I'm so sorry about your ma and pa," Leezie said to Ginny.

"Thank you. I'm managing."

"That lace on your collar is coming loose. Would you like me to fix it?"

"I've got some fresh gingerbread," Anne said. "Let me cut you a piece."

The family surrounded Ginny with attention. Soon, Leezie handed the baby to Charlie and took Ginny by the hand to show her to her room.

Meg excused herself and ran up to the piñon tree.

"We have the girl we always wanted, Jeb! She's Win's daughter. Remember Jeannette, the woman Win told you about? She had his little girl. She's so pretty; she has beautiful brown hair and Win's eyes — oh, Jeb, she looks just like him! She's lost the people who raised her, but don't worry, Gus, life hasn't scraped away her sparkle."

I hope she'll stay, for your sake, Meggie.

"Me, too, Jeb. I hope so, too." She wanted Win's daughter to stay and allow them to love her — to protect her. It would be as natural as breathing.

Chapter Sixty-Six: Win

Dawson-Avery ranch, two days later

Coming home held different meaning, now, from Win's earlier years roaming the wilderness. No longer just a visitor, he surveyed the healthy crop of timothy and checked the repairs he and Charlie made to a section of road that had washed out during the spring rains. With contented pride, he continued home. The thrill of seeing Meg never changed. Win rode across the low foothills, picking up his pace as he anticipated her warm welcome.

He knew, somehow, that their lives had altered as soon as he caught sight of the ranch. Meg sat on the porch swing, waiting for him. The dark-haired girl from his recurring dreams sat next to her. The vision had teased him through the years. He'd never understood it. But the vision was clear now, unmistakable. The girl with pretty, brown hair was his daughter.

They smiled at him as he bounded up the porch steps.

EPILOGUE:
MEG

Dawson-Avery ranch, 1927

Ginny lived with Win and Meg until she married. She gave birth to a daughter, whom they named Jameson.

Win and Meg traveled occasionally in their senior years, but didn't wander too far from home. Win continued to address conservation groups that became popular when Teddy Roosevelt was president, and lectured at universities. His favorite story — the one he told most often — was about meeting a curious Arapaho named Gray Wolf, who had seen a white woman ride horseback better than most men. He told Meg that when he'd won over the audience, he'd remind his listeners that the plight of the American Indian had not yet been resolved satisfactorily. Occasionally he complained that he'd never change opinion, but Meg assured him real change took time.

Before Gray Wolf died, he attended one of

Win's lectures. He sat next to Meg in the audience with his rough, gnarled hand held gently in her own. Win said he thought he saw Jeb in the audience, too, and Gray Wolf and Meg looked at each other and smiled — it came as no surprise to either one of them.

Eventually, Win declined invitations to speak, claiming that travel had become too difficult.

One spring, just before the lilacs bloomed, Win died. He caught a cold that winter and wasn't able to shake it. He and Meg spent hours by the fire. She read every book they had in their library out loud while he rested. She buried him in the family plot up by the old piñon tree, leaving a space for herself in between Jeb and Win.

She had been left behind, Meg complained. Gus, Jeb, and Win were having way too much fun up at the saloon, drinking whiskey and playing cards. Her grandchildren only knew her as a gray-haired, wrinkled old woman, although her children may have noticed how her blue eyes still danced when she spoke about the people she loved, both living and gone. None of them had known her as a young, spirited woman, racing their grandfathers across the Colorado high plains, letting go of the reins and spreading her arms wide, riding her horse with perfect balance. But she remembered.

Meg sat on the porch swing. A breeze lifted the pages of the open book in her lap. They fluttered back and forth, as if an impatient spirit reading along was nudging her to continue. Meg rested her reading glasses on the pages to quiet them. The book didn't hold her interest. Today she preferred the company of her memories — memories as rich as any story in a book. She closed her eyes and, with her toe, set the porch swing in motion and slowly rocked back and forth. She thought of the day Jeb finished it and proudly watched her test it for the first time. He said it would last generations. He was right.

Close by, two pine finches chirped raucously at each other, while, in the distance, a meadowlark sang its lilting, melodious song. The breeze gave up on the pages and swirled through the lilac bushes. It picked up the familiar scent and laid it gently in her lap like a gift. Lilacs always reminded her of Win. The wrinkles on the woman's face deepened as she smiled, like soft, worn folds of a love letter saved for years, reread and refolded hundreds of times.

Every room in the house, except the porch, had changed over the years to accommodate the needs of the growing family. The porch, however, was the welcoming arms of the home — the first to embrace family and friends when they arrived, and the last to let go of them when they left. It cradled the weary and comforted the brokenhearted. It was the place where joy was shared and burdens were lifted. It was where Meg loved to sit and rock and remember.

The telegram in her apron pocket said her granddaughter was arriving today, bringing good news. The breeze persisted in trying to get her attention and loosened a strand of her thick, gray hair, tossing it about, teasing her, unwilling to be ignored. The woman brushed the hair from her face with the same patience she had quieted the restless pages and grinned. Someone was here with her, waiting.

She opened her eyes, sat up straighter, and peered down the road as a brand new 1927 Model T Ford rumbled into view. Her granddaughter pulled into the yard and honked the horn, causing Meg to jump with surprise, but then she tilted her head back and laughed at herself.

"Jamie, honey, you sure know how to

make an entrance!" Meg clapped her weathered hands together as the young woman turned off the engine and hopped out. "Look at you, driving that modern machine!"

"This will be old news by next year. Ford's making a new model." Jamie winked at her grandmother. "I got a good price."

Meg laughed and held out her arms. The young woman ran up the porch steps like a little girl to receive her hug. "Oh, Grandma Meg, it's wonderful to see you!"

"I hear you have good news."

Jamie sat down next to her on the swing. She brushed her own short, bobbed hair from her face. "It's done, Grandma. Your wish came true. I've got the papers with me. Do you want to see them?"

The old woman took her granddaughter's hand. "No need. I believe you if you say they're in order. We've been waiting a long time for this day."

" 'Protecting what you love is as natural as breathing,' you've always said."

Meg tilted her head at Jamie. She squeezed the hand of Win's true legacy and then looked up into the foothills and smiled wistfully. "Let's go tell the boys."

Meg had been waiting for this last loose end. She took Jameson's arm and they walked slowly up the hill to the piñon tree.

Gray Wolf never became a US citizen, but, in 1924, Native Americans were given citizenship without having to give up their tribal alliance. Gray Wolf's grandson, the son of Warrior Travels Far and patriarch of a small Arapaho family, now legally owned the canyon and mountain just beyond the Dawson ranch. Jameson had the legal paperwork in hand.

Now they were on their way to the old piñon tree to tell the good news to Gus, Win, and Jeb. Meg was glad everyone else was busy and she could be alone with Jamie. She had grown accustomed to her grandmother speaking to her ancestors and was the most amenable to her peculiar ways. When they reached the top of the hill, Jamie helped Meg get comfortable on the weathered bench. Then she explained the legal contract out loud to her, "So the boys can hear, too," Meg asked. Jamie finished and fell silent.

Meg stared up at the mountains, lost in her memories, listening to the spirits. "At one point in your grandfather's life, he worried that there'd be no evidence of his ever being on this Earth." Meg turned to Win's granddaughter. "You are good evidence, my dear. You also did a fine job with this legal matter. We've been waiting for this day for a long time."

"I'm glad you're happy, Grandma."

"I hope you understood all of that, boys." Meg addressed the headstones. "Mighty complicated stuff, giving back to the Indians what was theirs in the first place. At least our ranch won't be swallowed up by towns and people. It will forever be next to a place for wild — Oh, Jamie . . . can you hear them? Gray Wolf, Sharp Eyes . . . One Who Waits . . . all of them . . . They're singing!" Meg chanted the Arapaho song of celebration along with them. Jameson waited patiently. When Meg was finished, she looked straight into Jamie's young, fresh eyes. "There's only one thing left that I wish for . . . and that is when I join the boys, I'll be young again, like you are right now. I want to race them across the flats and let go of Biscuit's reins." The old woman tilted her head back with eyes closed. A breeze loosened a strand of hair and tossed it around her head.

"It must have been wonderful, Gram. It must have been grand."

It was grand, Meg thought, as grand as life could be. The chanting faded away in her head and it was quiet again, except for the breeze. She heard the breeze call her.

"Well, honeybee," Meg said to Jameson, "we're going to celebrate tomorrow. You and your mama will be here early?"

"We wouldn't miss it! Aunt Leezie said to come first thing in the morning."

"I should think that will be a good time." Meg stood up, a cue to Jamie that it was time to leave.

"I'll walk you back to the house, Gram," she said, holding her arm out. But Meg wrapped her arms around her and gave her a warm hug instead.

"No, no, that's all right," she said lightly. "I'd like to stay up here awhile. Wash will be along soon and will walk down with me."

Jamie embraced her grandmother. "If that's what you want. You sure you'll be OK?"

"Absolutely." Meg grinned. "Good-bye, darlin'."

"Bye, Grandma Meg," Jamie said as she started down the hill. She turned to wave. Meg waved back and sat down on the bench next to the gravestones.

A little while later, Washaneekomosema, an old Pawnee, chanted an Arapaho death chant to build a bridge for his long-time white friend to enter the spirit world. When he laid her between Jeb and Win, he noticed a hint of a smile on her face.

The breeze picked up suddenly. Wash heard the sound of thundering hooves and joyful laughter in the wind.

ABOUT THE AUTHOR

M. M. Holaday is a former reference and rare-book librarian. She loves books for their power to educate, influence, and entertain. She also loves the tallgrass prairie. She and her husband are restoring the native ecosystem on their farm in Missouri. This is her first novel.

The employees of Thorndike Press hope you have enjoyed this Large Print book. All our Thorndike, Wheeler, and Kennebec Large Print titles are designed for easy reading, and all our books are made to last. Other Thorndike Press Large Print books are available at your library, through selected bookstores, or directly from us.

For information about titles, please call
(800) 223-1244

or visit our Web site at:

http://gale.cengage.com/thorndike

To share your comments, please write:

Publisher
Thorndike Press
10 Water St., Suite 310
Waterville, ME 04901